PURSUIT

A Novel

by

Rudy Apodaca

PURSUIT

May you enjoy the good life!

ISBN: 1-4033-8570-X (e-book)
ISBN: 1-4033-8571-8 (Paperback)
ISBN: 1-4033-8572-6 (Dustjacket)

Library of Congress Control Number: 2002095167

This book is printed on acid free paper.

Printed in the United States of America
Bloomington, IN

1stBooks – rev. 02/06/03

Also by Rudy Apodaca

The Waxen Image

Grateful acknowledgment is made for permission to use
the following copyrighted material:
Excerpts from *Our Own Worst Enemy* by William J. Lederer,
© 1968, and published by W. W. Norton & Co., Inc.,
New York, New York. All rights reserved. Published by permission.

Special acknowledgment to noted Southwestern artist
David Rothermel for permission to use his oil painting
as part of the dust jacket and cover design.

First Edition

Dedicated and in honor and loving memory
of my parents, 'Mundo y Elisa, who gave me not only life but the
will, strength, and vision to live it to the fullest.

ACKNOWLEDGMENTS

There have been many persons along the way who have helped me in my writing career. But in trying to acknowledge their help and support within a confined space, I find myself having to limit my notes of appreciation to a select few.

First and foremost, I owe a debt of gratitude to my four children, Cheryl, Carla, Cindy, and Rudy. They've always supported and encouraged me in my legal, judicial, and writing careers to the fullest, more than they'll ever know. Through the years, each in her or his own special way has lent a hand to me as a parent when the going may have gotten a little tough.

My dear and gracious friends from New York City, Norman Keifetz and Joyce Engelson, I thank from the bottom of my heart. They've always been there for me and have forever offered their support and encouragement, as well as their wisdom, advice, and professional suggestions with all of my writing, including this book.

My thanks go to Keith Wilson, a great poet and my good friend, who not only read and critiqued this book but has many times offered encouragement and moral support when needed most. I owe special thanks to Raven Valencia, Avelicia Gonzales, Julie Alban and Jana Barberio who were kind enough to proofread and comment on this work, including its numerous revisions. I appreciate their assistance in making this book possible.

Of course, I'd be remiss if I failed to thank my *tocayo* and fellow-writer, Rudy Anaya, for his support and friendship through many years, as well as the kind words he has said of this book. It is with much humility that I acknowledge the help of Tony Hillerman, world-renowned novelist, whom I respect for his skills as a storyteller. I thank these two fine writers, not only for their willingness to read the book, but because they've always shown an interest in my writing and have been willing to offer their help and expertise when I've called upon them.

Finally, where would I be without my beloved and devoted wife, Nancy, who has been a strong influence in my life in more ways than she could ever imagine? I confess that early on in our marriage, I took for granted her giving and caring nature. Many times, she spent hours upon hours alone, either reading, doing daily chores, or otherwise occupying herself, while I sat upstairs in my studio pounding away at my laptop keyboard into the small hours of the morning. My heartfelt gratitude goes to her for putting up with me when I found myself consumed and compelled to finish a scene or a chapter or even the whole book, no matter its toll. My lovely Nancy—she's one gracious and honorable lady.

CHAPTER 1

THEY parted on the front steps of the courthouse. The two attorneys, John Garcia and his co-counsel, Edmund Runyan, had defended the third man in a wrongful death action and had arranged to meet him later when the jury reached a verdict. John and Edmund began their short jaunt to the law offices of Simms, Connally, Bradley & Dunn down the street in the Hyatt Office Tower.

The afternoon was sunny and cloudless, but the cool breeze blowing steadily from the northwest left no doubt fall would soon arrive. In contrast to the stuffiness of the courtroom the two men had just left, the brisk air and bright sunshine caressed their faces.

Across the street, a man hurried into a dark-blue Ford Thunderbird. John thought it was the same man, a stranger, who had rushed out of the courtroom at the end of the trial. He wondered if the car, occupied by another person behind the wheel, was the same one he had seen parked near his home a few days ago. Not wanting to draw attention to himself, he observed the driver peripherally to see if he recognized him, but he couldn't see the man's face because of the sun's glare. A simple case of allowing his imagination to get the best of him, he concluded. So he dismissed it.

The two men slowed their pace as they cut through the lobby of the Hyatt Regency, a twin companion to their office building alongside it. Edmund left John to retrieve a case file he had left in his car in the underground garage. John took the elevator to the twenty-second floor.

At 55 years of age, he was one of Albuquerque's most successful civil defense lawyers. His firm, of which he was a stockholder, was one of the largest in the state, with some 45 attorneys occupying plush offices not only in Albuquerque and Santa Fe but in Las Cruces to the south.

The elevator opened into the reception area. He spotted his secretary, Lynda Lopez, chatting with the receptionist at the front desk.

"Hi," she greeted him with a pleasant smile. "I heard the jury just got the case." She was a petite woman with short, dark brown hair.

"You heard already?" he asked, not surprised.

She nodded. "It's nice when one has a friend at the clerk's office. Marcella just called."

He grinned. "Figures."

She laughed, then glanced at a Mexican-American, middle-aged couple and a young woman seated at the far left of the large room. "That's Mr. and Mrs. Reinaldo Soliz," she whispered, "and their daughter. They've been waiting for over an hour to see you."

John gave a rushed glance across the room. "Did you tell them I was in trial?" he asked. It upset him when prospective clients showed up with no appointment.

She nodded. "They insisted waiting. I'm sorry, John, but it seemed important to them to see you. I didn't have the heart to turn them away."

"That's fine." He sighed, then eyed the family. They were watching him. Mr. & Mrs. Soliz nodded at him and smiled. He returned the smile, then instantly felt guilty for being annoyed. Perplexed, he wondered if he knew them.

"You don't remember Mr. Soliz, do you?" Lynda said.

"Vaguely. Who is he?"

"You handled a workers' compensation case for him about eight years ago."

"Now I remember. What do they want?"

"They wouldn't say—just that it was urgent."

He thought of walking over to greet them but decided against it. "Let me go into the office and take a look at my messages. Tell them I'll see

2

them in a few minutes but explain that we're awaiting a call from the courthouse."

She nodded. "Okay."

During the two-week trial, he spent the evenings preparing for the next day's testimony. So he had given some semblance of order to the disarray of papers covering his desk. He even managed to return some phone messages. Clients felt slighted when their calls weren't returned, even when Lynda made clear he was in trial. So he usually tried returning what calls he could. Long ago, he had accepted this act as an important part of letting clients know he cared.

Several years ago, the Simms firm had lured him from a small firm he had helped form, having begun his law practice within months after he had completed a one-year clerkship for a New Mexico Supreme Court justice in Santa Fe. He had applied for the clerkship while still on active duty in Vietnam as an infantry officer with the U. S. Army.

His six-foot, broad-shouldered and medium frame hadn't changed much, even from his high school days when he had played football and run track at Albuquerque High. Years of working out with regular exercise at the health club and tennis kept him in good form.

He possessed rugged facial features, strong bone structure, and a medium olive skin complexion. Almost always well groomed and dressed, he bought his wardrobe right off a store's racks with little alteration, but his suits fit him as if they had been specially tailored. His good looks and intelligence had made him appealing to the opposite sex.

For the most part, his law practice had followed the plan he had set out for himself. He felt reasonably comfortable that, with few exceptions, he directed the cases he handled.

For that reason, he was a little dismayed upon hearing why the Solizes were there. They wanted him to represent their son, Bernardo, in a criminal case. He hadn't handled one in years.

Bernardo had been indicted for the attempted murder of a young woman stabbed by an assailant who had asked to come into her house to use the telephone. John remembered the incident because it had made headline news. The victim was the mayor's married daughter, so the story received more news coverage than usual. Albuquerque's mayor was a colorful politician who had experienced unusual popularity with his constituents. His daughter had been stabbed several times and had miraculously survived the assault. A defense lawyer from the Public

Defender's office had been appointed to represent Bernardo. The P. D., as court-appointed counsel was often referred to, wanted Bernardo to plead guilty to a lesser offense before the jury trial, which was two weeks away.

John explained to the Solizes and their married daughter, Carmen Fresquez, that he hadn't practiced criminal law in eight years. He was trying hard to hide his displeasure upon hearing the purpose of their visit. That he now felt exhausted from the long day in court didn't help.

"Even if I wanted to represent your son," he explained in Spanish, "this firm doesn't handle this sort of case. The P. D. probably could handle it better than I could."

"But he wants Bernardo to plead guilty to a lesser charge," Carmen Fresquez said in perfect English. The elder Solizes had spoken to John in both Spanish and English, but he sensed they felt more comfortable conversing in Spanish, and so he accommodated them. Besides, he thought he could convey his understanding better in Spanish. It had something to do with the nature of the language, he believed.

"There isn't necessarily anything wrong with copping out to a lesser offense," he said in Spanish. He liked the Solizes, and, because he was beginning to feel compassion for them, he wanted them to know he cared. But he sensed his tiredness weighing him down, and he hoped they wouldn't misinterpret it as a sign of indifference.

"*Pero mi hijo no hiso esa cosa tan terrible, Señor Garcia,*" Ramona Soliz pleaded. "But my son didn't do such a terrible thing." She held her two gnarled hands in her lap, rubbing them nervously, as if in pain. John studied the woman. Her face displayed the anguish she had apparently suffered throughout her son's ordeal. "Bernardo was at our home with us," she continued.

John listened attentively, liking the woman's soft-spoken nature. He forgot his tiredness and was now glad he was lending an ear. They obviously were getting some satisfaction in his listening to them. But how could he help them? "Is that true?" He was addressing Carmen.

"Uh huh," she said, nodding. "And we got people to prove it." She brushed her long, thick black hair away from her face.

"Who could testify on your brother's behalf?"

"My Mom, Dad, and myself. And, of course, Bernardo and his wife. My two sisters and my husband weren't there. He was picking me up after he got off work."

4

"Your brother's married?" he asked, surprised, for he had learned moments ago that Bernardo was 18 years of age.

"Yes."

"I assume he's told the P. D. all of this?"

Carmen nodded.

"*También a la policía le decimos eso,*" Reinaldo Soliz said, looking off in space dejectedly. "We also told that to the police." It was the first time the man had broken his silence, except for the few words of greetings he had spoken when Lynda had ushered them in. Studying the man's face and listening to his voice had refreshed John's recollection of the time when he had represented him. He remembered him as a hard worker—one of the best in his company. He was now a foreman for the company, he had proudly told John earlier.

"And what did they say?" John asked.

"They didn't believe us," Ramona said in despair. She grimaced sadly, as if trying to hold back tears.

He now realized the woman reminded him of his mother. It was the inflection of her voice and the movement of her head, more than her physical appearance, that triggered the realization.

"I don't think even Bernardo's lawyer believes us," Carmen volunteered. "That's why he wants Bernardo to plead guilty."

"Or he may have concerns that a *jury* won't believe the alibi," John explained. "I can see that as a potential problem in this case." He spoke slowly, leaving no doubt he was taking a serious interest in what they were telling him.

"You see," he continued, "it isn't enough for your own attorney to believe you and Bernardo that he was at home when the stabbing took place. He's got to be convinced the jury will believe the alibi. Surely you realize it's what the jury thinks that counts."

He became aware of showing some impatience, and he felt disappointed in himself. It was his exhaustion causing it, he realized, but he again worked hard not to let the Solizes feel unwanted.

"But we're telling the truth!" Carmen said in a firm, almost insolent voice.

"I appreciate that, but the truth is, you—and by that, I mean all of you—are what we know in court as potentially biased witnesses."

"What does that mean?"

"It means anytime you have family, especially parents, vouching for a family member's whereabouts, it often causes problems of credibility, at least to jurors. They may believe family members are just trying to protect one of their own. And a prosecutor, you can be sure, will try everything to remind jurors of that."

"That's why my parents would like for you to take the case," Carmen said. "They have little money, but somehow they'll manage to pay you."

He turned to Reinaldo Soliz, who sat there quietly. The man's sunken eyes, surrounded by a leathery, wrinkled face, looked up at him. Even if by some stretch of the imagination he decided to represent Bernardo, he was sure of one thing. He couldn't accept any money from these poor, decent people who didn't deserve the misfortune thrust upon them by events involving their son, whether or not he was guilty.

"*Por favor, Señor Garcia, hable con nuestro hijo,*" the man pled. "Please, speak to our son. He'll tell you himself he didn't do this thing."

The more words he heard coming from the lips of Reinaldo and Ramona Soliz, the deeper empathy he felt. Unconditionally, the elderly couple believed in their son's innocence, and their presence here was but a first step in helping him. He could tell there were no limits to what they would do to help. They apparently felt Bernardo was worthy of their seeing a lawyer. John wondered if he was deserving of such loyalty.

His thoughts brought back memories of his criminal law practice, when he had encountered similar loyalty many times over as family members and friends of an accused came to his or her side to offer help. He had forgotten that, years ago, he had come to believe there was no better way of finding out how true your friends were than to be charged with a crime. He recalled several of his clients had to carry the load alone, abandoned by family and friends. Obviously, Bernardo wasn't one of them.

He looked at his watch; it was already three o'clock. "I'll tell you what," he said, leaning forward. "I'll have one of our paralegals get a copy of the police reports on this case. I'll review them, and then I'll go visit Bernardo in jail." He wanted his words to sound comforting but not to raise false hopes.

"Thank you, *Señor Garcia*," Ramona said. For a moment, he noticed a twinkle in her sad eyes. She even smiled, something she hadn't done before. And it pleased him to see the edges of hope forming on her face. Seeing this gave him a spark of energy, as well as a pleasant satisfaction.

"*Muchísimas gracias, agradecemos su ayuda,*" Reinaldo added. "Many thanks, we're grateful for your help."

Now he felt uneasy. He knew there was every chance he might decline to take the case in the end. "I want you to know," he cautioned, "that I haven't yet decided to take the case. Fair enough?"

"Fair enough!" Carmen repeated.

He stood up and walked around his desk.

"We're appreciative just for your speaking to us," Ramona broke in. She stood, pushing herself up from the soft-cushioned chair, and held John's hand gently in both of hers. "*Dios lo bendiga, Señor Garcia,*" she said with a smile. "God bless you."

"In the end, we hope you decide to take the case," Reinaldo said. "But if you don't, we'll understand. Thank you ever so much for your time."

He ushered them out of the office into an adjoining conference room. "Lynda, my secretary, will get information from you—names, addresses, phone numbers—things like that. I'll be in touch with you tomorrow." He shook their hands and left the room.

Back in his office, he asked his paralegal, Mike Murphy, to get the police reports and news accounts of the incident. He made it clear he needed them that afternoon. The kid knew his way around the legal system well. He then called the Public Defender's office to inform Bernardo's court-appointed attorney that he might enter the case. He told the P. D. a courier would pick up copies of the police reports, newspaper clippings, and any other documents that might help him before he saw Bernardo. The attorney cooperated.

He next telephoned the county detention center to arrange his interview. Even that had changed since he had last handled a criminal case. Back then, the place was known as the county jail. Modern names for modern facilities, he thought. The modernization hadn't impressed him. Jails were still jails, no matter what they were called.

A few minutes after four, the call from the courthouse came—the jury had reached a verdict. Within minutes, John and Edmund were back in the courtroom with their client.

An anxious look appeared on John's face as the bailiff ushered in the last few of the jurors into the jury box. He knew the cause of his anxiety. He couldn't detect in the face of one or two jurors a sign that he had won or lost the case—a faint frown, a subtle, yet inescapable avoidance of his

7

stare. He reminded himself the jury had deliberated for only two hours. Usually, the less time the jury took to reach a verdict was a good sign for the defense. He tried to relax, realizing he was standing almost at military attention—straight and unyielding.

Robert Thomas, the trial judge, read the verdict form to himself, then gave it to the deputy clerk. The jurist looked up and glanced toward the back of the room, looking at no one in particular. "Madam clerk, would you please read the verdict," he said in a loud, forceful voice.

After identifying the proceeding, the deputy clerk announced, "We, the jury, find for the defendant."

John relaxed, breathing once again. His hands felt a bit clammy with sweat.

When the last of the jurors was escorted out, he turned to Edmund, who let out a big grin. They and their client exchanged handshakes. John then walked over to the two opposing counsel and shook their hands.

These were always awkward moments for him, but they were what was expected after every trial. Doing it never came naturally. An absence of this ritual meant an unacceptable insensitivity. He had been on the losing side before, and it wasn't a good feeling.

He next turned to their client. "I'm sorry it turned out this way for you, Mr. Bombach," he said. He extended his hand to the widower, whose wife had died as a result of a horrible two-car collision.

"Thank you," the man said. "Me too." His sad eyes met John's, then he turned away.

John couldn't help feeling sorry for the man, whom he had grown to like during the course of the lawsuit.

Moments later, as he and Edmund walked out of the courthouse, he looked across the street, recalling the man he had seen getting into the car. His curiosity could turn into an annoying suspicion if he allowed it, he warned himself.

When he and Edmund entered the reception area, Lynda was there again to greet them.

"Congratulations, gentlemen," she said with a wide grin.

"Don't tell me—Marcella?" John asked.

"She called me seconds after the verdict was read. I've already spread the word around here."

"I bet you wouldn't have been so efficient had it turned out the other way." He grinned.

She laughed. "Probably not."

He started walking down the hallway to his office when he bumped into Dick Dunn, one of the managing partners.

"You came through again, John," Dick said, shaking his hand.

"Thanks," he replied.

"Edgar just left for depositions in Phoenix. Asked me to congratulate you."

He thanked Dick, opened the door to his office, and entered.

He scanned his messages again before calling his wife, Demi, to tell her of the verdict. She sounded happy for him. He spoke to her for a short time and told her he wasn't sure when he'd be home.

He had never gotten serious about a woman until about eight years into his law practice. That was in 1981, when he had volunteered for the task of interviewing and hiring his old firm's externs. It was in the spring of that year that he interviewed a bright, young law student from the University of New Mexico School of Law. Her name appeared as Demetria Christina Flynn on the application he had reviewed just before she entered his office. He was surprised when she appeared, a well dressed, personable, 23-year-old with a smile that was faint, yet mesmerizing. She possessed grace and displayed a refined quality but not to the point of appearing too confident.

Speaking in a formal, yet friendly manner, she seemed at ease during the interview. She appeared eager to learn, a quality he considered essential but often absent among the younger attorneys. The young woman made such an impression on him that he offered her the clerkship right after the interview. He often wondered, and she had since quizzed him in jest, if he had hired her because of his admitted, strong attraction to her the moment she had walked in the door.

She clerked for the firm that summer, and the following year she became Demi Flynn-Garcia soon after taking the New Mexico bar exam.

Mike Murphy came through. The paralegal had the reports, witnesses' statements, and news accounts in his office before five o'clock. As John cleared his desk to make room for the documents, it occurred to him that, no matter how noncommittal he had been with the Solizes, he was all but hooked. He also realized that, if he should turn them down, they'd have nowhere to go—no one else to turn to. But in trying to help their son, what was he getting into? What of his colleagues? How would they react

9

to his taking the case? And what about Demi? What would *she* have to say? Recently, she had made pointed remarks that he seemed overtaxed at the office. She suggested it was affecting his disposition at home. And now he was considering taking a criminal case pro bono.

CHAPTER 2

HE began his review of the Soliz case by reading the newspaper account that had appeared in the Albuquerque Journal the morning after the incident. *"Mayor's Daughter Stabbed; Manhunt Begun,"* the headline read. The assault had occurred several months ago in late Spring, but he vaguely remembered the facts of the case. He recalled that, as he had read the front-page account of the stabbing back when it happened, he remarked to Demi how the news media sensationalized the news involving persons in the public eye or their families. The thought reinforced his belief about skewed or uneven news reporting that tainted its accuracy. How objective was the news media when placement or repetition of a story was based on an editor's or news director's subjective opinion of the story's importance? He read the article.

> Albuquerque Police are continuing their investigation and have started a manhunt for a young man sought in a stabbing of a local woman Thursday night at 3241 Amherst NE.

The stabbing incident is reported to have occurred at about 8:00 p.m. Thursday, as the victim, Patty Gregory, 26, was washing her car in the driveway of her home. Ms. Gregory is the married daughter of Albuquerque mayor David Phillips.

According to police reports, the offender was described as a Hispanic male, of a slender build but with broad shoulders, 5'6" tall, with dark, curly, clean-cut hair. He was wearing a white T-shirt and blue jeans.

Ms. Gregory was taken to University Medical Center where she was admitted with stab wounds in the small of the back, the stomach and left breast, according to hospital officials, who said today the victim is still in serious condition.

Police initiated a dragnet after the incident, combing the residential streets near Roosevelt Park, where the offender was last seen.

The offender is unknown to the victim, police said. Police reported that the man approached Ms. Gregory from the sidewalk and asked if the house across the street was for rent.

Ms. Gregory, a local real estate agent, started to talk with the man. The man told her that he had just recently returned from California after being away from Albuquerque for several months and was temporarily staying at 3022 Walker, NE, a fictitious address, police said later.

The offender reportedly asked Ms. Gregory questions to see if her husband was home, before he left the area.

Ms. Gregory reported she went into her home to get a towel to dry the car and was there a few minutes before she went outside again.

As she stepped onto the patio, she again saw the offender, who asked if he could use her phone. Ms. Gregory said she grew suspicious and frightened and tried to get back in her house, but the man ran up and grabbed her around the chest, pulling her into the kitchen.

In the struggle that followed, police said, Ms. Gregory was stabbed with a hunting knife with a five-inch blade several times. The struggle continued as Ms. Gregory began screaming.

Believing the man intended to kill her because of her struggle, Ms. Gregory went limp, feigning unconsciousness. The offender then ran from the house.

As the offender ran south on Amherst, police reported, Ms. Gregory managed to get up from the kitchen floor and screamed for help. Several neighbors then came to her aid and called police.

One passerby claimed to have seen the offender and followed him. The witness said the offender was on foot and went west on Monroe to Mountain, south on Mountain to an alleyway and then through Roosevelt Park.

Other witnesses saw the man double back through the park when he saw a patrol car enter the area. The suspect was not seen after that, police reported.

Police said the man was Hispanic and speaks English with no apparent accent.

Detective David Morales is heading the police investigation of the case.

John read several other newspaper accounts, then came to the last one headlined: *In Knife Case–Teen Surrenders.* This item reported that Bernardo had turned himself in after a four-day investigation. It also stated that an arrest warrant for attempted murder had been issued late Monday afternoon after the Thursday incident. Bernardo was identified as the prime suspect through photos that had been shown to the victim and witnesses. The article noted he became a suspect when police authorities received an anonymous phone call tipping off the police that he should be questioned in connection with the stabbing.

Before leaving for the detention center, John had just enough time to read through the police reports. They included both sworn and unsworn statements from several witnesses, including two statements from Patty Gregory. One of them made brief mention of the anonymous phone call. Most damaging of the evidence against Bernardo was Patty's identification of him as her assailant, first by photograph, then in a police lineup.

Reviewing the reports, John thought the process used by police to get the identification was suspect. That was something to look into. But the fact remained that, despite inconsistencies in description, the reports left no doubt the victim had made a positive ID of her assailant. The alibi problem had now become a much bigger hurdle. The case was a challenge, that was certain.

He wasn't in the attorney's booth more than a minute when Bernardo was brought into a companion booth. The two small cubicles were separated by thick, reinforced glass and a small grated opening to talk through. Although the news accounts and police reports had reported Bernardo's height at about 5'6" to 5'8", John was surprised at the small stature of the young man who sat in front of him. Not only was he much shorter, but he had a slight build. His thin and small face was pockmarked, and his hair, rather than being curly as reported, was more on the kinky side. John couldn't see the broad shoulders described by witnesses. Bernardo also possessed soft, almost kind, eyes, not those of one who would have stabbed Patty for no apparent reason.

John introduced himself and explained why he was there.

"Bernardo," he began, "I haven't yet decided to represent you so I'm not technically your attorney. However, what you say to me still comes within the attorney-client privilege, which means I can't tell anyone what you tell me except with your permission. Do you understand?"

Bernardo nodded. "Sure. My sister told me you were coming to see me."

John wasn't surprised Carmen had been there to report even the slightest glimmer of hope. But hearing it from Bernardo reminded him the Solizes were banking on him. He couldn't resist his first question. "How tall are you?"

"5-3."

"I thought so." He took out a legal pad and micro-cassette recorder from his briefcase. "I'm going to take notes and record this conversation. Okay?"

"Sure, why not?" Bernardo appeared more relaxed now. "Does this mean you're gonna represent me?"

Even Bernardo's hopes had been raised, he thought. "I want to ask you a few questions, first, if you don't mind. I'd like to satisfy myself that I can help you." As he had been reading through the police reports and news accounts earlier, the one thought that had lingered in his mind was motive. The facts of the assault seemed rather bizarre—a young man approaches a woman washing her car to ask about a rental. The woman has never met him before. They carry on a conversation. He leaves, then returns and asks to use the phone. Afraid, she starts entering the house, and he begins to stab her for no apparent reason. No rape, no robbery. What was the motive?

Now, for the first time, he realized the young man in front of him couldn't provide an answer. Not if he confirmed that he was at home at the time Patty was fighting for her life two miles away. Unless, of course, Bernardo confessed he had committed the crime, which was unlikely. Why, then, couldn't he decide if he was going to represent the boy? Because, he now realized, he wanted to first hear the alibi from Bernardo himself. But more importantly, he wanted to find out if Bernardo was credible—that a jury could believe him.

"I need to ask some personal questions," he said. "Is that all right?"

"Yeah, no problem."

He first asked preliminary questions—weight, color hair, color eyes, education, and background. Bernardo had no criminal record. John learned that the candid photo of Bernardo shown to witnesses had been

14

taken by a police photographer when the boy had been questioned at his home. "I understand you're married," he went on.

"Yeah."

He learned that Bernardo's wife's name was Beverly, that they had no children, and that she wasn't Mexican-American but Anglo. They had left Albuquerque for California a little more than six months before, where Bernardo hoped to find a job. Unsuccessful, they had moved back to Albuquerque and were living with his parents. Although Bernardo wanted to look for a place of their own, he and his wife weren't financially able to move yet. The assailant's description given to police by witnesses didn't at all describe Bernardo. But this tidbit, that he had just returned with his wife from California, matched up with what Patty had said of her assailant. Coincidence?

John decided to get to the heart of the interview. "Did you do it, Bernardo?" It was an essential question. Most criminal defense attorneys realized not all clients were candid with them. It wasn't unusual for criminal defendants' attorneys, especially public defenders, to believe their clients had lied about their innocence, even to their own lawyer. But ethically, it was important to ask the question. Besides, even if a client denied guilt when asked the pointed question, there were often signs that could show otherwise.

As he had suspected, Bernardo appeared shocked by the query. The boy sighed for a brief moment. It wasn't a sigh of relief but one of desperation.

"You mean, did I try to kill that woman?"

"Yes, did you stab her?"

"No way, man. I was at home with my family." He displayed a defiant, almost hostile look.

"Your parents and sister told me that. But I wanted to hear it from you."

He spent the next hour delving into details—times, dates, and specific events and actions in the Soliz household before and after the time the stabbing occurred. The assault had taken place when it was still light out, even though the sun had set. The complaint and offense report prepared by Police Officer Steven Tanner confirmed he was dispatched to the scene at about seven after eight. Other reports verified the telephone call to the police from a neighbor took place within seconds of his having seen Patty fall in her neighbor's front yard.

15

Bernardo told John that the P. D. had documented his account and his family's accounts of his whereabouts that evening. They had eaten supper around seven. Cheese enchiladas had been the main dish. They finished eating around seven fifteen or seven twenty. After supper, Bernardo went into the living room adjoining the kitchen and watched television. He watched TV until about ten past eight but didn't like the movie that had begun at eight. At that time, he decided to go into the back room behind the house where he and his wife had been sleeping. He stayed about thirty to forty minutes there before returning to the main residence.

"So no one saw you for that time?" John asked.

"I guess not."

Thirty to forty minutes, he thought. Even though this gap in time occurred after Patty was stabbed, it was a gap nonetheless. But that wouldn't have given Bernardo enough time to leave and do all that Patty's assailant had done. A good prosecutor, though, might be able to persuade a jury that Bernardo was either incorrect about the time when he went out back or how long he stayed there, outside the others' presence. Or worse, that he and his family were lying.

"I don't think I have to tell you it's important you be absolutely sure about when it was you were out in the back room. Once again, are you certain about the times?"

"Yeah. I remember, and my lawyer noted it down."

"And, the rest of your family—their accounts as to time agree with yours?"

"They should—that's what happened."

"Yes, but when persons go about their business at home or elsewhere, they don't go around checking their watch every ten minutes or so, just in case someone later inquires. See what I mean?"

"Yeah, but that night we remember we had red enchiladas for supper, and I remember what I watched on TV and when my sister and mother returned from picking up tortillas and cheese. That's why I'm sure about the time."

"What about later when they were looking for you with an arrest warrant? Did you compare notes with other family members then, so that each of you is certain about the time?"

"Yeah, I'd say that."

"By the way, Bernardo, the police reports indicate an unknown person called the police suggesting they talk to you about the stabbing. Do you know anything about that?"

"No, sir." He hesitated, then cleared his throat. "I have no idea what that's about."

The boy was now acting somewhat defensive; even a bit edgy. John thought he noticed a realization in Bernardo's face that he was acting that way, and his appearance changed. He gazed at John with a pair of desperate eyes John well remembered from days long gone when he had interviewed others in the same jail.

"I didn't do what they accuse me of, Mr. Garcia!" Bernardo pleaded. "Please help me. My lawyer—I don't think he believes me 'cause he wants to work out a deal with the district attorney and for me to say I did it when I didn't."

Bernardo's eyes gave John a penetrating, yet soft stare. "Please, believe me. I don't want to go to prison for something I didn't do!"

John believed him. He thought of the pathetic faces of Reinaldo and Ramona Soliz sitting in his office earlier. Again, he found it unbelievable he was interviewing this young man and considering whether to represent him in a trial two weeks away.

As he studied Bernardo's face, the answer came swiftly—he had never before been placed in this untenable position by a poor family seeking his help as a last resort. It was pure and simple.

He felt a slight adulation when he saw what he interpreted as not only hope but relief in Bernardo's eyes when he told him he'd take the case.

"Thank you!" Bernardo said. He closed his eyes, then looked up to the ceiling in apparent disbelief of what he had heard.

Before leaving, John went over preliminary matters concerning his attempt to get court approval of an appearance bond to release Bernardo for the two or four weeks before and during the trial. As John was leaving, Bernardo thanked him again, this time with a broad smile.

He left the detention center about six o'clock. As he entered the center's lobby, he was confronted by two camera crews from KOB-TV and KOAT-TV. He couldn't believe his visit to the jail had leaked out, although it shouldn't have surprised him since he had experienced similar situations before. The news media had their sources, he realized—that's all there was to it. After all, this case involved the mayor's daughter, and he might as well prepare for unwanted publicity.

He was tempted to ask who had informed them he was there, but he thought better of it. The fact was that the news crew was there, and he'd have to deal with it the best way he knew how. He wouldn't even have to worry about telling his colleagues he was going to represent Bernardo. They'd learn soon enough on the ten o'clock news.

He confirmed he had agreed to represent Bernardo pro bono because his family had asked him to. He answered the rest of their questions, even the sensitive ones dealing with Bernardo's representation by the public defender's office.

"Was Soliz not satisfied by their representation?" one newsperson asked.

"That had nothing to do with it," John responded, unable to hide his annoyance. He didn't like being put into the position of having to answer for someone else. "Parties in litigation have the right to change counsel, for whatever the reason. I'm representing Bernardo because his family asked me to. Let's leave the P. D. out of it."

At the office, the first thing he did was to call Demi to tell her he'd be home late.

"Oh, John, the children have their school's open house this evening," she said.

"You didn't say anything about it earlier," he said.

"I had forgotten. I tried reaching you later when Crystal reminded me. But would it have made a difference?"

There was a moment of silence as he contemplated the obvious annoyance in her voice. She had intended not to hide it, he was sure. "I stepped out for an hour or so," he finally answered, ignoring her rhetorical question. "I'm sorry, Demi. Would you mind going without me? I promise I'll go with you next time."

"Please don't make a promise you're not sure you can keep!"

"You're right." He sighed, resigned to the fact his children were going to be disappointed.

"Shall I keep something warm for you?"

"Don't bother. I'll grab a sandwich. See you tonight. I love you— bye." As he hung up, he realized he had no right to expect her to be understanding when he decided at the last minute to work late. The fact that she too was an attorney had helped during the early years of their marriage, for she knew first hand the pressures and unforeseen time constraints of their profession. But in recent years, the *working late at the office* theme had been played once too often to expect empathy when it

18

interfered with the children's activities. She was more tolerant when the children weren't involved.

He reviewed the criminal rules of procedure and other sources that evening. He also studied the new rules of evidence and case law dealing with criminal trials. As he worked, he sensed an excitement brought on by delving into what to him was a new area. He viewed it as a challenge. Although it had been a long day and he had just completed a ten-day trial, in a weird way his work on the case breathed new life into him. It was ten minutes of ten when he left the office for the twenty-minute drive home.

As he pulled out into the street, he didn't notice the blue car parked across the street from the garage exit. The driver of the Ford pulled away from the curb and followed John's car as it drove off down the street.

CHAPTER 3

DEMI stepped out of the shower into a pair of slippers and a white robe. Her delicate, white skin looked almost tan against the sheer whiteness of the robe. In front of the mirror, she brushed the fine strands of her long hair to remove the few kinks the conditioner hadn't removed. When she finished, she walked into the master bedroom and out into the hallway. She entered Crystal's bedroom.

"Ready for bed?" she asked her twelve-year-old daughter, who sat against the bed's headboard reading a book.

Crystal looked up and smiled, then lay the book down on the night stand. "Yes, Mommy, I'm really tired," she said.

Demi sat on the edge of the bed and stroked her daughter's soft hair. "So I noticed. You had a long day. It was nice meeting your new teachers."

Crystal pulled her pillow down from against the headboard and rested her head on it. "I wish Daddy had been there."

"Oh, sweetheart. He did too but couldn't make it this time. You understand, don't you?"

"Sure."

Demi smiled. "Goodnight."

"Goodnight, Mommy."

She kissed her daughter on the forehead and turned off the bed lamp before leaving the room and closing the door.

"Okay, stinker," she said to Johnny as she entered his room.

The boy was in bed, his school books near the foot of the bed, but he was playing with a model airplane.

"Finish your homework?" she asked, frowning as she glanced at the books.

The eight-year old looked at his mother with an impish grin as she picked up the school books off the bed and placed them atop the dresser. "I did it all, Mommy," he said. "Honest." He nodded, as if to add emphasis to his words.

"I believe you." She smiled as he settled into bed. "Sleep tight and don't let the bed bugs bite." Leaning over him, she held the sides of his face with both hands and kissed him on the cheek.

He kissed her back, then gave her his usual squeeze around her neck with both arms. "'Night, Mommy. Pleasant dreams."

She smiled at him, then stood up and walked to the light switch by the door. "Pleasant dreams to you, honey." She turned off the light, closed the door, and returned to the master bedroom.

She turned on the portable television set near the foot of the bed to catch the ten o'clock news before going into the bathroom to apply a facial moisturizer and brush her teeth. She glanced at the clock—it was a few minutes past ten. For an instant, she thought of calling John to see when he'd be home but decided against it. When she finished brushing her teeth, she took off the robe and hung it on a wall hook, exchanging it for a pale blue nightgown. Placing the nightgown on top of the vanity, she glanced at the soft reflection of her naked body in the moist mirror.

"Pure, silky-soft skin," John would often say when he caressed her bare shoulders and back, referring to what he considered her *well-proportioned and beautifully-constructed body*, a phrase he had coined.

The trim figure she saw in the long mirror had borne her two children. Those who knew her often complimented her by telling her she looked years younger than her 43 years. Although she appreciated the flattery, she wasn't going to indulge herself in the denial that her face, as well as her skin elsewhere, had developed a few wrinkles. She applied the moisturizing lotion first to her arms and shoulders, then to her firm breasts. The aerobic exercises and weights at the health club had paid off—her body possessed a firm muscle tone.

She rubbed the cream against a small mole just above her cleavage. It had been there for as long as she could remember. She had often remarked to John that the mole seemed to have gotten larger, and at times she complained it was a little tender. For that reason, she suggested removing it, but he insisted she leave it alone.

He laughed once when he was running his fingertips over the slight contour of the mole as they lay naked in bed after one evening of passionate lovemaking. That had happened before they married, before he confessed to her that he was captivated by the softness and delicate beauty of her skin.

"What are you doing?" she asked as he stroked the mole at the edge of her breast. She felt embarrassed when she realized he was focusing on the blemish and instantly clasped his hand.

"Besides many other things about you," he answered, "this birth mark, or whatever it is, just happens to turn me on."

She considered his spontaneous comment humorous, yet complimentary. He confessed to her that he had first noticed the skin blemish one particular night when he had taken her out to a state bar function before their engagement. It was even before they had slept together. That evening, she wore a rather low-cut black dress that revealed her cleavage and the upper part of her firm breasts. He noticed the dark mark right away, he told her, and found it difficult to take his eyes off it the entire evening. She laughed when he confided to her that he wanted to make love to her then and there but had fought the urge even later in the evening when they were alone. Reason prevailed, he told her, and he resisted, much to his surprise, until the right moment came later.

"What do you like most about my body?" she had once asked him, half in jest. Her question had been an obvious effort to extort a flattering comment from him, but it was a night when they were both in a giddy, fanciful mood.

"Many things," he said, grinning. "But if you forced me to choose, I'd say it would be between those striking, dark brown eyes of yours and that sensuous mole. If it were anywhere else on your body, I'm not sure I'd find it so sexually stimulating."

"Moles can't be sensuous, silly," she replied, laughing.

"Not all—granted. But that particular one—most definitely!"

She had grown up in Tesuque, a community set in the foothills of the picturesque Sangre de Cristo Mountains near Santa Fe. Often, during their early courtship, John called her *La Norteña*, the Northerner, referring to Northern New Mexicans, who at times were looked on as a proud breed all their own—even a little standoffish.

As a single woman, her mother, Guadalupe (Lupe) Andrea Serna, worked for the Los Alamos Laboratories in Los Alamos about twenty miles from Tesuque. It was then that she met Demi's father, Andrew Flynn, a retired Army sergeant who also worked for the Labs. Andrew Flynn was much older than Lupe when they married. The couple had two daughters, Demi, and her younger sister, Lourdes.

Demi's father, who had been a heavy smoker, died of lung cancer when Demi and Lourdes were in high school. Lupe was now retired and living on her own and her late husband's pensions.

Although Demi had strong, Mexican-American features, including her black hair and dark eyes, which she inherited from her mother, it was from her father that both she and her sister inherited their white skin. It was the combination of the Latin features and the striking, soft color of her skin that gave her the stunning quality John so admired.

She enrolled at the University of New Mexico in Albuquerque the fall of the same year she graduated from high school. With her mother's financial help and part-time and summer work, she was able to complete her degree work in four years.

At age 24, she graduated from the law school at UNM three years later. Had she realized the difficulties caused by attempting to take final examinations and studying for the bar exam, while trying to prepare for her and John's wedding, she would have postponed the wedding. Instead, impatience led to a wedding in September. She was the happiest she had ever been when the bar exam was behind her and she and John could begin their lives together. Somehow, she managed to survive that hectic summer.

Because of his workload at the firm, they delayed their honeymoon, a trip to Hawaii, until October. It was during the honeymoon that they learned she had passed the bar exam. She became a member of the bar at swearing-in ceremonies in Santa Fe the first week of November. She didn't know who was the proudest at the occasion—she, her mother, or John. He had choked on his words when he moved her admission.

She slipped on the transparent nightgown and began blow-drying her hair. When she finished, she caught the tail-end of the newscast. The television news anchor had just mentioned John's name. Curious, she hurried into the bedroom.

"Bernardo Soliz, an 18-year-old, married man," the newscaster reported as she sat at the foot of the bed, "was charged in May of this year and later indicted for the attempted murder of Patricia Gregory. Ms. Gregory is a local realtor and the daughter of Albuquerque Mayor David Phillips—" As the announcer spoke, video footage, taken sometime after Bernardo's arrest, showed a young, Mexican-American male, presumably Bernardo. In handcuffs, he was being led through a side entrance into the county courthouse by several, uniformed police officers. As the footage was shown, Demi was confused by the mention of John's name. The answer soon came.

"This afternoon, Channel 7 spoke to local prominent attorney John Garcia, who confirmed he would enter an appearance as attorney for Soliz tomorrow." As the newscaster finished the sentence, a shot of John being interviewed flashed on the screen. He was explaining that, at the request of Bernardo's family, he visited him at the detention center and decided to represent him at the upcoming trial. The newscaster repeated the several questions asked of John, which were followed by the video footage of John's responses. The announcer reappeared on the screen.

"Soliz' trial is scheduled to commence in thirteen days," the announcer continued. "Efforts to reach the Public Defender's office and Soliz' court-appointed attorney were unsuccessful. Channel 7 will keep its viewers informed of any additional details as they develop. In other local news,—"

"I can't believe this!" Demi said out loud, shaking her head. "What is he *thinking?*" She turned the volume down when she thought she heard footsteps coming up the stairs. It was probably John, she thought. Great timing—he'd be able to answer her questions. She stepped into the bathroom and turned off the light. When she turned around, he had entered the room.

He smiled at her. "Hi, honey," he said. He kissed her on the mouth.

She managed to hug him even though on the verge of losing her composure. "Hi," she said, not hiding her indifference. She looked down at the briefcase he carried. "You plan doing more work at home?" She forced a smile, but she was sure it did little to convince him she was anything but pissed off.

He grinned, she surmised, because of her facetious comment. It also occurred to her that he might think her coolness had something to do with his missing the open house.

"Not at all," he replied, placing the briefcase against the wall. "Just habit, I guess."

"I just saw you on TV."

"Oh, yeah, the Soliz case." He seemed surprised. "For the life of me, I don't know where those news guys get their tips." He took his suit coat off and loosened his tie.

"A *criminal* case," she said, ignoring his rhetoric. She pulled the bed covers back, turned on the night lamp on her side of the bed, and sat on the bed. "You haven't done one of those in a long time—think you'll be up for it?" She found it more difficult to hide her displeasure and grew concerned she might hit the ceiling on what had by now become a sensitive issue for her. The depth of her anger surprised her, but she hoped she'd stay in control and not go ballistic.

"I'll just have to." He shrugged. "That's why I'm late—catching up with my own crash course." He bent down, held her by the shoulders, and kissed her forehead. "What a terrific forehead you've got. And you smell sexy, too."

She resisted him, then let out a soft, but forced laugh. "Quit trying to distract me with compliments—you're awfully good at that." She had learned that his attempts at compliments were his way of relaxing in anticipation of her voicing displeasure over something he had done to upset her. Tonight, it was having to face her disappointment for his having taken on the Soliz defense. She sensed he was preparing himself for a mini lecture. Well, she thought, he deserved much more.

"Am I?" He sighed. "Is that supposed to be *your* compliment?"

His attempts to turn the tables on her annoyed her, especially when she believed they should be serious. His remark pushed a button for her, and she found herself overreacting.

"Don't act like a smart ass with me, John Garcia!" she blurted out. The loudness of her voice surprised her and forced her to notice the door into the hallway was open. She closed it.

She stepped into the bathroom as the tears began. She knew their cause—she was upset for losing control. Picking up several tissues, she returned to her side of the bed and reclined against the headboard, dabbing at her eyes.

"Don't get so upset," he said as he undressed. "And I also wish you wouldn't resort to name calling. That doesn't help."

"Damn it, John, don't turn the tables on me like that. Besides, I have a perfect right to be upset. And angry, too. On top of everything else, don't you think accepting a criminal trial taking place in two weeks is getting you into an overload mode. We've talked about your workload before, and you've promised you'd try doing something about it."

"I know we have, but only because *you* keep thinking it's a problem. I suppose tonight it didn't help that you heard about it on TV. Surely you realize I was planning to tell you. I figured you'd be upset, but you don't have to go ballistic."

"How dare you say that!" She was already disappointed in herself, but it didn't help being reminded of her overreaction by the victim of her wrath. "I've tried to contain my anger, and I could kick myself for not succeeding. But that doesn't change the fact I have a right to be angry. This exchange gets right down to the heart of the problem. And it's getting more serious." She paused. "Worse yet, we're not doing a damn thing about it!"

"I'm sorry about what I said." He took her arm, but she pulled back. "Demi, if there was a way I could take that back, I would." He sighed. "Of course you have the right to be angry. I didn't mean to trivialize it, even if I don't see it as serious as you do. It's just that I got a little defensive because—" He paused. "—I guess because I was hoping you wouldn't be so upset."

She dried her tears. "Well, doesn't that tell you something? Doesn't my getting this upset show you how bad I think things are? Or isn't *that* important to you?"

He stood up. "Of course it's important to me. Why would you even think otherwise?"

She shook her head. "Your attitude, I guess. You seem indifferent about all of this, as if nothing's getting through to you."

He held her by the arms. "Listen, I admit getting off on the wrong track. I know it's important to you. Maybe we should let things cool off a bit and continue in the morning. Is that all right with you?"

She dried her tears again and nodded. "I suppose so. But definitely tomorrow, not later."

"That's fine with me." He gave her a brief hug and stood up. She turned off the lamp on her night stand and got under the cover.

He took his suit and shoes into the walk-in closet, then went into the bathroom to brush his teeth, closing the door behind him. In a few minutes, he returned, turned the ceiling light off, and got into bed. Although awake, she lay still, facing away from him. He turned off his lamp and said goodnight, but she didn't reply. She realized he probably suspected she wasn't asleep yet and might consider her silence a bit childish, but she didn't care. To her, it was a way of emphasizing that what she considered a serious issue wasn't going to be blown off.

Outside, two men sat in the blue Thunderbird parked a half block away. The driver noticed the upstairs light go out.

"They must've turned in for the night," he said. "Shall we head out?"

"Let's wait another ten or fifteen minutes," the other whispered. "I hope someone at headquarters knows what they're doing. A week's gone by with no sign of activity."

"You think we're on a wild goose chase?" He lit a cigarette.

"We'll know soon enough." He sighed. "You're not thinking of smoking that thing in here, I hope?"

"Hold your horses. Getting a little edgy, aren't we?"

"I'm tired, okay?"

"I'm stepping out."

"Keep it quiet. We don't want to draw attention."

"Don't worry. I'll be back in a jiffy."

CHAPTER 4

DEMI awakened to the sound of the shower. She glanced at the clock on the night stand. It was only six. She was surprised John was up already, for he hadn't activated the clock's alarm the night before. He hadn't even bothered going downstairs to check the lights and the door locks, almost a nightly ritual. Unlike her, he had gone to sleep soon after turning off his lamp. She had lain awake for an hour before dozing off.

She was surprised she felt fully awake and rested this morning. She jumped out of bed, put on her robe, and walked down the hallway to wake up the children. She experienced more difficulty than usual. She spent a couple of minutes straightening up their rooms, waiting to make sure they had gotten up. Afterward, she went downstairs and set the breakfast table before going back up.

John wasn't only out of the shower but nowhere to be seen. She assumed he had gone into his study across the hallway. She took out a clean set of underwear, picked a suit to wear, then walked into the bathroom to take a quick shower. The room was stuffy, so she opened the window.

Out of habit, she looked out and spotted the dark blue car as it pulled up to the curb a half block down the street. She waited to see if anyone stepped out. No one did. She was certain it was the same car she had noticed a few days ago on two separate occasions, and she knew it didn't belong to any of the neighbors. It was one of their car pools, she guessed but decided to mention it to John. She entered the shower stall.

Although she had received several job offers from Albuquerque law firms soon after her admission to the bar, Demi saw no reason to rush into law practice. Instead, she wanted to enjoy the first months of her marriage without the complexities of a new job. It wasn't until a year after her marriage that she began working with Herman Weingarten, a 64-year-old sole practitioner.

She and John had met Herman at the state bar's annual convention soon after they returned from their honeymoon. She liked the man's homespun attitude and down-to-earth nature. Besides, she opted to work for a one-lawyer office because she was well aware of John's long hours at his own firm. She joked with him that one lawyer in the family enmeshed in the legal profession's rat race was one too many.

She stopped working when she became pregnant with Crystal and didn't return to work with Herman until Johnny began kindergarten. By then, Herman was 78 years old and had lessened his practice. But that worked well for both of them because she wanted to work half or three-quarter days and only a few days a week. For the last three years, she had worked mornings four days a week, including Fridays, but sometimes she'd work until mid-afternoon. The short hours allowed her to do whatever shopping or errands she needed to get done after work, then be home in plenty of time before the children arrived home from school.

Crystal and Johnny had just finished eating their breakfast when John appeared in the informal dining area right off the kitchen. Demi was in the kitchen.

"Hi, guys," he said.

"Hi, Daddy," they said in unison. Crystal gave her father a hug.

He placed his hand on Johnny's head and messed up his hair. "You almost done?"

"Yeah," Johnny answered.

John joined them at the table.

"Did you and Mommy have a fight last night?" Crystal said. She spoke as if stating a fact, not asking a question.

"Why do you ask?" he said, showing surprise at his daughter's candor. "Were we a little loud?"

Crystal shook her head. "No, I was asleep when you got home." She bit into a piece of toast. "I can just tell."

He didn't appear surprised, for he and Demi hadn't yet greeted each other, which was unusual. "We had a slight disagreement, that's all." He paused. "Sorry I missed your school's open house," he added, glancing from Crystal to Johnny. Johnny shrugged.

"That's not what you argued about, is it?"

"No, honey, not at all. It had to do with my work."

"What about it?" Johnny jumped in.

Before he could respond, Demi appeared with a pot of coffee and orange juice for John and herself. The kitchen and the dining area were separated by a broad, open doorway.

"Mommy thinks Daddy's working too hard at the office," she broke in. "Nothing for you kids to worry about. Right, Daddy?"

She planted a quick kiss on John's temple, as if to convey to the children that the two of them could work beyond their misunderstandings and act civil to each other. Rarely did John not go along with that tactic, for he thought it a good practice. Demi had made it clear she disliked arguing in front of the children, especially if they suspected the argument revolved around them. She poured the coffee and sat down.

"That's right," John said, smiling at her. "We've been through this before, 'kiddos.' No two persons can agree all the time." He grinned. "After all, what about you two rascals." He poked Johnny in the ribs. The boy let out a short laugh and moved away.

"Good morning, hon," John said to Demi.

"And good morning to you," she said, forcing a smile.

A few minutes later, Crystal and Johnny hurried upstairs to finish getting ready for school.

Demi waited until the children said goodbye and left to catch their bus before mentioning the car. She wanted to continue last night's discussion but thought her concern about the mysterious vehicle was the simpler of the two and might help relieve any tension that may have spilled over from the night before.

John swallowed the last bite of his toast and gave her a worried look. "Was it a blue Thunderbird?" he asked.

"I couldn't tell the make," she replied. "But it was blue. I saw it the other day too."

"Is it still there?"

"No. I looked out later, and it was gone."

"Why didn't you tell me this before?"

"I didn't think much of it then." She studied his face. "You've seen it too, haven't you?"

He appeared amazed at her uncanny ability to read his body language. He nodded. "A couple of days ago. Then I saw what I thought was the same car outside the courthouse yesterday. I dismissed it until you just mentioned it. Now, I'm thinking, a coincidence it isn't."

"What's going on? Are they watching the house? You?"

"I haven't the foggiest idea."

"It's a little scary. Should we call the police?"

He shook his head. "Maybe we're overreacting. Besides, I'd like to know what we're dealing with before getting the police involved, if at all. I'd be afraid they'd screw things up."

"The police?"

He nodded. "One loses faith in those guys after you hear about so many screw ups. I've got a better idea."

"Like what?"

He wiped his mouth with a napkin and didn't reply. He stood up and bent over to kiss her on the mouth. "You look mighty seductive in that bathrobe with nothing on underneath," he said and growled. "I feel like ravishing you on the table."

"Well, don't just yet. What do you say we continue where we left off last night."

"Anger and all?"

She frowned. "No, without it. I promise I'll be civil, but I should tell you I don't appreciate the humor you try to inject into something so serious."

"I do that, I think, when I'm nervous."

"I know." As her own sign of peace, she offered him her hand as they walked up the stairs.

"For openers," she began when they reached the top of the stairway, "why don't you tell me what Dick and the others at the firm had to say when they found out you're handling this case?"

"I haven't told them yet. They probably first heard about it last night like you did, if they were watching the newscast."

She closed the door to the bedroom behind them and sat on the edge of the bed. He sat next to her and took his shoes off. "I plan telling them at our meeting later this morning," he continued.

"That'll be the least of your worries," she said. She gave him a serious stare. "You know I don't like saying things to you that make me feel like a nagging wife, but—"

"I've never known you to be a nagger."

"Thanks for saying that."

"Sorry I interrupted. Whatever you were going to say, I'm sure I'm deserving of it."

"I only wanted to emphasize what I said last night before losing my cool. Don't you think taking on a trial at this time is going to add to your stress at work. It'll make it much more difficult to try working things out. I'm referring to the time we should spend with the children. I don't see how taking on more work than you can handle is going to help us do that. Even if the case was going to bring in more income, which it isn't, there's too much to lose when it comes down to Crystal and Johnny." Their eyes met. "Now I *do* sound like a nag."

"Not at all." He placed his arm around her. "I agree the pressure I've been under hasn't been good for us. But I can't see this case adding to the kind of pressure that's hard to deal with."

She noticed him eying her breasts, which were partly exposed because of the way she was sitting on the bed. He leaned over and kissed her along her cleavage. "What do you say we continue with this discussion after getting stark naked?"

"No," she quipped, "no distractions. We'll not only continue it but *finish* it." She was relieved they seemed to be making some headway.

"Fine, but first let me get comfortable." He took his suit and shirt off and laid them across the chair. Within seconds, he was laying alongside of her.

"How can you keep a straight face," she continued, "and tell me this case won't add to your pressures."

"You know the kind of pressure I'm talking about. This case will mean more work, of course, but I can handle that with no problem."

"And by adding to your work, you'll have less time for your family. Honestly, John, I don't think you even realize there's a problem here, much less know how to handle it."

"First, let's make sure we're on the same wavelength. What's the problem you're referring to?"

"Why, the one we've talked about before—your spending more and more time in the office and less and less time with the children."

"Doesn't everyone at some point in their career find that to be the case? It's practically universal."

"Of course. But when it gets out of hand, most people try doing something about it. That's my point—you're not!"

He frowned. "Things aren't getting that bad, are they?"

"I beg to differ, but they are! At this rate, considering you're in denial about this, things will get a lot worse before they get any better. Unless we do something."

"You really *are* worried about this, aren't you?"

She nodded, then sighed. "Let's approach this from a different angle. Have you given any more thought to Dan Conniff's proposal?"

"I take it you're referring to the federal judgeship?"

"Yes." She folded the pillow to prop up her elbow, then lay on her side facing him.

"What has that got to do with what we're talking about?"

"Plenty. We're talking about the pressures of your job and that they're getting worse. I'm trying my best to convince you I'm unhappy about what this is doing to us. That's why I got so upset last night. Doesn't there come a time when most persons feel they've paid their dues and shown everybody they too can do it? You've earned a right to slow down a bit. And the judgeship too, if you want it."

"So have a lot of other lawyers, at least, from their perspective."

"I've no doubt. But the fact is, so do you, and Dan has committed to you that he'll be happy to recommend you to the White House."

"Well, that's the clear message I've gotten. But you know how politics works. There would be others with political influence wanting the job. Dan would get pressure to appoint them too."

"But his loyalty to you goes way back."

She was referring to the fact that U. S. Senator Daniel Curtis Conniff and John had attended high school together, where they had been the best of friends. Dan's parents financed his four years of undergraduate work at Harvard. John wanted a change in his surroundings, but his parents

34

couldn't afford anything other than a state school. So he attended NMSU in Las Cruces.

The two of them had stayed in touch throughout college. Both graduated in the spring of 1967, and both headed for law school the following fall—John to Georgetown Law Center in the nation's capital and Dan to the law school at the same Ivy League school. A few years later, John's law firm had been a big contributor to Dan's senatorial campaign. John himself had spent many hours coordinating Dan's party nomination in the Democratic primary and in the eventual election. So Demi was correct—the two men's loyalties went back a long way.

"That's right," John said in response. "I have no reason to believe he wouldn't recommend me for the job, if I want it. Quite frankly, at the moment I'm not sure I do."

"When will he have to make a decision?"

"Not until the middle of next year. The appointee would take office late summer."

"You've got time to think it over—but not a lot."

He nodded. "You'd like for me to take that judgeship, wouldn't you?"

"In the end, I want you to do what *you* think is best. It's your decision."

"Demi, you're a lawyer. You must realize that job has its own pressures. I wouldn't go for it with some fantasy that it's a cushy job."

"I know. I've heard about the demanding caseload in the federal courts. But even then, I'd guess a judge's schedule is more structured. With all due respect to our federal judges, as hard as they may work, I don't see them burning the midnight oil like you." She paused. "They have their law clerks do that for them."

He grinned. She realized he agreed with what she had said, despite her humor.

She spoke again. "Honestly, John, it would free up your evenings and weekends."

"I've thought about that. You haven't often complained about my work. But it's starting to bother you that much?"

She sensed he realized he had asked the question before, and she didn't reply right away. She finally nodded. "Not for me, as much as for Crystal and Johnny. They're at that age where they have social lives of their own, not only at school but elsewhere. I can be there for them, but they need you too. I'm not saying this to make you feel guilty, so please don't take it that way. But I sensed they would have liked for you to have been there last night. As they get older, they'll need you even more.

"Remember last summer, when we planned to take them to Disneyland and Sea World, and you ended up not flying with us due to one of your cases? Even though you later joined us, it put a damper on the vacation because of the uncertainty you'd be there."

He placed his hand on top of hers and squeezed it. "So it's getting that bad?"

"Yes, I'll say it again—it's getting that bad." She paused to let it sink in. "I don't even think you take enough time to visit your own mother."

"I try to see her at least once a week."

"Yes, but for short periods of time. Thank God she has two daughters who spend quality time with her. If you were home earlier in the evenings, I'd invite her to have dinner more often instead of once a month. Even then, it's next to impossible to find a week night you'll be home early."

"Now you're making me feel guilty about my mother. Thank God she's forgiving."

"I hadn't intended to mention this. Although I admit I've had it on my mind and would have said something sooner or later. I suppose your taking on this new case brought it on. To me, agreeing to help this boy shows how driven you are. You just can't be all things to all people that walk into your office." She stopped. "Now I'm beginning to sound a little selfish."

"You're not. I realize my family should come before my job." He paused. "I'll think about that judgeship, all right?"

"That's really the point of all this."

"Believe me, I've gotten the point." He smiled. "Now, can we get down to our other, important business?" He moved closer to her. "I may still be flinching from last night's fireworks," he said, "but not enough to prevent me from taking you in my arms and telling you 'I love you.'"

"I know you do—and I love you."

He kissed her on the lips, then embraced her as he kissed her neck.

She returned his affection, kissing him on his shoulder. "I hope you'll never tire of holding me in your arms like this," she said, weakening from the touch of his moist lips on her sensitive skin. She purred. "And more, until I can't resist you and want you in me."

Many years before, during the early years of their marriage, she learned that he liked for her to suggest to him when she was being turned on by his foreplay. Teasing and encouraging words from her stimulated his desire for her even more, he once told her.

He aroused her as he ran his tongue along her neck, then into her ear. He pulled her bathrobe down below her shoulder, exposing her left breast and nipple. She felt her swelling nipples harden as he ran his wet lips around the nipple of her exposed breast. She felt orgasmic and wanted him inside of her. But she resisted the temptation, for she knew their bodies well—together, they would build up the frenzy in anticipation of the eventual climax to their lovemaking. Experiencing multiple mini-orgasms during foreplay wasn't exceptional for her. It was rare when she didn't experience several during aggressive foreplay on his part. At this moment, she sensed that he wanted her more than usual; sensing that brought on her orgasms even more. For her, their lovemaking was filled often with a series of them that later reached an incredible climax as he ejaculated in their final moment. In the end, they always reached orgasm together.

She herself dropped the other end of her robe, exposing her other breast to him. He soon lowered his open mouth below the breast and onto her firm stomach. She shivered in ecstasy as the fingertips of his right hand began their trek up along the inside of her thigh, en route to her clitoris, which she knew he'd soon stimulate to titillate her even more.

It had been a week since they last made love. For that reason, she savored the long drought with the gratification that, this morning, their lovemaking would be particularly meaningful. She just lay there, vulnerable to his every desire. Only when he had penetrated her digitally did she reach her hand for his groin, the beginning of her own titillation of him.

After their lovemaking, she stayed lying naked on the bed as he dressed again. She stood up and put on her bathrobe to accompany him downstairs.

"You never did finish telling me what you were planning to do about that car," she said as she straightened his coat collar.

"I'll tell you later," he said, "once I'm sure we can do it."

"Do what?"

He looked at his watch. "Got to run."

"John, don't go yet, damn it! What are you thinking of doing?"

"Calm down. Don't get upset before we know there's anything to worry about."

"Maybe I *am* overreacting. But promise me you're not doing anything foolish."

"I won't, I promise." He kissed her on the mouth, then smiled. "That was a great way to make up."

She returned the smile. "You'll give some thought to what we talked about, okay?"

"Don't worry, I will. Meanwhile, I feel committed to the Solizes. I hope you understand."

She shrugged. "Believe me, I'm trying."

He nodded.

After he left, she spent a few moments at the table pondering the turn of events. She wanted to believe there was a reasonable explanation to the mysterious car. Moments later, as she rinsed the dishes and placed them in the dishwasher, she turned her thoughts to her discussions with John.

She felt a little guilty for not leveling with him. What she had said about his work keeping him from the children was true. But she had painted only half the picture because she, for herself, not just the children, resented that he was spending more hours at the office. She learned long ago to be understanding. As an attorney herself, she appreciated that the demands of the occupation created a problem for those with a family. An occupational hazard, some believed.

In the past few years, she had known several attorneys whose marriages had ended in divorce due to the pressures of the profession. In the past year, it had passed her mind that what was happening in John's law practice would create a vulnerability in their marriage that might end in a permanent breakup. The thought was frightening. An overwhelming anxiety came over her as she contemplated that possibility.

She sat down and picked up a napkin to wipe the droplets of sweat that had collected on her forehead. Never, she said to herself out loud. John wouldn't let it happen. *I* wouldn't let it happen!

As John drove to the office, he thought of Demi's comment about his mother. Impulsively, he turned at the next corner, detouring from his straight path to the office. He headed north to his mother's house.

She lived off Edith Boulevard, north of Central, not far from where he had attended high school. If he didn't visit with her this morning, he didn't know when he'd next get a chance to. He wanted to see her, but he hoped the urge wasn't caused by guilt.

As he rounded the corner of the neighborhood where he had grown up, he spotted her outside her modest stucco home. Juanita was rearranging several flower pots along the edges of the tiny porch. She too began her day early, he thought as he pulled up near the dilapidated wooden gate leading to the small front yard.

She appeared preoccupied with her morning chore but apparently heard the sound of the tires as he brought the car to a halt on the mixed sand and fine gravel bordering the narrow asphalt street. Right away, he noticed the surprised look in her eyes turn to joy as she recognized him. She greeted him with a big *abrazo* at the gate.

"Mi'jo, what a pleasant surprise!" she said with a bright smile, not hiding her delight. *Mi hijo*, Spanish for "my son," had been shortened for many years by Chicano parents to the abbreviated but incorrect *mi'jo*. John and his mother always spoke in Spanish when they were alone together.

"Good morning, *Mamita!*" he said as they parted. He kissed her on the cheek. He often addressed her with his own term of endearment. Literally, the word translated to "little" mother.

He opened the screen door for her and followed her inside. She walked into the kitchen, the usual family hangout, and offered him coffee. He accepted.

"Please sit down, Johnny," she said, pulling out a chair from the kitchen table with some effort.

"I'll get the coffee, Mom," he insisted. "You sit down."

"Hush, I can manage. Now sit, sit."

He grinned and sat down. He knew better than to argue with her in such matters, for she enjoyed doing things for her children.

As she gathered cups and saucers, he studied her. She appeared somewhat frail to him this particular morning. The sweet, almost pungent or vinegary odor of the kitchen filled the air. It was the unique scent of his mother's kitchen that had been there as long as he could remember. This morning it brought back nostalgic memories of her as a much younger woman hovering over the kitchen stove when he was but a small boy. It was a pleasant odor, one he always associated with his parents' household.

Watching her pour him a cup of coffee, he wondered if he half-imagined her frailty. Her body did appear smaller, and he even wondered if she had lost weight since he had last seen her. Her face, despite the many wrinkles that had appeared in recent years, possessed a soft complexion, not leathery. She wore no makeup this early in the day. He rarely saw her without it and speculated that might be why she appeared vulnerable.

"Here you are, Johnny," she said as she brought his coffee. She poured a cup for herself, then joined him at the table. "Now tell me, how are the children?" She sipped her coffee.

"They're fine, Mom," he replied, putting his cup down.

"And Demi? Last time we talked on the phone, she didn't seem herself."

"Oh, really? In what way?"

"I asked about you—how you were doing. She said you were doing okay, but I sensed she seemed troubled when I asked about your work."

"Oh, that." So now even his own mother was noticing things weren't right. *That ought to tell me something,* he said under his breath. "Yes, she's concerned I'm working too much and not spending enough time with Crystal and Johnny."

"Are you?"

"I suppose. We've talked about it. I just didn't realize it was affecting her to the point others could tell. I'm glad you mentioned it."

"So am I, but I don't wish to get involved in your affairs. You'll work things out, I'm sure."

That was her way of suggesting he better tend to the problem before it worsened. "How about you? How have *you* been?"

She looked up from her cup. Their eyes met, and she hesitated, as if giving extra thought to her reply. "I was tempted to say the usual 'I'm fine' but why tell you something that's not true. Feeling my age more with each passing day, I'm afraid." She took another drink. "But I try not thinking about it and stay busy. Yet, at times, when there are a few aches and pains to remind me the years are adding up, it's difficult not to think about it."

"Does it bother you, *Mamita?*" He took a sip. "The fact that you can't do as much as you used to, I mean."

"I believe God gives us the strength to accept the limitations of old age." She wasn't looking at him as she spoke but instead stared beyond him and past the wall across the room, as if contemplating her idea of God. "If it weren't for one's faith, I think it'd be harder. Especially without your father." A sudden sadness came to her drawn face, and her brow wrinkled ever so slightly.

40

"Do you ever get lonely, *Mamita?*" He paused. "Living here alone, with Dad gone."

"It was that way at first after he passed away. I still miss him terribly, God bless his soul." She paused, as if reflecting on some memory. "Especially on some special occasions more than others. But that too passes, if one has faith in God. He makes all things possible, and I'm grateful for that." She forced a smile. "Why do you ask, *mi'jo?*"

"I couldn't help notice you seemed sad a moment ago."

"What you probably noticed is my worry, not sadness. I've no reason to be sad. And I have no reason to be lonely either, for I have you and your sisters. That in itself is a blessing."

"What worries you, *Mamita?*"

She looked away again, and he noticed her eyes fill with tears.

She took a Kleenex from her pocket to wipe her wet eyes. "Of becoming a burden to you and your sisters," she said finally.

He placed his cup down, knelt in front of her, and took her hands in his. "You're not a burden. Why would you think that?"

"Perhaps not now. But I still have enough of my senses to know I will someday soon." She looked up into his eyes. "When I spoke a moment ago about the limitations that come with age, I realized how hard it already is for me to do many things around the house I used to find easy to do. I try, but I can't. So I know the day will come when I will no longer be able to live alone."

New tears appeared, and she wiped them away. "That's when I'll be a burden, Johnny," she said, her voice breaking. "It's—not—a pleasant thought." She looked at him with saddened eyes.

He too now felt sad, seeing his mother share her most private thoughts. He found it difficult not to cry and felt the tears welling up in his eyes.

"Of course not," he found himself saying, "but try not thinking that far into the future. The fact is, though, you'll never be a burden. I promise. No more than you thought of us in that way when you raised us. If and when that time comes, when you can't do things for yourself, we'll do whatever's necessary. But please take that one thought away from your mind—we'll never think of you as a burden. Please tell me you believe me."

She smiled at him. "I do, *mi'jo.* Thank you for saying it—that's more reassuring than you'll ever know."

"Meanwhile, we want you to enjoy the years you have left when you can still do things on your own." He had been using *we* because he knew his sisters shared his feelings.

"But I do, son. I don't want you thinking I don't. Every day I wake up, I thank God for his blessings. I'm proud of all of you. I tell you, son—you are a blessing to me until the day I die."

"I know you feel that way." He embraced her. As he held her in his arms, he felt a deep, heartfelt compassion for her, and tears came to his eyes again. Holding her by her shoulders, he pushed away from her and met her renewed gaze. "*Mamita*, listen to me," he said, choking on his words. "You've been a pillar of strength in this family ever since I can remember. Even when Dad was alive, you were that way. I've always admired you for that trait, and it's always given me strength in my own life. I'd guess that's why you're worried about the limitations you're confronting."

"That's so true."

"You don't need your children's permission to get old."

Despite her own tears, she laughed at his remark.

"You laugh," he continued, "but think about it. I think you're feeling guilty because you believe you'll be a burden. Please don't look at getting old as your fault."

She wiped the remaining wetness around her eyes, then took the Kleenex and wiped away his tears. "I'm happy you came this morning, Johnny. And I'm glad we talked. It's been worrying me."

He stood up. "I'm glad we talked about it, then."

Because of this turn of events, he decided to stay longer. He called Lynda and asked her to tell Dick Dunn and the others to start the meeting without him.

He needn't have worried, for she bounced back to her usual self, apparently relieved she had gotten something off her chest that had been bothering her. They spent the rest of their time catching up on their lives since he had visited a couple of weeks before. He left her as he had found her—with a bright smile on her face as she waved goodbye to him from the front door.

He was half an hour late to the firm's weekly management conference. After the meeting ended, he was about to announce that he had agreed to represent Bernardo when Dick beat him to it. He had caught the newscast.

"Are you sure you want to get involved in something like that?" Dick asked. "I realize we all cherish our independent ways in this outfit, but it's been a while since you tried a criminal case."

"I gave it serious thought, believe me," John replied. "After sleeping on it, I feel good about my decision."

"You had quite a day yesterday," Edmund broke in. "A favorable jury verdict, then taking on something different." He smiled at John, then glanced at the others.

"Yeah, it *was* quite a day," John said. "As a result, I won't have as much time to savor yesterday's victory."

"I hope you won't mind my saying this," Dick said, "but I understand you're taking the case pro bono."

John made an effort to smile. "That's right. Is there a problem with that?"

Dick shrugged. "None for the firm. But I hope *you're* not biting off more than you can chew."

"Well, to be honest, the same thought crossed my mind. But don't worry, I won't let it have an adverse effect on my hours, if you're wondering."

"I'm not concerned about that." Dick placed his hand on John's shoulder in a friendly gesture. "It's just that I know you too well—it's your workload and its effect on *you* that I'd be worried about, not the firm's hourly output. Surely you know that."

"It's good to hear you say that. I just wanted to make clear I had no intention of hurting the firm." He felt a slight uneasiness because he wasn't sure Dick was leveling with him—he might be concerned about the case's effect on his work but couldn't find the courage to say it.

"I'm certain you'll enjoy doing it. I wish I had the guts to try that." Dick picked up several files off the conference table. "Good luck with it." He sounded sincere enough.

"Can I be 'second chair' on this one?" Edmund asked in jest, a wide grin on his face.

John let out a soft laugh. "No sense putting us both under the gun. I'll be burning the midnight oil for sure. Besides, as you heard, the pay's going to be lousy."

After the meeting, John met with Lynda to discuss the day's schedule. Afterward, he made several calls on the Soliz case, including one to the attorney in charge of the P. D. office and the one assigned to represent

Bernardo. He told them he planned entering an appearance as Bernardo's attorney. They were cooperative. He also had Lynda make the initial contacts and prepare the necessary documents to post an appearance bond so Bernardo could be released from jail pending trial. No sooner had he finished placing his last call when Lynda delivered a large pile of paperwork requiring his attention.

"I decided to hide these from you yesterday," she said, setting the load on the corner of his desk. "I'll need your instructions on the files I've flagged that require action today."

"I'm always prepared for this after a trial," he said. "Thanks for your short-lived kindness."

"You're welcome." She made an awkward attempt at a curtsy, then walked to the door.

"Oh, Lynda, would you please get in touch with Guy Zanotelli? If he's available, I'd like to have lunch with him."

Lynda nodded and left. Within seconds, she buzzed him to tell him Guy was on the line. After Guy congratulated him for his victory of the day before, John explained he had a favor to ask of him and wanted to treat him to lunch. Guy said he was available, and they made arrangements to meet at a restaurant midway between their offices. As John hung up, a chill came over him. Was he doing the right thing in getting Guy involved in this, he wondered. Could he help find out if he was being stalked? Well, he'd soon find out.

CHAPTER 5

GUY'S full name was Giuseppe Gulio Ẓanotelli. He was a well-known, successful criminal attorney who had befriended John since his first years of practice. A devout Catholic of Italian-American descent on both sides of his family, Guy grew up in Albuquerque when it was a sleepy little town. As a teenager, he helped his father in the grocery business during the closing years of World War II. His paternal grandfather had immigrated to the United States from Italy in his twenties. He settled first in New York City, but his yearning for the open country he had left behind led him out West.

Guy's humble beginnings, together with his assertiveness, which some perceived as too forceful, had influenced his decision to become a lawyer.

His zeal, as well as his advocacy skills, helped him gain a fine reputation as a criminal attorney. This was so despite the fact he had also gained notoriety as short-tempered and impatient, not only with his clients but with other lawyers. One could tell when either or both of these two traits surfaced because his use of profanity increased.

He was one of a small group of excellent criminal attorneys nationwide, and for that reason his work took him to the West Coast, New York City, Chicago, and Las Vegas. On occasion, he attended Las Vegas' shows highlighting well-known entertainers and celebrities, often in the company of his clients.

In the legal profession, it wasn't uncommon for the public to perceive the character of attorneys by the clients they represented. But nowhere was this perception more real than in criminal law. The universal *rule* unwillingly promulgated by society, attaching guilt by association, was most evident in criminal defense work. It was inevitable that Guy's ties with his clientele, reputed or perceived to have strong mob connections, soon brought into question the good character of Guy himself. It was the *Albuquerque_Journal* that first began reporting about a few of the clients Guy represented and their supposed ties to alleged crime syndicates. His purported associations did nothing to affect his successful practice or the respect his legal colleagues, including John, held for him.

Although Guy's suspected affiliations with criminal organizations were often the topic of small conversation in locker rooms and golf courses, John believed the connections were more imagined than real. He knew his friend to represent his clients with vigor, no matter who they were, or even, what they were suspected of having done. His interest was to practice law and to make money doing it. If this meant representing a person who lacked credibility or honor in the eyes of the public or the *Journal*, then so be it.

Nevertheless, John wasn't blind to the reality that Guy had certain connections he himself didn't. Those connections were needed for what he had in mind—finding out if he was being tailed and by whom. They met at a small restaurant just off Central Avenue.

An incessant smoker, Guy had selected a table in the smoking section and was smoking a cigarette. He stood up to greet John. "Good afternoon, my good friend," he said. They shook hands, followed by a big hug from Guy.

"Nice to see you, Guy," John said. "Hope you haven't been waiting long."

Guy motioned to the empty chair across the table. "Not long at all—enjoyed the quiet moment to myself."

They sat down.

"Let me buy you a drink." Guy pointed to his glass of scotch.

John shook his head. "Got to keep a clear head—lots of work piled up after the trial."

Guy nodded and looked at him with eyes that conveyed he knew the post-trial scenario too well. He sipped from his glass. "What's this I hear about you representing that Soliz fellow?"

"You've heard that already?" He laughed.

"In a criminal case, no less."

He nodded. "Yeah. How did you find out?" He picked up a menu and offered one to Guy, who waved it away.

"I already know what I want. I mentioned to one of the fellows at the office that we were having lunch. He told me he saw something on TV."

"That's when the guys at the office first heard about it."

"Are the bastards upset?" Guy put out his cigarette.

He pondered Guy's question, recalling what he considered as Dick's ambivalent assurance. "Hard to tell," he said finally. "They might be a little envious, though."

Guy extended his hand to him. "Well, my friend, welcome back to the real world. You've been with those friggin' insurance lawyers far too long."

He indulged Guy's kidding by taking his hand. The waiter appeared with a glass of water for him and then took their order.

Guy continued. "Is the Soliz case what this is about—why you wanted to have lunch?"

John shook his head. "Not at all."

"You think you can help the poor kid. From what I heard, the victim's ID'd him pretty convincingly."

"I should have known you'd know about the case."

"You know me well enough to know I make it my business to know. Even if it means reading it in the fucking *Journal* just before wiping my ass with it after taking a crap!"

"My client claims he was at home when it happened, and his family backs him up."

"That'll help only if you're able to discredit the gal's ID. Is that possible?"

"I'm going to try."

"Well, let me know if I can help. You need an investigator? Mine's damn good." He gulped the rest of his scotch.

"Thanks—I'll let you know if I do."

47

He spent the next few minutes explaining to Guy how it happened that he had agreed to represent Bernardo.

"Really gutsy of you," Guy said when he had finished. "I'm beginning to see you in a new light." He grinned.

John smiled. "I'll take that as a compliment. Thanks."

"You're welcome," Guy said and grinned. "Anyway, what's on your mind?"

"I've a favor to ask on something else that may be serious."

The waiter arrived with their order.

"That's why I'm paying for this lunch," John continued. He waited for the waiter to leave. "Let's eat first—we'll talk about it afterward."

During lunch, they caught up on news about the other's practice and their personal lives. Guy had gone through a painful divorce recently and was still showing his bitterness over the settlement provisions he believed benefitted Sally, his ex-wife, more than him.

"So now you've gotten first-hand knowledge of how our poor clients feel," John said.

"Damn her," Guy said. "After twenty-five years of marriage and four lovely children. I think she was just trying to get even with me. She still thinks I dumped her for some young chick." He sighed, then lit another cigarette. "So, let's move on to a more pleasant topic. What gives?"

"Like I said, I have a favor to ask."

"John, if I can do anything for you, you can count on me. How can I help?"

"Demi and I may be blowing this thing out of proportion, but I think someone's tailing me." He stopped to let Guy absorb that he was troubled. Guy said nothing. "We've both noticed the same car. Several times at the house and at least once near my office."

Guy had been listening intently. "How long has this been going on?"

"The last three days or so—that we've noticed, anyway." He drank some water.

"Any idea what it's all about? A case you're handling maybe?"

"No idea at all. It's puzzling." He paused. "And, a little scary. I don't like the idea of Demi having to worry about what's going on. The sooner we find out, the better."

"Have you contacted any of your friends in law enforcement?"

"Demi suggested doing that, but I'd rather not."

"You're like me in that respect. Don't trust the pricks."

"That sums it up. I thought maybe you knew someone who could—" He paused, uncertain what he wanted to say.

"Tail them?"

He nodded. "Yeah. I figured if anyone knew persons who could do that, you would."

"You figured correctly, my friend. I've got just the two individuals in mind to do the trick. Give me a day or so at most. It's possible I can line something up by tomorrow."

"Guy, I'd like to find out who these fellows are. But promise me—no rough stuff."

"Don't worry." He took one last drag of his cigarette and put it out. "Friggin' cigarettes. Wish I could quit—I'm up to two packs a day."

John looked at his watch. "I've got to get going."

He picked up the tab, and Guy grabbed it from him.

"It's my treat, Guy."

"I won't hear of it. It'll be my pleasure." He threw a five-dollar bill down on the table for the waiter.

They walked toward the exit. John waited in the waiting area while Guy paid the check at the cashier's counter. When Guy joined him, they walked outside.

"By the way, I almost forgot," Guy said as he slipped a Certs into his mouth, "About that federal judgeship. Anything going on with that?"

"I'm flying to D. C. next week to meet with Dan Conniff. There's a fellow from the White House he wants me to meet—or rather, Dan wants *him* to meet me."

They began walking toward the traffic light on the corner. "I know Conniff's your friend," Guy said, "but can you trust the guy?"

John grinned. "Yes. We go back a long way. Why do you ask?"

"Only because I've known him to do some things that gave me pause. You don't mind my questions, do you?"

"Not at all."

Guy patted him on the arm. "But if you trust him, that's what counts."

"He plays the political game, just like everyone else. But in politics, you can't possibly please everyone. On the judgeship, it's his shot, assuming the White House finds no skeletons in my closet."

"And we've all got those, my friend."

"Why did you ask about the judgeship?"

49

"You heard Justice McBride died of cancer two weeks ago, right?"

"Yeah, I meant to attend his services in Santa Fe but couldn't cut loose from trial. What about it?"

"A few of us were mulling it over the other day at the golf course. Your name came up as a possible replacement."

He grinned. "Really? I'm flattered. But I've never given the state Supreme Court any thought. Especially now, when Dan Conniff wants me to consider the new federal vacancy."

"Well, let me know if I can help with that."

"Thanks. I haven't decided to go for it. Demi would like for me to."

"You better listen to her. She's one smart lady. But you should still consider an appointment to the Supreme Court. If you later decided to go for the federal appointment, your being a justice on the state court would be a great stepping stone. Tell me you'll at least think about it. A couple of the fellows I spoke to are close to the governor. Your appointment would be a 'cinch.'"

"I doubt that, Guy, but I'll give it some thought. Don't hold your breath, though."

Guy laughed. "I won't. Bounce the idea off Demi, why don't you?"

"I'll mention it. But I've got a whole lot of stuff going on right now—this trial and—"

The pedestrian light turned to WALK, and Guy noticed. "Think about it, okay?" He was rushed to beat the light. "Listen, on this other matter, I'll get in touch with you tomorrow. For your and Demi's peace of mind, I hope we get to the bottom of it soon."

"Thanks, you're a true friend. Bye."

"*Hasta luego, amigo.*" Guy hurried across the street.

John began his walk to his office. Taking his time, he pondered the federal judgeship Demi suggested he consider, as well as Guy's comments on the recent Supreme Court vacancy. All this on top of everything else. Never before could he recall so much happening at any given point in his life. He wasn't sure he'd look forward to the idea.

The prestigious Simms firm had long ago established a reputation as one of the city's finest civil defense law firms. A predominant amount of its legal representation was oriented toward defending personal injury and wrongful death cases. For the most part, this line of work entailed the firm being retained by a sizeable number of liability insurance carriers to defend their insureds, usually large corporations that by virtue of their size exposed themselves to the many risks of litigation.

During his early years with his old law firm, the type of work performed by individual attorneys was less structured. In the years that followed, however, specialization became a trend. The practice of law thus experienced a change of major proportions. The so-called general practitioner, a past trademark, was replaced by a more sophisticated system in which clients expected more from specialists. Given the growing complexity of the law as it evolved, the change wasn't surprising.

Before joining the Simms firm, John represented mostly criminal defendants. But, because typically those clients had little money, this line of work became a drain on the firm. As each law firm got caught up in mushrooming growth cycles, the curse of billable hours showed its ugly head. Firm members were expected to work hard and long hours to assure a minimum in gross receipts. And so, after 16 years of doing criminal defense work, despite the fact that he enjoyed it, he gave it up. Besides, the specialty created an unavoidable stigma in the world of public perception.

He often wondered what his life, particularly his marriage, would have been like if he hadn't accepted the firm's offer. When the pressures of the firm's demands took its toll, he would daydream of life as a sole practitioner, now a rare breed. But the thought of going at it on his own was just a fantasy because he had too much invested in the firm. His salary and annual bonuses weren't easy to give up. For this reason, there were times he felt trapped. A judgeship might be an out.

On his return to the office after his meeting with Guy, he prepared the necessary pleadings to enter his appearance in the Soliz case. He also worked out the posting of the property bond on the Soliz family's residence to permit Bernardo to be released pending trial. He himself took the release order to the detention center, since he had arranged for the Solizes to be there. He met Beverly, Bernardo's wife, at the brief family reunion in the detention center's lobby. Reinaldo and Ramona Soliz thanked him several times for getting their son out of jail. Ramona even hugged him as they said goodbye.

He next visited the Public Defender's office to thank Bernardo's public defender for his cooperation and for making the case file available to him the day before. He learned he hadn't been given all of the case's documents, so he left there with additional material. When he returned to the office, he reviewed the new stack of papers.

The documents included a set of handwriting samples taken from Bernardo. The Albuquerque Police Department wanted the samples to compare with the handwritten note the assailant had left behind. In the assailant's own handwriting, the note contained the address and phone number of Patty's real estate office. In the struggle, he had dropped the note. The month before, the police had received the FBI report, stating the samples taken were inconclusive. It suggested, however, that Bernardo may have pressed hard against the pen to alter his writing style.

The file also contained a police report concluding that the only fingerprints found in the Gregory kitchen had been those of Patty and her husband, with the exception of a set of unidentified prints that didn't belong to Bernardo. Finally, the file included a short narrative and various photographs taken at a police lineup shown to three individuals— Patty, and two witnesses, Carol Niewold and Rebecca Medina.

Patty's positive ID of Bernardo wasn't surprising to John since, during her stay at the hospital, she had already identified a candid photo of the boy as her assailant, among several photographs of others fitting the description. Although she made the ID at the lineup, nothing altered the fact that the description she gave to police on the day of the assault didn't match Bernardo's. John knew he was going to have to capitalize on this difference.

Likewise in Bernardo's favor was the fact that neither of the two other witnesses, Carol and Rebecca, was able to pick Bernardo from the lineup or photos as the young man they had seen fleeing the scene. Carol had been driving south on Amherst when she saw Patty fall to the ground. At the same time, she noticed the assailant running south on Amherst and then onto Monroe before crossing into the park. She followed him in her car. She said in her statement that she got a brief look at his profile after he had slowed down. As he trotted through the park, she said, he evidently noticed some activity on the far side, so he backtracked, and she then lost sight of him. She also gave a description of the man's physical appearance, which didn't match Bernardo's.

Rebecca, twelve years old, was on the sidewalk alongside the park when she noticed the young man crossing through the park. She confirmed Carol's account that the suspect backtracked before disappearing from her line of vision.

From court documents, John noted that Robert Keith, an Assistant District Attorney, was assigned to prosecute the case. He telephoned Keith, whom he knew vaguely, to introduce himself and to arrange the interviews of those who had viewed the lineup or photos. He also planned to interview Special Investigator David Morales, who worked the case, and Police Officer Steven Tanner, who was the first officer to arrive at the scene.

The following morning, Keith scheduled interviews with the two police officers in the afternoon. Lynda also contacted Patty, Carol, and Rebecca's parents to arrange for John to interview them at their homes later in the day.

That afternoon, when he returned to his office from having visited with the two police officers, there was a message Guy had telephoned. He asked Lynda to return the call.

Guy always spoke in a low, resounding voice. "Did you talk to Demi about the Supreme Court vacancy?" he said when John picked up the phone.

"Is *that* what you were calling about?"

Guy laughed. "No, but I thought I'd ask. Have you?"

"To be honest, no, but I've been terribly busy. I will the first chance I get. I promise."

"Do it soon, brother. We'd like to get your name out there to try to dissuade others from filing or even considering going for it."

"How much time have I got?"

"A couple of weeks, at the most."

"Okay, I'll be in touch." He sighed. "Have you got anything on this other thing?"

"As a matter of fact, yes. Everything's set, my friend."

"Okay. Fill me in so I'll know what to expect."

"First of all, I'm making certain inquiries of my own."

"What kind of inquiries?" He wiped the sweat off his hands.

"Trust me, okay? The kind that might shed light on who's tailing you. It's a long shot, but I thought it'd be one way of solving this puzzle. Now let me explain what I've planned locally."

He cleared his throat. "I've made plans to have two men who can be trusted keep an eye on you. Beginning this afternoon, as a matter of fact."

John's hands were still sweaty, and he wiped them again. It surprised him he was nervous, until he reminded himself he was in a phase of his life unlike any other—he was being followed. And now, Guy was adding a twist—having the two men tailing him in turn followed by two individuals who were strangers.

"Who are these guys, anyway?" he asked, knowing Guy might gather he felt he should get to meet them at least, if not approve them for the task. "They're not a couple of ruffians, are they?"

"Trust me, John, for Pete's sake." He paused. "To answer your question, believe me when I tell you they're responsible and good at what they do. After all, we don't know what we're dealing with here, so it's best to prepare for the worst."

"Let's hope it doesn't come to that." He sighed. "Forgive me if I sound distrusting. It's just that I've never been even remotely involved in this sort of thing."

"I understand, my friend. That's why you've got to trust me. I wouldn't do anything that would place you or your family—your lovely wife—in jeopardy."

He heard Guy exhale close to the mouthpiece, obviously letting out a puff of smoke.

"You won't even know these guys are around," Guy continued. "That's how good they are at their business."

"I hope they don't carry guns. I'm beginning to think this wasn't such a good idea."

"I don't blame you for being a little up tight. But face the alternative—it's either doing something now about what you suspect is happening or just waiting for something worse to happen without knowing when it'll occur. Which would you rather have?"

"Neither, if I had a choice."

"You actually don't have one in these circumstances."

"I suppose you're right." He took a deep breath.

"But if you want, I'll cancel the plan. Just give the word."

He was silent. He knew what Guy was telling him made sense. Guy's plan was preferable to the other choices available to him—doing nothing or contacting the police. "No, what the hell," he said finally, "let's get it over with. What do *I* have to do?"

"Nothing. Just go about your business. Don't even act as if you know you're being tailed. Okay?"

"Fine. Thanks for your help, Guy. I appreciate what you're doing, although I may not have sounded like it a moment ago."

"I understand. But let me assure you—these guys will know what to do and when to do it. Be patient, and we'll get to the bottom of this."

"It's in your hands."

"I'll be in touch."

"Okay."

"So long."

He kept the telephone handset to his ear. He heard the click on the other end as Guy hung up. He was still sitting there mesmerized when the dial tone activated. For a moment, he thought of calling Demi to let her know of Guy's plan, but he decided to delay telling her until later. He guessed she would disapprove of the plan. Besides, he hoped a few pieces of the puzzle would soon unravel, and he'd have something more concrete to tell her.

As it happened, those pieces started falling into place sooner than expected, at dusk the following day. John was returning to his office by way of an almost deserted side street. He had attended a deposition at an attorney's office on a case scheduled for trial in late fall. As he crossed the street in the middle of a secluded block, not far from his office, he noticed two men walking in the same direction on the other side of the street.

Approaching an intersection, he glanced across the street and noticed two other men standing in the shadows of the recessed entrance to an office building. Although they were visible from John's angle, he realized they were out of sight of the two men trailing behind him. He was shaken when he sensed what was about to happen—the two persons following him were about to fall into a trap.

In an instant, he felt his heart beating faster and his hands getting clammy. Despite his nervousness, he tried acting oblivious to what was taking place. Yet, he grew concerned his stilted gait would betray him.

He turned the corner where a building abutted the sidewalk, dropping out of sight of his pursuers and the two men lying in wait. He was tempted to stop dead on his track but forced himself to continue walking at a slower pace. When he heard muffled voices and what was evidently a scuffle behind him, he stopped. He turned around but could see nothing, for the building hid his view. The noise came from where he had seen the men hiding. They had made contact.

Gripped by a terror that something terrible was about to happen, a part of him told him to run as fast as he could away from there. But another thought came to mind—the mystery of why he was being followed would soon come to an end. His need to learn the truth overcame his urge to flee. And so he stood his ground.

CHAPTER 6

HE rounded the corner before realizing he was taking a risk. He wasn't even sure the two men he spotted lying in wait were the ones tailing his own stalkers. But he soon found out they were. They had intercepted the two men.

The contact occurred just past the entryway where Guy's operatives were hiding. One of the stalkers was wrestled to the sidewalk, where he lay flat on his stomach. The larger of Guy's henchmen made certain he remained there by holding both arms behind him, a knee pressed hard against the small of his back. The other one held the second man against the building wall. Both aggressors appeared huge, explaining why Guy had been confident they could do the job.

John hurried across the narrow street. "You fellows have some explaining to do," he said to no one in particular. He approached the man held against the wall, who grimaced from the lock grip.

"Who are you?" he continued. "Why have you been following me?"

The big fellow holding the man tightened his grip.

Finally, the man spoke. "If you'll ask your two ruffians here to let us," he said wincing, "we'll show you some ID."

John motioned to Guy's cohort. "Let him get whatever he wants to show us."

The big man slackened the grip but kept his hold as he turned his captive to face John.

"Slow and easy, buddy," the big man said. "Don't try anything foolish!"

John had been concerned the commotion would cause a passing motorist or passerby to call the police. Although the street seemed otherwise deserted, he wanted to avoid any embarrassment the incident might draw if someone were to stumble upon them. With that in mind, he signaled the other of Guy's operatives to allow the other man to get up. By then, the first man had pulled a wallet from his coat pocket, unfolded it, and held it toward John.

"My name is James Kelly," he said. "I'm a special agent for the Central Intelligence Agency." He motioned toward his companion, who was now held against the building. "My partner too is a CIA agent. Fletcher Quigley."

"CIA!" John exclaimed. "Why in hell are you fellows following me? Scaring the daylights out of my wife? You'd better have a good reason for this shit!" He felt not only anger but fear. Anger because he had hoped this whole thing had been a bad dream. Realizing that it wasn't brought on the fear. Had he heard the man correctly? He was dumbfounded. And this was no dream.

"Believe me, Mr. Garcia," Kelly answered, "the least of our intentions was to alarm or scare you or your family." The formality with which the man spoke seemed out of place, even comical, considering the circumstances. "I can also understand your anger. We just didn't expect your finding out like this. Agent Quigley and I are on special assignment with orders to perform surveillance and protect you, if necessary."

"Protect me! From what?"

"Now that you've found us out, I'd like a chance to explain."

"Go ahead!"

"This really isn't the place. It'll take a while. Is there somewhere close by where we could talk—in private?" Kelly glanced at his captors.

Right off, John thought of his office but was concerned a colleague or one of the staff members might still be there working late. He then realized Kelly and his associate, Quigley, were still being held captive. He turned to the man holding Kelly.

"Their ID looks okay," he said. "You can turn them loose."

Both men released their hold on the two agents.

"There's a restaurant-lounge at the Hyatt Regency," John said.

"That would do fine," Kelly replied, "as long as we can speak in private. But what we have to tell you is very sensitive and so the fewer persons involved, the better." He motioned to Guy's henchmen. "Could we talk without your buddies here, or is that out of the question?"

John turned to the two men.

"That's up to you, Mr. Garcia," one of them said in a low, scratchy voice. "Whatever you tell us to do, we'll do."

"Well, I think they're on the level. I appreciate your help."

The other operative walked up and held his hand out to John. "Glad we could help," he said.

They shook hands.

"We'll be on our way," the first operative said, shaking John's hand. "You know how to get in touch with us should you need us."

"I sure do," John replied. "Thanks."

The two large men buttoned their sports coats and disappeared around the corner.

The man identified as Fletcher Quigley brushed his clothes off and approached John. "Fletcher Quigley," he said. "I too apologize for what you must view as an intrusion."

"That's a hell of a way of putting it," John said.

Kelly came up to him. "I'm sorry we've caused you worry." He held his hand toward him, and they shook hands. "Feel free to call me Kelly. Fletcher here is known by his surname also—Quigley."

"Quigley?" John asked, turning to Kelly's partner.

"Yeah, just Quigley," the man replied.

"We can cut the formalities. Just call me John."

"Thanks, John," Kelly said. "Well, shall we head out? I know you're anxious to hear us out."

"You bet. The restaurant's just down the street. They've got good food there, if you fellows haven't had anything to eat."

"Sure. We can grab a bite while we talk."

At the restaurant, *McGrath's Bar & Grill*, the hostess seated them in a booth at the far side of the main dining room. John excused himself to telephone Demi. He told her that he had found out who was tailing him and was meeting with them to obtain more information. He was vague about who they were because he didn't want to concern her any more than she already was. She prodded him, but all he told her was that the two men worked for the federal government. She pleaded with him to be careful, and he promised her he would be.

The three of them ordered drinks. John ordered a scotch and soda. Kelly and Quigley both ordered gin and tonic. The waiter took their food order when their drinks arrived.

As John sipped his scotch, he studied his impromptu dinner companions. Both had similar deep blue eyes, except that Kelly's appeared larger, caused, John thought, by Quigley's squinting of his. Kelly was the taller of the two. He was about John's height and weight and looked to be in his early sixties. His blond, almost white hair was thinning at the top, and he kept it trimmed short. He was of a ruddy complexion, and John noticed he had big hands with swollen joints—the kind that would make it hard to button a shirt. The agent spoke with the distinct, resounding cadence reminiscent of career officers John had known in the military.

Quigley was much heavier, or so it appeared due to his smaller size. He wore rimless glasses that appeared too small for his round, broad head. His hair had turned white, and he wore it longer than Kelly did his. Because of the white hair and the roundness of his face, the agent reminded John of a staff sergeant he had known at Ft. Benning, Georgia. Both men wore suits that were wrinkled, especially Quigley's, which was light weight.

Kelly spoke first after a brief moment of awkward silence.

"I must admit to you, John," he said, "that your two friends took us by surprise." He grinned for an instant.

"'Ambushed us' would be more descriptive," Quigley added and laughed.

"Who were they?"

"Honestly," John said, "I don't even know their names. A friend made the arrangements. I asked few questions. As a result, I got few answers."

"Can your friend and these fellows be trusted to keep this quiet?"

"If you think that's necessary, sure."

"Good."

As John sipped his scotch, he found it hard to relax. He realized that, even if he learned nothing more from Kelly and Quigley, he was rid of the ominous fear of being followed by unknown persons. It relieved him to know their identity. Now, in place of that fear, was first, a sense of curiosity but more importantly, a grave concern over the startling event now taking place. It was bizarre, the idea of two CIA operatives following him. He pondered its implications.

He took a big swallow of his scotch. "I know you guys work undercover," he said. "But this thing is new to me. It was a relief to find out who you fellows were. But I'm still more than a little mystified. Would you explain what this is all about?"

"Don't blame you a bit," Kelly said. "The agency doesn't have all the bits and pieces yet, so what we can tell you at this point is rather limited, I'm afraid."

"But we hope to get more info as the case progresses," Quigley added.

"Some information is better than none," John said. "Shoot—I'm listening."

Kelly swallowed what gin remained in his glass. "You want another drink?" he asked John.

"No, thanks." He gestured toward his glass, which was half full. He took a small sip.

"Let me first say that it was always our intentions, in fact, it was spelled out in our directives, to approach you at some point and brief you on what was going on. But—"

"So what's going on?"

"—we needed to be sure about a few things first."

"Like what?" He could tell the two agents sensed his impatience.

"It's also not our intent to intrude into your private life any more than circumstances require. However, certain intelligence has come into our hands that's made it necessary."

"What intelligence? Give it to me straight, for God's sake!"

"We have reason to believe your life will soon be in danger, if it isn't already. That's basically the reason for our surveillance—plain and simple."

"My life in danger? Can you be more specific?"

"I want to take it one step at a time to give you as clear a picture as we can."

He shook his head in disbelief. "This is getting more confusing by the minute. To think I was relieved a moment ago finally knowing who you guys were. What about my wife and children? Are they in danger too?"

"I'm afraid so."

John sat there contemplating Kelly's revelation and the effects it implicated. "This is unbelievable." He sipped his drink. "I've got more questions, gentlemen. Why do you think we're in danger? And from whom?"

Their dinners arrived. Kelly and Quigley ordered another round of drinks and again offered one to John, who declined. When the waiter left, Kelly spoke.

"We have reason to believe you or members of your family may be victims of a kidnaping plot. You may be at risk of injury and possibly even death."

He didn't bother taking a bite of his food. As he pushed his plate aside, he thought of Demi and the children at home this moment—at the dinner table, or having finished, the children doing their homework begrudgingly, and Demi in the kitchen cleaning up. The thought that they could be in danger spiraled through his mind.

"Are you telling me my wife and kids may be kidnaped or hurt as we sit here?" he blurted out.

"My honest answer, yes. That possibility exists. But it's much more likely that it's too soon for that to happen. Don't worry, though. We've got that covered. As we speak, your house is under surveillance by two of our agents."

"So my family's safe, at least for now?"

"I think we can assure you of that. But in this business there are no guarantees."

"But how can you be sure your surveillance won't place them in more danger by drawing attention to the fact that your agency is on to something."

Kelly nodded. "Let me put it this way. Without our men there, if our intelligence is correct, whatever could happen would happen without us being around. Our job is to make sure your family remains safe. In other words, you and your family are much better off with us doing our job. I'm tooting my own horn, but we'd like nothing better than to earn your confidence on this point."

"And just what is the information you've come across to make you suspect this?"

The waiter returned to check if they needed anything. John ordered another scotch and soda. Now, he really needed a drink.

Kelly drank some water and swallowed bites of his sandwich. "First, let me ask *you* a question," he said. "As you may have guessed, we already know quite a bit about you, including that you served with the U. S. Army in Vietnam in the early 70's. Is there anything—anything at all—about your tour there that you feel might explain why anyone would be interested in you."

"Are you telling me that this theory of yours has something to do with my serving in Vietnam? That was almost thirty years ago!"

"We're positive. Our sources tell us that much. What we don't know is what information these people are after. We think they're interested in you because of sensitive material you might have. Either something you know, something tangible you possess, like a document or set of documents, or that you might have access to, even if you're unaware of it. That's why I asked if there was anything about Vietnam—anything that happened there—that might shed light on this."

"None at all." He shook his head to emphasize nothing came to mind. "Not off hand."

"Well, we'll ask you to think about that, of course. But I take it nothing occurs to you at the moment that would cause someone to place value in what you know or possess."

"Absolutely nothing." His drink arrived, and he took a big swallow. He managed a faint smile. "I've never needed a drink as bad as I do now."

"We realize we're unloading heavy stuff on you rather quickly," Quigley said.

"That's an understatement."

Kelly gave him a pat on the arm. "Aren't you going to eat your dinner?" he asked. "Or have we succeeded in ruining your appetite?"

"Yeah, I guess I should eat something." He moved the plate closer, picked up a fork, and nibbled at his food. "Where did you fellows dig up what you now have? I'd like some specifics."

"We'll fill you in eventually. For now, let's just say your name came up on more than one occasion in connection with intelligence we received from Vietnam. Then we uncovered documents—more to the point, we intercepted them with the help of operatives at other locations. Pieced together, this information tells us you're targeted by a foreign power."

"A foreign power! You mean Vietnam?"

"No—another country. We don't have details. But, from the intelligence we've collected, it's evident these people believe you have certain information that's vital to them."

"Like what?"

"We're trying to figure that out. On that score, we were hoping you could help us. That's the reason why we've got questions of our own."

"I'll do my best to recall anything I can."

"At this time, we can only speculate why the information is important to them. My guess is that they want it because, if leaked, and by that I mean in the world of international affairs, it could either prove embarrassing or hurt their relations with other countries. It's probably more complicated than that, but that should draw you a picture of the implications involved. We're still collecting data. Sooner or later, I hope sooner, we'll begin to fit the pieces together. Such is the nature of the beast we're dealing with. We're talking to you a little prematurely, since we don't have all the facts we would have had this case taken its natural course."

"Is that a way of saying I upset things by forcing you to come out in the open?"

"I suppose so." Kelly seemed embarrassed. "Anyway, if these people think you have the information or that you know where to get it, they'll make contact soon." He sighed. "That's why we believe you and your family may be in danger. When it comes to espionage, and believe me, that's what this boils down to, these persons will stop at nothing to get what they want. Kidnaping, torture, snuffing out a life—these are the kinds of activities these people get involved in." Kelly paused and looked straight into John's eyes. "Can we depend on your cooperation?"

As he regarded Kelly's tone of voice, he sensed a renewed fear. "I'll have to give that some thought."

"Why your reservations?" Quigley asked.

"Well, for openers, you fellows don't appear very sure about what you're telling me. What if you turn out to be wrong?"

"Let's assume we are," Kelly jumped in. "Isn't it better to be safe than sorry? What would you have to lose if we offered you and your family round-the-clock protection?"

"Aren't you doing that already?"

"Not really. We need to set up electronic surveillance and make a much more concentrated effort to cover all possibilities. And with a lot more agents—agents specially trained for the type of surveillance we need.

As it is now, we've just gotten started because we're fairly certain we caught this in its initial stages before things really start moving."

"What would be the harm if we expanded our surveillance," Quigley added, "even if our intelligence is wrong?"

"I'd be concerned about the effect it would have on my family," John replied. "They'd worry over nothing, if you're wrong."

"If we scaled down the surveillance we had in mind, your children wouldn't even have to know about it."

"Yes, but that still leaves my wife, Demi. She'd be scared to death if she knew what you've told me." He studied their faces. "I don't want to burden you with my problems, but you don't know the pressure I'm under right now, even without you in the picture. This would add to it."

"But the cat's out of the bag already. You *know* why we're in the picture."

"Granted, but my wife doesn't."

"I thought she already knew about us?"

"She's seen your car and suspected you were following. And she knows I'm meeting with you tonight. That's all. I can figure out something to tell her to protect her from all of this. She'd worry if she had any inkling our children were in danger. I'd need something more solid from you, gentlemen, before putting her through that."

"We understand your reluctance. But we'd like for you to reconsider."

He nodded. "I'll do that, but let's assume I told my wife the truth and we agreed to cooperate. What would happen next? In other words, what would you want from us?"

"First of all, we'd ask for your permission not only to continue our surveillance but to expand it. We'd be discreet and stay enough in the background, at least at the start, that your family wouldn't even notice we were around."

"Yeah, like you hid the fact that you were tailing me," John said.

"We'd be a little more careful," Quigley added and managed a grin.

"Kelly, why did you say 'at the start'?"

"Because circumstances might change," Kelly replied. "Later, we might find it necessary to provide stricter surveillance that would bring our agents into your home."

"I see."

"Please tell us," Quigley said, "why don't you let your wife decide for herself whether she'd feel comfortable with the increased surveillance."

"Because, until you fellows provide me with something more than you have, I'm not willing to approach her. She'd want to know why the extra surveillance, including bugging our house and phones. I'd then have to explain your theory, as well as that our lives may be in danger."

"So you'd want more proof before you let her in on the whole picture?" Kelly asked.

"That's right. I'm sorry fellows, but I'm used to thinking like a lawyer. I'll need something more than what you've come up with so far before I cause my wife the extra grief."

"How much is enough to win you over?"

"That'll depend on what you provide."

"We'll see what we can do on that score, but in this business, nothing's clear cut."

"It's not in the law either."

"You'll reconsider, though."

"Yes, I will. Let's assume, for the moment, that I change my mind. On this subject of expanded surveillance, as you call it, what about your exposure to others? Would I have your assurance my family would be as safe, if not safer, than if your men weren't tagging along?"

"Affirmative," Quigley responded.

"You've got our word on that," Kelly added. "We have no intentions of placing your family at greater risk."

"That's good to know," John said. "What else?"

"We'd ask you to sign paperwork that would permit us to conduct our electronic surveillance and to tap into your phone lines, both at the office and your home."

"Would you have to install anything to do that?"

"Not at your office. At your house, we'd like to place transmitting devices in several of your rooms, but I promise, not in your or your children's bedrooms. This is just a precautionary measure in case someone breaks into the house. Small devices would also be placed on your vehicles so that we could keep track electronically at all times."

"What's prevented you from doing that already?"

"As we've suggested, we're in the initial stages of our work. Such an intrusion doesn't yet fit into the scheme of things." Kelly paused. "We'll get further into that in a moment. For now, let's just say we don't have the necessary approval to place tracing devices in your cars. Finally, we'll take care of the wire tapping electronically and by making arrangements with the phone company. All of this would remain confidential."

"Okay, I think I understand what to expect. I'd like some time to think about it, though. If I should decide to go along, Demi would have to agree to your plan, too. Bugging our house, for example. I'd have to let her in on what's going on."

"We'd insist. One other thing, though. It'd be important that both of you go about your lives as usual. That would mean 'playing dumb' and not acknowledging our presence, no matter what. It's imperative these individuals, if and when they make their move, don't have the slightest hint our agency is on to them. For that reason, it's imperative you tell no one of our involvement."

"My friend, Guy Zanotelli, who made arrangements for those men who confronted you, will know something's going on."

Kelly nodded. "That's fine. But besides him, don't let anyone know, all right?"

"That's not a problem."

"Of course, should you decide to go along with us, we'd like to get together with you and your wife on this point to answer any questions either of you might have. Would that suit you?"

"Sure."

"That'll be fine."

"I insist on one condition, though, whether or not I decide to cooperate."

"What's that?"

"That from this day forward you fellows keep me posted as you get more information. Not every day, but from time to time. As it is, this nightmare's going to keep us on needles and pins. I think knowing more would lessen our anxiety."

"I promise we'll brief you—every day, if we have to."

"No surprises then—no secrets?"

"Believe me, John, in spite of the fact that the nature of our work requires a certain amount of deception, that's the only way we'll operate with you—on the level. On your part, for now, we hope you'll try searching your 'memory banks' about your tour in Vietnam. Let us know what you might remember that could shed some light on the case."

"I'll give it a try."

"When you do, may I suggest you pay particular attention to the people you knew there—military or civilian. Make a list of persons you got to know, no matter how casual or distant the relationship. Jot down any facts about them, no matter how insignificant they appear."

"I'll do that."

"Good. One more thing—there's a sensitive item we should make you aware of. I noted a while ago that we hadn't gotten approval to place transmitting devices in your vehicles." Kelly glanced at Quigley. "This doesn't involve you but has to do with our own bureaucracy and federal agency jurisdiction."

"You're losing me."

"Quigley, why don't you explain?"

Quigley cleared his throat. "In general," he began, "the CIA's work is global. Our work is usually done outside the United States. That's because of the nature of our work."

"I knew that much," John said. "That's how you got the info that led you to me, right?"

"Precisely. But there's a fine line separating our jurisdiction from that of our sister agency domestically, the FBI. Where our work takes us to other countries, generally, theirs takes place in the U. S. With some exceptions, of course. For example, the FBI has offices in foreign countries. But its agents are there to pursue criminals wanted in this country and don't get involved in our area, even then."

"Which is espionage."

"In a manner of speaking, yes."

"Why is all this important?"

"That's where the agency jurisdiction concept Kelly mentioned comes into play. As a lawyer, you'll appreciate what we're getting at. As a rule, anytime the FBI's work requires intelligence searching outside the U. S., our agency steps in. By the same token, whenever our work requires effort here, we call upon the FBI to do that."

"I think I understand. FBI agents should be sitting here talking to me tonight, not the two of you. Is that right?"

"That's correct," Kelly replied. "And that explains our present lack of authority to tamper with your vehicles. We'd need FBI clearance. Actually, that agency would do it."

"What you fellows have done is to cross over the line, rather than requesting the FBI to do it." He studied Quigley's face. "Does that mean you guys are in 'deep shit'?"

"Well, not exactly," Quigley said, grinning. "The FBI's already been notified of our initial work on this case. We anticipate their eventual involvement. You're right, of course, about our crossing the line. But it's often a rather gray area. Sometimes, the work each agency does crosses over into the other's jurisdiction. Because of time limitations, it happens that neither agency contacts the other for help at the beginning. But there's a coordinated effort by both agencies in the end."

"But I gather you're not at that point. You haven't involved the FBI, have you?"

"Not yet," Kelly answered. "That's why we wanted to mention this to you now. Because we had to act fast, we got our director's approval to move on this right away, without the FBI's help. But their own director's aware of our actions. Yet, we're limited in what we can do and still maintain a working relationship with the FBI. Keep in mind this was a covert surveillance until you found us out. Eventually, if our work reveals a plan against you and your family, as we suspect, then FBI agents would take complete control of the case. It would be within the FBI's jurisdiction at that point. When that happens, we'll let you know."

"But would you fellows still be involved?"

"We'd have to get approval from the FBI director. But going on experience, I think we can assure you he'd okay the joint effort."

"I can see it's a sensitive subject."

Kelly stood up. "I'd guess we've exhausted you for the night. Any other questions?"

"When will I next hear from you?"

"Not until we've got something new to report. We'll keep you posted on developments. Meanwhile, although we don't need your approval, we ask that you go along with the limited surveillance we're doing until you decide whether you'll okay what we've discussed. If and when you give the word, we'll start on our expanded surveillance."

"What if I said 'no' to even your limited surveillance?"

"To be honest, until we hear anything that would indicate we're on the wrong track, we'd probably continue, since we wouldn't be taking any intrusive action."

"That's what I figured."

Kelly insisted on paying the dinner tab. "It's all on 'company' time," he said when John suggested paying for his portion of the check. "It's the least we can do for intruding in your life."

Before they parted, John told Kelly and Quigley of his planned trip to Washington, D. C. the following Wednesday. Demi was to join him on Friday, and they expected to return late Saturday night. They planned to leave the children at home with a reliable woman who had cared for them before. He wanted the agents' assurance they'd do nothing to cause the care giver or the children to suspect anything was wrong. Kelly assured him that wouldn't happen.

"After all," he reminded John, "we need your cooperation, and we'll do nothing to jeopardize that."

At home that evening, John informed a stunned Demi of the startling discovery. But he kept from her the true basis for the surveillance and minimized its importance. He explained the agents only wanted to ask him questions concerning certain information about his tour in Vietnam. He knew she wouldn't accept that explanation.

"What sort of questions?" she asked, bewildered.

"About individuals I may have known there."

"But why?"

"They've got some kind of investigation going." He wasn't lying to her, he convinced himself, but just holding back information by not telling her all of Kelly and Quigley's revelations—revelations that might change the way they lived, even though he didn't know yet the extent of that change.

Demi still wasn't satisfied. "But why wouldn't they just contact you by phone?"

"As opposed to tailing me?"

"Right. Why all this 'cloak and dagger' stuff?"

He shrugged. "That's just the way they operate."

"Just what about these persons you knew in Vietnam?" she persisted. "What kind of information would you have?"

"They didn't ask me about anyone in particular. They just want me to search my memory banks to see what I can come up with that might help them."

"What did you tell them?"

"I told them I'd try. They said they'd get in touch with me later." He smiled at her. "Now, I suggest you not worry. I'm not going to. It's their problem, not ours."

No matter his attempt to play down the contact made with the special agents, she was upset. She told him she considered the agents' appearance in their lives an invasion of their privacy—unwelcomed visitors. Finally, she calmed down after he reminded her the identity of the persons following him was no longer a mystery and that the agents meant no harm. Although she agreed, she insisted the children be kept in the dark— that they be told nothing about the turn of events. They wouldn't understand, and it was too much to ask of a child, she said. He agreed. Yet, he couldn't help wondering whether he had done the right thing in withholding information from her.

CHAPTER 7

JOHN had rarely visited the nation's capital since his graduation from Georgetown Law Center. He held fond memories of his life there, even though as a student always in need of a few extra bucks. When Crystal was just over a year old, John and Demi left her with Demi's mother, and they took a week off from their jobs to fly to D. C. for his 20th year reunion at Georgetown.

On that occasion, they visited the place where the ugly red-bricked edifice occupied by the law school had once stood, a parking lot built in its place. She was both amused and saddened as she watched him walk on the bare lot, staring at the surroundings with nostalgia. She was humored when he walked up to the vacant spot where a small, greasy sandwich shop owned by a Greek immigrant had stood around the corner from the law school. He had eaten lunch there often. He also pointed across the street from where the main entrance to the law school had been, where he took his shirts to be laundered by an Asian gentleman. The structure still stood, unoccupied and in disrepair.

Reminiscences of his and Demi's trip there filled his mind as the plane he boarded in Denver from Albuquerque made a wide loop over the capital before its approach to Washington National Airport. It was a cloudless, sunny evening, and so all of the famous landmarks were visible— true symbols of the nation's history.

He was surprised at the short wait to pick up his one piece of luggage. From the baggage claim area, it was a short hop by courtesy bus to the Hertz rental station, where a car was waiting for him. Dan's administrative assistant and personal secretary, Stella Chavez, arranged for his hotel accommodations at the Hyatt Regency on New Jersey Avenue, near Union Station. The hotel was within walking distance of Dan's offices in the Hart Senate Office Building.

The plan was for Dan and him to meet at the senator's offices late morning of the following day. At noon, they would travel to the *Occidental Grill*, a restaurant on Pennsylvania Avenue, just a stone's throw from the White House, where they were to meet with Christopher Dunlevy, Deputy Counsel to President James Madison Henning. Chris was second in command in the White House Counsel's office, right under the President's Chief Counsel, Aaron Riley. Dan had spoken to Chris many times concerning John's candidacy for the upcoming U. S. District Judgeship vacancy and had faxed John's resume to him at the White House. Dan had asked Chris to meet John, and so the informal luncheon was scheduled for that purpose.

Dan had also suggested John join him and his wife, Candace, for dinner that evening. John knew he'd be exhausted, not only from the flight but from the events of the week before. He had spent Saturday and Sunday of the past week preparing for the Soliz trial, which was to begin on Monday. He declined Dan's invitation, explaining he hoped to spend a quiet evening in his hotel room resting and going over a few files from work. But even during the flight, he hadn't bothered opening his briefcase due to his tiredness.

On his arrival at the hotel, after unpacking and taking a quick shower, he telephoned Demi to let her know he arrived. After dining alone at the restaurant located on the top floor of the hotel, he returned to his room. For a couple of hours before turning in, he relaxed watching TV. He brought a book along to read, but tonight, his comment to Dan was no exaggeration. He was exhausted and didn't need a book to fall asleep.

He slept late the next morning. After breakfast, he took a stroll before finally walking to the Hart building.

On entering the senator's offices, he was happy to see a familiar face behind the reception desk. Susan Blakely looked up from her word processor.

"Good morning, John," she said with the same bright smile he remembered. "Stella's expecting you. I'll let her know you're here."

"Thanks, Susan," he said.

Susan picked up the phone and buzzed Stella. He sat down and chatted with Susan until their conversation was interrupted by several phone calls.

As he reached for a magazine, he heard a door open. "Hello, John," a voice said.

He looked up and saw Stella Chavez approaching with a big smile. He stood up to greet her. "It's good to see you, Stella," he said.

"It's good to see you too—it's been a while since you've been here." She hugged him.

"You've changed offices since I was here last."

"Well, you know how that is. With retirements and changes in seniority, senators get their pick—better views, easier access, larger space. With the latest move, we came out ahead in all three categories." She took his arm. "Let's go into Dan's office, shall we?"

Stella was still as attractive as ever, he thought when he found himself staring at the striking curvature of her body as she led him down a narrow corridor. She wore a pale blue suit. Her auburn hair was cut short, revealing the tanned skin of her neck. What John had always liked most about her was her perfect, glistening white teeth that accompanied her beautiful smile.

He followed her through a doorway. "I overheard Susan tell someone Dan's on the floor for a roll call vote."

They entered the private office.

"Yes, but he called less than a minute ago to ask if you were here. They've just finished the roll call. Should be here any minute. Have a seat."

He sat in a chair in front of a large desk.

She sat in a companion chair next to him, crossing her legs and pulling her skirt down. "Tell me, how are Demi and the children?"

"They're doing fine. Crystal and Johnny are growing up fast. It's unreal." Her question made him wonder what other information he could provide about his children. Did he know enough of their current activities? Or was he being a bit hard on himself?

They chatted for a few minutes, catching up on each other's lives.

"I understand Demi's joining you tomorrow," she said and stood up.

"Yes. Dan's arranged for us to attend a big reception at the White House."

"I know. How exciting! I hope you and Demi have a lovely time."

"We're looking forward to it."

"Listen, I wish we could visit more, but I've got to run." She gave him a hug. "The senator should be in—" The door opened and Dan entered. "Speak of the devil and he appears," she joked.

Dan smiled at her, then walked up to John. "Sorry you had to wait," he said. John stood up and shook Dan's hand. "How was your flight?"

"A little tiring," he said. "But I had a good night's rest."

"I'll say my goodbye now, John," Stella said. She waved.

"Thanks, Stella. See you later. Bye."

She walked out the door without a sound.

"Please sit down, John," Dan said.

Instead of sitting at his desk chair, Dan sat in the chair next to John.

He was an inch or two taller than John and much thinner. Dan possessed sandy-colored hair, which he kept trimmed short. His tailored suits accentuated his lean frame. At times, he seemed a little too thin to look completely healthy. Yet, his facial skin was almost without wrinkles, which made him look younger than his 55 years.

"How do you manage staying so trim?" John asked. "You must be the envy of the senate."

Dan laughed. "Far from it," he replied. But to answer your question, I still play handball and jog at least twice a week." He gestured. "But look who's talking."

"Trouble is, Demi cooks all that swell but fatty Mexican food, and she fixes it often."

"How is she?"

The question reminded him of Kelly and Quigley's entry into his and Demi's life. Yes, how was Demi, he asked himself. It terrified him to think she and the children could be in danger. If, of course, the agents' suspicions were warranted. Had he done the right thing in refusing additional protection? And in keeping the truth from Demi to prevent needless worry? The thought of telling Dan about the turn of events passed through his mind. But he dismissed it, remembering Kelly's admonishment. He'd honor the agents' request, even though he thought their theory was wrong. What could he possibly know or have access to that a foreign power wanted to get its hands on?

He was tempted to confide in Dan, probably because there seemed a curious sense of security or comfort in divulging the sudden intrusion to a friend in Dan's position. But that sense was false, he concluded, for there was nothing Dan could do that the CIA couldn't.

"Demi's doing fine," he finally answered. She's still working half-days and seems happy with that arrangement. It gives her more time with the kids." And now he thought it therapeutic to admit his domestic transgression to a friend. "God knows *I* don't spend enough time with them."

"It's tough, isn't it, finding time for both a career and one's family?" Dan shook his head as he gazed at the floor. "Since Candace quit her job, things have been a little easier. Our two children, of course, are now old enough to understand the demands of this job."

"Sometimes I wonder how you do it, Dan. Having a family—being a U. S. Senator—with the political demands not just here but back home. It must be unbelievably stressful."

Dan smiled. "That, it is." He sighed. "But it helps if you like your work and you feel you're doing something meaningful. Otherwise, a good case could be made that it's not worth the effort." He laughed. "In fact, if I ever start feeling that way, that would be as good a sign as any that it's time to try my hand at something else."

"Good thinking." He paused. "Listen. I'm taking too much of your time. Are we still scheduled for lunch with Chris Dunlevy?"

"Yes, at twelve thirty. I've got a meeting at eleven." He glanced at his watch. "I better get going. Let's meet back here at noon. We can take a cab, okay?"

"I've got a rental."

"Don't bother. Believe me, it's easier taking a cab. I'll brief you about our meeting with Chris on the way." Dan stood up. "I'll see you at noon, then."

John stood up. "I'll be here."

They shook hands before parting.

The cab they rode came to a crawl at the first traffic light on Pennsylvania Avenue, where minor road repair created traffic congestion.

Dan had been eyeing the traffic in front of them, but he now turned to face John. "Let me tell you about our luncheon meeting," he began. "Chris Dunlevy is a great guy. Very loyal to the President and his boss, Aaron Riley. Chris already knows a lot about you, but I wanted him to meet you. Although the appointment's my call alone, after all, we are talking of a presidential nomination, and I'd rather you be their choice too."

Dan was referring to a longstanding tradition in federal judicial appointments. The U. S. Senator of the home state where the judicial vacancy existed, if a member of the same political party as the President, recommended an appointee to the President. Barring any exceptional circumstances, the President in turn deferred to the senator's choice. The President's appointment would then be subject to the advice and consent of the United States Senate.

There had been occasions when the White House staff grew concerned of controversy over a potential appointee. They would then express to the senator they preferred a different appointee less likely to encounter resistance from the Senate to prevent embarrassment to the President.

"I understand," John said in response to Dan's comment. "You know I appreciate your willingness to do this, even though I haven't committed to the job." Now would be a good time to explore the Supreme Court opening with Dan, he thought. "Something's come up that I ought to mention."

"Anything to do with the Supreme Court vacancy caused by Justice McBride's death?"

"How did you know?"

Dan grinned. "Just an educated guess. I heard last week that Guy Zanotelli's been throwing your name around to test the waters."

"Oh? I haven't said I'd apply—only that I'd think about it. What do you think of the idea?"

"You might consider doing it. It's a damn good appointment to fall back on in case you decide against going for the federal judgeship." He paused. "Or, for that matter, even if you later decided to go for the federal appointment. It couldn't hurt your chances of sailing through confirmation and probably would help."

"That's what Guy thinks."

"How does Demi feel about it?"

"I haven't mentioned it to her yet. I plan to when she gets here."

"I was going to bring it up if you didn't. Since you've asked for my opinion, I think you should do it. You've mentioned before about making a change. That's why I suggested you think about this new federal position. Now that this other door has opened, you should give it serious thought. Later, when the federal position's in place, I'll recommend you to the President."

"I'll consider doing that."

"That reminds me. No matter what comes up, don't let Chris know you may decide not to throw your hat in the ring. That's irrelevant at this point. What's important is that I'm confident you'd make a damn fine judge. The purpose of this meeting is to permit Chris to assess you in person. There's no question in my mind he's going to like you and that you're going to like him."

"What about Chris' boss, Riley?"

"He'll defer to Chris, I'm sure. My impressions are that Aaron's delegated judiciary and Justice Department appointments to Chris and will back his choices."

"Is that why it's not important for me to meet him?"

"I wouldn't say it's not important, but it's more important Chris gets to meet you. Besides, I think Aaron will be at the banquet. I'd be surprised if he wasn't."

"Demi's excited about tomorrow night. It'll be a first for both of us. We've never been invited to the White House for dinner and an evening with the President and First Lady. I took the nickel-and-dime tour once when I was at Georgetown. Thanks for arranging the invitation."

"Glad to do it."

Dan was right. John found Chris Dunlevy both likeable and friendly. He was a much shorter man than John had expected, possibly five feet, seven or eight inches in height—and stockier. Even in his suit, he appeared muscular. He wasn't overweight and didn't possess a protruding waist. Although he had a noticeable receding hairline, that fact didn't detract from his youthful appearance. John guessed him to be in his mid-forties.

After the three of them placed their order and exchanged preliminary small talk, there was an awkward but brief moment of silence. Chris broke it.

"I hope Dan emphasized this wasn't an interview, John," he said, smiling.

John liked the idea that Chris was addressing him on a first-name basis. Although he had felt uncomfortable and even nervous when they first met, Chris' demeanor put him at ease.

"He did," John answered. "But even so, I admit I expected some grilling." He smiled.

"Not at all. To be honest, we already know quite a bit about you. I commend you for your outstanding success as a litigator. As you might have suspected, we've done a little checking of our own. You're well respected as an attorney. From my standpoint, you have the ideal background to become a trial judge."

"I appreciate your saying that."

"Well, I'm sure Dan here agrees it's well deserved."

Dan grinned. "John knows we wouldn't be here if that weren't the case."

"I've always had a lot of respect for attorneys who plunged into trial work," Chris said. "As for myself, I suppose I was too timid out of law school. Hardly ever entered the courtroom."

"You make that sound like an apology," Dan said and laughed.

"Did I? I just meant I took a different tack in the profession." He smiled.

There was a pause in the conversation when the waiter arrived with their order. Before leaving, the waiter went through the customary *is-there-anything-else-I-can-get-for-you* inquiries. He received negative replies and excused himself.

Curious about Chris' background, John asked him about it. Chris spent a few minutes explaining how he ended up working for President Henning.

"Are you going to stick it out as long as the President's in office?" Dan asked.

"I think so. I even plan on taking a bigger part in his re-election campaign next year."

"Do you? I don't think he'll encounter much opposition in the Democratic primaries."

"There'll be some—the usual."

"But surely nothing major." Dan studied Chris. "Or do you know something I don't?"

Chris smiled. "Probably not. The problem's going to be with the Republicans. You've seen some of it already, both in and out of the Senate. After all, when you consider the ambitious, yet costly programs the President's managed to get through Congress, you pick up negatives and enemies along the way. That's more the case when social agendas are perceived as unpopular."

"Who does the White House think will surface as the Republican candidate?"

"There's no real consensus yet. Are you talking about what the President thinks?"

"Well, yes. But even you—what do you think?"

"Personally—" He stopped for a brief moment and glanced at John. "We're getting into sensitive stuff here, so let's keep it to ourselves, okay?"

"No problem." Dan turned to John.

John grew fascinated by the turn the discussion had taken. After all, he was listening to a private conversation involving a high official close to the President of the United States. The idea of being privy to it intrigued him, for he was learning firsthand, not from watching a news program on TV or reading a columnist's story.

"Listen," he said. "I've always considered this entire discussion just between us."

"Thanks, I appreciate that," Chris said. "My strong gut feeling is—and this happens to be the President's thinking too—is that your southerner in the Senate, that SOB Emory Condon, will be the Republican nominee. I think that's the guy we're going to have to worry about."

"I tend to agree with you, Chris," Dan said, "but it's too soon to tell how well a Republican from the south will do in other parts of the country."

"Where's Senator Condon from?" John asked no one in particular.

"South Carolina," Chris answered. U. S. Senator Emory Monroe Condon. A West Point graduate who went on to distinguish himself in the military."

"That's interesting. I knew a *Monroe* Condon from the South when I was stationed in Vietnam. He was a full-bird colonel."

"That's the one. Went on to a distinguished career in the Army and was a decorated war hero in Korea, as well as in Vietnam. Served two tours in Vietnam, as a matter of fact." He paused to take a drink from his tea glass. "When were you in Vietnam, John?"

"From '70 through most of '72. My tour got extended a few months."

"Yeah, Condon was there then. That was his second tour of duty. It was during his first tour a few years before that he was decorated in the infantry. Changed branches due to a minor injury he got during a rocket attack. During his second tour, he was given a desk job in procurement."

"That's when I knew the colonel," John said in amazement. "That's right, I remember he was in procurement. It wasn't my area, but I sometimes dealt with the man through my job. But it may not be the same fellow."

"We're definitely talking about the same man. We've learned a lot about him the past year. If anyone's a contender for the Republican nomination, we're going to learn all we can about him or her. For example, we've already verified there was only one Emory Condon in the U. S. military during the Vietnam conflict. So the fellow you knew has to be the Senator Condon who's Dan's colleague in the Senate."

"Hmmm, interesting," Dan remarked. "Is the Colonel Condon you knew from South Carolina, John?"

"All I recall is that he was from the South. Had the southern drawl to prove it too." He paused in reflection, then shook his head. "It's strange how you lose track of people you once knew, then come across their lives in a different setting. So the colonel became a United States Senator. Impressive. I guess I don't keep up enough with national politics. Now I vaguely recall hearing his name a time or two on TV. Never a picture, though. But I never dreamed it would be the same guy I knew in Vietnam. Besides, I knew him back then as *Monroe* Condon, not Emory."

"That's right," Chris said. "For some reason, he used his initial "E" in the military. He went by 'Emory' and dropped the 'Monroe' part when he entered politics. Anyway, he retired a year or so after his second tour in Vietnam. He returned to South Carolina a military hero, and, while his name was still fresh in the public's mind, ran in a crowded field in a Republican congressional race and beat out the field by a wide margin. He unseated the Democratic incumbent who experienced some local problems. He later ran for the senate and won handily. Since then, he's been very popular with his constituency. He also wields a lot of power as Minority Leader. An ultra conservative in more ways than one."

"That's just the way they like them in South Carolina," Dan commented and smiled.

"And now you tell me he's a prime contender for his party's presidential nomination," John said. "This is too weird. I've never known a presidential candidate before."

He shook his head in disbelief but kept to himself the thoughts that were now filling his mind. Vietnam—a short period of his life so long ago.

On occasion, he had read and heard accounts of Vietnam veterans who had come home scarred for many years, mentally or physically. He knew of a few who had survived the war, only to be haunted in the mental health clinics by traumatizing memories of what they had seen or experienced in that Godforsaken country so far away from their homes. He considered himself fortunate to have been spared such torturing, painful remembrances that had a devastating, debilitating effect on the lives of so many others.

The time he had spent on foreign soil had returned as reality in his present life. First had been the frightening, bizarre revelation that he was being followed. Not by someone seeking to harm him, but by those who sought to protect him from someone unknown. Did those unknown persons intend to harm him or, worse yet, his family. It was true indeed that some persons' past often returned to haunt them. At the moment, he didn't know why they'd want to harm him. But he hoped he'd soon find out.

And now, he had learned something else. Someone from that same past, an old acquaintance and fellow officer in the U. S. Army, whom he had forgotten in the intervening years, was surfacing as a serious contender for the Presidency.

During the first few years after his return from Vietnam, his memories of that country and the people there were more than vivid recollections. In a strange way, they were still very much a part of his life on his return home. But then he became involved in his practice. It was then that his life in Vietnam began to leave his consciousness and to transform itself to faint and vague memories, as if but a dream.

Those memories were now resurrected, jarred from deep within. Were these unconnected revelations pure coincidence? Surely they had to be.

The reflections raced through his mind as he sat there with Dan and Chris. When he came out of his reverie, he grew embarrassed, for he felt both men sensed he was in deep thought of those days long gone. They waited for him to say something.

"I hadn't thought about my time in Vietnam for quite a while," he finally managed to say. "That talk of the senator made me lapse into a past I'd rather leave alone." He forced a smile.

Dan spoke first. "That's all right, John. That friggin' war scarred many persons by the time it was over. You're one of the lucky ones. A lot of our veterans came back permanently changed—and not for the better."

"Ugly war, wasn't it?" Chris added. "I wonder if this country will ever live it down?"

John realized Chris wasn't expecting an answer. Both he and Dan had apparently misinterpreted the reason for his reverie. Knowing that made him feel isolated and emphasized what he'd have to keep to himself.

Chris glanced at his watch. "I've got to head back." He stood up and picked up the tab the waiter had left. "Lunch is on me, fellows." He extended his hand to John. "It's been a pleasure meeting you, John. I'm glad we finally got a chance to meet." They shook hands.

Dan stood up and reached over to shake Chris' hand. "Will we be seeing you tomorrow night at the banquet?" he asked.

"No, I wasn't invited to this one." He grinned. "Even we on the inside need special invitations. Aaron Riley will be there, though. You can introduce him to John. I'll let him know you'll be there."

"That'll be fine," Dan replied. "Thanks again for meeting with us."

"My pleasure." He turned again to John. "I ordinarily wouldn't say what I'm about to tell you." He glanced at Dan. "If you want the judgeship, and Dan here recommends you to the President, which at this stage appears to be a certainty, you've got my support."

"Thanks, Chris," John said. "You've caught me by surprise; I don't know quite what to say."

"There's nothing more to say other than you want the job." He grinned.

When Chris departed, John turned to Dan. "I didn't expect him to commit himself."

"His mind works fast," Dan said. "He was 'assessing' you the whole time. You didn't realize you were being studied, did you?"

"That's for sure."

"I could tell he liked you." Dan stood up. "Let's head out."

"It appears the only one who has to make a decision now is me."

They left the restaurant.

"You'll have half a year to think about it, so you won't be pressed for an answer anytime soon. All I ask is that you give it serious thought."

"I'll do that."

CHAPTER 8

WHILE John waited for Demi's flight to arrive at Dulles Airport, he placed a call to Kelly. He had tried reaching the agent several times the day before, but there hadn't been a ring or response. He hadn't spoken to Kelly since their meeting at the restaurant.

He grew anxious they may have learned more to convince him that the threat against him and his family was real. Since that first meeting, he was also concerned the agents weren't only disappointed but upset he hadn't gone along with their plan. He was torn, however. On the one hand, he worried of the risk if the CIA's suspicions turned out to be correct. On the other, Demi was already upset with him for his having taken on the Soliz defense. Telling her the real reason for the CIA's sudden interest, he was convinced, would just add to the problem.

What she didn't know wouldn't hurt her. Or would it? His uncertainty made him eager to find out if the agents knew any more since the meeting at *McGrath's*. There was one other important reason he wanted to get in touch with Kelly—to tell him about Condon.

Unable to contact the agent yesterday, he had telephoned Demi at home Thursday evening to make sure she and the children were all right. She assured him everything was fine and that he had no reason to worry. For one, she hadn't laid eyes on the blue Thunderbird. In fact, she had seen no trace they were being watched.

He was relieved to hear that. "I suppose they're going to leave us alone, at least for now," he said.

Before hanging up, he verified her flight arrival, then spoke to Crystal and Johnny. After talking to them, a deep feeling of contentment overwhelmed him. It made him wish he was home.

That morning, he had finally succeeded in contacting Quigley. Kelly was unavailable, Quigley told him. As for John being unable on Thursday to reach the agent's number, Quigley explained the phone had malfunctioned, but they had since corrected the problem. Quigley suggested he contact them from pay telephones. They arranged for him to call Kelly later that day. Anxious, he made certain he arrived at the airport early to place the call.

"Hi, Kelly," he spoke into the receiver when he heard the agent's voice. "This is John Garcia."

"Contact!" Kelly said. "I apologize for the problem yesterday. It's taken care of."

"That's what I understand. I just wanted to check back with you to see how things were. It's a little unnerving not being able to reach you."

"Understandable." He paused. "Meanwhile, I wish you'd reconsider our offer to provide expanded surveillance and even let us contact your wife to level with her."

"Not just yet, Kelly. Not until I'm convinced they're in danger. I trust you'll appreciate my reluctance."

"What *did* you tell her about us, anyway? What does she know?"

"Just that you're interested in my getting information to you about persons I knew in Vietnam. Although she quizzed me, she seemed satisfied, so that's how we left it."

"Well, it's your call."

"I'm glad you see it that way." He cleared his throat, still attempting to hide his frustration over the phone malfunction. What if he needed to get in touch with them? He decided not to make an issue of it. So he changed the subject. "Will this be standard policy from now on, my calling you from public phones?"

"Yeah. We better not take any chances. I know it'll be inconvenient for you. Do you mind?"

"Not if you think it's best. I'm surprised you didn't ask to tag along with me here."

"Actually, one of our operatives has been on your tail since you stepped off the plane."

"You don't say."

"It's standard procedure. An agent will be tracking you during your trip."

"I hadn't noticed. Does that hold true for Demi and the kids?"

"Yeah."

"I figured as much from what you said before."

"For your part, keep an eye out for anything unusual or suspicious. If that happens, call us at once, and we'll see how you feel then about our suggestion. If you can't get to a public phone, by all means use whatever phone you can get to fast."

"If something like that should happen, I'll reassess my decision." He paused to recollect his thoughts. "Getting back to why I called. So everything's okay with Demi and my kids? Nothing's changed? I spoke to her yesterday evening, and she told me everything was fine. But I wanted to hear it from you."

"The minute we suspect they're in danger, I assure you we'll notify you before taking extra steps to insure their safety."

He *was* worried though and now realized that, no matter Kelly's assurances, nothing was going to change that. "Demi's plane should be arriving in a few minutes. One last thing. You'll be extra careful with your surveillance now that the kids are with the sitter, right? I'd hate for your men to do anything that'll make her or the children nervous or suspect something's wrong."

"We'll keep it 'low key.' I give you my word." Kelly spoke with apparent confidence.

The agent was only human, no matter how well he knew his business, and so slip-ups could happen. John decided not to let his concerns get out control, so he drummed it into his head that the sensible thing to do was to trust Kelly. Otherwise, he'd find it tough to get through the day without a bad case of nerves.

"How are things going there?" Kelly asked.

"Fine. Things went well yesterday. Had a good visit with Dan Conniff."

"How did it go with that fellow from the White House?"

"Very well." He remembered he hadn't yet told Kelly about Senator Condon. "By the way, I wanted to mention a coincidence that floored me during our luncheon yesterday. It has to do with my tour in Vietnam."

"Oh?"

"You asked me to start thinking about individuals I knew there—people I worked with. Well, at lunch, Chris Dunlevy mentioned a senator from South Carolina by the name of Emory Condon as a likely candidate the President might face in next year's elections."

After a brief pause, Kelly said, "Oh, yeah?" Another pause. "What about him?"

"It turns out that this Senator Condon, who Chris suggested has a good shot at the Republican Party's nomination for the presidency, is someone I knew in Vietnam. He was a full-bird colonel back then." He paused and waited for a reaction from Kelly. There wasn't one. "Have you heard of him?"

"Sure," Kelly said after another moment of silence. "As a public figure. I've heard his name mentioned in the news a few times. I had no idea he had presidential aspirations, though. Or that you even knew him." He paused again. "That *is* a coincidence. Small world, isn't it?"

He sensed Kelly was caught off guard at the mention of Emory Condon's name. He got the impression the agent knew something about the senator he wasn't telling him.

"Yes," he replied. "Quite a coincidence." Once again, he waited for Kelly to speak. "Why do I get this feeling you're keeping something from me?"

"As a matter of fact, I am. You've got good instincts. I'll tell you about it on your return."

"About Condon?"

"You'll just have to trust me."

"Well, if that's the way it's got to be."

He didn't bother hiding his frustration. He was too used to having others level with him. All this secrecy—was it necessary? He hoped Kelly realized his annoyance wasn't directed at him but at a situation he wasn't used to.

"Now you've got me wondering," he added, "but I suppose it must wait."

"It'll have to. But I've got something new I'll share with you."

"Oh?"

"Remember we explained our suspicions you were being targeted by a foreign country?"

"Yeah."

"We now believe it's the People's Republic of China."

"China! How certain are you?"

"We're not absolutely sure yet, but that's a reasonable assumption we're going on at this time based on new intelligence."

He looked at his watch. "I've got to go. Demi's plane has probably landed. One final question, though. You don't have our hotel room here bugged, do you? We want our privacy."

"No way. We wouldn't do anything like that without your approval."

"Just wanted to make sure." He paused. "Well, I better get going."

"Caio."

"Bye." He hung up.

The moment he arrived at the gate, passengers were beginning to deplane. Demi was one of the last ones. He felt happy when he spotted her. He waved. She smiled and waved back. He kissed her on the lips, then hugged her with more force than he was accustomed to. She appeared surprised by his public display of affection.

"I'm so glad you're here," he said. "I missed you."

"I'm happy to see you too," she said with a bright smile. She hugged him again.

"It seems like ages since I last saw you."

They walked down the concourse and entered the baggage claim area. They waited several minutes before her flight flashed on the screen. The baggage belt began to move.

"The kids okay?" he asked.

"They're fine," she replied. Didn't seem to mind that both of us would be gone for two days. In fact, I couldn't help feeling that this time they showed more independence than usual. A sign they're growing up, I guess."

He noticed a change in her expression. "Does that make you sad?"

"I hadn't thought of it in that way. But yes, it does make me a little sad." She smiled, then turned away, as if to camouflage a sentimental surge.

He moved closer to her, placed his arm around her, and pulled her close to him. "Well, let's enjoy each other's company without the kids. We're entitled to our time alone, aren't we?"

"I suppose so." She looked up at him and smiled. "I'm looking forward to the next couple of days."

"So am I."

On the way to the hotel, he told her of the prior day's events and of his visit with Kelly concerning Condon. He was careful not to mention the continuing surveillance or the agent's disclosure of China's possible involvement. This would be as good a time as any, he thought, to mention Guy's suggestion that he consider applying for the vacancy on the New Mexico Supreme Court, and so he did. When he explained Guy's and Dan's opinions that the appellate court position might strengthen his chances of smooth sailing through the federal confirmation process, she got excited. She wasn't surprised he had such strong support. What if he decided against going for the federal judgeship? Would he be happy doing appellate work, she wanted to know. He wasn't sure, he told her. She agreed the state judiciary was well worth considering and assured him she'd support him, whatever he decided.

At the hotel, he telephoned Dan's office to confirm the plan for the evening. He reached Stella, who was working late at the office. She informed him that Dan and Candace would meet them at the hotel lobby downstairs at six thirty. From there, they would travel by taxi to the White House and arrive there in plenty of time for the opening reception scheduled at seven. They would then be ushered from the reception area to the dining room, where the guests would be received by President Henning, the First Lady, and other dignitaries.

Meanwhile, Demi unpacked, undressed, and put on a housecoat and slippers to rest from the trip. By the time he was off the phone, she had climbed onto the bed and was watching the news on CNN. He went into the bathroom for a couple of minutes and returned wearing only his shorts and a T-shirt. He joined her on the bed, kissing her on the forehead.

"Are you excited about tonight?" he asked.

"I sure am," she said. "I've been looking forward to it since you left. I've never even met a President of the United States, much less at a White House dinner where we're guests. I'm nervous, though. Butterflies and all." She placed her hand on her stomach. "Aren't you?"

"A little. Good thing we'll be only two out of a couple of hundred guests there."

"Obviously, based on what you said Chris Dunlevy told you, you're not going to be scrutinized by anyone tonight."

"That's right. We're there to have a good time. Let's plan doing that, shall we?"

"Let's." She grinned, then turned serious. "What about this senator you knew in Vietnam. You think he'll be there?"

"I don't know. Didn't even think of asking Dan. I have a feeling it's not a function where protocol requires the President to invite a potential opponent in next year's election."

"And you said Kelly plans to fill you in on something having to do with the senator's connection to the CIA's inquiries?"

"He didn't say he had any particular information about a connection. What happened was, after I mentioned Condon's name and that I had known him in Vietnam, I sensed something had clicked for him. What he actually said was that he had information about the senator, but he didn't connect it to their interest in me."

He paused in thought. "It's quite a coincidence, isn't it—my finding out like this about someone I knew back in Vietnam? At a time when the CIA is questioning me about what I may recall of individuals I knew there."

"You don't think there's a tie between the senator and what Kelly's working on?"

"It'd be too much of a coincidence. I doubt it. Yet, my thinking about Emory Condon, after Chris resurrected his name, has jogged my memory. It's brought to mind two other men I got to know in Vietnam. One was involved with Condon's work in procurement. The other wasn't in the Army."

"Who?"

"The first was an Army staff sergeant. He worked under Condon. A fellow by the name of Leroy Etcitty. Leroy had worked in administration when I first arrived in Vietnam. I was attached to Army intelligence at the time. But he got orders transferring him to procurement under Condon a few months after my arrival. He and I became good friends, though, so we stayed in touch. Come to think of it, that's the way I first met Colonel Condon—through Leroy. By the way, he was a Navajo from New Mexico. Raised somewhere near Farmington—in Shiprock, I think. He was a career noncommissioned officer, and I've no idea what happened to him." He paused, caught in the memory of times long past.

"Who was the second?" Demi asked.

"Pardon?"

"You said two persons had come to mind. Who's the second?"

"Oh, a guy by the name of LaPierre. Henri LaPierre. He was a French journalist I befriended who was covering the war for a French magazine or newspaper. In fact, come to think of it, I also met him through Leroy Etcitty." He sighed, for the vague memories seemed to originate in a dream dreamed long ago. "Anyway, when I next talk to Kelly, I plan telling him about Leroy and Henri. Ever since he prodded me for names, some things are slowly coming back to me."

"Do you remember that much about them to be of help?"

He shrugged. "Bits and pieces are coming back to me. I recall, for instance, that Henri was working on a big story, but a problem arose. Things are a bit fuzzy, but I hope they'll clear up."

"Would either of these men be the source of the information Kelly's trying to uncover?"

"I'm not aware of anything they would have known that would interest the CIA."

"Maybe they had access to the information and your involvement was that you knew them. They never passed any information to you?"

"Wait a minute. What makes you think Kelly's interested in information someone passed on to me? I never said anything to make you think that."

"I merely assumed it from what you said—that the CIA was interested in finding out about the people you knew during the war. Why else would they want you to remember individuals you got to know there unless they want to know what you learned from them, either on your own or from what they may have told you?"

John reflected on her explanation, relieved he hadn't slipped by telling her more than he had intended. He now realized he was dealing with her inquisitive nature and keen insight. "That's a big leap, isn't it?"

"I suppose, but—"

"I don't know what to make of it," he interrupted, deciding to change course so she wouldn't pursue the subject. "But I'm sure that in time I'll remember details about these two guys. I'm surprised I hadn't remembered Leroy before now." He paused, saying nothing for a long while.

"Penny for your thoughts," she finally said.

"I was thinking how strange that one goes through life so immersed in the present. Events that happened in the past—and the people that were part of your life back then—they seem so irrelevant. As if the past never happened. Even when you start remembering more, it all seems to be but a blurred part of some dream. Yet, there's the realization that they weren't a dream but actual events that were once a part of your life. Does that make any sense to you?"

"I'm not sure." She smiled. "But remember, John—I'm not quite as old as you are. So you're a few years ahead of me in the 'wisdom' department."

"You smart aleck." He grabbed her, then kissed her.

She cuddled up to him, and he wrapped his arms around her warm body. They lay there in each other's arms for a long while. He wanted to make love to her and sensed she wanted him to. He began rubbing her back. She too apparently sensed his desire, and she nibbled at his neck with her soft, moist lips. She raised her head and looked into his eyes. Then her mouth met his, and they kissed with a powerful passion.

"I missed you, John," she whispered into his ear, then kissed him on the mouth.

He could feel the tip of her tongue moistening his lips. He opened his mouth, allowing her tongue to enter. He just lay there, letting her take charge. She turned him on his back and straddled him, her breasts just touching his hairy chest. She then began to rub her soft belly against his groin. He remained motionless, relishing the moment as she continued her sensual movements.

In their lovemaking, he was usually the active participant in foreplay, and she, the passive one. It was rare that she was the active one, as she was now. When she would do that, he relegated himself to remaining passive as she stirred their carnal desire for one another. The anticipation titillated him when she played this role.

She had told him once that it aroused her when he would lay there motionless, permitting her to do whatever her passion directed. He shivered with excitement as she moved the tip of her moist tongue down his neck and onto his chest, then onto his sensitive abdomen, where the warmth and softness of her mouth bit into his taut skin.

Afterward, they lay in bed for what remained of the late afternoon. He even managed to fall asleep for a short while. He woke up to the sound of her taking a shower.

He was surprised they were in the hotel lobby a couple of minutes before six thirty. They had experienced a last-minute rush getting ready. Her evening gown had wrinkled on the flight, and she had spent over half an hour ironing out the wrinkles.

"You look absolutely ravishing, darling," he said as they waited for Dan and Candace.

She smiled. "Thank you," she said. "I have a slight confession to make, though. I bought this gown for this occasion. But please don't ask how much I spent for it."

"Whatever the cost, it's worth seeing you in it. It looks great on you."

"You're looking mighty spiffy yourself." She reached over and picked out a thread hanging to the sleeve of his tuxedo.

They had been waiting there a minute when Dan entered through the revolving doors. He embraced Demi. She returned the hug and kissed him on the cheek.

"It's so good to see you again, Demi," he said.

"It's nice seeing you," she replied.

Dan smiled. "Candace is out in the cab. Ready?"

"Ready," John said.

They exited through the revolving doors.

For Demi, the evening turned out to be one of the most enriching and memorable events she had ever experienced. The guests were received by military officers in dress uniform, before being ushered into a broad hallway leading into the Blue Room, where the reception was to take place. John and Demi, both nervous, followed Dan and Candace through the receiving line afterward. It was there that Demi enjoyed the highlight of the evening when Dan introduced them to President Henning and the First Lady.

"Look what beauty comes to us from New Mexico, Penny," President Henning remarked to the First Lady.

"My dear, how lovely you look," the First Lady said as she held Demi's hand. Mrs. Henning wore a pale blue gown and a rhinestone necklace with matching earrings. She was befitting the elegance of the occasion and stood there with such grace, Demi thought.

"It's not often that the President's correct about non-political matters," the First Lady continued, "but on this occasion, I simply must agree with him. Please forgive his flirtatious conduct, my dear. Thank you both for coming." She smiled at John as she took his hand.

Demi was so thrilled at what she considered such personal attention that she only managed a smile and an awkward *thank you.*

She had never seen such elegance, not only in the interior decorations, but in the evening attire, from the President himself, whose presence was very much felt, and his striking wife, to the butlers that served an eight-course dinner and the formally-dressed orchestra members that played at the dance following the banquet. She was uncertain whether the President and the First Lady would remain for the dance. They had slipped out as the banquet was winding down but appeared a half hour later just before the dance was to begin. The President and his wife danced the first dance, a waltz. They danced alone at the beginning but were soon joined by others as the President motioned them onto the floor.

They left the White House a few minutes before midnight. Enjoying the cool night air, they walked down the street for more than a block before finding a cab. Dan suggested they stop for a nightcap at a café-lounge Candace and he frequented often, and John and Demi accepted.

CHAPTER 9

THE bailiff half-shouted in a deep, resonant voice, "All rise."

Everyone in the room stood as District Judge Scott D. Walker entered the courtroom. The jurist followed the court reporter and his law clerk through the doorway leading out of his chambers. Closing the door behind his broad frame, he looked about the courtroom, as if assuring himself the scene was set—everyone in their place. He walked up the two steps behind the bench, sat in the high back chair, and swivelled it around to face those in the room.

"Bailiff," the judge said in a resounding voice, "you may bring in the jury." He stood up.

The bailiff opened the door leading into the jury room, and the jurors entered the courtroom.

"Please be seated," the jurist announced as the last juror took his place. He himself sat, adjusted his reading glasses, and opened the file he had carried into the room. He glanced at the file, then turned to the jurors.

"Ladies and gentlemen," he said. "After you were sworn earlier this morning, I gave you certain instructions. Before we took a recess, I admonished you not to discuss this case with anyone, including your fellow jurors. I wish to remind you that instruction will remain in effect throughout this proceeding until the time comes for you to deliberate on a verdict." He cleared his throat, then turned to the attorneys seated at the two counsel tables.

"Mr. Keith, is the state ready to proceed?"

He was addressing the prosecutor, Robert Keith. Keith sat at the table nearest the jury box. At the second table sat John and Bernardo. The youth wore a dark pair of dress slacks and a beige sports coat. He didn't wear a tie but instead, a pullover knit shirt. The knit shirt fit tight, accentuating his small, lean body.

John had insisted Bernardo wear a sports coat. When the boy revealed he didn't own one, John gave him the money to buy it. Bernardo's almost frail body contrasted with John's broad-shouldered and taller frame. John wore a dark blue suit.

Keith stood up. "Your honor," he said, "the state is ready." He cleared his throat. "May it please the court—earlier, the state invoked the rule." He turned and motioned toward those seating in the gallery. "I notice there are a few persons who've been called as witnesses, particularly members of the defendant's family, who are seated in the audience."

Judge Walker nodded.

"Is the defense ready to proceed?" the judge said, turning to John.

"The defendant is ready, your honor," John answered.

Judge Walker then addressed the gallery. "Ladies and gentlemen. Those of you who have been called to testify mustn't be present in the courtroom during the proceedings until such time as you yourselves are called to testify. You may sit outside in the hallway until you're called."

Even before the judge completed his remarks, several of those in the audience, including Reinaldo and Ramona Soliz and their daughter, Carmen, had begun walking to the exit. Patty, Carol, and the youngster, Rebecca, were among the few in the audience leaving the gallery.

John turned to the Solizes. As Ramona Soliz' eyes met his, he nodded to her and smiled, assuring her everything was fine and that he was going to do his best to represent her son. She returned his smile, but he could tell she was nervous.

"Mr. Keith, call your first witness," Judge Walker said as a deputy sheriff dressed in khaki uniform ushered the last witness through the swinging doors in the back of the courtroom.

Keith stood up. "The state calls Officer Steven Tanner of the Albuquerque Police Department," he said, turning to the deputy sheriff standing at the doorway.

Seated in the witness box, Officer Tanner answered Keith's preliminary questions concerning events that had taken place after the stabbing. Through the officer's testimony, the jurors learned that, when he was dispatched to the scene, he was half a mile away. He arrived in less than a minute and began administering first aid to *the victim*, whom he found lying on her stomach in her next door neighbor's yard. Without exception, police officers referred to a victim of an assault as *the victim*, both in written reports and in their testimony.

Someone had already covered Patty with a blanket. The officer found a puddle of blood on the grass. Drawing back the blanket, he tore the victim's blouse with a knife from his first aid kit to examine the stab wounds. He described a large wound in the small of the back, from which the victim was bleeding.

He then asked her if she was in pain. In a weak voice, she stated that she was. She informed him she had been stabbed by her assailant several times in the front. Turning Patty over on her back, he unbuttoned the front of her blouse to examine those wounds.

He found two wounds in the abdomen and one to the side of her right breast. In fractions of inches, he described the size of those wounds. Two of them were bleeding *profusely*—the same word the officer had used to describe the large wound in the back. The other one wasn't bleeding as much. As he administered first aid, Tanner asked *the victim* questions concerning her assailant's description.

The prosecutor brought out testimony from the officer showing that, despite the wounds and pain, Patty was coherent, lucid, and able to answer questions with little difficulty. The officer expressed surprise that she was able to do so, for he had attended to other victims in the past when they had been hysterical or incoherent and thus incapable of explaining what happened.

Keith laid this foundation apparently to prepare the jury for later testimony concerning Patty's description of her assailant and her identification of him at the lineup. The fact that she *kept cool*—Tanner's own words—would lend strength to her description and identification of Bernardo as her attacker.

After an ambulance arrived to take Patty to the hospital, the officer then entered the Gregory residence and observed blood and a towel lying on the kitchen floor. Keith showed Tanner several photographs. The officer identified them as showing various angles of the kitchen's interior. Photographs of the exterior front of the house and the yard where he found Patty were also shown to the officer. They were taken an hour or so after the stabbing had been reported, near dusk, when it was much darker. For that reason, Keith had Tanner explain that, at the time he arrived, it was still daylight and visibility was unobstructed.

When Keith completed his direct examination, John cross-examined the police officer. He first asked him preliminary questions concerning his experience and his tenure with the police department. He then asked questions to clarify the facts testified to by the officer and to make certain that any loose ends were tied up. Keith hadn't asked Tanner many follow-up questions to obtain more detail on the officer's testimony.

The havoc a witness could cause to a lawyer's case or theory by *painting himself or herself into a corner* with specific testimony was a potential problem a good trial attorney tried to protect against. One of attorneys' worst nightmares in trying a case occurred when their witnesses testified they were certain about a particular fact that later might be proven doubtful, or worse yet, untrue. In John's opinion, nothing could discredit a witness's testimony overall more than to prove to a jury with reasonable certainty that he or she was lying or mistaken about some specific fact, even when that fact wasn't particularly significant or relevant.

On the other hand, juries were known to forgive or accept the few honest mistakes made by witnesses in their testimony, for that showed them to be human. In attempting to discredit a witness, lawyers had to be careful they didn't cross the line and badger or mistreat a witness. If they did, the tables could turn if the jury was forced to feel sympathy for the poor witness and possible distaste if not contempt for the insensitive interrogator.

As John continued with his questions of Tanner, he contemplated Keith's tactics and realized that, not having tried a criminal case against Keith, he was unaware of his methods. He convinced himself that his concern was more a part of opening day jitters than something that would play a significant role in the outcome of the trial. Besides, he thought, Keith knew little about him, so that somewhat evened the score. John was having lunch that day with Guy. He had meant to ask Guy about Keith a few days ago, but it had slipped his mind. He would ask him at lunch.

His thoughts now, as he cross-examined Tanner, were the same ones he had concentrated on when he made his opening statement to the jury earlier that morning. Those thoughts were that what he said, how he said it, and how he acted as Bernardo's lawyer during the trial would play an important part in how the jurors perceived his client's case. The jurors would later be instructed by the judge that their sympathies weren't to play a part in their deliberations. Any good defense attorney knew, however, that it was a good defense strategy to try obtaining the jurors' sympathies for a client as subtly as possible, rather than to antagonize them by conduct they disapproved of.

In preparing for the trial, John came to realize he could use a part of Tanner's testimony to help Bernardo's defense. After asking the officer questions concerning what each of the photographs depicted, John began to make an important point. He wanted the policeman to commit to the fact that Patty was able to describe her assailant without reservation, despite her condition. In his opinion, her description wasn't of Bernardo. This was important in creating reasonable doubt in the minds of the jurors. He didn't want Keith to explain away any discrepancies in the description by claiming Patty's condition prevented her from being accurate. Committing Tanner on this point would prevent Keith from doing just that.

"Now, Officer Tanner," John asked, "you stated earlier that Ms. Gregory gave a fairly specific description of her assailant?"

"Yes, sir," Tanner replied. He was tall and broad and appeared to be in his early thirties. John could tell he was a well-trained and disciplined officer.

"Without getting into what she told you, would you say she appeared certain about the specifics of her description?"

"Yes, sir."

"And, of course, you testified in response to one of Mr. Keith's questions that she wasn't only calm as you were talking to her but coherent as well."

"Yes, sir. Although she did appear to be in considerable pain."

Tanner knew his job well, John thought. He was being respectful, not just in his words but in his tone of voice. But in volunteering that Patty was in pain, the officer was also laying the groundwork for Keith to later

101

suggest her discomfort may have affected the accuracy of her description. Although John had no intentions of getting testy, he surmised the officer had long ago taught himself to remain calm and unaffected by an interrogator's relentless questions.

Like most seasoned trial lawyers, John had learned the hard way that you couldn't afford losing control or becoming angry at a witness like Tanner. Otherwise, the witness usually came out *winning* in the eyes of the jury. In the heat and excitement of a trial, where emotions ran high for both witness and cross-examiner, it was an easy trap to fall into.

John knew better. "Would it be accurate to say, Officer Tanner, that Ms. Gregory had no doubt at all concerning the description of her assailant?"

"None at all, sir."

Two could play this game, he thought. Now, he wanted to emphasize another important point—that the stabbing had occurred when it was still clear and there was sufficient light for Patty to get a good look at her attacker. "Now, sir, did I understand you to say that, when you arrived there, it wasn't only daylight, but clear?"

"That's correct."

"The reason I'm asking, officer, is that these photographs appear to show the residence and the surroundings during night time. They were taken much later, I take it." He picked up the photographs from the exhibit table and started going through them.

"Yes, sir. It took a while to get the photographer at the scene. He was off-duty at the time."

"So these photos really do accurately depict what was there—what they purport to show. With the exception of the darkness, of course."

"It wasn't nighttime when the photos were taken. It was dusk. In fact, we had plenty of daylight to conduct a search of the area for a weapon. I think we searched for an hour."

"You *think?*"

"Well, no, sir, that was a poor choice of words. I'm fairly certain it was around that time. I didn't time it."

"You didn't find a weapon, I take it."

"No, sir, we didn't."

John intended later to show Patty's description of her assailant didn't describe Bernardo in several respects. This bit of evidence was important to plant the inference in the jurors' minds that Patty might have been accurately describing to the policeman someone other than Bernardo. A corollary to this inference would be that she was mistaken when she had picked Bernardo in the lineup. With that in mind, John asked the last few questions of the witness.

"The reason I'm asking these questions, Officer Tanner, is that Ms. Gregory gave you a rather specific description of her assailant, one with which she appeared to be comfortable. At the time when this terrible thing happened to her, she could have seen clearly the person attacking her, wouldn't you say?"

"Yes, sir, she sure could."

"That fact, and her good memory, of course, would explain why she was able to give you a detailed description."

"That's correct, sir."

"So the darkness or shadows in the photographs wouldn't have been factors in how well she could see her assailant."

"No, not at all."

"So should it be established during the course of this trial that there might be some inaccuracies in her description, they couldn't be attributed to the fact that she couldn't see well in the dark, could they?"

"I don't think so, sir."

"There you go again, Officer Tanner, thinking—"

Keith stood up. "Objection, your honor. Argumentative."

"Objection overruled," Judge Walker said. "This is cross-examination, Mr. Keith. I'll permit Mr. Garcia some leeway."

"Thank you, your honor," John said, glancing at the judge. "I actually have no further questions. Thank you, Officer Tanner."

Keith next called Detective David Morales to the stand. John glanced at his watch as Morales made himself comfortable in the witness stand after taking the oath. It was already eleven fifteen. Because he was meeting Guy, he hadn't planned working on Morales' testimony during the lunch hour. Yet, he felt well prepared for the detective's testimony. He knew what Morales was going to say on the stand by heart now.

He had spoken to Morales several times on the phone, aside from the detective's interview at police headquarters. He had disliked the man from the moment Ramona had described in tears how he had bullied her family when he visited her home searching for Bernardo. He had treated them rudely and had even threatened harm to Bernardo if he didn't turn himself in.

Even over the telephone, the detective's arrogance was easy to detect. At police headquarters, he wasn't only uncooperative, but insolent, obviously upset Keith had directed him to comply with John's requests for information about the case.

As Keith began his direct examination of Morales, John was hoping the detective's aloofness would come across. His initial replies to the prosecutor's questions were polite and professionally handled, even though he appeared a little nervous. But as Keith began asking the detective to trace his steps after his arrival at the scene, John noticed that, as Morales relaxed, he began slipping into his usual self, displaying a touch of his arrogant nature. John was pleased at this turn of events but hoped that during his cross-examination, he'd succeed in causing the officer's negative trait to come through even more.

Morales arrived at the scene at about eight twenty. In response to Keith's questions, after explaining he was in charge of the investigation, the detective developed the following scenario.

The day after his visit to the scene and his initial interrogation of *the victim*, he learned of a suspect. That suspect was Bernardo. On one day alone, just two days after the stabbing, he spoke twice to Bernardo. On one occasion, he was accompanied by the department's photographer, who took a candid photo of Bernardo as he was entering his brother-in-law's car. Morales later placed the photograph with nine others showing individuals with similar physical characteristics and then went to the hospital where Patty had been admitted to the intensive care unit.

Previously, on the day following the attack, he was at the hospital to obtain a physical description of the assailant from Patty. That same day, after having taken Patty's statement, Morales returned twice with several mug shots and other candid photographs of other male subjects. From those particular photographs, Patty failed to identify her assailant on the day following the attack.

Bernardo's photo hadn't been among those first groups of photographs shown to Patty. Keith next handed another group of photographs to Morales, marked as State's Exhibit 7, which included the candid photo taken of Bernardo. That photograph was numbered "9". The prosecutor asked Morales to explain the manner in which Patty had looked through the pictures.

The detective testified that, as Patty viewed each picture, she placed the photos to one side of the bed. When she arrived at the eighth picture in the stack, she threw it aside and said without hesitation, "That's him right there." Based on that identification, Morales prepared the necessary affidavit and obtained a warrant for Bernardo's arrest.

Keith then elicited from Morales that another series of photographs were taken of Bernardo after his arrest. These photos, State's Exhibits 8 through 12, purported to show parts of Bernardo's body. The pictures showed scratch marks on the neck, the left wrist, and the left elbow.

Morales also testified that the day before these particular photographs were taken, the day after the stabbing, when he had spoken to Bernardo, Bernardo's hairdo was different from that shown in the photographs. The detective also compared the manner in which Bernardo now wore his hair in the courtroom—Bernardo's hair on the day after the stabbing had been curly and even a bit kinky, rather than straight as it appeared in the courtroom. On the day of his arrest, Morales said, Bernardo's hair had been straight, and he wore a part in it. The obvious inference Keith wanted the jury to make was that Bernardo had combed his hair differently the day after the stabbing. The next inference to be drawn, of course, was that Bernardo had changed his appearance to make it more difficult to point him out as Patty's assailant.

As John sat there listening to the comparisons, he realized he could do nothing to stop such tactics. He knew that if he objected, the judge would most likely overrule his objection, and he might be perceived as trying to keep the truth from the jury. His only viable option was to negate the inference the best he could through cross-examination and the testimony of other witnesses. Bernardo, for one. John himself didn't think the photographs showed any significant changes in Bernardo's hair style, and he hoped the jury would agree. During the trial, he would have to try pointing that out in subtle ways.

The use of subtleties in courtroom examination could prove helpful. It might give jurors the impression they themselves had drawn from the evidence that which was important, instead of their having been spoon-fed the noteworthy evidence by the interrogator. An astute and competent examiner could succeed in that tactic most of the time. Jurors felt more comfortable with evidence perceived not to have been forced upon them, but as important points they themselves had gleaned from the evidence.

Morales next explained that, to obtain Bernardo's height, which was shown in the arrest report the detective had prepared, Bernardo was placed standing against a wall at the detention center indicating measurements in feet and inches. The height shown in the report was therefore accurate. Bernardo's weight, however, was a different matter. The report showed Bernardo weighed 135 pounds. Keith was obviously concerned that his true weight was only 108 pounds. For that reason, he had Morales explain that, to obtain the weight of 135 pounds shown in the report, he had merely estimated and hadn't weighed Bernardo with a scale. It was a wise move.

A good attorney, during his examination of a witness, should be aware of the case's weaknesses and anticipate opposing counsel bringing those weaknesses to the jury's attention. It was often well worth the risk for attorneys to bring out the weaknesses in their own case and to offer reasonable explanations for them. Doing so minimized any damage opposing counsel's fresh reference to those weaknesses might make.

Keith had just begun asking Morales questions concerning the police lineup when Judge Walker interrupted to stop for the noon recess.

"Is this a good time to take a break in this witness' testimony, Mr. Keith?" the judge asked in a tone of voice that was declaratory rather than suggestive.

Keith looked at his watch. "It certainly is, your honor."

Judge Walker directed the jury, Morales, and counsel to be ready to continue at one thirty.

CHAPTER 10

WHEN John arrived at the restaurant, Guy was seated at a corner table smoking a cigarette.

"Being late is becoming a habit for me," John said as he sat across from Guy.

"No big deal," Guy said as he put out his cigarette. "Just got here myself." He picked up the two menus on the table and handed one to John.

"How's the trial coming?" Guy scanned the menu.

John glanced up. "Fine. Moving faster than I expected."

Guy put down the menu. "I'm not too hungry—just having soup and salad."

"That's what I'll have. I hardly ever get hungry when I'm in trial." He put the menu aside.

"Especially this one, I bet."

He nodded. "I must admit—I started off a bit nervous." He took a drink of water. "Keith's got Detective Morales on the stand."

"Dave Morales?"

"That's the one."

"That little prick! Don't take that fellow lightly. If you do, it'll be a bad mistake. He may be an asshole, but he's smart."

"Sounds as if you know him quite well." He grinned. "Thanks for the warning."

The waiter came and took their order.

"What's your sense of the case?" Guy said. "Is there a chance you can get the poor kid off?"

"Considering the victim's ID," he replied, "and a few other things that are against us, I'm sure glad the burden of proof for the state is tougher than in a civil case. That's one advantage of representing a client in a criminal case."

"Yeah, but the majority of criminal defendants are guilty, my friend. That kind of balances things out."

"I suppose."

"You think you can convince the jury there's reasonable doubt?"

"Our chances are fair. There are several areas I can stress. The ID discrepancies, for example. And Carol Niewold—she failed to identify Bernardo at the lineup. Then, of course, there are our alibi witnesses."

"Well, if other things are in your favor, maybe they'll buy the alibi." He paused and lit a cigarette. "But family testifying on alibi—if that's all you got, I doubt you'll convince a jury."

"I'm thinking of putting Bernardo on the stand."

"You are? Does he have any 'priors'?" He was referring to whether Bernardo had a record of convictions.

"His record's clean. Besides, I think his denial will sound genuine."

"I hope you win it."

Before their order arrived, they spoke of Keith. Much to John's surprise, Guy considered him a competent prosecutor. Guy usually set high standards. For that reason, it wasn't often that he had anything good to say about another attorney, especially prosecutors. Guy suggested John not underestimate Keith. They paused while the waiter served their order.

"Tell me about your trip to D. C.," Guy said as they began eating.

"It was successful, I think," he replied. "He drank some tea. "The meeting with Dunlevy went well. He told me the job was mine if I wanted it."

"Let me know if I can help you at this end."

"I appreciate your offer." He ate a couple of spoonfuls of soup. "I've actually got Dan's support all the way."

"That's what counts. And you told me before you trusted the guy. That's important." He took a sip of water. "What about my suggestion you consider the Supreme Court vacancy? Got a chance to talk to Demi?"

"I mentioned our conversation to both Dan and Demi." He went on to explain they were both supportive of the idea.

"Swell. That's the first time your friend, Dan Conniff, has agreed with me on a matter as important as this one." He grinned. "Are you going to do it?"

"Not so fast, Guy. I'll need more time, but it helps having Demi on board."

"And your buddy, the senator. Maybe I'll have to rethink my opinion of him." He took another sip. "You said you two go back a long way. How far back?"

"Since high school. We were good friends even then and played football together. Dan was my favorite receiver and we relied on one another. Trust was important to us."

"When was that?"

"'61–'62—around then."

"That's about the time I took a two-year sabbatical from practice. Otherwise, I'd have known about you guys back then when I kept up with high school sports." He speared two pieces of tomato from his plate, chewed on them, and swallowed. "I can appreciate the friendship that develops in sports. Just remember, though, life's more than a football game—more's at stake."

John nodded, deciding not to continue the dialogue that reflected Guy's dislike for Dan. "*You* took a sabbatical? Doesn't sound like the Guy Zanotelli I know."

"Law practice was different back then—more laid back. Cases didn't seem as complex and judges were more relaxed. Today, it's different." He paused. "Now, there's a helluva lot more money to be made in this business. But there's also a lot of shit to put up with."

"What in the world did you do during those two years?"

"I'll tell you in two fucking words—*enjoyed life*! Traveled. I couldn't take that much time off today if my life depended on it."

"I know I couldn't."

"Listen, I've got some important information to pass on." Guy wiped dressing from the edges of his mouth as he finished swallowing. "I told you I'd be making my own inquiries."

"I remember." He took a mouthful of salad.

"I've got these friends in New York who make it their business to know about these things. We trade favors once in a while, but they owe me at the moment. I asked them to find out if the Mafia or another outfit was doing surveillance of an Albuquerque attorney. That's exactly the way I put it—or if they knew about any activity of that sort taking place here."

"Holy shit, Guy—the Mafia! I don't want them involved."

"Hold your horses. It's being done discreetly. Besides, they're not involved."

"I hope not."

"Anyway," Guy continued, ignoring, John thought, what he considered John's unwarranted concerns, "the Mafia has nothing going on in this state. But in checking this out, my connections learned that the Tong organization has in fact hired professional 'thug-types' to travel here for unknown reasons. That supposedly took place just a day or so ago."

"Tong!" John exclaimed. "Isn't that the Chinese equivalent of the Mafia?"

"That's the one."

"I find it hard to believe that organization's activities would have anything to do with what Kelly and Quigley are investigating."

"Maybe not. It's a long shot, granted, but I wouldn't write it off. Sounds like a lead your CIA friends should check out."

"I suppose." He hoped it turned out to be nothing more than a coincidence. Yet, he grew afraid. Kelly had said his agency now believed the People's Republic of China was involved. Was there a connection? Tong was an outfit made up of Asians.

Guy looked at his watch. "I've got to get back to the office. And I know you've got that trial to get back to. What's with this fellow Kelly and his *compadre* Qui-Quig—"

"Quigley."

"Whatever. Anyway, can they be trusted?"

"They're federal agents, Guy—our own government!"

"How do you know they're on the level? Have you checked them out—their credentials?"

"Only when they first identified themselves."

"Those are easy to forge. In my book, you're too trusting."

"Well, I saw no reason not to."

"Well, shit, even assuming they're legit', will they level with you? Keep you informed of what's happening?"

In response to Guy's question, John summarized the events of the past week. He told him of the apparent coincidence involving Senator Condon.

Guy shook his head. "*Amigo*, sounds as if your whole friggin' past is coming back to haunt you."

"You've got that right."

"Tell me this. Do you want my people to do anything else?"

"Not at the moment. I appreciate the offer, though. And I can't thank you enough for what you've already done."

"Don't mention it. I'm glad to help you and your lovely family."

"I'm meeting Kelly and Quigley this evening. They're supposed to give me the latest rundown on Condon's involvement in any of this shit."

"You just give me the word if you want my people in on it. I'll do anything to help. After all, I've got my own connections in Washington."

"I'll let you know."

"If you don't mind, I'll do some checking around. Without Kelly and Quigley knowing, how about my having someone verify they're providing you with proper protection."

"I don't need protection, Guy! Not even the CIA's. I just want this mess to be over. You mean checking up on them?"

"Yeah. For openers, why the FBI isn't involved."

"I told you—the FBI may get involved." He hesitated. "I want this thing played down. Getting others involved, I don't know if that's—"

"It'll be done cautiously, John. Kelly and Quigley won't learn about it."

"Promise?"

"You have my word." Guy lit a cigarette. "Meanwhile, when you meet with these guys tonight, I suggest you tell them of the Tong operatives coming here from the Big Apple."

"Yeah, sure." He shook his head in dismay. "Even though I'd rather not believe there's a connection, I suppose I should tell them."

"You seem more worried than the last time we talked."

"That's because I hoped this mess would die down, not get worse."

Guy gave him a somber look and nodded.

It was one fifteen when they left the restaurant. Guy let John pay the tab, a rare event. They parted just outside the exit. John barely had enough time to return to the courthouse, check for messages with Lynda, and review his trial notes before testimony continued.

Keith spent most of the afternoon questioning Morales. The prosecutor's questions centered on the detective's role after Bernardo was arraigned before a magistrate. Morales first described the scheduling of the police lineup. The lineup had originally been planned for a Monday, but it was then moved to the prior Friday. Carol had seemed confused at the lineup and not only failed to identify Bernardo as the person she had seen fleeing the Gregory residence but had picked out another participant in the lineup instead. Keith therefore elicited from Morales that he didn't have sufficient time to get participants for the lineup.

Keith wanted to lay the blame for any confusion on the public defender, who had insisted the lineup be moved up to Friday. The mixup could lead to a possible inference that it was the sole cause of Carol's inability to identify Bernardo, or at least a factor.

Morales then made a mistake. Not a big one, but a mistake nevertheless. It could have been a genuine slip up, but John thought it might be intentional. Responding to Keith's questions concerning the lineup scheduling, the detective stated at one point that the prosecutor's office wanted the lineup scheduled the Monday before the Friday when it occurred. The public defender, on the other hand, had wanted it postponed. John knew from reviewing the public defender's case file that it had been the public defender who wanted the lineup to take place as soon as possible, and Keith had wanted to postpone it.

John made a note of this discrepancy to correct it during cross-examination. He wanted to make certain the jury didn't interpret it as suggesting that either Bernardo or the public defender was attempting to avoid the lineup confrontation altogether. That was why John suspected the detective's slip up might have been intended. Morales may have wanted to convey Bernardo's avoidance, thus suggesting guilt. John wanted the jury to believe the opposite. The fact that the public defender had insisted on an early lineup could form the basis for the inference that Bernardo had nothing to hide; he was eager to prove his innocence.

Morales next identified three photographs of the lineup participants consisting of fourteen subjects, all males, including Bernardo. Only two persons were asked to view the lineup—Patty and Carol. They were taken into the room separately.

Patty identified Bernardo, third from the left, as her assailant. She did so with no difficulty. Carol, on the other hand, identified an individual standing to the left of Bernardo, after taking considerable time to make

112

her selection. The young man she had chosen was about the same height as Bernardo, but stockier, almost approaching medium built.

Keith took great pains to have the detective emphasize that Carol took considerable time before identifying the person she selected. The tactic was the prosecutor's way of permitting the jury to believe or infer that, although she had selected the wrong man, she must have agonized over her selection because she was unsure. It was a good way for Keith to minimize the damage to his case.

From John's point of view, the mistake made by Carol was a plus for the defense. She had selected an individual who came closer to the description given by Carol herself and the victim. John would later hammer away on this point.

Morales also testified of the city map the assailant had handled and on which he had written Patty's work address. She had suggested to him he could check at her office for possible rentals in the area. The map, the handwriting specimens, and Bernardo's fingerprints were forwarded to the Federal Bureau of Investigation's laboratory in Washington, D. C. for analysis.

The FBI report received from the federal agency stated that only two different sets of prints found on the map were identifiable—those belonging to Patty and her husband. The agency hadn't uncovered any prints on the document matching those of Bernardo.

The handwriting analysis was also inconclusive—the agency had been unable to learn if the address written on the map was in Bernardo's handwriting. The report suggested two factors were involved in the inconclusive analysis. First, the address was short, and so it didn't provide a sufficient specimen of characters from which a considerable number of differences could be detected for comparison purposes. Second, the report suggested the handwriting specimen taken from Bernardo appeared as if he had made an effort to change his penmanship. As a result, the FBI requested a second sampling from Bernardo, which Morales obtained and resubmitted to the agency.

When the second batch of handwriting samples was taken, the detective requested Bernardo to relax as he wrote the address repeatedly. Bernardo appeared to comply, Morales testified, but the results of the second test were also inconclusive.

John began his cross-examination of Morales the latter part of the afternoon. He first clarified it had indeed been the public defender's office that insisted on scheduling the lineup as soon as possible and the prosecutor's office that wanted to postpone it.

He next asked questions concerning the relative positions of the male subjects shown in the lineup photographs as compared to the list of those individuals participating in the lineup. The subjects were first placed in the same order as their names appeared on the list. During the public defender's momentary absence from the room, however, the order in which the subjects stood in the lineup was reshuffled at someone's request. Morales couldn't remember who requested the realignment.

John brought out this information for two reasons. First, he didn't want the jury confused into thinking the photographs showed the subjects in the same order they were listed. Second, and more important, he wanted the jury to know a change was made during the public defender's absence from the room. That fact, by itself, wasn't significant. Additional testimony or evidence, however, might surface during the trial that might form the basis for an argument that the state or the police weren't dealing at arms' length. The showing of such tactics could damage the state's case, no matter how slight.

Next, John questioned Morales about the pictures he had shown to Patty at the hospital.

"I believe you testified you showed ten photos to Ms. Gregory at the hospital," he asked, picking up the photographs.

"That's correct," Morales replied. Not only did he not address John by *sir*, but he spoke with considerable confidence. If he handled his questions just right, John thought, he'd have no trouble bringing out the detective's flippant manner.

John walked toward the witness box as he flipped through the black-and-white pictures one by one. "Now, Detective Mora—by the way, do you prefer being referred to as 'Investigator' or 'Detective.' I ask because I've noticed that at police headquarters and in some of these documents, you're referred to as Investigator."

"Both are correct. Technically speaking, my title is Investigator, but most people refer to me as Detective. Take your pick. I answer to either."

In asking the question, John was taking the risk he'd be perceived as too picky. But he couldn't resist the opportunity, for his intuition told him Morales would answer with a bit of aloofness. His instinct was correct. "Well, I think it's easier to refer to you as Detective, so I'll use that, if you don't mind."

Morales shrugged.

"Now, in looking at the photos," he went on, "I notice they all appear to be mug shots, except one." He handed them to Morales.

Morales shuffled through the photographs. "That's correct."

"In fact, the green tags on the pictures themselves appear to be covering certain numbers, don't they?"

"They do." Morales attempted to return the photos, but John, acting as if he hadn't noticed, walked away, then turned to face the detective.

"Did you take those photos from a *mug shot* book?"

"We took them from our files at headquarters," Morales corrected him, evidently not comfortable with the use of the term *mug shot*.

"With the exception of one photograph, isn't that correct?"

"That's correct."

"And that one happens to be of the defendant, Bernardo Soliz."

"True," Morales said without looking at the pictures he still held in his hand.

"Don't take my word for it, Detective." He approached Morales. "Take another look and pick out Bernardo Soliz' picture, if you will."

Morales looked through the photographs and picked out Bernardo's. "Here's defendant's picture."

"Now, *that* isn't a mug shot but in fact a candid photo, isn't it?"

"That's obvious," Morales replied and nodded.

"It's the photograph you testified earlier was taken of Bernardo Soliz by the police photographer when you visited him at his parents' home. Isn't that correct?"

"That's correct."

"Now, sir, do you honestly believe that's a fair way of showing these pictures to Ms. Gregory." He took the photos from the detective. He put his arms up so the jury could see the faces of the photographs and shuffled through them, Bernardo Soliz' photograph on top. "Isolating Bernardo Soliz' candid picture from the mug shots, thus drawing attention to it."

"I believe so."

"You don't feel that procedure tainted Ms. Gregory's identification?"

"Not at all."

For an instant, he thought of asking the judge's permission to show the photographs to the jurors so they themselves could notice the difference. He decided against it, however, for he didn't want to distract the jurors as they passed the photos around while he continued his examination.

"Detective Morales," he said, "please correct me if I don't recall your testimony quite right. Earlier, in response to Mr. Keith's questions, I believe you said you showed Ms. Gregory an 8-by-10 wedding picture and other pictures along with that wedding picture."

"That's true."

"Those 'other pictures', as you called them, were actually mug shots, weren't they?"

"They were."

"From a mug-shot book."

"Correct."

"And isn't it a fact that out of the mug shot book, Ms. Gregory identified a photo of a person who wasn't Bernardo Soliz?"

"Out of the mug shot book?" The question had been clear, but Morales seemed to want more time to think of an answer.

"Yes." He spoke fast, not wanting to give Morales extra time.

"I believe she picked a person with similar characteristics."

"What did she say when she picked out the photo? That it looked like the man who attacked her?"

"No, she didn't."

"What then did she say."

"I can't recall her exact words, but to the best of my recollection, she said something to the effect that the person had similar characteristics. But I understood her to mean it wasn't the subject."

"And by 'subject,' I assume you mean the person who assaulted her."

"Yes."

"Whatever your understanding of what she meant, however, she didn't say that, did she?"

"Didn't say what?"

"That the photo wasn't of the person who attacked her."

"No, she actually didn't say that."

"And you didn't bother asking her if that's what she meant, did you?"

"No, I don't recall that I did. As I said, that was just my take on what she meant."

He decided not to pursue this line of questioning further. He was satisfied he had made his point with the jury, and it was time to leave well enough alone.

In response to additional questioning, Morales admitted his error when he testified he saw Bernardo on the Monday following the stabbing. He had stated he compared Bernardo's length of hair the previous

116

Saturday, when the detective saw him at his parents' home, to the hair length on the following Monday. John reminded him he had obtained the arrest warrant late Monday afternoon, and that, when he had gone to the Soliz residence to serve it, he didn't find Bernardo there.

The truth was that Morales didn't see Bernardo until Tuesday morning, when he had turned himself in at the office of the judge who issued the arrest warrant. This wasn't a significant point, but the mixup by the detective showed he wasn't immune to making mistakes.

John also pointed out the discrepancies in the hair description, the weight of 135-140 pounds, and the height of 5' 6" to 5' 7". These descriptions had been included in the APB, the all-points bulletin sent to law enforcement agencies in the Albuquerque area. Morales denied knowing that Bernardo, with shoes on, was 5' 3" tall and weighed 108 pounds. When the detective testified the description had also included the reference to the assailant being broad-shouldered, John asked him to look at Bernardo and tell the jury if he thought Bernardo was broad-shouldered.

Keith objected before Morales could answer, which John had expected, but again he had made his point. He wanted the jurors to observe Bernardo themselves and form their own opinions whether his slender, short client could in fact have been the person who assaulted Patty with such violence. Just as important, did he fit the description given initially of the assailant?

John also succeeded in eliciting testimony from Morales that he failed to inform Bernardo on the Saturday after the incident the true purpose of his visit to the Soliz residence. Instead of asking Bernardo's whereabouts on Thursday evening at the time of the incident, the detective went to the residence under a pretext. He asked Bernardo questions concerning Bernardo's knowledge about a particular incident the detective was investigating that supposedly had occurred the prior night.

The real reason for the detective's visit was to take the candid photograph of Bernardo. It was taken as Bernardo hurried into a car and while the photographer sat unnoticed in the detective's automobile. That's why it turned out to be a blurry profile. According to the state's case, the poor quality of the picture was the reason why Carol hadn't been able to identify it as that of the person she had seen running from the Gregory residence. This, despite the fact Patty had managed to pick out Bernardo's photo without a moment's hesitation.

John reemphasized Morales' earlier testimony during Keith's direct examination that the results from the fingerprint and handwriting analysis were inconclusive. But he also asked the detective if any prints other than those belonging to the Gregorys were discovered by the FBI analysis on the map. Morales admitted three distinct sets of latent prints were found by the federal agency, just two of which belonged to the Gregorys. The third set didn't belong to Bernardo.

When asked if the prints of anyone else who may have handled the map were sent to the FBI for analysis and comparison with the third set found on the map, the detective admitted no such prints were sent. When John asked why not, Morales became defensive, explaining that many persons in Patty's office could have handled the map. He insisted he sent the most logical sets of prints to the FBI—the Gregorys' and the defendant's.

John's questions left no doubt in the jury's mind that the third set of prints belonged to an unknown person. This fact left the door open for him to argue later that the prints could belong to the real assailant. That would never be known because the police failed to submit to the federal agency print samples of other persons who may have handled the map. Equally important, Morales failed to mention the existence of the third set of prints during Keith's direct examination. John later wouldn't let the jury forget what he considered as something less than full disclosure.

Even though Patty identified Bernardo as her assailant from the candid photo, as well as from the lineup, Morales also testified that, when she was shown the mug shot book and other photos before, she had picked out one or two pictures who she said resembled the man who attacked her. Carol and Rebecca too picked out a couple of photographs of male subjects they thought resembled the man they saw on the day of the attack.

John introduced the various photographs as exhibits, and Judge Walker admitted them into evidence. The exhibits, John thought, showed heavier, broad-shouldered males who contrasted in both facial features and size to Bernardo. He intended to point out these discrepancies during closing argument and argue that these fine points showed there were many areas in the state's case creating reasonable doubt, as Judge Walker would later define the term.

He also introduced into evidence a composite drawing made from a composite kit on the day of the assault. The drawing had been based on the description and guidance given by Carol at the same time the artist was attempting to compose the drawing. The finished product showed a person with short hair on top, as if the person wore a "flattop," a style popular in the fifties. In the composite drawing, the flatness was even exaggerated by use of a straight line.

John used this fact, together with the assailant's description in the APB that he had "short hair on top," to question Morales about Bernardo's hair length and style in the courtroom as compared to when the detective first questioned him. Although Morales attempted to neutralize the discrepancies with replies that were vague and noncommital, John hoped the jury would focus in on them even more. He surmised the detective's vague responses would affect his credibility.

On redirect examination, Keith attempted to rehabilitate his witness with questions aimed at clarifying what he considered to be *loose ends* in Morales' testimony. In an attempt to discredit Bernardo's family, who he knew would testify later as alibi witnesses, he ended his interrogation by questioning Morales about one of his visits to Bernardo's home.

"Now, Detective Morales," he said, "on that occasion, did you inform anyone at the Soliz residence that you had a warrant for the defendant's arrest?"

"No, I didn't," Morales replied.

"And you had determined from prior inquiries that Mr. Soliz wasn't home, is that correct?"

"Correct."

"Was there any conversation involving Mrs. Soliz, the defendant's mother, concerning the whereabouts of her son or her turning him in, that you may have overheard?"

John stood up. "Objection, your honor," he said. The question calls for hearsay. Ramona Soliz is here as a witness, and she alone can testify to what she may have told someone else."

"The objection is overruled," Judge Walker said in a deep voice.

Keith rephrased the question for emphasis. "Did you overhear Mrs. Soliz say anything as to her own attitude toward delivering up her son to you?"

"I can't recall the exact words," Morales replied in cue, "but I heard her tell one of the family members that she would never turn him in and that they wouldn't tell us where he was located under any circumstances."

"So you didn't find the defendant's family cooperative?"

"Not at all," the detective replied, emphasizing each word.

"I have no further redirect, your honor." Keith sat down.

John realized Keith was attempting to paint the Soliz family not only as protective, but deceptive as well, willing to harbor a wanted suspect. Such uncooperative conduct could be used by a skilled advocate to infer guilty knowledge, an attempt to hide an important fact from the jury, or worse yet, guilt by association on the part of the defendant. Showing a defendant's family in a bad light limited a jury's sympathy for the defendant's side of the story.

John was certain that, when Ramona Soliz got on the stand, she'd clarify the context of what she may have said, and thus, he hoped, gain sympathy for members of the Soliz family, who were trying to protect a person they believed innocent. He therefore wanted to lay groundwork for her testimony by asking Morales about the incident.

"Just a couple of questions, your honor," he said, approaching the witness stand. "Now, Detective Morales, in addition to speaking to Mrs. Soliz that Monday afternoon when you had the arrest warrant in your possession, you also had spoken to her that morning, hadn't you?"

"Yes, I had," Morales replied.

"Now, when did you overhear her comment that she wouldn't ever turn her son over to you?"

"In the afternoon, after the arrest warrant was issued."

"Isn't it a fact, Detective Morales, that earlier that morning, when Bernardo Soliz wasn't there, Mrs. Soliz told you at that time that she didn't know where her son was?"

"I believe so. But I can't recall."

"Which is it, Detective? Do you believe she said it, or you don't recall *what* she said?"

"She said something to that effect."

"And isn't it also a fact that, when she told you in the morning she didn't know where her son was, you replied that, when you found him, you were going to kill him?"

The question didn't shake the detective. Instead, he replied. "I did not!"

"Do you deny saying that?"

"I sure do."

"So if Mrs. Soliz were to take the stand and testify under oath that you indeed made such a threat, she would be incorrect, is that your testimony?"

"Yes, it is."

120

"But if she had interpreted what you may have said as a threat, would it surprise you if later that day, when you returned with the arrest warrant, she would have made the statement you told Mr. Keith you overheard?"

Keith jumped to his feet. "Objection, your honor! Calls for speculation."

"Sustained," Judge Walker bellowed.

"No further questions, your honor," John said. He walked back to his chair and sat down.

CHAPTER 11

THE trial recessed late that afternoon. John huddled with the Solizes outside the courtroom to give his impressions of the first day's testimony. They were neutral, but he believed he was laying the groundwork to create reasonable doubt. He felt satisfied the day's testimony had helped do that. The Solizes appeared hopeful and relieved the trial had begun.

Outside the courthouse, he watched them walk to their car. Whatever the trial's outcome, he hoped he'd feel he had done all he could when it was all over. That was important to him.

As he walked back to the office, he reflected on that first day. It had exhausted him. Ordinarily, he would have looked forward to going home to relax. How many times before had he felt that way? But he was meeting Kelly and Quigley, and, although tired, he anxiously awaited seeing them.

After that first meeting, although curious, he had intended to ignore and even avoid the agents and their limited surveillance, for he considered it a nuisance. He had walked away thinking he'd ignore their warnings and go on as if nothing had changed. But as the days passed, he found himself drawn to their web of intelligence. With it, they would get a clearer picture of whether the danger was real. Why, he asked himself, was he so affected. Because, he surmised, at some level he must have feared they just might be right—someone was after him or soon would be. A part of him told him the CIA didn't make those kind of mistakes. The fact that he found himself unable to call off the meeting tonight convinced him he was hooked on finding out anything that would shed some light on the issue. It was more than mere curiosity; he had a vested interest in their work.

Now, he faced another dilemma. Would there come a time when he would have no choice but to divulge everything to Demi? Would it be better to tell her now rather than later? Whatever he did, one thing was certain—she'd be pissed. First, for his having kept the truth from her. Second, for the added pressures they would bear due to the intrusion.

His thoughts returned to the meeting this evening. He was eager to learn what the agents would tell him about Senator Condon. He also wondered how relevant or helpful his memories of Henri LaPierre or Leroy Etcitty would be.

It was uncanny—much of what had happened in Vietnam was now coming back to him. He was surprised how many ordinary, everyday events of his tour he had suppressed.

It occurred to him he had just now managed to "turn off" the emotions connected to his client's trial, replacing them with his own concerns for what was going on in his personal life. Didn't that transference, though, take place often in the daily tasks of a lawyer? How many times before had he turned off the energy expended in one case only to have to turn on the spigot of energy to flow in another? Times too numerous to count.

But he wasn't now concentrating on another client's case. As matters progressed in what he now encountered on a personal level, would he be able to turn off the flow of energy needed to deal with his own problem and shift it to Bernardo's trial? He couldn't allow his problem to affect his concentration on his work, he said to himself as he walked back to his office. Otherwise, he'd fail the Soliz family.

At the office, he returned several calls before phoning Demi to remind her of his meeting. He promised he'd go home right after the meeting. It was a promise he intended to keep, fully aware there had been times in the past when he was home much later than he had estimated. He looked at his watch. They had scheduled a seven o'clock meeting at *McGrath's*. He had about an hour before the meeting. He spent the time preparing for the continuation of the testimony the next day.

Kelly and Quigley were already at the restaurant when he arrived. The agents were cheerful when they greeted him, although they appeared haggard. He guessed he looked the same to them. Quigley put out his half-finished cigarette as John sat down.

"You look tired," Kelly remarked.

"That's because I am," John answered. He sighed, then smiled. "I was just thinking the same thing about the two of you."

"That's because *we* are," Quigley said.

"How's the trial going?" Kelly asked.

"It drained me," John said. "If I hadn't been anxious for you to fill me in on Condon, I'd have canceled our dinner and gone home."

The waiter delivered three glasses of water and left menus.

John took a sip of water. "Well, as I said on the phone, I've got a few things to tell you, but I'd like to hear what you have to say first."

"Fine," Kelly replied. "Quigley, why don't you fill John in on what we have on his old acquaintance, Senator Emory Condon, formerly full-bird Army Colonel E. Monroe Condon."

"All right," Quigley said. "We've suspected some of this information for a while, but verified it a few days ago." He paused to drink some water. "It seems our senator served two separate tours of duty in Vietnam, almost two years apart."

"That's what I learned from Chris Dunlevy," John said. "Doesn't surprise me. He was the Gung-Ho type."

"I believe the senator had something other than patriotism in mind," Kelly broke in.

"What do you mean?"

"We're not definite," Quigley replied, "but we think there's a connection between what we suspect Condon was doing during his second tour and the reasons why someone's after you."

John threw up his hands. "Why am I not surprised out of my friggin' mind and at the same time not find what you just said too incredible to believe? I know that's somewhat contradictory, but this whole thing is beginning to seem that way."

"Probably because of the coincidence the senator's name came up in your discussions with Dunlevy," Kelly explained.

"That's likely. Then you gave me a hint with your silent treatment on the phone. Yet, a connection seemed improbable."

"Possibly because it may lend credibility to our theory that someone is after something they think you have." Kelly paused when the waiter came to take their order. After they ordered, he continued. "In other words, we're putting real life faces of actual people to our theory."

"What's this about Condon not being motivated by patriotism?"

"How much do you recall of Condon's line of work?" Quigley asked.

"I knew he was in procurement. That's about it."

"But what you might not have appreciated is the tremendous power he wielded in that job. At the time, there was an enormous amount of U. S. dollars involved in procurement. We've uncovered documents providing information about millions upon millions of supplies, including anything from weapons to foods to medicine. These supplies were intended not only for our own troops but as assistance to the South Vietnamese and other countries in Southeast Asia. It seems our financial aid to the region was enmeshed with our military operation in the area."

Quigley paused when the waiter delivered their drinks. "Colonel Condon," he went on when the waiter left, "was directly accountable for these millions of dollars in supplies."

"Why is that important," John said, "and what does it have to do with me?"

"We've gained access to previously classified documents that many millions of dollars of these supplies were unaccounted for after the U. S. pulled out of Vietnam."

"Are we talking embezzlement?" he half whispered and glanced about the dining room. "And are you next going to tell me the colonel was involved?"

"We can't say that. But we're not ruling it out either. Later, we hope to have more information to form a few conclusions. To either clear him or implicate him."

"One thing's for sure," Kelly added. "Many supplies vanished with no trace whatever."

The waiter arrived with their food order. Quigley cut a piece off his New York Sirloin, which was bloody red throughout. He shoved it into his mouth.

"Let's switch," Kelly said. "Suppose you tell us what *you've* got."

John nodded as he swallowed his first bite. "First, I'll tell you what Guy Zanotelli had to say at lunch." He told the agents of Guy's offer to

126

probe his contacts in New York and then explained the outcome of his inquiries—the Tong operatives traveling on an unknown mission to New Mexico.

"That's interesting but not surprising," Kelly said. He sipped his coffee and turned to Quigley. "What do you think?"

"I agree," Quigley answered. "You see, John, Communist China has never had any direct involvement in espionage or other 'discreet' activities in this country. That we know of, that is."

"I'm losing you," John said. "You made it plain the other day you suspected the Chinese were in on this. Are you now saying they're not?"

"Not at all. The Chinese go way back in history and culture, so they've had hundreds of years to develop their skills. They're wise—very much so. And astute, hardly ever making mistakes. They're also quite aware they 'don't fit in' well into the mold and culture of this country. For that reason, they've been known to hire U. S. born operatives to do their dirty work here."

"The Tong organization," Kelly added, "fits in nicely into China's way of doing things. Direct involvement by the Chinese in these sorts of activities, if discovered, could prove embarrassing to them in the international community."

"Well, now, I suppose another set of real-life faces creeps into the scene," John said.

"And those faces represent the group we've suspected all along. Your friend's information confirms our suspicions. For that reason, we should begin the protection we've offered so we can be ready when they make their move."

There was no end to Kelly's insistence, John thought. The agent's comments deserved a response. "I'll admit this latest development has got me a bit concerned. But we still don't know for sure Guy's information is correct. I'm not willing to change my mind just yet."

"Actually," Quigley cut in, "I think this turn of events is fortunate for the reason I noted a moment ago. Our agency has always found the Chinese to possess a high intelligence, political ingenuity, even brilliance, not just in foreign affairs, but just as important, in the world of espionage. For that reason, we've found it difficult to overcome their methods—to 'out smart' them, so to speak. Such isn't the case with Tong. Although of Chinese extraction, Tong members have been too detached from

Mainland China and don't share their ancestors' acumen. They're apt to make mistakes that the Communist Chinese never would."

"That's right," Kelly agreed. "Ironically, in hiring the Tong operatives, China jeopardizes its operations by proxy in this country. It has always risked failure here in exchange for keeping its hands clean from potentially messy affairs, should its agents be caught red-handed in the U. S. For that reason, I'd rather have Tong to deal with than the Chinese themselves. So I think we've got some refreshing news from your friend."

"I suppose," John said with some irritation, "assuming his information's accurate. Yet, we don't know there's a connection."

"Can Zanotelli be trusted with this information?" Quigley asked.

"That's funny. He asked the same thing about you."

The two agents smiled.

John hated to admit it, but instead of his troubles disappearing, these unwelcomed events continued to grow. Even so, a part of him was tempted to end it all tonight by just telling the agents he wanted no part in their plan and walking away. But his better judgment told him that wouldn't make the problem go away. He may as well accept it—there was no quick resolution.

He felt his throat dry, so he sipped some water. "Don't worry, Guy can be trusted," he finally said. He took a big breath. "I suppose I should tell you about these fellows I knew back in Vietnam."

"Yeah," Kelly said, "I've been anxious to hear that."

He told the agents about Henri LaPierre.

"When I first thought of him while in Washington, I vaguely remembered he was working on a big story. But since then, I'm remembering more and more—details I had forgotten."

"I was hoping that would happen," Kelly remarked.

"Anyway, Henri was secretive about this big story he was working on. Leroy Etcitty, the other fellow I'll tell you about later, introduced me to him. Henri was friendly in a weird way. By that, I mean he was outward at times; often, he appeared preoccupied and withdrawn. For some reason, he became attached to me and would sometimes invite me to go have a drink at one of his favorite Saigon hangouts. It was on one of those occasions that he told me about his story. He had one too many drinks, and I'm sure that's why he was loose with words and told me about a matter he would have otherwise kept guarded." He related that one conversation with the French journalist.

It had been a muggy day in Saigon. A cool drink at Henri LaPierre's favorite bar sounded refreshing to John when Henri asked him to meet him there. At the bar counter, Henri looked at John through narrowed eyes. The room was poorly lit, except for a ceiling flood light near the side of the counter. The light made the journalist squint.

Henri was small in stature with long, wavy black hair he was always sweeping back from his forehead. Despite his size, he was full of energy, bold, and even outspoken. What annoyed John about him was his hair—it was long and cut in such a way that much of it seemed to block his vision.

The Frenchman was drinking an exotic punch drink—his favorite. He knew the bartender, who would double the amount of vodka he used in the drink. Henri was so inebriated that he was slurring his words now as he spoke of the story he was working on.

"What's it about, this story of yours?" John asked.

Instead of sweeping his long hair back with his hand as was his custom, Henri snapped his head back, forcing the hair away from his forehead. "That, my dear friend," he said in almost perfect English, "are facts that should be left known only to me, the journalist." He pointed to the side of his head, as if to emphasize that the secret must remain with him.

"Then why mention it?" John sipped his drink.

Henri held his glass up in the air and pointed to it. "Probably because I've had one too many of these." He set the glass down on the counter and turned on his stool to face John, a sad, almost glassy look in his eyes. He possessed dark eyes that complemented his jet black hair, and they appeared even darker still in the dim light.

"But that's just partly true," he continued, still slurring his words. "I think it bothers me terribly—what I'm working on, I mean. Telling you I've got a big story, in a strange way, helps me cope with its ugliness."

"That big, huh?" John commented, more curious now than ever. "Just what kind of story is it that makes it ugly?"

They had been at the bar for several hours, and he had begun to grow a little bored with their conversation, which, until now, had focused on what he considered trivia. What Henri was telling him now, however, stirred his interest.

"I like you too much to endanger your life with what I know, John." He swallowed the rest of his drink. "Let's leave it at that, shall we. Me and my big mouth, as you Americans would say."

"I didn't mean to pry," John said. "It's just that I'm curious. You made it sound so intriguing. And I thought you wouldn't have mentioned it unless you trusted me."

"I trust you." Henri held up his empty glass to the bartender, gesturing for another round, then turned to John. "Another?"

"I'm fine, thanks." He sipped again from his drink.

"Trust has nothing to do with this, but you're my friend." He put his arm around John's shoulders. "And that's the point. As a friend, I want to protect you."

"Protect me from what?" John asked, even more curious.

Henri spoke as if to avoid slurring his words. "Protect you from knowing too much about something important. Not only to South Vietnamese officials but to your country."

"If it's that important, why not report it to the proper authorities."

"All in due time." The bartender delivered Henri's refilled drink. "Thanks," he said in French and grinned. He took the drink and raised it toward the bartender, as if to toast him. He sipped from the overfilled glass.

"The subject matter of my story is important, really," he said. "In the many months I've been working on this project, I've accumulated a good deal of information. I just need to verify some figures and extremely sensitive material. If I'm successful, my friend, I'll tell you this much—there just might be serious criminal activity on the part of certain important individuals in both your country's military and the South Vietnamese government. It'll have significant international implications. That much, I'll reveal to you."

Henri patted John on his shoulder. "But I've told you too much," he said with a smile. "So, I ask you, please do as you Americans say—keep it 'under your hat.' That way, you won't give anyone the impression you know something that might prove risky to you."

"That sensitive, huh?" John asked. "Henri, I respect your reasons for not telling me more."

"Thank you. Yes, it's very sensitive, I'm afraid. So much so that I'm getting a little worried of knowing what I know."

They left the bar right after that conversation and took a cab to the journalist's office. Henri decided to spend the night sleeping in a cot that he kept there. From there, the cab driver took John to his living quarters on base.

As the weeks passed after Henri LaPierre's cryptic revelations at the bar, John became preoccupied with his own work and lost track of the journalist. Meanwhile, as the rocket attacks and bloody skirmishes continued throughout the countryside not far from Saigon, the already volatile political picture in Saigon itself was worsening. The South Vietnamese government and the military, as well as the political climate and the relations between the U. S. military and the South Vietnamese officials, were growing more unstable day by day.

One day, through Leroy Etcitty, John learned Henri had lost his job as a foreign correspondent for the French newspaper he worked for. Henri needed John's help, Leroy told him. Leroy arranged for John and Henri to meet. Within a few days, Henri telephoned him, and they met in a remote location near the outskirts of Saigon.

"What happened with your job?" he asked a nervous Henri.

"Believe me, John," Henri replied in a halting voice, "it's better if you know nothing about it. After this is over, possibly I will tell you. For now, I need your help."

"If it's anything I can do, you know I'll help. What's the problem?"

"The Vietnamese officials are giving me a big hassle about my leaving the country. Not without considerable delays, which I can't afford at the moment. I believe my life's in danger the longer I stay here. I need the necessary papers, John! Can you help me get them?"

"To leave the country?"

"Precisely. Can you help me get them processed without much delay? There's not much time, and I may be endangering your own life by your being here."

"Calm down, Henri. Of course I can help."

"How long will it take?" He took his eyes off John just long enough to look around. "We must end this conversation now."

"Maybe tomorrow. Contact me at this number first thing in the morning." John scribbled a number on a note pad, tore the page, and gave it to Henri. Trembling, Henri grabbed the piece of paper and stuck it in his pocket.

"Thank you, John. Someday soon, I'll explain all of this so that it makes sense. At the moment, it hardly makes sense to me, except that I know I must leave the country." He embraced him, which surprised him for Henri had never before shown that level of emotion toward him.

"I'll wait to hear from you tomorrow. Goodbye."

"Goodbye. Thank you again."

They parted. The following day, he received the anticipated call. He gave instructions to Henri where to pick up the documents he would need to fly out of Saigon.

"If things don't go as planned," Henri said, "I might contact you. I may ask you to do something else for me, if you will permit me to ask you that one last request."

"If I can help you again, Henri," John said, "please don't hesitate getting in touch."

"Let us hope to God it won't come to that, my friend," Henri had said before hanging up.

The Frenchman had left the country in fear for his life.

"That's the last time I saw him," John said to the agents. "Anyway, I have no idea if that will help." He glanced at Quigley, then at Kelly. "I don't understand, though. Let's assume Henri's connected in some way to what's happening now, however remote. Why now, after so many years, would anyone be interested in any of this, including, if your theory's correct, Communist China?"

"Damn good question." It was Quigley who answered.

"It sure is," Kelly agreed. "I can speculate; it might have to do with something that's happened or is about to happen that's resurrected China's interest. An event unknown to us may have triggered that interest. I've a feeling your question, as well as several others, will be answered the minute we uncover what that might be."

"I hope so, Kelly," John said. "And it would ease my mind if that happened soon."

CHAPTER 12

THEY ordered after-dinner drinks. John sat there transfixed by his reverie of Henri LaPierre. So far away and long ago those events had happened. Yet, he now recalled them as if they had taken place yesterday.

Kelly broke the silence. "So that was the last time you saw him. Did you hear from him again?"

"Yes," John answered. "I received three or four letters from him. The first one was a postcard with a short note, thanking me for helping him get out of the country. He wrote that I saved his life. In the letters that followed, he wrote of putting together the finishing touches on his story. I remember him saying he had contacted a news magazine or journal about publishing his work. Thinking about it now, I realize he was obsessed not only with the story itself but with its long range effects when published."

"Did he ever say whether his story involved supplies or procurement?" Quigley asked.

"I don't remember." He paused in thought. "Are you suggesting there might have been a connection between Henri's story and the embezzlement you suspect Condon was involved in?"

"It's a possibility," Kelly replied, "but at this point it's too great a leap to conclude that."

"According to John," Quigley broke in, addressing Kelly, "LaPierre spoke of possible criminal activity involving the military. Because of that common factor, I think we should look into his story."

Kelly nodded. "Absolutely. We should pursue it. What about his termination with that French publication he worked for in Saigon? Did he mention that again or say anything leading you to believe his firing had any connection with what he was working on?"

"I'm surprised I remember as much as I do." He thought for a moment. "No, he didn't say anything like that. Come to think of it, though, he did say something about suspecting his firing was caused by the persons he thought meant to harm him before he left Vietnam in such a hurry."

"I'd guess these were individuals who didn't want his article published," Quigley interjected. "Getting him fired might have been the first step in assuring that. At least for a while."

"But he wasn't close to finishing it at that time," John said.

"That wouldn't have mattered. They might not have wanted to risk it."

"Good point," Kelly added. "That would also explain LaPierre's suspicions that the same individuals wanted to harm him after he was fired. They wouldn't have wanted his work to be published elsewhere, so they may have wanted to get rid of the story's source."

"And to think I thought he was blowing the whole thing out of proportion. Somebody might have been after him, according to your theory."

"Well, we should look into that. Anything else you recall about his letters?"

"Not now. Except for gleaning from them what I've already told you, they were cryptic."

"That's typical when a person suspects someone's trying to harm him," Quigley said.

"Did he ever tell you his location or provide a return address?" Kelly asked.

"Not that I recall." He paused. "Now that I think about it, he never included a return address. I distinctly remember noticing there was no sign of where he was living. I made a mental note at the time that he was being a bit paranoid not letting anyone know his whereabouts."

"He knew the letters could end up in the wrong hands," Quigley volunteered.

"What about postmarks?" Kelly asked.

"I couldn't make out the postmarks." John drank some water. "And I suppose you're wondering if I saved any of the letters. The answer is 'no.' I'm afraid I didn't."

"Were you still in Vietnam when he wrote?"

"Yes. I stopped receiving his letters while there; none after I returned to the States. But I made it a point to look for the story with his byline. I never saw it. In time, I forgot all about it."

The waiter picked up what remained of the dirty glassware and dishes. He left the check. Kelly dropped a $100 bill on top of it.

"You know, Quigley," John said, "you asked if Henri had mentioned anything about his project involving procurement. As I said, he didn't. But interestingly enough, the other fellow I planned to mention, Leroy Etcitty, might be able to help us on that score. Leroy worked in procurement under Colonel Condon. He knew Henri much better than I did."

"That's an interesting coincidence," Quigley said. "Maybe he can help us fill in the blanks."

"There's more. Leroy told me once that Henri had asked him questions about his job, especially the paper trail involved—how supplies were accounted for and how the process worked. I haven't the foggiest idea whether Henri's questions had anything to do with his story. Come to think of it, after Henri fled the country, Leroy told me his questions led him to believe Henri was interested in inventory discrepancies and the apparent ease with which supplies could be embezzled."

"That's something to follow up with Etcitty," Quigley said. "I don't think it was coincidental that LaPierre was quizzing Etcitty about his job in procurement when he was doing a story on alleged illicit activities in supplies."

"Reasonable assumption," Kelly said. "But we still can't tie LaPierre's story to procurement." He smiled at Quigley. "Yet, I'd be willing to bet ten to one we'll find a connection."

"I wouldn't take the bet."

"Leroy also told me Henri was stepping on a few toes in procurement," John said. "He said even Colonel Condon was annoyed. Condon used to refer to Henri, according to Leroy, as 'that annoying little

135

Frenchman with the distasteful accent.' Although I don't remember Henri having a strong accent."

"You've provided us with valuable information, John," Kelly said. "Don't you think so, Quigley?"

"I agree," Quigley replied. "Shouldn't we brief John on the bits and pieces we now know that might tie in the Chinese with the questions we've raised about procurement?"

"Yeah, I think he's entitled to hear what little data we have on that," Kelly said.

"You were vague on the phone, so I suspected you knew more than you were telling me."

"Well, I apologize for that. I'll let Quigley fill you in."

"What we have at the moment," Quigley began, "is tentative intelligence that isn't verified. So we're not guaranteeing its accuracy. We suspect, however, that millions of dollars in medical and arm supplies may have been steered into the hands of the Chinese Communists. These had been earmarked for our own troops in Southeast Asia, as well as for aid not only to the Vietnamese Army but other countries there."

"You're kidding me!" John said. "That's heavy stuff you're unloading. How would China be tied in to something like that in Vietnam? Other than being involved in boundary disputes with the North Vietnamese, what connections would China have in South Vietnam?"

"At the time of the war, there was a Chinese minority in Saigon that was loyal to Mainland China. These loyalists were a merchant class that were influential in that country economically. China was cash-poor at the time, and it wouldn't be beneath it to try filling its coffers with the help of its loyalists in South Vietnam."

"But surely you don't suspect that someone like Condon would be tied into such a scheme? The guy's an ultraconservative, and back then he was no different. He probably despised the Communists, whether Russian or Chinese."

"I'd guess you're right," Quigley said. "He wouldn't align himself with them. But we're not talking ideology. We're talking greed for the almighty dollar. In this business, we never eliminate any possibility until we've got enough to rule it out. Until then, we intend to keep an open mind on what Condon was capable of back then. Even if it included ties with the Chinese in illicit activities."

Kelly shrugged. "I think Quigley's right. I suppose that, not unlike politics, greed can create strange bedfellows. Besides, there were many diversion schemes going on at the time. So it's conceivable, assuming both Condon and China were involved in the illicit activities, that neither knew of the other's involvement."

The agent motioned to the waiter. He ordered a cup of coffee and asked John and Quigley if they wanted any. The both declined.

"But we'll find out sooner or later," Kelly added.

"For God's sake, Kelly, I'm hoping it's 'sooner.'" John felt a slight dizziness, overwhelmed by the growing gravity of the turn of events. The nightmare thrust upon him by Kelly and Quigley the prior week appeared to be mushrooming into a confusing scenario involving broader implications than he could have ever imagined. He sensed a loss of control over his life and the future—and just as important, in assuring his family's safety.

"I realize this whole thing seems to be getting worse and much more confusing to you by the day," Kelly said. He reached over and patted John on the arm. "That's why we're going to try to get some answers soon. That's not going to make the threat go away, but I think the more we know and the sooner we know it, the better you'll feel."

He paused and appeared to study John for a moment. John saw in his eyes that he understood. None of them said anything for a long time.

Finally, Kelly spoke. "Based on what you've told us, John, I think this French journalist, LaPierre, may be the key."

"To what?" John said.

"To our finding out if Condon or China, or both, were involved in any illicit activities, either in some kind of joint effort or separately. What we've told you up till now is preliminary, and our sources could be leading us astray. But as Quigley said, we've got to follow all possibilities until other information tells us we're on the wrong track."

"I couldn't begin to guess how any of this ties in to me." He sighed.

"Well, getting back to the Frenchman," Kelly offered, "I think he may be the answer to that too. Let's look at what we've got so far. Our sources tell us China may have been involved in benefitting from the embezzlement of millions of dollars worth of supplies destined for Southeast Asia. Another source gives us reason to suspect that our Colonel Condon, now Senator Condon, may also have been involved in missing supplies. Granted, these two possibilities needn't be related. But we can't rule out a connection yet.

"Now, we have this Frenchman, who was working on a 'big story.' Your pal, Etcitty, told you the journalist was stepping on the toes of persons in procurement, where the ordering and distributing of these missing supplies were handled. Etcitty also said that Condon was annoyed by what he perceived as LaPierre's meddling into their operation. LaPierre asked Etcitty questions concerning procurement, and Etcitty told you he thought LaPierre was particularly interested in some discrepancies and the ease with which he thought supplies could be misdirected from their intended destination.

"As Quigley and I agreed earlier, it's not such a big leap to assume LaPierre's inquiries about procurement practices had to do with his story. You said he told you it implicated certain persons in serious criminal activities."

"And how, may I ask," John said, "do I fit into that picture?"

"Their main interest may be LaPierre. They might only suspect you know something about him or his story. So at this juncture I think it's important to find out what the journalist's article was about. We'll have to track his movements after he left Vietnam."

Kelly appeared to ponder the possibilities. "Your Native-American friend may be our source to LaPierre. What happened to *him* after Vietnam?"

John shook his head. "When I returned home, I was interested in two things. Plunging into my legal career and forgetting the Army and Vietnam. I put that behind me. Leroy was a career, noncommissioned officer, but I'd guess he retired long ago."

"Why don't you sleep on it to see what else you might recall about him. Meanwhile, we'll try to locate him."

"Let me give that a try. I'd guess he returned here because of his cultural ties."

Kelly shrugged. "That's up to you."

"I'm still curious about China's interest in information it thinks I might have after all these years. You said a while ago it might have to do with a recent event. I was wondering if you think it has anything to do with Senator Condon?"

"Excellent question," Quigley said. "Congress has been resisting China's efforts to become a member of the World Trade Organization. That's a possibility, I suppose."

"And, assuming Condon was involved criminally back then, even if not in complicity with the Chinese, do you think China may have known about his activities?"

"We'll check that out," Kelly replied. "In fact, we've got a few of our operatives looking into that as we speak. Condon's role in current-day politics may be important too."

"We'll soon find out," Quigley assured John.

"Well, I think we've covered enough ground for one night." Kelly stood up. "Thanks for your help, John. Are you sure you want to check into Etcitty's whereabouts? Our agency has the resources."

John stood up. "Yeah, I'll get on it tomorrow."

"We'll wait to hear from you on that."

CHAPTER 13

THE Soliz trial recessed at eleven the next morning. Judge Walker had scheduled an emergency hearing on an unrelated case, and he rescheduled the trial to reconvene at two o'clock.

John was glad for the long break because he had a few tasks at the office. He also hoped to have lunch with Demi.

Back at the office, he made a few phone calls and discussed with Lynda the scheduling of depositions on several pending cases. When they finished, he asked her for the Farmington telephone directory. He then telephoned Demi's office. She was free for lunch, her secretary told him, and would meet him at the *4th Street Café*, a small downtown restaurant just off Central Avenue.

Lynda returned and left the phone directory on his desk while he was on the phone. Finding out whether Leroy was in the state turned out to be easier than he had anticipated. He knew that, unless Leroy had a phone listing, he might have to resort to a more time-consuming search—automobile licensing, tax, and voting records.

As it turned out, the phone directory contained Shiprock listings, where he thought Leroy may have settled. Shiprock was a small Navajo community about thirty miles west of Farmington in the northeastern part of the state. It was known as the Four Corners area because it was the one place in the United States where the respective corners of four states, New Mexico, Arizona, Utah, and Colorado, shared the same point in space.

John looked under the E's. There it was—no address but a phone number nonetheless. Now to find out if he had the right Leroy Etcitty. He picked up the phone and dialed. After the third ring, an answering machine became activated. He recognized Leroy's recorded voice right away. After identifying himself and greeting the absent Leroy through his recorder, he left both his office and home phone numbers and asked Leroy to call him as soon as possible.

Lynda buzzed him from the front office to tell him Dick Dunn wanted to see him for a few minutes and had asked if he would drop by his office before leaving for lunch. He looked at his watch. It was eleven thirty, so he'd have to hurry if he was going to meet Demi at noon. He found the door to Dick's office open, and he peeked in to see if his colleague was at his desk.

Dick looked up, saw him at the doorway, and motioned for him to enter. "How's the trial going?" he said.

They shook hands. Dick offered him a chair.

"Fine," John replied as he sat down. "Judge Walker has good control of the case, and things are going at a smooth pace."

"Good." Dick moved forward in his chair and leaned his elbows on the desk. "Thanks for dropping by. You got lunch plans?"

"Yeah, I'm meeting Demi. Care to join us?" He was trying to be polite, and the invitation came out before he realized he wanted to spend the time alone with Demi.

Dick must have thought as much, for he declined. "What I've got to talk to you about won't take long. You have a few minutes, don't you?"

"Sure, we're meeting just around the corner. What's up?"

Dick stood up, walked to the door and closed it, then returned to his chair. "I was just wondering if this trial has you a little up tight?"

That was vintage Dick Dunn, he thought; got right down to the point without any "beating-around-the-bush" crap.

He found himself irritated by the question. It didn't surprise him, for he had sensed Dick wasn't happy he had undertaken the Soliz defense.

142

"I was a little stressed at first but I've relaxed." He paused and looked straight into Dick's eyes with an expression that didn't disguise his irritation. "Why do you ask?"

"It's just that you've seemed upset the last few times I've seen you around the office. I wasn't too concerned at first, but then Edmund happened to mention he too had noticed. I thought of asking Lynda but then decided it'd be best talking to you."

"I don't know what to tell you except that I was a little worried about the trial right before it started, but I've got that under control."

During the past several days, he thought he had done a good job so far of hiding his worries over the CIA's sudden appearance. Had he been unsuccessful? "Dick, I didn't realize it was that noticeable. I'm doing fine, and you needn't be concerned."

"Well, I was beginning to worry. I hope you don't think I'm trying to meddle, but it's my job to see that thing's are running smoothly in the firm."

He thought it would be best to end the discussion with the least tension possible. It annoyed him, though, that the events causing the recent stress in his life seemed to be affecting his demeanor at work enough for his colleagues to notice. He wondered if he could better mask his anxieties.

"Thanks for being concerned," he said finally. "I have no problem with you doing your job. But there's no reason to worry."

"Fine, I'm glad it's nothing serious. I also wanted to discuss two other matters. They're not major concerns, but I think I should mention them as long as we're talking along these lines."

John looked at his watch. It was fifteen minutes of noon. He'd have to cut the conversation short soon.

"You know, Dick," he said, "if it's something serious and involved, perhaps it'd be best to continue this discussion later." He looked at his watch again, certain Dick could sense the slight discomfort in his voice.

"This won't take long, John, I promise. And since I can tell you're a little irritated about this conversation, I think it'd be better if we got it over and done with."

"Fine. What concerns?" He was unable to hide his impatience.

"I only wanted to mention them. After that, nothing more will be said." He cleared his throat "First, in spite of your assurance when you first took on the Soliz case, I'm a little worried your involvement will in fact have an effect on your billable hours."

"I wouldn't worry about that, either. My promise to you that the trial wouldn't affect my input holds true."

"I'm sure you'll make it up on weekends or at night, but at what price to you? I'm not talking about loss of hours to the firm but about your trying to squeeze them in every week. Consider me a friend, in spite of the unpleasantness of what we're discussing. I'm concerned you'll be working too hard to make up for missed time."

Dick sighed, then placed his hands on the arms of his chair and sat back, evidently more relaxed now. "I don't care if you get pissed off for my saying this to you as managing partner. But, as I said, this is part of my job, and I'm going to do it. The bottom line is, damn it, I'm still your friend and I'm concerned about your well being."

He realized Dick had a valid point. "I'm well aware of the problem you've noted, and I'll keep it in mind. What's your other concern?" He couldn't help glancing at his watch.

"Well, that one, I admit, doesn't have to do with your welfare. It has to do with the firm's welfare; that too is my business. I should have talked to you about this when you first decided you'd be taking on the case. But the fact is, it didn't register at the time."

"Am I doing something that's affecting this office in a negative way?"

"I don't know how to answer that, John, but hear me out. I realize you're committed to represent this youngster and commend you for that. I expect you'll fulfil your obligation to him and finish this case. But I'd like to ask you a favor, and it's nothing more than that, believe me."

"And what's that?"

"Before you take on any more controversial cases, as I believe this one is, think about the adverse publicity your representation might cause the firm. A couple of attorneys in town have commented on it."

"Commented on what?"

"Think about it. I believe you'll agree this firm needn't relish the kind of publicity cases like this one can bring. We've always been low-key. We can do a better job for our clients that way. And we've always managed to keep a low profile. I think it works best for everyone."

"I can appreciate what you're saying." He meant what he said and wanted not to sound defensive. He was surprised at himself for realizing with little hesitation that Dick had a valid point. "I must admit, what you've brought up didn't occur to me either when I first took on this case.

Now, having had time to reflect, I can see there could well be repercussions. I'm glad you realize I can't jump ship now."

"Absolutely. I wouldn't expect or want you to."

John checked the time again. "I've got to go, Dick." He stood up and extended his hand to let his partner know there were no hard feelings. They shook hands. "I realize I may have acted a little pissed off when this talk first started. But I want you to know I appreciate you were looking after my welfare and the firm's."

"That's fine," Dick said. "Thanks for understanding." He patted John on the shoulder as he opened the door. "Damn, I'm glad this discussion's over."

John smiled. "Me too. I don't envy this part of your job. Don't worry about me, okay?"

"Whatever you say, John." He paused. "One suggestion, though. Why don't you leave room for Demi and your children on weekends, instead of trying to meet your work quota then? You can catch up later."

He walked out into the hallway. "I'll think about that."

"Fine." Dick smiled. "Give my best to Demi."

"I will."

Demi was waiting for him when he arrived at the restaurant. She wore a light blue suit, one of his favorites. The periwinkle blouse she wore was low cut, and around her neck was a two-strand faux pearls. She had on matching pearl earrings.

"You look exquisite," he said, kissing her on the mouth. Her lips were moist and had a sweet, pleasant taste. He found the slight scent of her perfume alluring.

She smiled at him. "Thank you."

They ordered.

He told her of his unexpected talk with Dick, even though he realized he might be setting himself up for another barrage from her. When he finished, he again was surprised he had come away from it without feeling the least bit resentful. She had been listening with interest but said nothing.

After the waitress brought their order, Demi asked if he had been successful in locating Leroy Etcitty. He told her of his phone call to Shiprock.

She apparently sensed he was elsewhere in thought. "John, I can tell you're preoccupied." She smiled. "Are you thinking of the trial or about your talk with Dick?"

"Neither. You're right, though, there's something I can't seem to get off my mind."

"What?"

"It's about Leroy. When I heard his voice on the answering machine, it was the first time in thirty years that I had heard it. It was eerie and brought back memories of him that made me realize I had blocked out so much about that part of my life. It's beginning to dawn on me why."

"That's understandable. It was a terrible war that broke the hearts of many."

"I've never before realized I felt that way about our country's involvement there. I don't think you've ever heard me speak against it."

"You never even discussed the war, John, much less the fact that you may have opposed it."

"It began sinking in last night, when I met with Kelly and Quigley. As I was telling them about Henri and Leroy, I realized my tour in Vietnam had been unpleasant. It dawned on me I didn't have good things to say about our military role there. Not long after I returned to the States, I was aware of the antiwar sentiment prevalent back then and growing by the day during the last few years of the war. Although I had no opinion one way or the other during my tour, I later concluded this country had no business being there, at least not militarily. I now realize that this negative sentiment grew in me, and I think I later began to feel guilty for being a part of it. So much so that I found it easy to forget those years and the people I knew back then."

"But you shouldn't feel guilt. You had no control over it."

"I know. I'm not even sure I ever felt guilty, at least not on a conscious level. I'm just speculating that subconsciously I may have felt some guilt. That might explain why I blocked out Leroy and Henri."

They both ordered coffee after the waitress took their empty plates. Neither of them said anything for what seemed a long time. It wasn't an awkward silence, though. He used the time to reflect on what he had said to her and decided to leave the philosophical question of responsibility for the Vietnam war effort to historians and philosophers. He was also tempted to tell her everything he had learned from Kelly and Quigley and risk whatever wrath she unleashed. But he decided to hold off, still

146

hopeful the agents would soon come across information that would prove their initial suspicions wrong.

When they left the restaurant, he had just enough time to pick up the Soliz file and his briefcase at the office before heading back to the courthouse.

As he walked to his office, his thoughts were on Leroy Etcitty. Would he be willing to cooperate? Even so, would he be able to help? He hoped his old friend would have information that would be helpful to the CIA. Did he know anything about Henri or Condon that he himself hadn't already provided to the CIA?

He recalled a conversation with Leroy when the Native American had hesitated telling all he knew about Henri's inquiries of procurement practices. The conversation had taken place in a small bar and restaurant in the heart of Saigon where John had gone to meet a few friends for cocktails and dinner. He arrived early and was sipping a drink at the bar, waiting for his fellow officers. Leroy was walking from the restaurant side of the building to the street exit via the lounge when John spotted him. He called out Leroy's name.

"Sit with me for a minute, Leroy," he said as Leroy approached. "Let me buy you a drink."

The two men shook hands.

"No, thanks," Leroy said, "I don't drink." That was the first time he learned Leroy didn't touch liquor.

Leroy was a hefty man, not quite six feet tall but much stockier than John. He had a pockmarked face that gave him a certain air of ruggedness. His swarthy facial features and complexion were distinctly Native American and his shiny black hair and bushy eyebrows that almost met above his nose left no doubt he was Indian. His thick mop of hair was cut short, an Army requirement, but that didn't detract from his Native-American features.

He always walked around with a somber look and a distinct frown that gave the appearance of either being angry or in deep concentration. But if one ever got him to smile, which wasn't difficult to do, his face lit up, and one would realize he wasn't only likeable but possessed a healthy sense of humor. It was when you got him to laugh that the outward, somber appearance evaporated, and you were left with the image of a friendly person.

"What are you doing here alone?" John asked. "I thought you didn't like coming into Saigon by yourself."

Leroy smiled. "I don't ordinarily. But once in a great while, I make an exception. I met Henri LaPierre for dinner. He just left a minute ago."

"Why don't you sit with me and relax for a moment?" He patted Leroy on the shoulder. "You seem a bit uptight."

"I plead guilty." Leroy sat on the stool next to him.

"What's going on?"

Leroy spun on the stool and faced away from the bar, his back leaning on the counter. "Friggin' Henri's been questioning me a helluva lot about the procurement practices in our department. He's working on some story and asking a load of questions. He's getting all the higher ups on our staff jittery 'cause he's been asking questions."

"Yeah, I knew he was working on that project. I'm curious, though. How sure are you that his inquiries are connected with what he's working on?"

Leroy looked at him straight in the eye. "Why do you ask?"

"Only because he's told me he's been working on a story but didn't tell me much about it. I'm just curious, that's all."

"Listen, John, I'd rather not say. I shouldn't have agreed to meet him tonight. He had too much to drink and was telling me more than I needed or even wanted to know."

"Why does that upset you?"

"Because," Leroy said, rubbing his hands, "in my position, I figure the less I know about what he's delving into, the better."

"What do you mean?"

"Hell, he seems to think something improper is going on in my unit's offices, and the way I see it, I'd rather not know a damn thing about it. I do my job, and I don't want to know if anything illegal is going on."

"Just knowing about it won't implicate you."

"I don't want to take any chances. I feel uneasy anytime someone gets suspicious about anything that close to me. I'd rather not know if others are doing something they shouldn't be."

"I appreciate what you're saying. Be up front with him. Tell him his questions make you uncomfortable."

"First off, he's a friend. And I don't want him thinking I have anything to hide. I've leveled with him and given him plenty of information during the past few months. I don't want him thinking I'm being uncooperative, that's all." Leroy stepped off the stool. "Listen,

John, I've got to go. I shouldn't have burdened you with this. And I'm not going to tell you all I know because I figure the less *you* know, the better off you'll be." He extended his hand, and they shook hands.

"I hate to see you in such a predicament, Leroy," John said. "If you feel that way about it, I'd talk to Henri if I were you."

Leroy shook his head. "Yeah, well, it's a sensitive thing for me, but I'll give that some thought." He patted him on the shoulder. "See you around."

Leroy walked out of the bar.

That cryptic conversation had taken place a month or so before John helped Henri get out of the country. He and Leroy never broached the subject again. Now, almost thirty years later, he hoped Leroy wouldn't be reluctant to provide what information he possessed that could unravel this puzzle.

The trial continued at two o'clock, and Judge Walker informed counsel they wouldn't recess until six that evening. The jurist ordered a fifteen-minute break at four thirty, and John called Lynda at the office for messages, hoping Leroy had called. Leroy had in fact returned his call, Lynda told him.

"I told him you were in trial all afternoon," she said, "and would he please leave a number where he could be reached later. He said he'd try you again at home this evening because he wasn't planning on being home."

"Thanks, Lynda," he said.

That evening, in the tiny community of Fruitland, twenty miles east of Shiprock, Leroy Etcitty drove off U. S. Highway 64 onto the unpaved parking lot of the *Zia Lounge*. He had made plans earlier to meet some friends there. Shiprock was on the Navajo Reservation. For that reason, it was dry—booze wasn't sold there, neither packaged nor over the counter. To find the nearest place that sold liquor, one had to travel ten miles east along U. S. 64 to the *Hogback Trading Post*, where only packaged liquor was sold. The *Zia Lounge*, found ten miles further east, was the closest place booze was served over the counter. Most of its patrons were Native Americans. The tavern's other attractions were its four pool tables and its frozen food heated in a microwave oven. Pizza was a favorite. Although Leroy didn't drink, his friends did. He'd meet them at the *Zia Lounge* to exchange the gossip of the week while they played pool throughout the evening.

He parked his car, locked it, and walked to a public telephone anchored to the front wall of the tavern a few feet from the bar entrance. The sun had set a half hour before, but its orange-red glow was visible along the breadth of the horizon, where several mushrooming thunder heads had formed. In this open, almost desolate area, a slight cool breeze blew steadily from the northwest. He took a quarter from his pants pocket, placed it in the coin slot, and dialed the operator to place the call to John.

He wore a black pair of loose-fitting Levi's, a long-sleeve western flannel shirt, and a black Western felt hat with a sterling silver and turquoise trim around it. His face showed little wear since his days in Vietnam, but he had grown bulky around the waist. His swarthy face had a nervous look as he listened to the ring at the other end. A young girl's voice answered.

"May I speak to John Garcia?" he said into the phone.

"Who's speaking, please?" the young girl asked. John's daughter, he assumed. "Honey, I think your daddy's waiting for my call. Please tell him Leroy Etcitty is on the line."

"Just a moment, please," the young voice said. "Daddy, it's a Mr. Etcitty," Leroy heard the youth say.

In another moment, John's voice came over the line. "This is John. Leroy, is that you?"

Leroy grinned. "Yeah. It's good to hear from you, John, after so many years. Never in a million years did I think I'd be hearing your voice again. It's a shame we haven't kept in touch."

"It *is* too bad, isn't it? After I left Vietnam, I got so busy with law practice that I lost track of everyone I knew back there."

"I'm probably more at fault than you. After all, I spent another fifteen or so years 'in' after you left. I've been back in New Mexico since. I've seen your name in the newspaper a couple of times, and so I knew you were in Albuquerque."

Several times in the past, he had thought of reaching John, but that's as far as it got. He had been in Albuquerque on several occasions during the past few years, so the opportunity had arisen. For that reason, he felt guilty that it was John who had made the first contact. He was curious to find out why John was calling.

"Please tell me about yourself," John said. "What are you doing with your life now that you're retired?"

His curiosity would remain unsatisfied for the moment, he thought. It was time to get reacquainted. "I settled down here, doing a lot of hunting and fishing the first few years. Then I got tired of that life of leisure and learned a craft. I create silver and turquoise jewelry—at times work in gold, but usually silver. It's become a lucrative business for me."

"So it's not just a hobby?"

"Well, it started out that way, but I was told I was good at it, so I started marketing my work. Now, it occupies quite a lot of my time, which leaves little of it for hunting and fishing or other things. But I'm having the time of my life so I don't mind staying busy with a craft I enjoy."

"That's great, Leroy. A professional artisan-craftsman. Did you ever marry?"

"No, it was hard to find a Native-American girl during my thirty years in the Army. They just weren't around. When I got back home, I was too set in my ways, and there were few prospects. For a fellow my age, anyway. I have a little house out here in the country and live alone. My parents are dead, and my brother and sister moved away from here long ago." He paused. "What about you? I'd be surprised if you stayed single, a good looking guy like you."

"Yeah, I got married. We've got two children."

"That's great, John. Two little ones." He was happy he and John had made contact after so many years. "It's good to hear your voice." He wanted to find out more about John and his personal life, but that would have to wait. "I'm curious as hell why you called. Something tells me it wasn't just a social call."

"I'm sure you were surprised when you heard my voice on your machine. Listen, we can catch up on ourselves when we meet. That's why I called—I've got to see you so we can talk in private. The sooner, the better."

"Sounds like it's important. Anything the matter?" Now, he was even more curious.

"Well, it's important to me. Something's come up, and you might be able to help. I'd rather not talk about it on the phone. I could go up to Shiprock to see you."

"If you can meet with me this weekend, you won't have to travel that far. It so happens I'll be at Indian Market in Santa Fe. I've had a booth there for several years. We could meet there."

"That'll work. Demi might want to come along. We haven't been to Indian Market in a while. Saturday night would be best for us."

"That'll be fine. It'll be good to see you. I'm curious as hell what's come up, but you don't want to tell me over the phone, huh?"

"I'd rather not."

"I'll respect your wishes. I'll be in booth No. 104. Just come up Saturday night—I should be there after seven."

"Can you leave your booth? Why don't you join us for dinner?"

"I've got a helper, so I'll be able to take a break, and we can talk in private somewhere else. Thanks for the offer, but I've already made plans with friends early that evening."

"That's fine." He paused. "Listen, one final point."

"Yeah?"

"I won't get the chance to speak to you alone. I may not be doing the right thing, but I haven't told Demi everything about what I'll eventually talk to you about."

"Oh?"

"Yeah, I don't want her worrying about it."

"I understand."

"So keep in mind I'll tell you what she already knows. Later, I'll fill you in on the rest."

"That's okay with me, John."

"I'm looking forward to seeing you."

"Likewise. It's been good talking to you. So long."

"Thanks, Leroy. Bye."

He hung up, then walked the few steps to the *Zia Lounge's* entrance. His mind wasn't on meeting his friends for a few games of pool and a pizza but on his old friend. Whatever John's reason for calling him, he felt good hearing the voice of an old Army buddy. He'd be impatient for Saturday night to come around, not only because of his curiosity about why John had called but because he was eager to renew acquaintances with an old friend from the past. That realization made him smile as he walked into the tavern.

Down an isolated dirt road off the paved highway, a few yards away from the tavern, two strangers sat in the front seat of a car. The vehicle was hidden in semi-darkness. Although the light in front of the tavern was bright, its light rays reaching the dark car cast a dim shadow on the vague faces of the two men. But even in the darkness, the facial features were distinct enough to reveal the men were of Asian descent. The driver picked up a cellular phone from the seat, pushed the TALK button, and in perfect English spoke to someone at the other end.

CHAPTER 14

DEMI heard the doorbell as she struggled with one of her earrings. It was probably Eloise, the babysitter, she thought as she rushed to get ready.

"Crystal, would you please answer the door?" she yelled down the hallway, hoping her daughter was still in her bedroom.

"Yes, Mommy," Crystal shouted back.

She heard her daughter's rushed footsteps on the stairway leading down into the entryway.

She was glad she and John were going to Santa Fe for dinner. She couldn't recall the last time they had driven the sixty-mile drive to dine at the City Different. Later, they were to meet Leroy at Indian Market, and so she realized the time wasn't going to be completely theirs. Nonetheless, she hoped the evening together might relieve them of the excessive tension she felt had been thrust on them. Besides, she looked forward to meeting John's friend from his days in Vietnam. Even so, it surprised her John appeared so eager to talk to his former buddy.

"To get Kelly and Quigley off my back," he had explained to her when she had inquired why he seemed so anxious to meet Leroy.

"I didn't realize you felt that kind of pressure from them."

"I don't, actually. Doing this is my way of letting them know I'm trying to help by providing whatever information I can get my hands on."

"But will it be helpful to them?" she asked.

"That, we'll find out when I talk to Leroy."

"You're not beginning to worry about this, are you?"

"I'm anxious to bring this thing to a quick end."

"You're not holding back on me?"

"What do you mean?"

"You've told me everything you've learned from them?"

"I've told you everything you need to know."

"What's that supposed to mean?"

"Just that we don't need to inquire into their work."

She had left it at that and didn't ask any more questions. She realized that as long as he was obsessed with his attempts to gather information for the CIA agents, she couldn't expect him to concentrate on changing the structure of their lives so they could spend more quality time as a family. And that damn trial. Why did he have to get involved with that?

She wasn't sure she could go on acting as if nothing was the matter in front of the children. Yet, that was apparently what she had done, for Crystal and Johnny gave no sign they sensed anything wrong. It relieved her to know she was capable of putting up the necessary facade.

The concern she expressed to him the night she learned he had taken on the Soliz case was growing. She was certain that if she and he didn't soon make some changes, they would indeed be in serious trouble. She grew a little irritated at herself for allowing those feelings to surface at a time when she was looking forward to the evening. She loved him—of that much, she felt good about. And she believed he cared for her. Yet, she knew love alone did not a marriage make.

They left the house a few minutes before six. She had made reservations at *El Nido Restaurant* for seven. Without asking him, she sat behind the wheel of the car. "You can rest a little from the day at the office today," she suggested. He didn't resist.

As they drove off Tramway Boulevard onto Interstate 25 heading north, she thought the trip to Santa Fe would be a good time to catch up on the Soliz trial. Even though she had made it clear she thought it was a mistake to have taken the case, it was now a part of his work. And, after all, she had always shown an interest in his work.

"Why don't you fill me in on what happened yesterday at the trial?" she said as she accelerated the car and activated the cruise control. During the past week, he had briefed her every day on the case.

He sat in apparent comfort on the seat, which he had reclined. "I was hoping to get in a quick snooze while you drove," he said with a grin.

"No, you don't!" She elbowed him. "Now tell me about the trial."

"You won't believe what took place before we recessed yesterday," he began, gazing at the road ahead. He turned to face her. "And, damn, it's not going to help our case."

"What happened?"

"Remember Carol Niewold—the woman who saw Patty's assailant run from the scene?"

"Yeah. What about her?"

"She came back after the lunch break and approached Robert Keith. They were talking in whispers, but I thought nothing of it. I didn't begin to worry until Keith asked for a meeting in the judge's chambers. I sensed then it had to do with Carol's conversation with him."

"Don't tell me she's now willing to testify Bernardo's the guy she saw running away?"

"That's precisely what she wants to do! It was upsetting as hell."

"I can imagine. Is the judge going to let her? I thought she couldn't ID Bernardo?"

"She changed her mind." He slumped on the seat. "I was banking on her testimony."

"I suppose that's what the conference in chambers was about."

"Yes. It seems that during the week, after observing Bernardo go in and out of the courtroom, she's decided he's the one she saw that day. She claims she was mistaken not to have recognized him before."

"How sure is she now?"

"Well, she said she's positive Bernardo's the one she saw running from the house."

"Of course, she's known for quite some time now that Patty made a positive ID. Do you think she may have been influenced by her?"

"Possibly. She's always been aware Patty's confident about her own ID."

"You'll still be able to show that the descriptions both of them gave don't fit Bernardo."

"True."

"Besides, Niewold can be discredited by her failure to identify Bernardo in the first place. That should cast doubt on her changed testimony."

He nodded. "But I'd still rather have called her as my witness to counter Patty's positive ID." He straightened up, then sighed. "I've lost that edge."

She placed her hand on his knee. "You've still got an edge," she said. "I think the discrepancies in the descriptions and Carol's last-minute switch, as well as Bernardo's denial on the stand, will go a long way in winning over at least some of the jurors."

"Shit, I'd rather get an outright acquittal than a hung jury."

"I gather Judge Walker's going to let her testify for the state."

He nodded. "From the way the trial's going, I'd guess she'll take the stand next Tuesday."

"When is Patty testifying?"

"Probably Wednesday. I figure I'll start my 'cross' of her on Friday."

"Are you still glad you took the case? Now that there's been this turn of events, I mean." They had discussed variations of this question before, and he had always been emphatic that taking the case had been a good decision, despite the added pressure.

"Sure," he answered. He placed his hand on her lap. "I know my involvement with this trial has upset you—you've made that clear. And I don't want to minimize the negative effect this sort of thing could have on us." He patted her, then straightened up on the seat. "I appreciate that you've made the best of it. Yet, taking on the case has made me see my law practice in a different light. It feels good representing flesh and blood clients again."

"As opposed to—"

"—to big companies and insurance conglomerates. That's been the nature of my practice for the past eight years. I've been so busy representing 'corporate America' that I lost track of the other facets of law practice and that I could have made other choices. Handling this case, in a curious way, might make it easier for me to pull out of the firm and go for that Supreme Court vacancy."

"You think so?" she asked, not hiding her joy. "You're not saying that to appease me?"

"Not at all."

"What about the federal judgeship?"

"Both Guy and Dan claim I could go for one, then the other when it opens up."

"Don't you think you'd be criticized for leaving the Supreme Court after being there just a few months?"

"Possibly, but in politics, those things are done all the time."

"I realize that, but would *you* feel good doing it? After all, there's a matter of commitment."

"True." He thought for a moment, then shrugged. "I don't know how I'd feel. And on the federal bench, the work at the trial level and the higher pay would be hard to turn away from." He sighed. "But I'll have to make up my mind on the Supreme Court soon."

"When's the deadline?"

"Next Wednesday. You still with me on this?"

"Sure. I'm real excited for you. For us, really." She squeezed his leg. "I'm curious. How did taking the case make you see things differently?"

"It made me realize I was afraid of change. I'm so accustomed to the way I've practiced law that I haven't given much thought to making changes that could have a positive effect."

"It's natural to resist change. All of us succumb to that." She was pleased he was considering other options, something he hardly ever did. It was a good sign, she thought. "You've made me very happy, John. I think you've crossed a big hurdle."

"Don't jump the gun. I haven't yet decided on either position, though I'm leaning that way."

"I realize you didn't commit, and I wouldn't want you to until you feel good about it." She recalled the irritation she had felt earlier. Would she later be thankful for his decision to represent Bernardo? How ironic if that turned out to be the case.

Tesuque was an unincorporated village consisting of a grouping of houses and a few commercial buildings in a rural setting. It had its own post office fronting the narrow road passing through the village. The community was set in the foothills of the Sangre de Cristo Mountains northeast of Santa Fe, hidden by a growth of piñon, salt cedar, and other large trees and vegetation. Demi's mother lived a few miles south, just off Bishop's Lodge Road.

They arrived in Tesuque ten minutes past seven. The restaurant was packed. The hostess explained they were running behind schedule and suggested they sit at the bar-lounge to enjoy a cocktail while tables in the dining room were cleared. They found two empty stools at the bar. John needed to unwind from the long day, she thought, so she was pleased they were having a drink.

She had always enjoyed the atmosphere of *El Nido,* nestled in the heart of the village. The community had a foundry and was also the home of one or two galleries. At night, however, the only activity took place at *El Nido.*

The restaurant was housed in a single-story adobe building with a thick coat of whitewashed stucco. Its entryway led into a long, narrow dining room. The dining room had two fireplaces at each end that were found burning almost year-round during the cool Santa Fe evenings. Past the front dining room was the bar-lounge, followed by a doorway leading to yet another dining room.

John had suggested earlier that they not meet Leroy at the plaza until nine, so they had plenty of time to enjoy their dinner. She was glad they got to relax and enjoy what she considered a romantic evening in an inviting atmosphere.

They left the restaurant in plenty of time to arrive in downtown Santa Fe around nine. He didn't even bother attempting to find a place to park near the plaza, congested with cars crawling through the narrow streets. Avoiding the crowd of cars, he made a wide circle on Paseo de Peralta to park behind the Supreme Court Building.

As they walked the few blocks to the plaza, she thought of how different Santa Fe was from what she remembered as a youngster, when the town had but one traffic light. The block-size plaza with a gazebo wasn't unlike other town squares found in other small communities. But Santa Fe's plaza always bustled with pedestrian and vehicular activity.

For the most part, the buildings surrounding the plaza had remained the same, although most of the retail shops were different. Before, those shops had catered to the natives and an occasional visitor or tourist. Now, the stores catered to tourists and those who could afford their exclusive and expensive art, clothing apparel, and jewelry. Gone from the plaza were the clothing and department stores, old-fashioned drug stores, and, to the dismay of many of the natives, "the true culture of our people," as Demi had often heard Santa Feans complain.

The city had spread out, and countless commercial establishments and art galleries had sprung up over the years. The number of tourists packing the city had grown geometrically. So had the resentment of the blue-collar workers, mostly natives. They found themselves pushed aside into the outskirts and into mobile home parks as real estate prices and taxes soared. Californians and others from the Midwest and the East moved into the City Different, paying exorbitant prices for ancient adobe homes they considered charming and possessions they just had to have.

She had tired of the *trendy, artsy* Santa Fe, which in recent years had attracted Hollywood celebrities, as well as its share of mystics and a New Age element. She wished that somehow it could all change back to the way she remembered, but she knew that would never be. Besides, she pondered, what would happen to the natives and the local economy, which had grown to rely on the almighty tourist dollar. Alas, a number of the natives had grown to dislike and resent the presence of throngs of tourists, yet in a bit of irony depended on them for their livelihoods.

Demi and John entered the area surrounding the plaza, which had been roped off from vehicular traffic. It had been a long time since they had last visited there. During a big event, such as Indian Market, where hundreds of Native Americans from throughout the United States came to display and sell their wares, arts, and crafts, it became almost impossible to move through the crowds. People converged on Santa Fe from all over the world. And they came prepared to pay high prices for high-demand merchandise they considered unique.

They worked themselves through the thick crowd along the west side of the plaza, headed, they hoped, toward Leroy's booth. The booth turned out to be on the nearside, and so they avoided having to weave through the large crowd at the far end.

"There's Leroy," John said. "He's the taller one."

She stretched her neck and saw two men standing in the back of the booth. She studied the taller man. "He's not as old as I thought he'd be," she said.

"His hair's turned almost all white." As they got closer, John shouted over the noise of the crowd. "Leroy!"

Leroy looked up. Grinning, he walked to the front of the booth, reaching both hands across the counter to shake John's hand. He held on.

"How's it going, John?" he said with a wide grin. "God, it's good to see you after so many years." He released his grip.

"It's good to see you too," John said. "I like that white hair."

"You're looking mighty fine, yourself." Leroy pointed to his hair. "'Salt and Pepper' I think they call it. Comes with age. So does this." He patted his abdomen.

John took Demi by the arm and helped her get in front. "I want you to meet Demi."

She gave Leroy a bright smile. "Nice to meet you, Leroy," she said, extending her hand.

"My pleasure, Demi," Leroy said, taking her hand in both of his. "John, you did a bang-up job finding her." He gazed at her, then released his grip.

She glanced at the jewelry displayed in the booth. It was hard not to notice the fine quality of the craftsmanship. "You do beautiful work, Leroy."

"Thanks. I'm proud of what I do. I try doing quality work, and so I take extra time to complete the pieces."

"It shows."

"You're good at your craft," John added as he looked around the booth. "I admire your talent."

"Thank you," Leroy said. "I needed something to stay busy and couldn't see myself hunting and fishing the rest of my life. When I can get away to do that, I enjoy the outdoors more."

"I bet." John looked around the booth again. "I like your style. It's unique, don't you think, Demi?"

"It certainly is," she said.

"Thank you both for those nice words," Leroy said.

"Listen, is now a good time for us to talk?" John said. "We could look around a bit and come back later if you wish."

"That won't be necessary." Leroy turned to his young Native-American helper, who was assisting a customer. "I'm going with my friends, Gerald." He crouched down under the counter and came out in front of the booth alongside John and Demi. He placed his arm around John. Turning to Gerald, he said, "Let's see if you can sell everything by the time I return."

Gerald smiled and waved Leroy off.

John suggested they walk to *Vanessie of Santa Fe*, a spacious piano-bar lounge and restaurant on West San Francisco Street. The restaurant was frequented mostly by Santa Feans, for it was hidden in an out-of-the-way place, making it difficult for tourists to find. Once in a while, a group of tourists would stumble on it by accident.

They found a small table at the far corner of the lounge, away from the restaurant's busy dining room and the chatter of the crowd sitting around the piano bar listening to Doug Montgomery, a local entertainer.

The restaurant-lounge was a typical Santa Fe interior, stuccoed, earthtone walls with massive vigas crossing the high ceiling and two large fireplaces at opposite ends of the long room.

The waitress came and took their drink order. Demi ordered a Margarita, John a Scotch and Soda, and Leroy a 7-Up.

Leroy asked about John and Demi's extended families and their children. John described his law practice and explained how he and Demi met. The two men then exchanged stories about their tour in Vietnam. Aside from answering a few questions Leroy asked of her, Demi stayed out of the conversation and listened instead to John and Leroy talk about their days in the military. They ordered another round of drinks.

Admitting his curiosity had gotten the best of him, Leroy asked John what he wanted to talk about. John explained the unexpected events of the past two weeks. He then told him what the CIA agents wanted from him and of Condon's involvement in suspected illicit activities. Several times, he emphasized the confidentiality Kelly and Quigley insisted on.

He went on to brief Leroy on what he had told the CIA agents about Henri LaPierre. "They were hoping you could provide more information about him. Do you have anything else that might be helpful, other than what information you gave me in Vietnam?"

"Oh, I recall well about Henri," Leroy said with emphasis. "To me, it's as if it was yesterday, when I think of 'Nam." He drank his 7-Up through a straw, lifting the glass off the table with his huge hand, almost covering the entire glass.

"The CIA seems to think the project Henri was working on is one of the keys, if not *the* key, to what the agency is trying to uncover concerning Condon." ·

For a moment, Demi thought she noticed Leroy draw back as John spoke. He also appeared nervous for the first time that evening. She sensed it in his eyes, but then concluded she didn't know him well enough to take notice. Was it her imagination, she wondered. Or was it that the discussion had now turned serious and, for that reason, Leroy was displaying a different demeanor?

"I find it hard to believe," Leroy said, "that after so many years the story Henri was writing would have any connection with what's going on for you today. Yet, your CIA friends' theory about the story Henri was working on is on track." He took another sip of his soft drink. "Back in 'Nam, I kept you in the dark about Henri to protect you from knowing too much. As it was, I felt guilty for telling you as much as I did."

"Well, tell me now. Was Henri working on a story on procurement?"

"Yes. Except the word 'story' doesn't quite describe his project. 'Scandal' is more descriptive." Leroy put his glass down and leaned back. "He told me he stumbled on it quite by accident. At first, he intended to do a simple, run-of-the-mill article about the cost of the war. When he was gathering figures and other data, he came across several discrepancies. Serious ones involving considerable sums of money. That's how I came into the picture. Once he found these discrepancies, he bombarded me with questions."

"I recall you felt uneasy about it."

"Sure did. Anyway, Henri sensed I was avoiding his questions. He thought he could loosen me up by telling me his research led him to suspect that weaponry and even medical supplies were being diverted to an unknown destination—possibly a foreign power outside of Southeast Asia."

"That's what he told you? Did he use those words—*foreign power?*"

"Well, he said something like a foreign power or foreign country."

He seemed to weigh his reply, then continued.

"Anyway, I felt uncomfortable during the whole affair because, if it turned out that he was right—that illegal activities were going on—someone in my outfit would have to be involved. Under our organization's mission, we were responsible for distributing every single item shipped into the country to its proper destination, from helicopters all the way down to toilet paper and toothpicks. Nothing, absolutely nothing, came into the country without our authorization or knowledge. And it was our job to track every item and expenditure. So, if Henri's suspicions were correct, it followed that I had to know the persons involved. And I'd rather not have that kind of knowledge."

"Even now, you seem a bit edgy talking about it," John volunteered.

"Do I? I hadn't noticed." He attempted a smile. "Talking about it after so many years might have something to do with that."

"I'm sorry if this causes you any unpleasantness."

"Don't worry about it."

"Okay. Tell me, do you think Condon might have been involved?"

"Damn, I thought I knew all there was to know about the colonel, so I'd be shocked if he was. But if Henri was right, it would take a person in a position of considerable authority, like Condon, for such a quantity of material to disappear like that."

"I'll ask you a loaded question." He finished what was left of his scotch. "From what you've told me, it'd appear to be unlikely for millions of dollars in supplies to be diverted without Condon knowing about it. Is that right?"

"Right. And that fact, alone, I told Henri, made me uncomfortable. After all, I worked right under Condon's chief of staff."

"Even if you said nothing else, I think what you've told me will be useful to the CIA."

"I've got more to tell you that I think you'll find interesting. Like I said earlier, I didn't want to create problems for you back then. Now, of course, if what I know can help you with these fellows from the CIA, I'm glad to cooperate. But in 'Nam, though I was tempted to tell someone, I kept my mouth shut because I was scared shitless about the whole business."

He turned to Demi. "Pardon my 'French,' Demi."

She smiled and gestured she had no problem with his language.

He continued. "In that kind of situation, knowing what's going on is the same as being involved, at least the way I see it."

"I understand your predicament at the time, Leroy," John said. "And I appreciate your willingness to help now."

"I'm glad I can help an old friend." Displaying a big grin, he patted John on the arm. "Please excuse me while I pay a visit to the men's room." He pointed to his empty glass. "This stuff passes right through me."

"Go right ahead."

Leroy stood up and walked toward a marked hallway leading to the restrooms.

CHAPTER 15

WHILE Leroy was away, they sat there for a moment, enjoying the last bars of a piano melody. When the music ended, she leaned closer to him to be heard above the noise of the crowd.

"Was it just my imagination, or did Leroy get nervous?" she said.

"He did seem a bit jumpy," he replied. "Probably for the reason he gave, though—talking about past events has a way of resurrecting the emotions that went with them."

"I suppose you're right." She picked up her drink. "Doesn't he drink liquor? He ordered nothing but 7-Ups."

He shook his head. "Not since I knew him in Vietnam. I tried buying him a drink a couple of times back then, and he flat out told me he never touched the stuff."

She reclined back in her chair. "That's interesting."

Makes you wonder, huh?" He smiled, twirling the ice in his drink with his straw.

"Of what" She took a sip from her glass.

"Of the 'drunken Indian' stereotype we hear so much about. Leroy disproves it."

"I thought that's what you meant. Yeah, I'd say so."

Before Leroy returned, she quizzed John about comments Leroy had said of Henri that were unclear to her. He filled in the gaps.

"But didn't you think what Leroy said pretty well connected the diversion to Condon's group?" she asked. "I understood him to say only the colonel's organization dealt with supply distribution in the Saigon area."

"I too got that impression." He paused in thought. "So if there was anything improper going on, it had to involve Condon's organization."

"But did it involve Condon himself? I suppose that's the big question."

"That's right. What Leroy told us points to Condon, I think."

Leroy returned. "So Condon's a U. S. Senator now," he said, apparently overhearing. He sat down and picked up his glass. "Can't say that surprises me. He loved the limelight."

"Did he?" John asked.

"Yeah." He smiled at Demi. "Sorry. Got a little delayed in there. Met up with a buddy of mine from Gallup. He's with a group over there in the restaurant."

"We were just going over what you told us. You said you've got other information. I'm anxious to hear about that, but first let me ask you a few questions about Henri's present whereabouts." He drank what was left of his Scotch and Soda. "Have you stayed in touch? Do you know where he is?"

Leroy set down his glass. "I knew you'd ask me that. I'll answer your second question first—I don't know where he is. That's the short answer."

"Wishful thinking. I had a hunch you'd say that."

"As to your first question, though, the fact is he and I did stay in touch after he left 'Nam. He wrote more to me than I to him. I received several letters when I was still in 'Nam. Then I got a couple at my next duty station at Ft. Bliss in El Paso."

"Did you keep any of his letters?"

"At the time, I did." He paused, as if contemplating John's question. "You're wondering if I still have them?"

"Yes."

"Damn, John, I don't know. To be honest, I doubt it. It's been years. And I've moved around several times. Of course, they're not the sort of thing I'd leave laying around the house. They'd be stored. I can check."

"I'd like for you to do that. For now, do you recall where he lived when he last wrote?"

"Now that, I remember. He was in Athens at the time."

"Athens?"

"Yes, Athens." He smiled. "You've got it—as in 'Athens, Greece.'"

"What was he doing there?"

"He got a job there after 'Nam."

"As a journalist?"

"That's right."

"What about his story?"

"He was still working on it. I recall his last letter saying he had completed it, except he was waiting for an important piece of information to arrive from 'Nam."

"From whom?"

"I have no idea. But I doubt it was from another journalist or a friend. He was working on it by himself and still secretive about it. Besides, the only real friends he had there were you and me. He stayed away from other journalists." He sat back upright in his chair. "Regarding the information he was waiting for, I remember that even when he was in 'Nam, there was a missing link; some kind of verification."

The waitress approached to ask if they wanted another round of drinks. John glanced at Leroy and Demi. They didn't want a refill. He asked the waitress to bring him the tab.

"Tell me, Leroy," he continued, "what you know about why Henri left Vietnam. All I ever knew was that he had lost his job. I never got the full story, even though I helped him get out of the country."

"And was he ever grateful to you for that. He claimed it saved his life."

"I know. He wrote me a short note later to thank me, and that's what he said to me. But, at the time, even you told me little about why he had to leave the country."

"I'll tell you why our dear friend lost his job. That's what I meant a while ago when I said I had something you'd find interesting." He began relating his story. "I had just returned to my living quarters after an exhausting day at work."

He was about to warm up day-old left overs when the phone rang. Because he felt tired, he was tempted not to answer it. But he remembered Henri had tried reaching him at the office several times earlier that day and had left urgent messages. He picked up the phone.

It was Henri. "Leroy!" his loud voice came over the phone. "I'm so glad I found you. I've been trying to reach you all day!"

"I know," Leroy said into the phone. "I was away from the office most of the afternoon, and things were hectic when I got back."

"That's quite all right. But I must see you at once. Can you come to my apartment?"

"Right now."

"Yes. It's of great importance to me! I wouldn't bother you otherwise."

He couldn't let down a friend in such desperate need and agreed to meet him within the hour. He hailed a cab in front of the NCO Club a block or so away from his quarters and went straight to Henri's modest apartment in the outskirts of Saigon, arriving there in half an hour.

"Thank you for coming," Henri said as he invited Leroy into his small living room and closed the door. "You're a dear friend."

"Please tell me, Henri," Leroy said, "what in the world has got you so worked up?"

"To 'get to the point,' as you Americans say, I've lost my position with the newspaper. My world's falling apart!"

"What happened." He spoke in a tone showing genuine sympathy.

"How clumsy of me," Henri apologized, "please have a seat." He pointed to the sofa. Leroy sat, but Henri remained pacing the floor. "May I offer you a drink?" He rubbed his hands.

"No, I'm fine. Now, why don't you calm down and tell me what happened."

"The maggots!" Tears appeared. "They've set me up! That's why I was fired."

"Who's set you up?"

"I believe it has to do with my project but have no proof."

"You mean the story about the missing supply shipments?"

"Yes." He took out a handkerchief from his pocket to wipe away the tears that were now on his cheeks. He blew his nose.

"How did they set you up?"

170

"The authorities raided my apartment this morning. They found drugs. Do you hear me? Drugs!"

"From the way you're talking, I take it they didn't belong to you."

"Of course not!" He paused and blew his nose again. He began crying once more, seemingly agonizing that anyone would believe he was a drug dealer. "I've never touched them, Leroy, you must know that. I've been set up, I tell you. Someone must have broken into my apartment last night when I was away and planted the drugs the police found this morning. It's easy to get into these apartments. The authorities arrested me like a common criminal!"

"How did you get out of jail?"

"My supervisor posted bail." He scowled. "Then the asshole asked me into his office and gave me the second blow of the day."

"Which was?"

"He pulled out documents and sworn statements accusing me of running a second business. Are you ready for this—pimping! Can you believe that?"

"That's incredible. What basis would anyone have for those accusations?"

"What basis, you ask?" He slammed his fist on the coffee table. "These scoundrels don't need that! Nothing but stinking falsehoods. That's all they need. And I'm the patsy."

"Seems to me that the patsies are your superiors for placing any credence on any of this. They'll believe you, won't they?"

"I've tried talking to them." He choked. "They want nothing to do with me! After the years I've given them; that's the loyalty they show me."

"But if you explained what's happening is because of the story you're working on, they'll realize you've been set up."

"No, no, I couldn't do that. You see, they don't know about this project. It's outside my directives—my assignments. It was something I was doing on my own and had nothing to do with the people I worked for. Although they might find it of interest, I'm afraid I'd still be out of a job for insubordination—not following company policy. The irony is that I can't use the cause of what's happened to me, the story, as my defense."

Leroy understood. "What are you going to do now?"

"My life's in danger, Leroy, and I must leave right away. Will you help me?"

"I can try. We'll need John Garcia's help, though. You want me to contact him?"

"Would you please?"

"I'll do it first thing in the morning and see if he'll meet with you."

"But I ask this one favor—please don't tell him what's happened. It's not only embarrassing, but I'm concerned for his safety. He's better off not knowing why I've been terminated."

"You might be right." He shook his head. "It's terrible, what's happening to you, Henri."

Henri nodded and said nothing more. Not knowing what else to say, Leroy asked Henri to call a cab.

Before he left, they made plans to meet again the following day after he had spoken to John. Still distraught, Henri closed the door as Leroy walked down the stairs to the waiting cab.

"And you know the rest," Leroy said when he finished. "I contacted you and arranged your meeting with him. I hope you don't mind my honoring his request not to tell you why he was fired."

The waitress had left the check on the table. John placed a twenty and a five on top of it.

"Not at all," he replied as he motioned to the waitress he was leaving payment on the table. "Tell me, did you believe him that it was a set up? For my part, I can't see him involved in drug dealing and pimping." He turned to Demi. "He wasn't that sort of guy."

"It had to have been." Leroy said. "No way was he involved with that shit!" He glanced at Demi. "Pardon my French, again. Why, the fellow didn't even smoke pot. And, as you know, that and sniffing cocaine were common occurrences in 'Nam—casual habits in the military and among some in the news media. Yet, there were those who didn't touch the stuff, and, believe me, Henri was one of them."

Demi sat there transfixed by Leroy's story, realizing the seriousness of the French journalist's predicament. What had ever happened to him, she wondered. Just as important, what had happened to his story? Despite the fact that John wanted this mess to end so he wouldn't have to deal with it any longer, she found the mystery not only interesting but intriguing. Fascinated, she decided to end her silence.

"What I don't understand," she said, "is why the persons Henri accused of setting him up wouldn't have harmed him in some other way.

After all, if someone felt threatened by what he was working on, wouldn't killing him have solved their problem once and for all."

"Good point," Leroy said.

"What Demi's brought up makes me wonder," John added, "about Henri's set-up theory. If we assume he wasn't involved in drugs and pimping, then the setup could have been the work of someone other than those who felt threatened by the damage his story could do. I say that because, if his story was going to create the big scandal he suggested to me, getting him fired wouldn't solve the problem for them. On the other hand, getting rid of him would."

"Maybe not," Demi said. "Without getting their hands on the story, whoever felt threatened by it wouldn't necessarily feel safe even if they eliminated Henri. If he was smart, he'd make sure his work would survive should something happen to him. Another thing. It's conceivable that if someone felt threatened, as a prelude they might have wanted to let Henri know they meant business. Getting him fired would be a way of doing that."

"Yeah, to scare him away from going public with the story," Leroy added. He turned to John and grinned. "Not only did you find yourself a beautiful lawyer for a wife, John, but a smart one at that."

"Why, thank you, Leroy. What a nice thing to say."

"I agree," John said. He smiled at Demi and squeezed her hand. "Leroy, getting back to what you might find back home. Would you check to see what you have by way of letters, phone numbers, addresses, and the like? Anything that might help the CIA."

"I'll do that."

"Good. They'll get in touch with you."

Leroy hesitated. "On that, John, if these guys don't mind, I'd feel more comfortable making contact directly with you. Is that okay?"

"I don't see why not." He stood up. "Listen, we've taken enough of your time. We'd better call it a night and let you get back to your booth."

"Don't worry about it."

Leroy took Demi's jacket off the back of the chair and helped her put it on. As they walked toward the exit, Leroy explained he had told his friend he'd join his group at the restaurant. When John told Leroy he was hoping to buy a piece of jewelry from him back at the booth, Leroy took out one of his business cards, wrote something on it, and gave it to John. He read the card. The note instructed Gerald to give a forty percent

173

discount on any purchase. He thanked Leroy and told him he'd get in touch with him soon. Before they parted, Leroy embraced Demi, then John. John and Demi exited the lounge as Leroy crossed the entryway to join his friends at the restaurant.

Outside *Vanessie*, the night air had turned much cooler, and Demi could smell the sweet scent of piñon burning somewhere inside a nearby dwelling. She was glad she had brought her coat. As they walked across the parking lot toward the narrow street leading back to the plaza, a man unknown to her approached from a car at the near end of the parking lot. Sitting in the vehicle was another person Demi also didn't recognize.

"Quigley!" John said as the agent got nearer. "Is that Kelly?" He glanced toward the car.

"No," Quigley answered. "He stayed in Albuquerque." The agent turned to Demi. "Hi, Demi. I'm Fletcher Quigley. I feel like I know you already." He extended his hand.

She took it. "Hello, Quigley, she said and smiled. "I'm glad to meet you finally."

"Likewise."

"The gentleman in the car," John said, nodding toward the vehicle. "I haven't seen him before." During the past two weeks, he had met several of Kelly and Quigley's confederates.

"He's not one of ours," Quigley replied. "He's FBI."

"Oh. I take it you'll be staying onboard working with them, as you had hoped."

"Right. The decision was made this afternoon. The agent in the car is stationed in Albuquerque, but there'll be several new ones coming in from other duty stations."

"So is this thing going to get bigger still?" Demi asked no one in particular but threw a disappointing look at John.

"I'm afraid so," Quigley answered.

She expected John to ask the agent why he was there, but he didn't. She herself perceived Quigley and his cohort's presence an invasion of their privacy. For the first time since she had learned of the CIA's interest in John, she understood why he wanted this unwelcomed intrusion to end.

"Why are you gentlemen here?" she asked. "Have you been following us?"

As she stared at Quigley, waiting for a reply, she noticed John wince.

The agent hesitated, as if caught off guard. "No, no," he finally said. "It's just that we considered it urgent to learn what you found out from Etcitty. Is there a place we can talk nearby?"

John cleared his throat. "We were walking back to the plaza," he said. "There's a restaurant-lounge on the way. Let us buy you and your comrade a drink."

"I'll walk down there with you." Quigley excused himself, went over to the driver of the car, and arranged to meet him later. The three of them walked to the restaurant.

At *The Palace*, over drinks, John briefed the agent on what Leroy had told them. He added that Leroy preferred dealing with him and that they had made plans to get together once Leroy checked if he found anything providing a clue to Henri's whereabouts.

It was then that Quigley made a stunning revelation. "As you might have guessed," he began, "ever since you told us about Etcitty, we've checked up on him regarding his tour in Vietnam."

"I can't say that surprises me," John said. "What *would* surprise me is if you told me the military still keeps documents that go back that far."

"Well, believe it or not, they do; especially involving Vietnam."

"What did you uncover?"

"That Etcitty could well have known of embezzlements Condon may have been involved in."

"I find that hard to believe. What did you learn?"

"That your buddy himself participated in some embezzlements of his own. We've discovered microfilmed documents tracing his signature on supplies that were later unaccounted for. Items that mysteriously disappeared from the army's inventory."

"Are we talking something major here or—"

"'Small potatoes,' really. But if he was involved even at that level, it's possible he was in on thefts of the magnitude we believe Condon may have been involved in."

"Why didn't you tell me this before I met with him?"

"We thought it'd be better to wait and see what he divulged to you first. Otherwise, we felt this knowledge might taint your discussions with him and affect your objectivity." He appeared to study John's expression. "Don't worry about it. On the positive side, it sounds as if you found him cooperative. That's a good sign."

"Yeah, a very good sign. Should I confront him with this? And if so, when?"

"Kelly plans to visit with you on that score."

After the agent left, John and Demi walked back to the plaza to visit some of the booths. The crowd had thinned.

"Did you know they'd be up here?" she asked as they made their way to Leroy's booth.

"I had an idea they might show up," he said, "so I wasn't surprised."

She said nothing else, even though it annoyed her to think these agents found it easy to pop into her family's lives. Besides, she could tell John was upset over Quigley's revelation about Leroy. After all, he had just reunited with an old friend. The adage *leave well enough alone* described what she thought was the best thing to do. Only if he brought it up first, she decided, would she say anything. Although she sensed an uneasiness about this whole affair, she surmised he had his fill for the night. She had too, for that matter.

At the booth, where Gerald was busy showing merchandise to other customers, they looked at earrings until she found a pair she liked. John thought the price was reasonable and didn't bother showing Leroy's note. Before leaving the plaza, they treated themselves to an ice cream cone at the *Haagen-Dazs Ice Cream Shoppe* on the south side of the plaza before heading home.

When John got to the office Monday morning, he felt nervous, and for good reason. He planned telling his colleagues he had decided to apply for the Supreme Court vacancy. He had made the decision Sunday afternoon after talking to Demi one last time.

The first thing he did was to visit Edmund Runyan. Over a cup of coffee, John told him of his decision. He had worked on the first draft of his application Sunday evening, he explained.

"I knew Dan Conniff had spoken to you of the new federal judgeship opening up next year," Edmund said, "but this took me by surprise."

"Had you heard?" John asked, suspecting word had already spread.

"Yeah, someone mentioned it last week. I figured you had been approached but weren't seriously considering it. I'd have brought it up if you hadn't."

"I suppose Dick and the others on the management team know too."

Edmund nodded. "Dick's upset you hadn't mentioned it to him."

"I should have, I know. But until a few days ago, I was lukewarm on the idea. Now that I've made up my mind, I'm letting you guys know."

"Believe me, John, I myself take no offense. You haven't told Dick yet, I take it?"

John shook his head. He had suspected Dick would be pissed if he had already heard, and there wasn't any reason to think he hadn't. That made them even, he thought, for he himself was pissed at Dick for their discussion the past week. Although he hadn't been upset at the time because he felt Dick was just doing his job, now that he had time to think about it, he realized how tied down he felt at the firm, and the discussion with Dick confirmed that. Had he been looking for a way out? He decided not to bother Edmund with that issue and instead told him he wanted to spend more time with his family.

"I don't blame you. Working for this firm will definitely prevent you from doing that. I'm glad I'm single." He took a deep breath. "When are you going to tell the others?"

"This morning. I'm taking a few hours this afternoon to finish my application; it's due Wednesday."

"I'm glad you're getting it over with once and for all. I was concerned you might decide to wait for the management conference tomorrow."

"Dick and Edgar aren't in yet. I left word I'd like to talk to them when they can cut loose." He drank the last of his coffee and stood up. "Thanks for the 'dress rehearsal.'"

"Don't mention it." Edmund got out of his chair and shook John's hand. "What are friends for." He smiled, then turned serious. "John, for whatever it's worth, let me say that you deserve the best the profession has to offer. You've shown your loyalty to this firm many times over. It's time you do something for yourself—and your family. As long as it's something you want. So don't let Dick or Edgar fill you with guilt. That, you don't deserve."

"Thanks for being my friend, Edmund." His face tightened.

Edmund noticed. "You really want this, right? You're not doing it just to get out of here."

He forced a smile. "I'm as certain as one can ever be. No, this isn't an anti-firm thing. But that doesn't mean I don't have second thoughts."

"Everyone suffers from those when making big decisions; they come with the territory."

The meeting with Dick and Edgar lasted almost an hour. It went much better than John had anticipated. Should he not get the appointment, John told them, he'd try for the federal position later. Edgar accepted John's explanations and responded favorably. Before he left, he offered his own, as well as the firm's, support to assure John's appointment. From Dick, John sensed different vibes, possibly, he thought, because of their talk the prior week.

The discussion had taken place in Dick's office, and Dick asked John to stay as Edgar left.

"John, please level with me," Dick said when Edgar closed the door. "I hope this has nothing to do with our talk a few days ago." He paused. "I was of the impression that had gone well."

"To be honest, the thought occurred to me too," John replied, "but I concluded it had nothing to do with it. Looking back at our conversation, although it annoyed me at the time, I admit I got pissed after the fact, even though I knew you were just doing your job. But honestly, Dick, this has been coming a long time. I need that change I told you and Edgar about."

He went on to explain his discussions with Demi and her concerns his work kept him from the family. He became convinced Demi's feelings were justified and that either of these two new positions gave him an opportunity to make changes important to his family.

"I'm relieved," Dick said when John finished. "The entire time you were talking to us a while ago, I felt guilty about our discussion the other day." Dick didn't offer the firm's resources in helping John with the appointment, as Edgar had. Did Dick consider it a *given* that Edgar spoke for the firm, he wondered. Still, he would have liked hearing it from Dick himself.

He felt no discomfort when they parted. Instead, he was relieved it had gone so well. It dawned on him he didn't care if Dick was displeased with his decision, recalling Edmund's suggestion. He broke the news to Lynda, who, although saddened he might be leaving the firm, was happy for him. The two of them spent the rest of the afternoon on the application draft he had worked on the day before. Lynda prepared a final, signed copy in time for the courier to deliver it to the chairperson of the nominating commission late afternoon.

CHAPTER 16

THE trial resumed Tuesday mid-morning. Before Judge Walker asked the bailiff to escort the jury into the courtroom to begin the day's testimony, he asked Keith and John to approach the bench. From Keith, he wanted to know how many of the state's witnesses remained to be called to testify and how much time the prosecutor anticipated each one to be on the stand. Keith told the judge he intended to call Carol as his first witness. He expected her testimony to take up the entire day, including his direct and John's cross-examination. He intended to put the victim, Patty, on the stand the next morning.

Asking Keith to outline the remaining testimony before he rested the state's case was the trial judge's way of committing him to his time schedule. The jurist wasn't unyielding or inflexible, however, and so he'd allow counsel additional time if necessary.

John appreciated the judge's firm style. Throughout the trial, he reminded counsel in subtle ways that he alone was in charge, without trampling on counsels' freedom to try their cases. He rarely abused his authority and usually appeared fair to both sides. Yet, on occasion, John had seen him lose control, as well as his patience. His demeanor in presiding over Bernardo's trial pleased John. After all, he had his work cut out for him. The last thing he needed was a judge who would make his job more difficult.

Carol wore a tan skirt of mid-length, a white blouse, and a matching, unbuttoned vest. Her hair, which John had mistakenly thought was shorter and lighter in color when he had spoken to her before, was shoulder length and had been styled professionally. It was obvious she had made an all-out effort to look presentable to the jury this morning.

After asking several preliminary questions, Keith requested she describe the path the assailant had taken from the Gregory residence. In detail, she described the assailant's actions as she pursued him in her car while trying to calm her six-year-old daughter. She guessed she had stayed within a hundred feet of the young man as she followed. She also estimated the time lapse from the moment she had first seen him to the moment she lost track of him was ten to fifteen minutes.

Later in his direct examination, Keith, apparently realizing she had misjudged the length of time by some five to ten minutes, succeeded in having her qualify her response. She corrected herself and said that only five to ten minutes had elapsed.

Even then, John thought, five to ten minutes was a long time, far more than he would have guessed had elapsed for such a short distance. He hoped the jury too would think the time estimate too long. He made a note to bring this out during his cross-examination.

So the jurors would have a clear picture of Carol's testimony, Keith used a map drawn on a blackboard. He asked the witness to trace her own path as she tried not to lose sight of Patty's attacker. The prosecutor introduced black and white photographs showing the actual streets from different angles. He also used photos of the park and the alleyway where the assailant disappeared before reappearing as he crossed the street into the park and then backtracking. The fugitive then disappeared for good from Carol's view, and she had no idea where he had gone.

Keith, John thought, realized John would make every effort later to point out the glaring fact that Carol had identified the wrong man at the lineup. The prosecutor couldn't escape that fact. For that reason, by artful use of his questions, he laid the groundwork with plausible explanations. He hoped the jury would understand why Carol was mistaken on the day of the attack and at the lineup, and not today, when she was expected to identify Bernardo as the person she saw fleeing.

"As you followed this person, Ms. Niewold," Keith asked, "did you ever have the opportunity to get a full front facial view of him?"

"My view," she explained, "was more of a side view because he kept turning sideways away from me, as if trying to hide his face. I'm fairly certain he knew he was being followed."

John could sense she had rehearsed. She seemed aware of the potential negative effect her previous misidentification might have on her testimony. There wasn't any question in his mind she was taking the first of many steps intended to explain her mistake away.

She spoke in a soft, pleasant voice. Her tone could convince the jury she was sincere and believable, subject to human error like anyone else and stating what she had observed without prejudice or ulterior motives.

When he had spoken to her a week or so before, she appeared sure of herself and even aloof. This morning, though, she appeared more than a little nervous and somewhat cautious in her responses, as if she felt threatened, a trait that could gain sympathy from the jurors.

"Did you have occasion, Ms. Niewold," Keith continued, "to go to the police department to provide a description to an artist who was drawing a composite of the assailant?"

"Yes, I did," she answered.

"There was previously introduced into evidence a composite drawing marked as Defendant's Exhibit 5." He picked up the exhibit and approached the witness stand. "Would you please look at that exhibit and tell us if that's the drawing you helped the artist prepare?"

She took the exhibit and examined it. "It's the drawing," she said, "but with one exception." She glanced at the jury. "The gentleman who was drawing this kept referring to the hairdo as a crew cut, and I kept insisting that it wasn't. So that part isn't based on the description I gave."

"Well," he asked, "as it turned out, that drawing is what you and the artist came up with, is that correct?" He was careful not to dwell too much on her qualified answers, for fear it would emphasize the discrepancies in her identification, as well as her attempt to minimize them.

"Yes, this exhibit is as close to the description that I could give at the time," she responded.

Another doctored-up answer, John thought.

Keith then referred to a photograph she also viewed at the police department and that she had selected as resembling the suspect. "Why did you pick this photo, Ms. Niewold?" he asked. "Was it the facial features or the hairdo or what?"

"Objection, your honor," John interrupted. "Leading."

"Objection sustained," Judge Walker said. "Mr. Keith, let the witness testify without putting words in her mouth."

"Sorry, your honor," Keith said, not sounding apologetic.

Once again, John thought, Keith was prompting the witness for a qualified answer. His purpose was to soften the fact that all witnesses who had seen the assailant gave a description of him that, John hoped, the jury would agree didn't describe Bernardo.

"It was the hairdo I was trying to explain to them at the time," Carol said after the lawyers' exchange with Judge Walker, without waiting for Keith to rephrase the question. "But unfortunately," she added, "that picture doesn't quite show what I was trying to describe."

Keith moved on. "Did you later have occasion to be called to the police department again to view a lineup?"

"Yes."

"How much notice were you given of that lineup?"

"Fifteen minutes."

John scrawled a note of her reply, for he realized Keith was again laying the groundwork to explain away the misidentification at the lineup.

"I hand you State's Exhibits 15, 16, and 17 and ask you if they show the lineup you viewed?" Keith asked.

She took the exhibits and examined them. "Yes, they do."

"Did you make an identification from that lineup?"

"Yes, I did. But I was under considerable pressure and—" She hesitated.

"What kind of pressure?" he asked, attempting to help her.

It didn't surprise John the questions and answers seemed rehearsed. What surprised him was that the answers were too pat, almost contrived, and he hoped the jury would think so too. But the responses had their purpose. How effective they turned out, the jury would later determine.

"I'm referring," she replied, "to the pressure of having such short notice, the lighting in the room, the fact that it was my first lineup. And of course, just having the police, the detectives, and the lawyers in that one room made me nervous. Then there was the matter of the hairdo being changed, which I didn't realize until I had made the identification and left the room." She singled out one photograph and held it up, as if to show it to the jury. "I would like this picture to be shown to the jury."

John sprang to his feet. "Objection!"

"Sustained," Judge Walker said. "The witness is instructed to just answer the questions."

"And you said you were very nervous?" Keith went on.

"That's correct," she stuttered, now more nervous than ever. John wasn't sure if her nervousness would gain the jury's sympathy.

"Were you as nervous at the lineup as you appear to be right now?"

"Perhaps more so."

Keith asked her questions intended to show she hadn't only failed to identify Bernardo but instead selected another individual. That person was standing next to Bernardo in the lineup. Once again, she emphasized Bernardo had styled his hair in a different way and that was the main reason why she didn't identify him.

When John realized Keith was about to ask her if the person she had seen on the day of the stabbing was present in the courtroom, he requested a hearing outside the presence of the jury. The brief hearing was held in the judge's chambers. John argued that Carol's in-court identification was tainted not only by all of the photographs she was shown before but by the fact she learned she had picked the wrong man in the lineup. Judge Walker ruled that her in-court ID would be permitted. He reasoned that, even though she had said one thing before and now was saying something else, it was a matter of credibility, which was for the jury to decide.

Back in the courtroom, Keith was permitted to ask her a series of questions leading to her identifying Bernardo as the man she followed on the day of the assault. The prosecutor seemed determined to create a certain picture in the jurors' minds—the image of Bernardo running away from where he had attempted to murder Patty.

In his cross-examination, John lost no time attacking Carol's credibility. It had been frustrating to sit there listening to Keith draw out testimony from her that Bernardo was the attacker. After all, before this turn of events, she was *his* witness ready to testify Bernardo *wasn't* the man she followed. Despite what she now claimed was a mistake at the lineup, she had moments ago pointed her accusing finger at his client.

John's initial questions focused on her chase, including the ten minutes she claimed it had lasted. It was only an estimate, she responded, for she wasn't looking at her watch, and she was also trying to calm her young daughter. He felt he made inroads with her confusing description of the suspect, including the purported change of hair style. After asking several questions relating to the photos and the composite drawing, he went on to her testimony of the lineup.

"You testified you were very nervous at the lineup, Ms. Niewold, is that correct?"

"I certainly was."

"And I gathered from what you said earlier that was the reason you picked the wrong man?"

"That, among others."

"Yes," he quipped. "Let's go to one of those. You said you only had a fifteen-minute notice to *rush* to the police department."

"That's right."

"So would it be fair to say it all happened very fast for you?"

"Yes. I had company for a late dinner when I was called, and I left immediately."

"And what time was that?"

"It was around three thirty, if I'm right."

"You were having a late lunch, then, not dinner?"

"Yes. I'm sorry."

"Do you recall what time you arrived at the police station?"

"No, I don't."

"Well, let me put it this way, Ms. Niewold. Isn't it a fact that you waited in Detective Morales' office at least an hour from the time of your arrival to the time you were asked to go to the room where the lineup was held?"

"That's true."

"So, although you may have been given a fifteen-minute notice, as you put it, you actually had a whole hour to calm down."

"Perhaps the time was there, Mr. Garcia, but I had the problem of being there and knowing why I was there. That didn't go away."

"But what I'm getting at, ma'am, is that surely you don't want the jury to get the impression you were rushed into the lineup room, do you?"

"Of course not. I hope I didn't say that." Her tone of voice betrayed her intentions, he thought, for it was exactly what she had meant to convey.

"You didn't say that, Ms. Niewold, but Mr. Keith's question, without more, might have given that impression. I'm just trying to clarify that one point, is that all right?"

"That's fine," she said.

"And taking it one step further, you don't want to leave the impression that you felt rushed in *making* your selection at the lineup, do you?"

"No, of course not."

He picked up the pace. "Now, about the lineup. A week or so before, did you tell Detective Morales without qualification that, if you had a personal view of the subject, you were sure you could make a positive identification?"

"Yes, I did."

"And when you told him that, you were well aware of your tendency to become nervous, weren't you?"

"Yes."

"Well, you had that direct, personal view of Bernardo Soliz at the lineup, didn't you?"

"Yes, except the hair style threw me off." She seemed flustered now.

He ignored her excuse. "And you didn't identify him as the man you saw running, did you?"

"That's right, but—"

"In addition, when you were viewing the lineup, you were told to circle the number representing the person in the lineup who you saw fleeing the Gregory residence, weren't you?"

"I believe they said 'if you see him or someone who looks like him...'"

He was growing frustrated with her tentative answers, yet he tried hard not to show it. "Now, Ms. Niewold, isn't—"

"—or had some resemblance." She appeared groping for the right words.

"Let me put it this way," John emphasized, "you *knew* you were there to see if you could identify the man you saw running on the day you gave chase, isn't that true?"

"Of course."

"And weren't you told that if you weren't certain, you weren't supposed to circle a number?"

"I don't recall being told that."

"Well, let's see if you recall this event as you were leaving the room after having identified the wrong man." He paused for emphasis. "Do you recall Mr. Soliz' public defender, his attorney at the time, asking you if you were certain of your identification?"

"No, I don't."

He was exasperated with an uncooperative witness. "Ma'am, do you deny being asked by the P. D. if you were sure, and you responded 'yes' and even nodded, to emphasize your answer."

"I-I d-don't deny it," she said, "I just don't recall it.

"When did you find out you had picked the wrong man?"

"A few days later. I called Detective Morales, and he informed me."

John left that line of questioning and proceeded to the physical description she had given to the police. To prove the many discrepancies concerning height, weight, and body build, he had Bernardo stand against the wall to measure his height, with and without shoes. He also had found and brought to the courtroom a pair of sandals similar to the ones Patty described her attacker as having worn. He asked Bernardo to put them on. He then used a tape measurer and ruler for the exact measurements and even placed a book on top of Bernardo's head to measure his height to his scalp, thus excluding hair thickness.

This was important, he believed, because Carol had implied that the assailant's hair style had increased the appearance of his height by well over an inch. Bernardo's hairline, in fact, was a quarter of an inch above his scalp.

No matter how grueling the questions, she wouldn't budge. No matter her discrepancy in the composite drawing, the photo identifications, as well as the lineup misidentification, she was certain Bernardo was the person she had seen on the day Patty was attacked.

On redirect, Keith was brief but effective. John anticipated Keith's strategy concerning John's use of the measuring tape and ruler. But he felt he should nonetheless risk using the devices to make his point. Keith somewhat neutralized the gains he may have made on these points.

"Now, Ms. Niewold," he began, "when you saw this man running down the street, he didn't have a book over his head, did he?"

"No, he didn't."

"He didn't have anything on his head?"

"No."

"And you didn't have a ruler or a measuring tape on you, did you?"

"I didn't."

"And the assailant didn't line himself up against a light pole, or—"

John was off his chair. "Objection, your honor!"

"Sustained," Judge Walker said.

"You were just trying to stay up with him," Keith went on, "while at the same time trying to calm down your six-year-old daughter?"

186

"That's correct," Carol answered.

The next morning, Keith began his examination of Patty.

When John first met her, he wasn't sure what overall effect she'd have on a jury. She was outgoing and assertive, two traits that had to make her an above-average real estate salesperson. She also appeared to be highly intelligent. To that, he would add that she possessed a considerable amount of common sense. Anyone who met her for the first time could also see she possessed much self-confidence.

There wasn't any question she was confident of her identification of Bernardo, despite any discrepancies.

The amount of self-assurance displayed by her, John thought, could work against her before jurors. He had seen many witnesses lose their credibility with a jury just because they came across as too sure of themselves. That occurred even when the facts suggested the witnesses might be wrong and should have shown some doubt or uncertainty before committing to a given set of facts.

This morning, Patty wore a modest dress that gave her almost a homely appearance, hiding her curvaceous body. On the two occasions John had interviewed her, she wore a suit with the hemline just above the knee the first time and slacks the other. She was petite, blond, and possessed vivid blue eyes, as well as what many would consider an attractive pair of legs. This morning, her legs were well hidden by the long dress she wore. Her long hair was pulled up in a bun in back, making her appear matronly. John was certain her appearance in court had been Keith's idea.

Although she had worn khaki shorts and a white blouse on the day of the assault, there wasn't a hint her attacker had attempted to assault her sexually. Rape victims often didn't fare well when they wore attire suggestive of even the slightest promiscuity, either at the time of the incident or while testifying in court, thus permitting an accused to contend the intercourse was consensual.

After the usual preliminary questions, Keith lost no time getting to the heart of Patty's testimony. With Carol, he had prepared both the witness and the jury with many questions before Carol had identified Bernardo. Not so with Patty. Instead of having her testify about some faceless assailant involved in the events leading up to the climatic assault, he went for the jugular—pointing right off to Bernardo as the actor in the drama.

He obviously wanted the jury to see *Bernardo* as he plunged the knife into his victim, not a faceless, nameless attacker.

After calling Patty's attention to the evening of the assault, he set the stage for Bernardo's entry into the scene as Patty was washing her car.

"Was anyone else at your residence at the time?" he asked.

"No, sir," she replied. "My husband was away on business."

"And did anything unusual—" He paused for effect. "Let me call your attention to the individual seated to the left of Mr. Garcia." He didn't yet refer to Bernardo by name or even as the defendant or the accused. "Did you have occasion to see that person on the night in question?"

"Yes, sir."

He addressed the court reporter. "Let the record reflect that the witness is referring to the defendant, Bernardo Soliz." Now it was Bernardo, not anyone else, at the scene. Keith turned his attention to Patty. "When and where did you first see Mr. Soliz that evening?"

"It was around seven thirty or sometime after that. He approached as I was washing my car."

"Had you ever seen him before?"

"No, sir. Not that I know of." She spoke with little emotion.

"What then occurred?"

"I didn't realize anyone was there until he got maybe ten feet away from me as he entered the carport. Then he said to me, 'Excuse me, ma'am, do you know if the house across the street is for rent?' He pointed to a house that was vacant at the time and that I knew was in probate."

Keith then showed her a series of photographs portraying various angles of the front of her house, including the carport, the front yard, the street, and portions of the houses across the street. John had no objection to the photos, so they were admitted as exhibits. Referring to the vacant house, Patty related her discussion with the stranger concerning his interest, and she informed him what agency to contact to see if it was for rent.

"'So are you looking for a place to rent?' I asked him," she went on. "He was extremely polite. 'Yes, ma'am. I just arrived from California and am looking for a place.'" She paused to clear her throat. "I went on to explain I was a realtor and worked for a real estate office. I told him our office didn't handle rentals, but I gave him our address anyway. Then I suggested he contact the Chamber of Commerce and gave him the names of several real estate companies that handled rentals. After several minutes of conversation, I asked him if he would like to have a map of the city."

"He said, 'Yes, ma'am.' I opened the car door because I keep a supply there. I took out a map and handed it to him. 'Do you have a pencil I could borrow?' he said. I opened the door again and retrieved a felt pen. Again, he asked me my office's address and wrote it down on the map, using the car to write on. He asked a few more questions, then thanked me. I had continued to wash my car as we talked, and when he walked away, I didn't pay attention where he went."

Prodded by questions from Keith, she then testified that the entire *meeting*, which was the term used by him during his interrogation to describe the event, had taken place about three to five minutes. Bernardo, she said, was wearing "straight legged blue jeans," a white crew-necked, snug fitting T-shirt, and a pair of sandals—no socks. The sandals had tire-type treads for soles about a half or three-quarters of an inch thick.

It took her several minutes to finish washing her vehicle. She then went inside the house to get a towel to dry off the car. Keith, again referring to the photographs, had her describe her actions as she entered the house and returned to the car. Afterward, she was standing in the patio, drying her hands, a few feet from the doorway leading into the house, when she looked up.

"I saw this same individual," she said, slipping by not referring to Bernardo. "He was standing near the rear of my car. He stared at me for a moment, then approached me."

"And by 'this same individual,'" Keith asked, "I assume you're referring to the defendant, Mr. Soliz, who had been there earlier asking about a rental?" John admired Keith's continuing tactic. Once again, he didn't want a yet-unknown assailant-to-be who would later be identified as Bernardo at the lineup. He wanted the jury to see the man's face as Bernardo's, and so he made sure she didn't slip again by speaking of an assailant that remained faceless.

"Yes, I'm referring to the defendant."

"What happened then?"

She took the hint. "The defendant, Mr. Soliz, said to me, 'Excuse me, ma'am, do you think your husband would mind if I used your telephone. I want to call and see if this place down the street is for rent.' Without thinking, I began to tell him my husband wasn't home, then realized I shouldn't. I was concerned about letting him use the phone. Making no

189

commitment one way or the other, I turned around and started going into the kitchen."

"Please relate what occurred next, Ms. Gregory."

"As I walked into the kitchen, I heard him behind me. When I had one foot on the threshold, I looked back and noticed he had moved rather fast, and I was surprised he was right there."

Until now, she had kept her composure, showing little emotion, nervousness, or even trepidation over the fact that her assailant was a few feet away. Even at the lineup when she identified Bernardo, the P. D. had told John, she had been very calm and hadn't displayed any of the nervousness that had affected Carol.

John had wondered before, as he wondered now, if she would display any emotion when she related the event that almost ended her life. Some witnesses suffered considerably from such a traumatic event. So much so that, in relating the event, they relived it. By a long shot, John was certain Patty wasn't one of them. Before the trial, he had predicted she would retain her composure. He was correct.

"The next thing I knew," she said, "he jumped me from behind. I felt his hand on my shoulder and then the knife entering my back. I started to scream, not so much from fright as from the stinging, burning pain. He then tried covering my mouth. To stifle my scream, I suppose. Then he shoved me forward into the kitchen and out of the patio.

"Inside, I continued screaming, not because someone would hear me, but because I thought it would keep one of his hands busy trying to keep me from drawing someone's attention."

Few persons in her predicament would have considered such a ploy. John wondered if she had really gone through that mental process when she was fighting for her life or had come up with the idea sometime later. No matter, he said to himself—for certain, she was an effective witness.

"Somehow, with my left hand," she went on without emotion, "I got hold of the knife still stuck in my back and pulled it out. He was still in back of me as we struggled, his right hand over my mouth and his left hand around my wrist, trying to force me to release the knife. As he forced me further into the kitchen, we both lost our balance and ended up on the floor."

Keith showed her photos of the kitchen and asked her to use them to show the jury where the scuffle had taken place. She seemed full of energy as she went from one picture to another, describing the scene in vivid detail.

"Did you still have the knife in your hand when you both fell to the floor?" he asked as he placed the photos on the reporter's desk.

"Yes."

"Were you bleeding?"

"Yes, I was. I could feel the wetness on my blouse."

He asked her to describe the knife, which she did in minute detail. John wasn't surprised she remembered it so well. He didn't intend to question her about it, however, so he didn't bother taking any notes of her description. The knife had never been found. Even a search warrant executed at the Soliz residence hadn't produced it. Bernardo had denied ever owning such a weapon when John had questioned him about it.

"What happened next?" Keith continued.

"I didn't have the strength to throw away the knife because his left hand was still holding on to my wrist. I remember thinking I mustn't let him have control of the knife. In spite of my efforts, somehow he got the knife back. That's when I started to struggle with all my strength, and that's when he stabbed me here." She pointed to her breast. "I rolled over and I think I then got the long gash in my abdomen as my weight pushed against it and he moved it across from one side of me to the other. Instantly, I felt the blood from the new wounds. It seemed to me as if it was gushing out. I remember thinking I was going to bleed to death."

John glanced at the jurors and noticed a couple of them grimace as they listened. The courtroom was dead quiet as Patty paused to catch her breath.

"Were you in any pain?" Keith said, breaking the pause.

"By that time, no. I felt numb. I could feel the cuts, and I knew I was bleeding because I could feel the wetness. That's when I started feeling weak—almost faint. At that moment, I realized I was losing control and that if that happened, he was going to kill me." She seemed caught in the frenzy of the event she was describing but not reliving. "I think that's when I decided it might be wise to give up my struggle and play dead. It was either that, I thought, or *be* dead."

"Did you believe at the time he meant to kill you?"

"Objection, your honor!" John said, on his feet. "She can't testify to the assailant's state of mind."

"That's correct, Mr. Garcia," Judge Walker said, "but I don't believe that's what Mr. Keith is asking. He wants to know *Ms. Gregory's* state of mind, not the assailant's. I'll permit the witness to answer the question."

Keith returned his attention to Patty. "Do you wish for me to repeat the question?"

She shook her head. Before answering the question, she turned to Bernardo and glared at him. "I truly believed he would kill me. That's when I got the idea that, if I played dead, maybe he'd do whatever he came to do, rob us or whatever. Just as long as he stopped stabbing me. And that's what happened—I let my body go limp, and he didn't stab me anymore. He just lay there for a moment, and I didn't dare move even a fraction of an inch."

She paused, as if considering her next words. "Then for no apparent reason, he started squeezing me hard, with his arms and hands wrapped around me. He wouldn't stop, and I recall almost blacking out from his strong hold. Then he stopped suddenly, and I heard him make a sound like a child makes when he's about to cry."

"You mean like a whimper?" Keith asked.

She contemplated the question. "No—no. He actually choked up and cried, and I felt him tremble against my body as he held me. Then he stopped making the noise and stood up. When he let go of me, I just continued playing as if I was dead and let my body drop to the floor. I heard him walk across the patio and into the carport. Realizing I was able to get up, I moved to the door and watched him as he passed the end of the carport."

"Were you standing up?" Keith asked in apparent disbelief she had the strength to do so.

"By that time, I was. I went out the door, thinking I might see him get into a car I could describe to the police. But when I got to the front yard, I was too weak to follow him. He took off running south, and I ran north screaming as loud as I could across my yard and into my neighbor's yard, where my legs gave out, and I fell. I looked up and saw a few persons across the street. I could see I had attracted their attention. One of them—a man—ran across the street to where I lay."

"Did he talk to you?"

"He asked if I was in any pain."

"Were you?"

"I told him I didn't feel a great deal of pain, but I was still faint. I asked him to call the police. He said someone had gone to telephone them and for me just to lie calm until they arrived."

She then went on to testify that she was tended to by Officer Tanner, to whom she gave a description of her assailant. Later, she gave the same description to Morales when he arrived. She estimated her assailant's height to be 5' 6" and his weight around 135 to 140 pounds. Keith asked her if, during her encounter, she had an opportunity to measure or stand up close to him to compare heights. She emphasized she had been bending over or squatting as she washed her car and talked to her would-be attacker. Keith also elicited from her that, from the actions and movements of her assailant, she believed him to be left-handed.

She described two tattoos on his right arm. The one on the upper arm, which was half-covered by the sleeve of his T-shirt, appeared to be initials of some sort, but she wasn't sure. The tattoo on the lower arm she couldn't describe too well either, except that it was blotchy with a whole lot of ink. She gave Morales descriptions of the tattoos when asked if her assailant had any identifying marks or scars on his body. Keith showed her photos taken of Bernardo's arms. They showed his right arm bear, but his left arm had two tattoos. She conceded she was mistaken the attacker had tattoos on his right arm. Although she couldn't be sure they were identical to the ones she had seen on her assailant, she insisted they were similar and in the same general area.

Mid-afternoon, Judge Walker recessed the trial for the day, even though Keith hadn't completed his direct examination of Patty. This time, the jurist's administrative responsibilities, not other court hearings, prevented him from continuing the testimony. The judge also explained before recessing that the next morning he'd be forced to recess again. There were several hearings he had to preside over in other cases due to the sudden illness of another judge.

John was relieved when he heard the jurist announce the early recess the following day because Leroy Etcitty had telephoned him during the lunch hour and left word he had found something he wanted him to see. Kelly insisted he discuss nothing by telephone but instead travel to Shiprock to see Leroy in private. Because of the trial, John knew that his first opportunity to go there wouldn't come until the weekend. Now that the trial would be recessed before noon, he'd be able to drive, or better yet, fly to Farmington and return that evening.

Before excusing counsel, Judge Walker obtained a commitment from Keith that he'd conclude Patty's testimony by eleven the next morning. The judge also instructed John to be ready to begin his cross-examination of Patty first thing Friday morning.

CHAPTER 17

KEITH wrapped up his examination of Patty as promised. She described her care and treatment during her eight days in the hospital. To stop internal bleeding, she underwent surgery. She testified of the various visits Morales made to show her photographs of subjects. When she picked out a photo from a mug shot book that wasn't of Bernardo, she emphasized she told the detective she was selecting the photo only to show the hair style, as well as the profile similarity. When shown the composite drawing, she explained to Morales that the drawing wasn't *right*—the eyes were too far apart and the top of the head appeared *chopped off.*

Finally, she described her identification of Bernardo at the lineup as well as her earlier ID at the hospital. To bolster her having picked out Bernardo's candid photo from among a dozen photographs, Keith had her describe for the jury's benefit how she had selected Bernardo's photo. She held the pictures in her left hand, she said, as her right hand picked up the one on top and threw it on the bed. She did the same with the next six photographs. When she came to the eighth photo, which was

Bernardo's, she flung it all the way to the foot of the bed and told the detective, "That's him!" It was a dramatic and unnecessary display of self-confidence. Yet, John feared it was effective, which in the end was what counted.

After asking several preliminary questions regarding the lineup, Keith handed her photographs taken of the lineup participants.

"Whom, if anyone, in that series of photos did you identify as your assailant? Keith said.

"Bernardo Soliz," she said with certainty.

"Were you given something, some paper, to mark your choice on?"

"Yes, I was given a printed sheet with a series of numbers."

"I hand you state's exhibit 18 and ask you to look at page two. Is that what you're referring to?"

"Yes. It's got my signature, and I made a circle around *Number Two*."

Once more, she anticipated the question. Some witnesses needed no prompting and played their role to a T. Patty was one of them.

"How long would you say you viewed the lineup before deciding the individual in the *Number Two* position was your assailant?"

"Oh, I'd say fifteen seconds after I entered the room."

"Is that all?"

"I spotted him right away."

"Did you have any trouble identifying your attacker?"

"Well, when I first looked, I did a double take because I noticed his hair style was different. It was combed over and parted instead of being combed straight back. But that didn't create any trouble for me, as far as that goes." Once again, she needed no suggestive questioning. She knew what Keith wanted her to say, and she was smart enough to know when to say it.

Keith wanted her testimony concerning the alleged change in hairdo to offer an explanation for Carol's mistake at the lineup. What Patty was implying was that she herself hadn't had any trouble with the new *hairdo*, but she could understand how someone else might.

"Is there any doubt in your mind today that Mr. Soliz is the person who assaulted you?" Keith next asked.

"Definitely not," she said.

"Was there any doubt in your mind the day you identified Mr. Soliz at the lineup?"

"None at all." She turned and stared at Bernardo, who in turn glared at her.

Her confidence hadn't faltered. To emphasize that point to the jury, however, Keith went on. "Do you recall having a conversation with the public defender after you made the lineup identification, who at the time was the defendant's attorney?"

"Yes, I do."

"And he asked you a question, did he not?"

"Yes. Mr. Soliz's attorney was right behind where I was seated to view the lineup. After I had made my mark and circled the number, and the men in the lineup were being dismissed, the public defender asked, 'Ms. Gregory, are you sure about your choice?' As I recall, my answer was, 'I'm as sure as I can ever be.'"

Keith's direct examination ended at ten thirty, and Judge Walker reminded John to be ready to begin his cross-examination the following morning. The trial was recessed until the following day.

John had thought of driving to Shiprock in his own car, but that meant spending some three and a half hours driving one way on a narrow, two-lane road. Concerned that the car trip would exhaust him even more, Demi suggested he fly up midday to Farmington on a commuter airline, rent a car there, then fly back that evening. He took her advice, realizing his insistence in making the trip in the middle of a trial displeased her. Early that morning, he asked Lynda to book him on a round-trip flight leaving Albuquerque around noon. She also arranged for a rental car at the Farmington airport.

Lynda knew he hadn't any prearranged business in Farmington, so, by way of explanation, he told her he had just learned that an old Army friend was terminally ill in Shiprock. He disliked distorting the truth but felt he had no choice. The day before, Kelly had informed him Quigley and an FBI agent would be leaving for Shiprock early Thursday morning and arrive there long before John's plane landed. The agents were to make contact with him sometime after he left Leroy's residence for the return flight home.

He was uncertain whether to reveal to Leroy on this particular trip that the CIA had uncovered documents linking him to several misappropriations of army property. A part of him wanted to give Leroy the chance to defend himself; to prove the agency wrong. Kelly suggested he wait until later to confront Leroy, but left it up to him. The agent also told him that if he decided to address the issue on this particular visit, he wait until after Leroy provided whatever information he was prepared to share with him. Kelly insisted he ask Leroy if he had any knowledge of illicit actions taken by Condon.

"He's already said he knew nothing of the sort," John said. "Or at least suggested he didn't."

"Ask him again," Kelly replied. "He's got to level with us! In the end, it'll be better for him."

"Surely the government wouldn't prosecute him after all these years?"

"If he cooperates, probably not. But that's not up to me or the agency."

"No, I suppose not," John said, ending the discussion.

Before he left his office for the airport, he telephoned Leroy, and they arranged to meet in Leroy's house between two and two-thirty. Leroy gave him directions. He drove into the little village of Shiprock a few minutes after two.

Leroy's small, modest home was just off U. S. Highway North 666, a highway connecting Shiprock to the town of Cortez, Colorado, located near the New Mexico border. Leroy lived in an almost desolate area a mile or so north of the turnoff linking U. S. Highway 64, the highway from Farmington to Shiprock, to North 666.

John had no problem finding the turnoff to Leroy's property, just past the Shiprock Post Office and the Navajo Community College. He turned off on the unpaved road just north of the Northern Navajo Medical Center. It led him up a hill past several isolated houses. Leroy's house was just past a small incline.

He found Leroy in the studio behind his house. The studio was a wooden structure he had built to do his work. It looked new. The stucco house and studio had no greenery around it, except for the sparse, native vegetation that grew wild in the region. As John walked up to the studio's door, a strong gust of cold air from the Northwest whistled past him. It blew past the pitched metal roof of the structure, then continued toward the crest of a small ridge on the far side of a fence running alongside the back of the studio.

At the exact moment Leroy was inviting him into his studio, a quarter mile away, Quigley and his associate pulled over to the side of the unpaved road. There, they'd wait until John's anticipated departure.

"So this is where you do your work," John said as he took off his coat. "It's roomy."

Leroy smiled. "Yes," he said. "I built this a couple of years ago when I outgrew an extra bedroom I used in the house." He offered him a chair setting near a small table and a refrigerator. "The house itself isn't much, but it's good enough for an old 'codger' like me."

As John sat, he looked around the large room, taking in the assortment of equipment. "I don't know about your house, but your studio looks like it's 'state of the art' to me."

"I wouldn't dare take you into the house," Leroy said, grinning. "It's a mess. I'm not a very good housekeeper." He glanced around the room, nodding his head. "But this studio is where my money has gone into and where I spend most of my time." He sat in a chair on the other side of the table. "Speaking of my work, Gerald told me you bought a set of earrings and didn't bother showing him my note."

"The price he quoted seemed reasonable." He smiled. "I hope I didn't offend you."

"You didn't. But I meant the discount as my gift to you and Demi. Had I been there, I'd have taken your money for the earrings you bought, then given another pair to Demi."

"I appreciate your generosity, Leroy. Demi liked you, by the way."

"And I liked *her*. Better hang on to her. She's a jewel."

"I plan doing that."

Leroy stood up. "Let me get you a drink." He walked to the small refrigerator. "I've got a couple of stale beers in here and some soda pop— Pepsi and Ginger Ale. I've been keeping the beer for when I have guests. I guess you might say I haven't had any in a while." He laughed.

John accepted the Ginger Ale, and Leroy fixed two glasses with ice. He sat back down.

"*Salud!*" he said, holding his glass up. "To renewing an old friendship."

"To us," John added. They tapped glasses and drank.

"I've had you on my mind ever since last week," Leroy said after taking a big swallow. He shook his head. "This thing that's happened after all these years—it's bizarre."

"I've thought about you too, Leroy. I dislike the idea of getting you involved in something that may prove dangerous."

"Don't give it another thought. I'm willing to do what I can to help." He took another drink of his Ginger Ale. "Tell me, though, why do you say this thing could be dangerous?"

"I guess now's the time to level with you." He gave a detailed explanation of the CIA's theory that he had access to information the Chinese government was seeking and of the agency's concern for his and his family's safety. He had resisted the agency's suggestions, he explained, to go on an all-out effort to provide protective surveillance. Finally, he told Leroy of the more recent suspicions that Tong might be involved.

"You've kept all this from Demi?" Leroy asked when he had finished.

He nodded. "But I'm having second thoughts. Maybe I shouldn't have downplayed this fucking mess. Each day, I seem to learn something that supports the CIA's suspicions."

"Fuck, John, it's your business, but you should come clean with this shit. With Demi."

"I was hoping it wouldn't come to that, but you might be right."

Leroy sighed. "And I guess I'll soon be adding fuel to the fire."

"Why do you say that?"

"Well, after our talk last week, I couldn't understand what possible connection all this had to do with Henri. Like you, I thought your CIA buddies' suspicions were overblown. But after what I found yesterday, I'm wondering if whoever's after you thinks Henri let you in on his story."

"Why?" He couldn't hide his impatience. "What did you find?"

Leroy walked to a small desk setting against the back wall. He pulled out a faded, worn envelope. "Much to my surprise," he said, sitting back down, "I found this old letter from Henri." He tossed the brittle envelope on the table.

John picked it up and recognized Henri's handwriting. The style was fancy, almost calligraphic, and he recalled the postcards he himself had received written in that same handwriting. Henri had used a fountain pen with a purplish-blue ink to write Leroy's address at Ft. Bliss, Texas. The return address appeared to be a residence—*Lydias 24, GR-14272*, in Athens, Greece.

His eyes were glued to the envelope. He finally looked up at Leroy. "Have you read it?"

Leroy nodded.

"Did you find anything else?"

"I found an old address book that's got a couple of phone numbers and a different address, but that's it. Meanwhile, why don't you read the letter? You'll find it interesting."

He turned the envelope over with care, then took out the discolored letter and began reading. "*My dear Leroy,*" the letter began.

I wish I had the time to tell you all that's happened to me during the immediate past. But alas, I've moved three times in two months and am getting ready to leave my flat in the morning to a place out in the country. You've been a dear friend, and I'll forever be grateful, but I have one last favor to ask of you. My most recent letters to John Garcia have been returned unclaimed, for I lost track of him after leaving Vietnam. I don't have his current address. It's a matter of great urgency that I get hold of him. I was hoping you'd know either his whereabouts or how to get in touch with him through military channels.

Leroy, I wouldn't bother you if it wasn't important to me. You've been loyal to me. I'll never forget that, but for what you and John did to get me out of that dreadful country, I'd probably not be alive today. I can't say much to you, except that I have some extremely sensitive information to pass on to John. He should contact my parents for that purpose. I don't wish to involve you, for you still have many years ahead of you in your military career, and I dread thinking what would happen if you had this information in your possession. Unlike you, John is not career military, and I know I can trust him also. Besides, he's a lawyer, and he'd know what to do with this information in these circumstances.

Please write as soon as possible to let me know John's address and phone number (better yet,

201

call and leave a message at the home of an acquaintance here in Athens: +301 77.79.725). Or if you can obtain John's address later and send it to me, that too would be fine. But I beg of you, please act soon. I await your reply.

Warmest regards,

Henri

P.S. —I've given you my current address, but my correspondence will be forwarded to me as soon as I know of my new residence. I presently have no phone but will have one soon at my new place.

When he finished reading the letter, he laid it on the table and looked at Leroy. He shook his head in disbelief. "I'm assuming you replied to it," he said.

"I had forgotten about that letter when we spoke last week," Leroy said. "It was so long ago. Yes, I replied to it. I now remember doing it. I told him I lost track of you after you left 'Nam. I don't recall trying to find out where you were at the time." He shrugged. "Much later, when I learned you were in Albuquerque, I had forgotten all about it."

"His letter raises more questions than it answers."

"Maybe. Don't you agree, though, it might answer one."

"What's that?"

"Your connection to him. If he was trying to pass on important information to you, don't you think that's why someone's interested in you? They might not know he never passed it on."

"You could be right."

"Even so, it still leaves one question unanswered."

"What?"

"Why the fuck are they interested in you after so many years?"

"I've asked that same question of Kelly."

"What did he say?"

"He suspects their interest was rekindled by something that's occurred recently. Something that might make the material useful to them now."

"Makes sense."

"Another thing's for certain—Henri was desperate when he wrote this." He picked up the letter and reread it. "'Sensitive information,'" he read out loud. "Wanted me to contact his parents. I didn't even know them. Sounds as if he was afraid he wasn't going to make it. He might have passed on the information to his parents." He dropped the letter on the table. "What do you think?"

"The same thing. When I reread the letter yesterday, I thought you might have met his parents, but then realized that wasn't likely. I too didn't know them, and I was closer to Henri than you were. He may have spoken of them once or twice, that's all."

"I agree you were closer to him than I was. But that raises another puzzle."

"Which is?"

"Since you were closer to him, if we're correct in assuming the sensitive information he referred to had to do with missing inventory, why wouldn't he entrust you with it, especially since he knew where you were and didn't know my whereabouts."

Leroy hesitated. "For the reasons he gave in his letter, I suppose."

"That you were still in the army and that, as an attorney, I'd know what do with it?"

"Yeah."

"I don't buy that. The fact remains he knew you better than he did me."

Leroy hesitated again, then spoke. "I want to confess something to you, John, and I suppose now's the time to come out with it." He swallowed and cleared his throat. "That one time our paths crossed at the bar in Saigon when I had met with Henri—do you remember that?"

"Yes. In fact, I was thinking about it the other day. You were very nervous about his quizzing you."

"Well, what I didn't tell you was why I really felt he was treading too close to home. I'm not sure you understand how prevalent thefts of supplies were in 'Nam." He paused, as if unable to get the words out. "I haven't been completely honest with you."

Leroy had just opened the door, he thought. Might as well help him out. "Are you trying to tell me you were involved in some way?" he asked.

Leroy nodded. "That's exactly what I'm trying to tell you." He let out a big sigh. "It embarrasses me to say this. But the truth is I found it so easy and that made the temptation greater. And so I did it. Not just once, but over and over again."

"But your career? You were willing to risk that?"

"That's just it. It was so easy to cover up that the risk wasn't even all that great."

"Maybe not at the time. But what about later?" He looked at him straight in the eye. "Like the investigation being conducted by the CIA now, for instance?"

"Are you suggesting your CIA friends have got something on me?"

He nodded. "I found out about it after our visit in Santa Fe."

Leroy looked away. "Shit!" After a long silence, he spoke, as if resigned to the very worst. "Do they intend to fucking prosecute?"

"They don't know the answer to that. It's out of their hands." He stopped as he sensed the depth of Leroy's concern. "For whatever it's worth, Leroy, as a lawyer, I'll make an educated guess that the statute of limitations would prevent them from filing charges against you. There's quite a lapse of time."

"Damn, John, this was 'peanuts' I was dealing with. Nothing approaching the level of what your buddies suspect Condon of doing."

"It was still wrong, Leroy!"

"I realize that."

"Do you still maintain you did nothing that would connect you to Condon's activities?"

"I swear to you, John, on my parents' graves. I never even suspected Condon. That's what got me so nervous when I found out Henri was working on that story; that someone that high up was involved." He sighed, then continued. "Anyway, that's why I think Henri didn't trust me and why he chose you to pass on the information to."

"You think he had evidence implicating you?"

"I can't say for sure, but I'd guess he had his suspicions. He knew these minor embezzlements were taking place all over the place. That's what perked his interest to begin with. He probably suspected I was too close to the problem to trust me."

John shook his head. "I'm relieved you decided to come out with this. I was struggling with how I was going to approach this issue with you."

"Did your CIA friends ask you to do that?"

"They left it up to me. Sooner or later, though, I think they were planning to confront you. The fact that you didn't wait for that to happen works in your favor, I think."

"In a strange way, I feel a big relief getting this off my chest."

"I'm glad." He patted Leroy on the shoulder. "We can talk more about it some other time, if you'd like, but for now, let's get back to Henri's letter. His parents—where did they live when he was in Vietnam?"

"In Paris, France, I think."

"We might be jumping the gun. I'm not sure he'd entrust this information to them if he himself felt threatened. Why get them involved if he thought there might be some danger?"

"Yeah, it wouldn't make sense. What I was wondering was whether any of this had anything to do with that hot story of his."

"I'd be surprised if there wasn't a connection." John took the letter and placed it in the envelope. "May I keep this? I'd like the CIA to take a look at it."

"Sure." Leroy walked to the desk and pulled out a small, black leather address book that was worn and cracked. He brought it back to the table and opened it. "Here's my old address book I found in the same foot locker. It's got a couple of entries for Henri." He handed the little book to John. "You can keep that too, if you want."

John looked through it. "I don't think that'll be necessary. I'll just jot down the address and phone numbers for Kelly and Quigley to check out." He took out his pen and a pocket notebook and wrote down the two phone numbers and Henri's second address.

For the next half hour, they speculated what may have happened to Henri and his writing project. John found it difficult to believe the story, if it had any credibility at all, wouldn't have found its way to some publication.

Their discussion returned to Leroy's confession. With obvious shame, he disclosed that he found the rewards of his illegal practices at the time easier to accept with little remorse because of their prevalence among others. He spoke of the active black markets in Saigon. American supplies, food, and armaments were sold in such places on a daily basis, but he never heard of the criminal activity Henri had spoken of. The PX's in Vietnam, Leroy said, were always losing merchandise that found its way to the various black markets where items were sold for twice and three times their regular price. He also recalled having read several articles on the subject after his tour in Southeast Asia. He described his own behavior as an aberration confined to *that blasted sewer hole of a country*. Once out of there, he said, he didn't even take a pencil home for his personal use.

John had lost track of time. He looked at his watch. It was already three thirty, and he had a return flight to catch at five thirty. Not only did he have to make the thirty-mile trip back to Farmington, but he had to meet with Quigley.

He stood up to leave and thanked Leroy.

Leroy accompanied him out of the studio. "I've been thinking," he said. "The danger to you and your family over this must be very real. I hope you tell Demi the whole story."

"There's a lot going on in our lives right now," John replied. "I hesitate adding to that. I'm hoping the CIA will stay on top of things without my having to add to Demi's worries." He got to his car. "But now I'm concerned about getting you involved. If you and I should have further contact on this, I'm going to ask Kelly if they shouldn't set up surveillance here for you."

"I doubt that's necessary. It's you and your family I'm worried about." He looked away, then returned his gaze to John. "And listen, John, I'm embarrassed after telling you what I did back then. I hope you're not too disappointed in me."

"Don't worry about it. You made mistakes, and I'm just glad you came clean with me."

"You really think there's a good chance they won't file charges?"

"I'll talk to Kelly again. From what you've told me, sounds as if they'd have to charge a helluva lot of individuals."

"Well, I'll take my licks if it comes to that."

John opened the car door and extended his hand to Leroy. "Keep an eye out, okay? Let me know if you suspect anything. I'll stay in touch."

Leroy took John's hand and gave it a tight squeeze. He followed it with a bear hug. "Thanks for being so understanding," he said.

"Think nothing of it." He got into the car. "I'm the one that thanks you for helping with *my* problem."

"Let me know what happens."

"I will. Bye."

"Be careful, John."

CHAPTER 18

BEFORE reaching Highway North 666, John spotted Quigley's car approaching from a private road on the left. He pulled over ahead of Quigley. The agent walked up to his car, but the FBI agent riding with him didn't exit. John took out Henri's letter from the envelope and gave it to Quigley. After Quigley read it, John tore off the page in his notebook containing the phone numbers and address he had taken from the address book and explained them to Quigley.

"We'll get on this right away," Quigley said, placing the papers in his inside coat pocket. "I'll call Kelly before leaving Shiprock. I doubt we'll find LaPierre in Athens after so many years, even if he's still alive. These international journalists don't stay in one place for too long."

"You think he might be dead?" John asked.

Quigley shook his head. "Hard to say. If his fears were well founded, I wouldn't be surprised if someone bumped him off long ago. For now, we'll go on the assumption he's still alive. What about Etcitty? Did you get a chance to confront him with what we had on him?"

"I didn't have to; he volunteered it." He related Leroy's admissions, as well as his emphatic denial of any knowledge concerning Condon's activities.

"Quigley, I've been thinking—doesn't it make sense these people might know I've made contact with Leroy and suspect he too knew Henri? Shouldn't the FBI assign one of its agents here?"

"We're on that. We planned doing it today because of your trip here, but we couldn't get an agent loose. One's being assigned here in the next couple of days."

"Good," he said with obvious relief. "He won't have to know about it, will he? I don't think he'd like the idea."

"It'd be better if he didn't. Especially since he now knows we have something on him."

John was tempted to address the likelihood that criminal charges would be filed against Leroy but decided to leave it for another day. "See you in Albuquerque," he said finally and began rolling his car window.

"Have a safe flight back."

He drove off, and Quigley followed behind at a slower speed.

As Quigley's car disappeared over the crest of the small hill, a maroon automobile approached the dirt road by way of the same side road Quigley had appeared from moments earlier. It was the same car and the same two Asian-Americans who had waited in the darkness outside the *Zia Lounge* in Fruitland the prior week. The slow-moving vehicle turned off the side road and eased onto the narrow road leading to Leroy's studio.

From the moment John's plane took off from the Farmington airport to when it landed, his thoughts were consumed by Henri's letter. He was still surprised Henri would have entrusted him with what he had termed *sensitive information*. What had he wanted him to do with it? Had he suspected Leroy's involvement? Is that why he had turned to him instead?

He was mystified more than ever as he drove home from the airport. Was the information Henri wanted him to have connected with his project? With such thoughts racing through his mind, he detoured from his way home and drove to the Albuquerque Public Library. He was curious about the black markets in Vietnam Leroy had mentioned. Why hadn't he heard of them? Leroy said he had read articles involving merchandise stolen from post exchanges. How extensive were these thefts? Did they involve military persons in high positions, as Henri had suggested?

At the library, he was directed to a section containing books on every subject dealing with the Vietnam War. He began his research by first reading the book titles without removing the books from the shelves, hoping they alone might give him a hint of the books' contents. He found none specific enough to suggest criminal activity. He then started pulling books off the shelves whose titles caught his eye as interesting, then skimming through their tables of contents.

In this manner, he went through roughly half the books when he picked one entitled *Our Own Worst Enemy* by William J. Lederer. The title alone intrigued him, and the author's name seemed familiar. He guessed he may have read other writings by him. When he opened the book, he came upon the page listing other books by Mr. Lederer. *The Ugly American* was among them, and John hadn't only read the book, which was coauthored by another writer, Eugene Burdick, but had seen the movie starring Marlon Brando. He noted that this particular book was published in 1968, long before the war ended in the 70's.

He took the book to a table, where he browsed through a few sample pages to get an idea of the subject matter. He recalled that *The Ugly American* had been critical of United States foreign policy and of the image portrayed by Americans on foreign soil. For that reason, he thought that even the chapter titles hinted at the author's criticisms of U. S. policies and actions during the Vietnam War—*The Deaf and Dumb American, The Humiliated American, The Anguished American*.

He gleaned sample paragraphs from those particular chapters. In the first chapter, Lederer made it clear the book was an indictment of the United States's techniques in Southeast Asia. He cited examples of American "bungling" and "foundering" and gave brief statistics showing why the Americans were losing the war. Basing his arguments on these statistics and several examples, he posed a rhetorical question. "Is it not obvious," he wrote, "that we are doing something wrong?" On the last page of the first chapter, he wrote:

> One of the reasons we have been so impotent in Vietnam is that we have allowed two additional deadly enemies to enter the war. These two additional enemies give tremendous support to the North Vietnamese and to the Vietcong. These two enemies of the United States supply North Vietnam and the Vietcong with war material and food.
>
> ...

209

> Even though these two allies of our enemy are among America's most
> dangerous foes, we have been helpless against them. We are afraid to
> take action to thwart their deadly actions. We do not have the
> courage or integrity to confront them.
> The two countries who are giving this support to North Vietnam and
> to the Vietcong are not Russia and Red China.
> They are South Vietnam and the United States. We are our own
> worst enemy.

"Hmmm, 'We are our own worst enemy,'" John repeated to himself.
Interesting statement. He wondered what Lederer meant by that. He felt
compelled to read on. It was in Chapter 6, entitled *The Generous American*,
that John found what he was searching for. It was there Lederer
contended that, because of the U. S.'s own mistakes and incompetence, it
was losing the war. The U. S. was doing that, first, by supplying the Viet
Cong, corrupt South Vietnamese officials, North Vietnam, and even The
People's Republic with civilian and military supplies, including clothing,
food, medical supplies, ammunition, and weapons. Second, by losing
billions of dollars in the process.

How so, John wondered. Excited by what he had found, he read on.
Lederer wrote that every government the United States ever tried helping
in South Vietnam had been inadequate and that one of the measures of
this inadequacy was the degree of governmental corruption. He went on
to tell of his first experience with the Vietnamese black market in Saigon.
Planning to go out with troops as a journalist covering the war effort, he
needed proper clothing and equipment. A friend took him to a large PX
in Cholon to purchase jungle fatigues and boots. Unable to purchase the
clothing and equipment at the PX because it had been out of them for
months, Lederer's friend took him through the streets of Cholon to a
"Tiny Black Market." They didn't find the equipment he was looking for
there. But they found hundreds of other desirable items stolen from the
PX and commissaries—radios, blankets, toasters, watches, cigarettes, shirts,
televisions, cameras, patent medicines, liquor, and cans of food of every
kind available through the commissaries.

In another place he visited that same day, Lederer found what he said
"looked like a U. S. Army ordnance ammunition depot." There, he found
what he was looking for and also found automatic rifles being sold for
$250, 105 mm. Mortars for $400, thousands of American-made rifles,

with an M-16 rifle selling for $80. One side of the store had uniforms for all services, including U. S. Navy diving equipment.

Reciting his first day's experience with the black markets to a friend later that evening, Lederer learned more. He referred to his friend as Tran Trong Hoc, an alias used to protect him at the time the book was published. Lederer recounted a conversation with his friend.

> He said, "What you saw is nothing. Go down to the waterfront some day and see how the big operators work. The whole South Vietnamese government—from Ky down—is involved."
> "Any Americans in on it?"
> "Plenty are becoming millionaires—exactly as happened when the U. S. Army occupied Japan and Germany."
> "How do you know?"
> "The black market in Vietnam is about ten billion dollars a year—all in American goods and monies. This could not exist without American collusion. It would be impossible. For example, everyone in Saigon talks about how La Thanh Nghe or Ky's cabinet has gotten about a million dollars in kickbacks from American pharmaceutical firms. There has to be American collusion. You couldn't lose ten billion dollars a year without it."
> I did not answer.
> "We'll go to the waterfront in a few days," said Tran Trong Hoc, "and watch the big operations."
> "Let's go now."
> "We have to plan it well. I need a few days. If we are not careful, neither of us will be alive to tell what we saw."

Lederer later found out the "Little Black Market" near the U. S. Embassy in Saigon was *small stuff* and that the South Vietnamese and U. S. governments tacitly considered it semi-legitimate. One U. S. official explained to him that "[w]e aren't too strict about it because in the first place we don't want to antagonize the Koreans or the Filipinos; the black market helps stop inflation. I don't know how, but that's what our economists say." The author noted that the Koreans and the Filipinos referred to by the official were involved at the time in black market operations, even though they were both allies of the United States.

Lederer decided to investigate PX practices. In doing so, he spoke with a colonel, a PX official who spoke on condition of anonymity. After being "given a small lecture on how newspapermen were always saying bad things about the PX," he described to the colonel the malpractices he had uncovered, and the colonel offered his explanation. Lederer wrote:

> The PX, [the colonel] said, employs over 5,000 Vietnamese women, because it is the duty of the United States to train these women in merchandising practices. It is America's duty to Vietnam. After the war is over, the women will know how to be skilled clerks in the stores of Vietnam and will be able to aid the commerce of the country. This seemed crazy to me. Any store which was run like the PX would soon go bankrupt.
> ...
> I pointed out to the PX colonel that the service was bad, that perhaps $75 million a year of merchandise was stolen or diverted to the black market largely because of employment of foreigners, including clerks, executives, truckers, longshoremen, and so forth. He denied that the service was bad—which is contrary to the opinions of his customers (who have no other place to shop). He denied that there was any sizable black-market leak from his stores.
> He denied that there was $65,000 worth of pilferage from the small Saigon PX. I myself had seen the Saigon PX's own estimates of pilferage. Either the colonel did not know what was happening in his own stores or he was lying.
> He said that another reason for employing over 5,000 foreigners in the PX's was to give work to worthy Vietnamese of good character, which helped the war economy. I asked him if he knew how the employment racket worked. He denied there was such a racket.
> The facts are, however, that each clerk employed has to get a recommendation from someone who is in the Vietnamese government. This recommendation has to be paid for—and the standard payment is approximately a month's wages.
> The colonel said he had never heard of any such thing.
> ...
> The PX as it is run now makes the United States a collaborator in the worst kind of corruption. Everyone—including the Americans—knows that some Americans involved are corrupt. They know that many Vietnamese clerks are corrupt; they know the Filipino and Korean PX assistants often are in cahoots with their friends.

Lederer also wrote that the PX foul-ups and the black market sales of millions of dollars of PX products were "almost microscopic" compared to what he found out later through his old friend, Tran Trong Hoc. His friend took him near the wharf along the river, where they saw several

American freighters discharging their cargo to barges alongside. The barges later carried the cargo to the wharf, where eight five-ton trucks were parked. Vietnamese longshoremen then began carrying the cargo off the barges and onto the trucks.

From their spying location, they could see that the cargo being unloaded into the trucks was American war material, including crates marked "Department of Defense, ELECTRONICS, this side up." When the trucks were loaded with 40 tons of U. S. electronic equipment, they began their journey up the Saigon-Bienhoa Highway, and then onto Old Route One, a highway leading to Cambodia and to Nhom Penh. The trucks reached their destination, Go Dau Ha, a village almost on the Cambodian-Vietnamese border. Later, another convoy of trucks arrived from the other direction. Swarms of laborers then appeared and began swapping the cargoes of the two convoys. Half an hour later, the loading and unloading were completed, and the Cambodian convoy began its trip back to Cambodia and the Vietnamese convoy traveled back to Saigon.

In those trucks were tons of Chinese merchandise—toothbrushes, tooth powder, vitamins, imitation Parker fountain pens, and many other items. Those Chinese Communist products were delivered to a warehouse in Cholon, on the outskirts of Saigon. That structure already stored stacks of tires for U. S. military vehicles, hundreds of bags of U. S. cement with USAID markings on them, and hundreds of bags of rice.

The next day, Lederer continued, he and Tran Trong Hoc returned to the Saigon wharf, once again within sight of a different pier. There, alongside a small Vietnamese steamer, were 1,500 tons of materiel—U. S. rice, U. S. sheet metal, bags of U. S. cement, drums of U. S. oil, and cases of ammunition. After a short while, stevedores carried the supplies aboard the steamer. The two men didn't wait for the supplies to be loaded, but Lederer wrote of Tran Trong Hoc's explanation:

> "There is no use in our staying longer," says Tran. "It will take several hours to load the ship. I just wanted you to see what goes on board. That ship leaves this dock every sixth day. It goes south, then up the Mekong River to Chau Doc Province, which also is on the Cambodian border. There, it off-loads; and the supplies go easily to the Vietcong—or whoever else needs and can pay for them."
> "What about the U. S. Navy?" I ask. "Doesn't the U. S. Navy inspect all the shipping along the coast?"

213

"Of course your precious Navy stops every ship and inspects it. But that inspection isn't worth a fart in a whirlwind. The ship's papers are in perfect order. The captain of the Vietnamese ship has a document, signed by Thanit Tung, saying that the ship is carrying urgently needed supplies for the South Vietnamese intelligence units near An Phu. Not a single American on any U. S. Navy ship speaks or reads Vietnamese. All your goddamn Navy can do is glance at the document with the Intelligence Force's letterhead and Thanit's signature. So, of course, your Navy permits the ship to go on. How in hell does the U. S. Navy know the ship's carrying black-market materiel stolen from the U. S. Army?"

"Does the steamer bring a cargo back?"

"Of course. It brings back the same Red Chinese products you saw in the trucks. There is a small fleet of steamers working this racket..."

John was astounded by what he read, even though it mentioned nothing about possible involvement of high echelon offices such as Colonel Condon's procurement section. It was clear many of the products destined for the several black markets thriving in Saigon and the surrounding area were stolen and embezzled without the help of American civilians or the military. But that didn't mean Americans weren't involved in other illicit operations. Most likely, Lederer had only uncovered the tip of the iceberg, John suspected. He guessed there were dozens of other ways thefts occurred that he hadn't uncovered.

The power to control the ultimate destination of U. S. supplies and equipment within Condon's procurement office was probably nothing less than awesome. Potentially billions of dollars could be diverted within any given year, John surmised. If that had been the subject of Henri's writing, it was no wonder he believed his story would reveal a significant scandal that would prove embarrassing to the United States and to others. Especially if he named the individuals. Had Condon been one of them? Following Leroy's lead might be a way of finding out.

CHAPTER 19

THE trial wasn't scheduled to begin until nine o'clock. Planning to go straight to the courthouse from home, John had picked up the Soliz file at the office on his way home from his visit to the library. When he had arrived home, he told Demi of his trip to Shiprock and his visit to the library. He had found her distant, and she seemed depressed, but he decided not to approach her on that. Ever since their return from Santa Fe, she had seemed moody.

This morning at breakfast, he attempted to discuss Henri's letter and its implications with her while the children were upstairs getting ready for school, but she didn't appear interested, and so he dropped it. He worried, for he was beginning to realize he was consumed not only by the Soliz trial but now by the questions raised in Henri's letter. With each passing day, he sensed that the level of his anxiety was worsening. Because he believed Demi was reacting to that tension he carried with him, he blamed himself, not her, for her demeanor. She had a meeting with a client at eight and, as soon as the children were off to school, she said a quick goodbye to him and disappeared.

He was left alone at the table with time on his hands, and he relished the leisure. With over an hour to get to the courthouse, he decided to read the *Albuquerque Journal*.

It was in the New Mexico & Metro section that he spotted the news item in the *Around New Mexico* column. The story's headline had *Shiprock* in it, which caught his eye.

MAN'S BODY FOUND ON ROAD NEAR SHIPROCK

SHIPROCK—A hit and run auto accident outside Shiprock early this morning left a Shiprock resident dead.

State police investigating the mishap said the accident occurred on a farm road designated Navajo Highway 364, 0.5 miles west of the road's intersection with Highway North 666. Early reports state that the body of Leroy Etcitty, age unknown, was found on the shoulder of the road.

Sgt. Rudy Tafoya of the State Police is investigating the accident together with Navajo police officials. The accident occurred within the tribal boundaries of the Navajo Nation. Based on markings at the scene, Sgt. Tafoya speculated that Etcitty, who resided in the vicinity, was walking along the edge of the road when a vehicle traveling at a high rate of speed hit him. The vehicle left no skid marks. Sgt. Tafoya said that initial tests showed Etcitty was intoxicated, causing the victim to walk into the path of the oncoming vehicle, whose driver fled the scene without reporting the accident. Tafoya further stated that arrangements have been made to transport the body to the Office of the Medical Investigator for an autopsy.

He sat there stunned. He reread the article a second and a third time. This was no hit and run, he said out loud. No way. His head was spinning, and he felt nauseous. His eyes filled with tears. They were tears of grief, but also of anger and guilt. Grief for the tragic loss of a friend who tried to help him and, as a result, suffered the consequences. Anger and guilt because he alone felt responsible for his friend's death. Leroy was the innocent victim of *his* actions. He had anticipated the risks of getting Leroy involved but not soon enough.

Still upset, he got up from the table and went into the kitchen to call Kelly. The agent answered within seconds. Barely able to articulate his words, John read the article to him.

"Get a hold of yourself, John," he half-heard Kelly say when he finished. "I know how you must feel." He paused. "We were to start surveillance in Shiprock tomorrow. I feel bad about this."

"It's *my* fault," he said. "I should never have gotten him involved."

"You're *not* responsible. Getting in touch with Leroy was essential. This threat against you is real, and it was inevitable that he'd be drawn into it. After all, he was a part of it from the beginning, even without knowing it. He was a character in the play, just as much as you were, and eventually was going to have to play his role."

"But his death needn't have been a part of that."

"We'll never know. I'm not trying to minimize this. Sure we can attribute it to your contacting him. Yet, once events over which we had no control were set in motion by those who mean to harm you, who knows what would have happened to him. They would have gotten to him in time since he was close to Condon in his work and because of his involvement in minor thefts."

"I don't know. Maybe you're right."

"Besides, we're not certain it wasn't just a hit and run."

"No way! It was foul play. I told you—Leroy never touched alcohol. The fact that the police think he was intoxicated tells me someone forced liquor down his throat to make it look like an accident—wandering onto the road in a drunken stupor. Besides, that spot where they found his body isn't anywhere near where he lived. I can't believe he'd be walking in that area. It was a set up, I tell you." He looked down at his hands and noticed they were shaking.

"We'll have someone look into it. I promise we'll soon find out what happened."

"I have a friend who's a state policeman. He could have a copy of the police report faxed from Shiprock."

"That won't be necessary. We've got our own sources. I'll contact you later. Meanwhile, go about your business and try putting it out of your mind. You're in trial, aren't you?"

"Right." He looked at the kitchen clock. It was eight fifteen; he'd better finish getting ready so he could be at the courthouse in plenty of time. "I'll be talking to you later, then?"

"Yes." Kelly hesitated. "John, one parting thought."

"Yeah?"

"If the investigation shows they got to Etcitty, then it's likely they'll make their move against you. You and your family need more protection, and I wish you'd reconsider our—"

"Which would still mean letting Demi in on it."

"Affirmative."

"Kelly, I've given that some thought and can't see how additional protection and electronic surveillance will make a difference. I don't want Demi and my children to be a part of this and—"

"But they already are. That's what I'm—"

"You're still conducting limited surveillance, aren't you?"

"Yeah, but—"

"That'll just have to do, then. I'm unwilling to have them worry over this. As it is, there's too much going on for us. I don't want to get into domestic stuff with you, but things are quite tense between Demi and me right now. I don't relish the thought of adding to our problems, okay?"

"I'm sorry to hear that. Fine, then."

"You'll get back in touch with me on Leroy, then?" he asked. "I've got to go."

"Yeah, I'll contact you."

"Okay. Bye."

"Bye."

On his way to the courthouse, he was relieved he had regained his composure but still felt irritable. While on the phone with Kelly, he wondered if he'd have to request a postponement of the trial until that afternoon or the following morning. He worried he wouldn't be able to question Patty effectively. Although he still sensed the loss, as well as pangs of guilt, symptomatized by an emptiness in his stomach, he was now confident he could put Leroy's sudden death aside and focus on the trial.

As he parked his car in the underground parking lot, he began getting mentally prepared for his cross-examination. Patty was an effective witness. But he had a clear image of the questions he'd ask to try weakening her effectiveness.

The trial started on time. After the jury was seated, Judge Walker asked the bailiff to call Patty to the stand. When she was seated, John walked up to the rostrum with his notes and note pad. He smiled at her. Again, she wore modest clothing—she wore a long, simple skirt and a sweater with full sleeves. Her hair was again combed in a bun.

Through his questions, he hoped to contradict Carol's testimony in several respects. With that in mind, he began by asking questions concerning the lighting during the lineup. She conceded the room was well lit, the faces of the lineup participants were plainly visible, and the lighting wasn't bright enough to strain a person's eyes. She was able to see the lineup without discomfort. Carol had said the bright lighting had distracted her.

He then focused on Patty's ID. "Now, Ms. Gregory," he asked, "I believe you testified that a couple of days or so after the assault, Detective Morales visited you at the hospital. He asked you to go through ten photographs, is that correct?"

"Yes, he did," she answered, exhibiting confidence even with those three little words. She seemed prepared to answer his questions, no matter their difficulty. It'd be hard to get her to stumble, but that wasn't going to keep him from trying.

He picked up the photos from the reporter's desk and handed them to Patty. "And these are those photographs, aren't they?"

"Yes."

"In examining those photos, Ms. Gregory, do you notice that all of them, except the one of Bernardo Soliz, have a green marking or tag?"

"Yes, they're different from the one of the defendant."

"Apart from the green marking, can you tell in what other way they are different?"

"I believe they're what police refer to as 'mug shots.'"

"While the one of Mr. Soliz, who you identified as your assailant, is a candid picture, isn't it?"

"Yes. It was obvious to me it wasn't a mug shot."

"Did you know then it was a quick picture taken when the police went to question him?"

"No, I didn't know under what circumstances it was taken."

"You hadn't been told the police had a suspect?"

"My recollection is that Mr. Morales said something about there being a suspect among the pictures and would I please take a look at them."

"And the candid photo stood out from that batch precisely because it was obvious to you it wasn't a mug shot and the others were?"

"As I said before, I was aware it wasn't a mug shot." She retained her composure, and there wasn't the slightest hint she'd lose it.

"Let me rephrase the question, Ms. Gregory." He tried hard to hide he was unnerved by her ability to stay calm. "Wasn't it apparent to you when you picked out Mr. Soliz' candid photo that it didn't even come close to your own description of your assailant?" He emphasized *your own description* because he knew she wasn't about to admit any discrepancies.

"No, I don't think it was apparent. To be honest with you, Mr. Garcia, I don't think it even occurred to me that the man in the photo didn't match the description I had given to the police. As I went through the mug shots, for example, I wasn't conscious of comparing their faces with the descriptions I gave to Detective Morales."

"You didn't say to yourself, 'My God, can't they do better than that?'"

"No."

"So are you saying the description you gave wasn't a factor when you chose Mr. Soliz' photograph?"

"Not in the slightest. The description I gave was over and done with, as far as I was concerned. It played no part in my choosing the picture of the man who stabbed me."

"What I'm getting at, Ms. Gregory, is this. Let's go along with your testimony and assume you weren't consciously aware of the description you had given and how it might compare to the individuals in the photos. How certain are you that you didn't select Mr. Soliz' picture solely because it differed from the mug shots in such an obvious way? And also because you realized Detective Morales had a picture of only one suspect in the array of photos?"

"That's a long question to keep track of, Mr. Garcia, but I'll try to answer it the best I can. I'm certain I didn't select defendant's picture for those reasons. I selected it because I remembered clearly the face of the man who attacked me."

He was certain that would be her answer, but there was a good reason for the question. She had already testified she was certain Bernardo was the man who assaulted her, and so he didn't mind reinforcing that fact in the minds of the jury. That was because giving the jury the option of another plausible explanation of why Patty chose Bernardo's candid picture was worth the risk of reinforcement, or so he reasoned.

He could argue that Patty's ID of Bernardo was tainted or suggestive because it stood out from the mug shots. He could do that even though she denied the differences had anything to do with her selection. He took another approach for the same reason.

"You didn't consider the array of photos in the least suggestive, then? That's your testimony?"

"They weren't suggestive to me, Mr. Garcia." She paused. "Yes, that's my testimony."

220

"That picture you selected of Mr. Soliz. It was clear to you at the time that it showed your assailant, wasn't it?"

"Yes, I could have identified it even under poor lighting."

"The fact is that you were positive when you tossed the picture toward the foot of the bed and said, 'that's the man' to Detective Morales, that it was a picture of your assailant."

"Yes, I was." She paused, as if searching how best to put her point across. "That's why I described to the jury how I selected his photo, so they'd get a clear picture of how certain I was."

"So it would be fair to say, Ms. Gregory," he continued at a faster pace, "that you got a clear image or imprint in your mind of the face you had selected."

"As I have an image of all of them."

"But specifically, you got an image of what the man whose picture you had selected looked like, isn't that right?"

"That's right."

He didn't let up. "So the fact is that when you walked into that lineup several days later and saw Bernardo Soliz, you knew very well he was the man you had identified, didn't you? The imprint of the person in that photo remained with you, didn't it?"

"I was aware he was the man who had stabbed me!" She spoke without hesitation. "I didn't pick him because I had selected his photograph at the hospital."

Her answer took him by surprise. Indeed, she was one smart woman, he thought.

"Ma'am,' he went on, "you were also aware that was the man you had identified a few days earlier, weren't you?"

"If the photo happened to be of the same person, yes." She knew well what he was getting at, and she wasn't about to help him make his point.

He fired off the questions. "Which you convinced yourself in your own mind was the person in the photo?"

"I believe you're drawing a conclusion for me."

"Just answer my question, Ms. Gregory," he demanded, accepting he had an uncooperative witness on his hands. "You were convinced in your mind that the man whose picture you picked at the hospital was the man who attacked you?"

"Yes."

"So you drew a picture in your mind of the man you had selected and that image was with you when you walked into that lineup, right?"

"The picture in my mind was that of the man who stabbed me, not the man in the photo."

Take another tack, he said to himself. "You felt committed to Detective Morales, didn't you? When you tossed that photo to the foot of the bed and said confidently, 'that's the man,' you were positive then that was the man who stabbed you?"

"As I am today," she responded.

"When you walked into that lineup, you saw Bernardo Soliz as the man in the photo you selected?"

"I'll say it once more, Mr. Garcia. I saw your client as the man who stabbed me. He may have looked much different from the man in the photo or even from the description I gave to the police." She paused. "But there he was, his entire body from head to foot."

Realizing he wasn't making any ground, he decided to move on. He brought out other facts from her he thought would clarify some important points and that he would refer to during closing argument. She conceded the incident occurred during daylight hours and that she got a good look at her assailant.

Delving into the description she gave to the police, he also brought out the various discrepancies concerning age, height, weight, body size, hair color, and hair style. She gave the approximate age of her assailant as 23 to 26 years, and Bernardo was barely 18. When he asked her to explain the discrepancy, she told him that, even in the courtroom, Bernardo appeared 23 to 26 years of age to her and didn't look like the eighteen-year-old man John insisted he was.

He asked her to explain why she had described her assailant's hair style as a "crew cut." She explained she was attempting to convey the fact that her assailant's hair was evenly combed straight back and cut the same length and nothing more. She explained away the term crew cut on her part as a poor choice of words.

He also reminded her that she had told the police her attacker had dark hair but not black. She agreed. The P. D. had told him that, when he had spoken to her at the hospital and asked her to be more specific about the "dark hair," she said to him that it was "certainly not black." Those were her exact words, the P. D. had said. John now confronted her with this conversation, but although she acknowledged it had taken place, he was unable to get her to admit she had said anything more specific than that her assailant had "dark hair."

Bernardo's hair was black. So was John's, or so he had always believed. Yet, in attempting to narrow hair color, based on her description, he was surprised and even frustrated when she refused to describe his own hair color, as well as Bernardo's, as black. She insisted it was a dark color having "shades of brown in bright light." To her, she said, that made it "not black," as she had told the P. D. John realized this was her way of explaining away the discrepancies between Bernardo's actual description and the one she gave to the police. She also reminded him she was either injured, in pain, or sedated when she gave the various descriptions.

Finally, he won a victory of sorts when he succeeded in getting her admission that she had mistakenly described Bernardo's tattoos on the right arm when they were actually on his left arm. John reemphasized that, when Keith asked her about the tattoos, she was unable to identify the tattoos on Bernardo's arm as the same ones she saw on her assailant's arm.

When asked if she had seen any other tattoos on the other arm or hand, she hesitated. He suspected she wouldn't commit one way or the other. Evidently unsure whether Bernardo had any tattoos on the other arm, she explained she hadn't gotten a good look at the attacker's "other" arm. It was a long shot, but John was hoping she would say she hadn't seen any markings on the other arm. If Bernardo happened to have those markings, and she had said she hadn't seen any, he was sure her credibility would be affected.

As it turned out, the only markings Bernardo had on his right arm were on the hand. Tattooed onto the knuckles, he had the letters L-O-V-E crudely done. To explain away the fact that she hadn't noticed those letters on Bernardo's hand, Patty emphasized she had been concentrating on his face, not his hands. Essentially, John surmised, she was telling him that in fighting for her life she shouldn't be expected to remember every detail. He was certain any reasonable juror would agree, so he didn't pursue the issue.

Instead, he decided to concentrate on her already admitted mistake. "Ms. Gregory," he went on, "you've admitted you must have been mistaken when you told Detective Morales that the tattoos were on the right arm, isn't that right?"

223

"I must have been," she replied. "All I can say for sure is that they were similar and were in the same general area of the arm."

"But maybe that's not the only explanation," he countered, pausing for effect.

"What do you mean?" she finally asked.

"What if you hadn't been mistaken. What if you really did see the two tattoos on your assailant's right arm? If that were the case, and we know for certain Mr. Soliz' tattoos are on his *left* arm, then it would follow you're mistaken about Mr. Soliz being the one who attacked you."

"That's not possible!"

"Why not?"

"Because I'd know that face anywhere," she insisted. "I'm right about the face; I was wrong about which arm I saw the tattoos on." She appeared offended.

He next moved to the height discrepancy. To do this, he asked Bernardo to stand up with his back against the wall. In this position, Bernardo was facing both the witness and jury. He then asked Judge Walker to permit Patty and Bernardo to stand within a few feet of each other so that their heights could be compared. The judge gave permission. When Bernardo and Patty were in place, John joined them to begin his new line of questions.

"How tall are you, Ms. Gregory?" he began.

"About 5-2."

"Now, I'd like for you to look at Mr. Soliz. At this distance, wouldn't you say he's about the same height as you?"

"Well, what can I say. To me, he looks taller."

He could tell she noticed the disbelief in his eyes.

"When I look at somebody, they look taller," she added.

Once more, she had decided to remain faithful to what she considered as her genuine perception at the time of the assault, just as she had with the weight discrepancy. If she was consistent in her testimony, he thought, she was hoping her error in judgment wouldn't only be understood but accepted as an honest mistake.

He believed that throughout her testimony, without knowing it, she was stretching the truth. In her eyes, it was justified because, despite whatever discrepancies existed in her descriptions, she convinced herself the right person had been charged and was now being tried. He had seen this courtroom behavioral phenomenon before. It was analogous to the ends-justifying-the-means notion.

He knew what she was doing, and he feared he'd find it difficult to hide his exasperation not only from her but from the jury. "Aren't you looking him straight in the eye, Ms. Gregory?"

"Yes."

"And other than his mop of hair on top, wouldn't you say—"

"I said he *appears* taller to me. When you go through life being short as I have, almost everybody seems taller than you are."

"Even when they're the same height?" he said in disbelief.

"Yes, even then. At least to me."

Who could argue with such subjectivity, he mumbled to himself. Even the jury might consider it the nature of human behavior. He decided to take another tact. "Realizing what you just said, Ms. Gregory, and looking at the defendant as you are now, why would you tell Detective Morales the man was 5-6 to 5-8, as compared to your height of 5-2? That's a difference of some four to six inches."

"Because that's what I felt he was at the time. I'd like to point out, Mr. Garcia, that the entire time, I was never as close to him as I am this moment. Besides, part of the time, I was bending down washing my car. He just appeared taller to me, okay?"

She paused, but he said nothing more, hoping she'd continue on her own accord. She obliged. "I guess you're wondering why I would say that. If I had to account for what appears as an inaccuracy in my statement, I'd ask that you imagine you're lying on the ground in front of your neighbor's yard, and you don't know if in five minutes you're going to be dead. In that situation, you think as fast as you can and say what you can, as well as you can. You don't necessarily have time to pick and choose or to deliberate between saying one thing over another."

"Officer Tanner said you were very cool when he arrived," he said, trying hard to remain *cool* himself.

"Well, I was."

"As it turns out, Ms. Gregory, I suppose you've just now come to realize a person of your height is going to appear four to six inches taller to you. Is that what you're telling the jury?"

"Yes, sir. It's fortunate I don't make my living judging heights, weights and distances, or I'd be out of a job."

"And can you assure this jury you're not basing your testimony on the sole fact that it's Mr. Soliz who's been charged with stabbing you, and, because he doesn't fit your description to the police, you're going to explain away your errors of judgment?" He realized he was taking a risk asking the question of such a forward witness, but her damaging ID left him no choice.

She didn't say anything for a moment, apparently contemplating his question. "I think I'd say in response," she spoke finally, "that my testimony is based on my own individual belief that this man is the person who stabbed me, rather than on my previous descriptions that have turned out to be somewhat inaccurate. What it amounts to, Mr. Garcia, as far as I'm concerned, is that no matter how accurate or inaccurate I was in my descriptions, you are *never* going to take away from me the memory of the man who tried to kill me, and I'm telling you—this is the man!" She gestured toward Bernardo standing inches away, who scowled at her in return.

He stopped his questions to permit her to return to the stand and Bernardo to take his seat.

"You admit then," he continued when she was seated, "that you were mistaken when you gave Detective Morales and Officer Tanner, not once, but on several occasions, the various descriptions of the man who assaulted you?"

She wasn't the kind of person who would ever answer that kind of question with a simple *yes* or *no*. She proved true to form. "If I am to accept," she began, "what you say to be his true height and weight, I admit that my descriptions turned out to be inaccurate. But, from my own frame of reference, I don't believe I was mistaken about what I sensed at the time."

"You differentiate between being inaccurate and being mistaken, Ms. Gregory?" he barked.

"Well, I suppose it's a question of semantics."

"Do you admit to having made mistakes in your life?"

"Yes."

"All of us do, don't we?"

"Yes." She paused, then added, "I made one big one that evening."

No doubt about it. She wasn't only intelligent; she was sure of herself. He was convinced she had made a vow before trial. She was going to make certain she overcame whatever obstacles her poor judgment in

226

measurements and descriptions had placed in her way. In the courtroom, she did this with her own conviction and belief that Bernardo was beyond doubt the person who had tried to end her life. She was a determined woman, and just as important, she was demanding justice. Nothing, absolutely nothing, was going to stand in her way of assuring that the man who had assaulted her would be convicted. And that man, in her eyes, was none other than Bernardo.

Despite his experience in examining countless persons on the witness stand with considerable success, he realized that in some respects she hadn't only held her own but had won this round. Nonetheless, he felt he had made some inroads, however slight, toward persuading at least one juror there was reasonable doubt. But one thing was certain—she had made his job harder.

He asked a few more questions to clear up a few important facts before turning the witness back to Keith.

The prosecutor spent the next few minutes rehabilitating his witness on a few points. Not that she needed rehabilitation, John thought, but that was the term used by trial practitioners in describing one purpose of redirect examination. The fact that Keith spent just a few minutes on redirect was a clear sign he believed Patty had done well. When that occurred, a good lawyer knew when to leave well enough alone.

She was Keith's last witness; when she stepped off the stand, he rested the state's case. It was mid-afternoon. To preserve the court record in case of an appeal, outside the jury's presence, John made several oral motions to dismiss the criminal charges and requested a directed verdict. As anticipated, Judge Walker denied the motions without comment. The jurist ordered a quick recess and instructed him to be ready to begin his case when they reconvened.

As his first witness, he called a deputy sheriff who had been present when the P. D. had gone to visit Bernardo at the detention center a few days after the attack on Patty. Realizing that Bernardo's hair was much longer than the "crew cut" length described not only by Patty but by Carol and Rebecca, the P. D. performed an important task at the time. Rebecca was the youngster who had been at the park with a friend when she saw Patty's attacker running through the park.

The deputy sheriff John called to the stand was an acquaintance of the P. D. who happened to be passing by the attorney's booth where the P. D. was waiting to confer with Bernardo. The deputy stopped to greet him

227

and the two of them exchanged a few words as Bernardo was being brought into the prisoner side of the booth. Identifying Bernardo as the person charged with the stabbing of Patty, the P. D. asked the deputy to note the length of Bernardo's hair, particularly on top. The deputy testified that Bernardo's hair in the courtroom now appeared a little longer than it was on the day he had seen him at the detention center. He estimated, however, that it had been at least 2 to 2 ½ inches long on top when he saw him in the booth. In any event, he didn't consider Bernardo's hair short on top as worn by the assailant. For certain, it wasn't trimmed in a crew cut or flat top style at the time, he said.

John next called a booking clerk who was present when the P. D. had weighed Bernardo. Once again, the P. D. was well aware Patty's assaulter had been described as weighing upwards of 126 pounds. Wanting to document Bernardo's weight a few days after the incident, he had requested special permission to have Bernardo weighed in his presence. According to the scale, Bernardo weighed less than 110 pounds with his clothes and shoes on. The P. D. had given John the page from his pocket calendar where he had documented Bernardo's weight, which he had the booking clerk date and sign for later verification. John showed the clerk the calendar page, and he verified his signature and that Bernardo's weight on the date shown had been 109 3/4 pounds.

The last witness John called that afternoon was Rebecca. Only twelve years of age, she was noticeably nervous as she sat in the witness chair, which wasn't uncommon for a youngster. Except for being friendly, there was little an attorney could do to calm such a young witness.

After a few questions, youngsters often begin concentrating on the questions asked and the answers they're supposed to give. They seem to put aside for the moment that they're the center of attention. Such a youngster was Rebecca.

He nevertheless realized he had to word his questions with care because he didn't want Keith to stand up and object. It had been his experience that objections often would tense up a young witness, who tended to view the objection as a discomforting disagreement or confrontation between the attorneys. Worse yet, young impressionable witnesses sometimes wondered what they themselves may have done wrong to bring on such confrontations.

Rebecca had soft, brown hair that hung four to six inches below her shoulders. She wore it straight with bangs. Her light-complected face was round and possessed a pugged nose and a few freckles. Signs of puberty weren't yet visible on her. Several times during his first few questions, John had to ask her to raise her voice so she could be heard, for she spoke in a soft voice.

He first laid the foundation for her important testimony. She was at the park with her mother's friend and her three children, she testified. They had been to an Albertson's a few blocks away. Having extra time before heading home, the friend drove to the park where her children could play for a while. They parked their car on the north end, facing west, and had just gotten out of the car when Rebecca spotted the man running through the park.

"Please tell the jury, Rebecca," John said, "what you saw when the man caught your eye."

"Uh—well," she stuttered, "he looked very upset—kinda jumpy, you know. He ran from one corner and almost all the way to the other corner. Then he turned and ran back, but I didn't see him go out of the park after that."

"Did you lose sight of him?"

"Yes."

"What happened then?"

"In a short while, a policeman came. We went over to see what was happening, and that's when the policeman asked me if I had seen anything. I told him I saw the man running. He asked us to walk down to Ms. Gregory's house, where I later talked to Detective Morales, and then I went to the police station."

"Did you meet Ms. Carol Niewold that evening?"

"I didn't meet her personally, but I saw her at the park and later at Ms. Gregory's house talking to the police."

"This man you saw running—did he appear scared or nervous?"

"Both."

"How exactly was he running? Was he trotting, running fast, or what?"

"Pretty fast."

"Did you see him well enough to give us some physical features?"

"Well, he was sort of skinny. He had dark brown or black hair. Had on a white T-shirt and blue jeans."

"So if you saw all that, you must have gotten a pretty good look at him, would that be correct?" A young witness often needed prodding, but he wanted to be careful not to ask leading questions that might cause Keith to object.

Rebecca nodded in agreement.

"Rebecca," he said, "the court reporter over there is taking down your testimony, and he can't take down your nod, so you're going to have to answer 'yes' or 'no.'"

"O-O-k-kay," she said. She had calmed down from when she had first taken the stand. "Uh-huh, I got a good look at him."

"Did you give Detective Morales a description concerning the man's height?"

"Yes, sir. I remember telling him the man was 6-8 to 6-9."

"You mean 5-8 to 5-9, don't you?"

She smiled. "Yes, 5-8 to 5-9."

"How did you arrive at that estimate, Rebecca?"

"Well, at the police station, my mother met me there, and so I measured the man to be between Detective Morales and my mother, who's taller."

He next asked her questions concerning the mug shot book and composite drawing. She agreed that the composite drawing resembled the man she saw, except that she thought the sideburns on the drawing were too long. She also was shown the array of ten photographs that included Bernardo's candid photo. When asked by Morales to pick the one that resembled the man she had seen running through the park, she selected three photos, one of which was Bernardo's candid photo. When asked to select the one of the three photos that most resembled the assailant, she chose one of the mug shots and not the candid photograph.

John picked up Bernardo's candid photo. "Why didn't you select this one?"

"Because," she replied, "I didn't think he looked that much like the man I saw."

"You know who the man in that picture is, don't you, Rebecca?"

"Yes, sir."

"Who is it?"

"Bernardo Soliz," she said, glancing at Bernardo.

"The man sitting at counsel table?"

"Yes."

"Now, let's see if I have this correct. Out of the ten, you picked out three. Then you picked out one of the three, is that correct?"

230

"Yes."

"Then what happened?"

"After I picked the one, Detective Morales showed me the picture."

"What picture?"

"The picture of Bernardo Soliz."

"Let's make sure I understand," he said, emphasizing his words for the jury's benefit. "Do you have any idea why he asked you to look at Bernardo's photo after you had chosen another one?"

Keith was out of his chair. "Objection!" he said. "This witness can't—"

"I apologize, your honor," John said to the judge. "I'll withdraw the question." He returned his attention to the young girl, who still appeared startled by Keith's objection. "Now, Rebecca, you saw Bernardo Soliz this afternoon when you came into the courtroom, didn't you?

"Yes, sir," she answered in a soft voice.

He smiled at her, gesturing upward with his hand as a signal for her to speak up. She returned the smile and nodded that she understood. "I'll ask you, Rebecca," he went on, "to look at my client, Bernardo Soliz, right now. Is this the man you saw running through the park?"

"I don't think so."

"Why don't you think so?"

"Well, for one thing, he's too short. And the man I saw had something like a crew cut, I think."

He asked a few more questions before turning her over to Keith. The prosecutor elicited testimony from her that she was more than a few feet away from the man she saw running through the park and that the man had been running "very fast." She admitted that, for those reasons, she didn't have the opportunity to see the assailant eye to eye or within a few feet standing up. Keith then attempted to get her to admit there were also trees and shrubs obstructing her view, but she said that wasn't the case.

On redirect, she reaffirmed that, even though she hadn't gotten a good view of the man, the view she did get was good enough. Based on that, she was certain Bernardo was too short. After her testimony, Judge Walker recessed the trial until Monday morning.

Before leaving the courtroom, John took the time to gather Bernardo and his family to plan for their testimony the following week. He answered their questions concerning the testimony that day. Bernardo was particularly interested in his assessment of Patty's testimony, for he too realized she hadn't budged, convinced Bernardo was her attacker. John decided he better level with them—Patty had been an effective witness. Her unrelenting and damaging ID would prove difficult to counter. His cross-examination of her, he felt, hadn't done the trick. He wondered if Bernardo already sensed how close he was to a conviction. He prepared him for the worst.

It was past five when he contacted Kelly. The agent confirmed John's suspicions that Leroy was the victim of foul play. One of the FBI special agents was a close friend of the forensic pathologist in the Office of the Medical Investigator. Preliminary tests showed Leroy's body had wounds that the pathologist believed were inflicted by trauma unrelated to the car accident.

John grimaced as Kelly described the wounds. A traumatizing disbelief revisited him. "Was he tortured?" he asked.

"We can't conclude that from the preliminary report. We'll get more details for you as soon as we can. But for now, I can tell you the pathologist didn't say he knew how some of Leroy's injuries were caused. We may never know."

Before John hung up, Kelly arranged to brief him later that evening on Quigley's upcoming trip to Greece. When he hung up, he was dejected again. His conversations with Leroy during the past week, even their phone conversation when they had first made contact, resurfaced. In the past, he had hoped Kelly was wrong about potential risks—that nothing terrible would happen to anyone close to him. But it had—to someone he himself had gotten involved.

He hadn't yet telephoned Demi because he didn't want to spoil her day with the tragic news. It would alarm her, he was certain, and he dreaded telling her because it was bound to make matters worse between them. But tell her he must.

CHAPTER 20

SITTING behind a massive desk in his private office, United States Senator Emory Monroe Condon listened to his visitor. The Minority Leader's stately offices were located in the Senate wing of the Capitol. Hidden in the shadows of the dimly-lit room, the senator's visitor spoke in a low, deep voice. An avid cigar smoker, Senator Condon held a lit cigar. He had puffed away for several minutes, filling the air with noxious smoke.

The senator was dressed in a cream-colored wool suit that stood out in the darkened room. Preferring lighter colors, he often wore tailor-made suits of a light material. Earlier that week, he had returned from a four-day excursion to the Bahamas, and his recently-acquired tan contrasted with his light suit and silky white hair. Without fail, his hair was trimmed short every week at the basement barber shop in the Russell Senate Office Building.

His private suite was on the west end of the Senate wing's second floor. A fireplace adorned the space between the two large windows overlooking the Mall to the west. The Capitol roof of the rotunda could be seen through a window on the south wall. The office was decorated with fine antique furniture and large oil paintings dating back to the 1700s. As Minority Leader, the senator earned the luxury of the spacious office. Not a working office, it was used primarily to greet foreign dignitaries, as well as high-ranking government officials and corporate executives.

The Capitol's Senate wing office was provided with a small staff in outer offices along the perimeter. Condon, however, did most of his work at his offices in the Russell Building, the oldest of the upper chamber's buildings on Capitol Hill.

In the shadows, the visitor coughed from inhaling the pungent smoke that saturated the room. From the outline of his broad frame, one could tell he was a large man, reaching about 6' 3" in height. Pausing the exchange, he pulled out a handkerchief to wipe his eyes and clear his sinuses.

"I must speak to maintenance about the ventilation," Condon said, clearing his throat. "I see the smoke is getting to you." He stubbed out the cigar on an already-filled ashtray.

The visitor let out the last of a cough, clearing his airway. "That's quite all right, Emory," he grunted. "But you should have that looked into." He paused to wipe his nose. "Either that or do away with smoking those nasty cigars in here."

"Sorry about that." Condon pushed the ashtray aside and reclined in the high-back, soft leather chair. Resting his elbows on the massive arms of the chair, he clasped his hands and rested his chin on his interlocked fingers. "You were telling me about some investigation you've come across. Please continue."

"Yes, by sheer accident. Extremely sensitive material I just learned about. Pure happenstance, really." The man put the handkerchief away in a back pocket. "As you know, the CIA Director orally briefs President Henning every week on the clandestine activities of his agency. From time to time, the Director follows up his briefings with a written memo to the President. By some quirk, a copy got misrouted to me. I destroyed it after reading it."

"And you said the memo mentioned me?"

"More than that, in fact. According to it, you're the subject of an investigation by the CIA and possibly the FBI. I say 'possibly' because the memo referred to one of the FBI's deputy directors."

"You must realize this is purely political hype. We're less than a year away from · the primary elections, and they're scavenging for dirt. Something they can use against me because the President considers me a potential threat in next year's elections."

"Please tell me, Emory, is there any dirt to be found?"

"That depends. You more than anyone else should know they'll blow anything out of proportion if it'll hurt their opponent. But I'm curious. Did the memo suggest what about my past they're interested in?"

"Yes—something they suspect occurring at some point in your military career. Specifically your tours in Vietnam."

The expression on Condon's face changed. Until now, he had appeared amused, if not indifferent, by what his visitor had told him, even suggesting he believed his political enemies were groping in the dark, having nothing to target. But his visitor's reference to the senator's military tours in Vietnam changed his amusement to one of apparent concern.

"Oh, really!" he managed to utter. He paused, as if refining his thoughts. "What about my tours there?"

"That, I cannot tell you. There were no particulars. The memo stated, however, that although the investigation was ongoing, nothing concrete had so far been uncovered." The visitor's eyes penetrated the smoke still hanging in the air and appeared to glare at Condon. "Emory, you're going to have to level with me." A look of concern was evident in his eyes. "I realize you're a highly decorated, retired member of our Armed Forces." His voice became louder. "But for God's sake, is there anything about your military career in Vietnam, or elsewhere for that matter, that could prove embarrassing or worse yet threatening to you and the office you hold? Anything at all?" He pounced his fist on the senator's desk in apparent frustration.

"Listen carefully, for I'll say this only once!" Condon was now angry. "I'm not going to waste my time discussing this matter further. I'm damn proud of my service to this country, whose laws I swore to uphold when I took the oath of this office. I've dedicated the best years of my life to the citizens of this country and my beloved South Carolina. So I'm not going to dignify any supposed dirt these blasted, witch-hunting Democrats are itching to throw my way by spending your or my time worrying about it. I'm not going to get one bit concerned about these fucking pussies investigating me. Let them scrutinize my record all they want, for all I care!"

"Fine, fine." Condon's visitor leaned forward on his chair, preparing to stand up. "As long as you're satisfied they couldn't uncover something that might adversely affect or worse yet destroy our plans. They're too important to me."

"And need I remind you they're important to *me*!"

"Fine, Emory. That's all I wanted—your assurance that nothing negative would be revealed should this investigation continue."

"You have my assurance." He smiled and squinted his eyes almost shut. "Now, if you don't mind, I'd like to end this unpleasant discussion. Was there anything else?" It was obvious by his tone he was annoyed. He leaned forward on the chair but didn't stand up.

"No, nothing else." He stood up, taking the hint the discussion was over.

"Good." Smiling, Condon stood, walked to the front of the desk, and extended his hand.

The taller man took the senator's hand. As an added gesture of friendship, Condon placed his other hand over the visitor's hand and shook it with both hands.

"You know," Condon said as he escorted his guest to the door. "You shouldn't be such a worry-wart. It doesn't become you or the high office you hold."

The visitor appeared not to have appreciated the remark. "Really, Emory," he countered, "I thought you knew me better than that. I believe you should be glad I opted to discuss the memo with you." He opened the door, then looked at Condon with obvious disapproval. His tall figure became silhouetted against the brightness of the wide hallway, where two men apparently waited for Condon's visitor to appear.

Condon got closer to his visitor and spoke so as not to be overheard. "Believe me, I am. It's just that I'm a little annoyed to learn of an investigation I consider nothing more than a witch hunt for muck intended to hurt my political chances next year."

"I appreciate your irritation," the tall man replied in a low voice. "But I hope you appreciate the importance of my visit."

"I do. Pardon my anger. Believe me, it wasn't directed at you."

"There's no need for an apology, Emory. I realize that in these situations, one is often tempted to punish the messenger." He smiled. "Have a good night."

Condon laughed. "Good night to you too." He walked behind his desk, took a deep breath, and picked up the phone. He sat in the chair and dialed.

Quigley's plane landed at the Hellinikon International Airport in Athens at dawn Monday morning. The Boeing 747 had taken off from LaGuardia International Airport late Sunday night. The flight stopped in Rome for an hour or so. Feeling cramped from the long trans-Atlantic flight, Quigley exited the plane there to stretch his legs while the plane refueled and took on new passengers before continuing on.

Greece's counterpart agency to the CIA and the FBI all rolled into one, known as the KYP, had arranged to have someone meet Quigley at the airport when his plane arrived. As Quigley entered the concourse on deplaning, he spotted the KYP agent holding the piece of white cardboard spelling *Quigley*. The agent introduced himself as Leonidas Kahiasvili but asked Quigley to call him Leo. He escorted Quigley to the baggage area.

While waiting there, Quigley asked Leo if he had any word on Henri LaPierre's whereabouts. Leo answered that he knew nothing of Quigley's business in Athens. He had only been instructed to pick him up at the airport and assist him during his stay.

After Quigley retrieved his luggage, the two men went through customs, where the Greek agent displayed his ID and was permitted to pass unhindered by the inspectors, with Quigley tagging along. Quigley was exhausted from the trip and jet lag, so he appreciated the special treatment and welcomed not having to stand in the long line to be inspected by the customs officials.

It took Leo a half hour to drive from the airport to the *Gran Briton Hotel*, located in downtown Athens.

It was where foreign dignitaries stayed, Leo remarked. "And," he added, "CIA agents too."

Reservations were made for Quigley to spend Monday night. The return flight was booked through Paris the following morning in the event his search in Athens proved fruitless. In Paris, the plan was for him to try finding Henri's parents, assuming they were alive.

After Quigley registered, he arranged for Leo to return in an hour. The two men were to have a quick breakfast before driving to the Athens Police Department, where they were to touch base with one of the detectives there assigned to help Quigley. Leo soon departed, and Quigley went up to his room to take a shower and rest before beginning what he was certain would be a long day.

Before flying out of Albuquerque en route to LaGuardia to catch his trans-Atlantic flight, he experienced considerable difficulty getting in touch with the KYP. The contact was necessary protocol to request the agency's assistance in finding Henri. With the KYP's help, Kelly and Quigley hoped the Greek agency, as well as the local police in Athens, could get an early start in attempting to find Henri. As it turned out, Quigley was forced to leave Albuquerque for LaGuardia before arrangements with the appropriate individuals at the Greek agency were completed.

At LaGuardia, while awaiting to board his flight to Athens, he succeeded in contacting Leo's boss. It was then that the agent gave the KYP the information it needed to track Henri's movements since he had last written to Leroy.

At the police department later that morning, a uniformed deputy escorted Quigley and Leo through a semi-dark corridor to the office of the chief of detectives, Nikolaos Papadakis. Papadakis, wearing civilian clothes, greeted them with a big smile at the doorway to his office. He explained that instead of assigning an underling to help Quigley, he took on the task himself. Quigley appreciated the chief's interest, he told him. The chief was a small man with a receding hairline and of swarthy complexion.

His office was rather small, and the walls needed a new coat of paint. It was furnished with a few pieces of plain furniture that had seen its finest days long ago.

"Would you pronounce your name for me?" Quigley asked after the chief had gestured for him and Leo to have a seat. The two agents sat in the two arm chairs located in front of a gray metal desk. The chief sat behind the desk.

"Please, Mr. Fletcher Quigley," the chief said in broken English and smiled. "Ni-ko-la-os Pa-pa-da-kis. But save yourself the trouble of trying to pronounce it. In the Hellinic language or Greek, as you Americans refer to us, those under me call me 'Chief,' so you are free to do likewise. Or, if you prefer, just call me 'Nick.'"

"I see. That'll be fine, then. 'Chief,' it'll be. You may call me Quigley." He was amused when the man had addressed him by his full name—"Mr. Fletcher Quigley." "That's what *my* associates call me back home."

"Very good. Quigley, it will be." He opened a desk drawer and pulled out a bulky brownish folder. "Now, gentlemen, let's get down to business, shall we." He placed the thick file in front of him and opened it. "Quigley, the request we received yesterday from the KYP, Leonidas' agency, stated you were attempting to locate a French gentleman by the name of Henri LaPierre. A journalist originally from Paris, I understand."

"That's correct." The fact that Chief Papadakis had the file in his desk drawer suggested to Quigley that the chief knew something of Henri.

"I regret to inform you that you may have come to Athens for nothing."

Quigley's heart sank. "But the file." He glanced at the folder. "You must have infor—"

"The gentleman is dead, I'm afraid," the chief interrupted.

Quigley's expression conveyed his disappointment. He wasn't surprised. Yet he had kept his hopes up that Henri wasn't only alive but that he'd be found soon. "It doesn't come as a shock to me, but I'm disappointed nevertheless."

"I can see that. Truly, Quigley, I didn't wish to be the bearer of bad news."

He sighed. "We were hoping to find him, of course, for he could have been a great help to us." He eyed the file. "How long has he been dead?"

"He died almost thirty years ago, I'm afraid." The chief shuffled through the papers in the folder and read from one of them. "July of 1973." He made eye contact with Quigley. "Let me explain about this particular file. The case was under the jurisdiction of the provincial police department, which has authority over the district or area where the death of Mr. LaPierre occurred. That's an agency that polices the outlying areas of Athens, much like, I believe, the county sheriffs in your country function."

"How is it you have the file, then?"

"Well, at the time of this particular incident, we were called into the case because it was suspected the death might be related to another death that had occurred within our own jurisdiction a week or so earlier. As it turned out, our department determined the cases weren't related, but the investigation continued coordinated between the two departments. That occurs frequently. The provincial police sometimes call upon us to assist them in these serious cases because they often don't have the resources we do."

The chief squared the loose papers back in the folder and pushed it toward Quigley. "You're free to look through the file we retrieved from our warehouse yesterday. By the way, we did locate a Mr. LaPierre who lives in Athens at present, but we've verified he isn't the man you're looking for. When our records and those of other sources we checked didn't turn up your Henri LaPierre, that's when we checked our old investigation records." He gestured toward the file. "What you see in that folder is all we have on the man you're seeking."

"May I?" Quigley asked, gesturing to the file.

"But of course." He smiled again.

Quigley picked up the file.

"What you will glean from there," the chief went on, "is that Mr. LaPierre burned to death in a mysterious fire. Arson and murder were suspected, but the case was never solved. The file was closed a few years later. I've taken the liberty of contacting the detective who was assigned the case at the time. He worked the case with the provincial police, and you'll see his name, Christos Petropoulos, on the entries. He's now retired but still lives in Athens. The incident happened long before I started with the department, and so I knew nothing of the case. When we found the file, I contacted Detective Petropoulos. He was kind enough to brief me on the case."

He stood up. "Take all the time you need. Let me leave you and Agent Kahiasvili for a moment to tend to some other business. Of course, what you'll see in the file is written in our own language, but I trust Agent Kahiasvili will translate the reports for you." He grinned at Leo.

The chief took a few steps toward the closed door and stopped. "By the way, Detective Petropoulos has agreed to make himself available to you today and has even volunteered to show you where Mr. LaPierre's body was found, if you think it'd be helpful."

"If you don't mind," Quigley said, "I'd like that very much."

"Fine, I'll make the arrangements."

Quigley thanked the chief, who then disappeared into the hallway. He handed the folder to Leo. "Would you do the honors?"

"Surely," Leo said and took the file.

The KYP agent took half an hour to study the reports, jotting down notes as he read. From time to time, Quigley glanced at the notes, only to realize Leo was writing in Greek, a language baffling to him.

After Leo finished reviewing the documents, he spent the next ten minutes summarizing their contents to Quigley.

Henri had burned to death in a fire on July 28, 1973. The mysterious death occurred in a rural community outside Athens. To get to it, Quigley learned, one had to go through the mountains surrounding Athens into farm country. The fire was confined to the small dwelling rented by Henri.

The police reports at the time left no doubt the fire was started intentionally, for heavy traces of gasoline residue were found in several containers recovered from the debris. An arson expert determined the fire was set by hand. In fact, the evidence of arson was so overwhelming that it was apparent whoever killed Henri meant to leave solid proof of their deed behind. The investigators concluded someone wanted all to know Henri had been murdered.

Not only were the entire contents of the dwelling destroyed, but Henri's body was burnt beyond recognition. Dental records obtained from Paris were used to identify the remains. Examination of the dwelling's contents and furniture, however, revealed that the place had been ransacked before being set afire. Evidence was also uncovered that led the investigating team to conclude Henri was tortured before his home was set ablaze.

The initial report in the file listed his next of kin as his parents, Paul and Marie LaPierre, of Paris, France. Their address and phone number were listed in the report, and Quigley made a note of them as Leo finished his summary.

Quigley had brought Henri's letter to Athens. The postmark on the envelope showed it was mailed on July 15, 1973, just 13 days before Henri's fiery death. The agent concluded he was dead by the time Leroy received the letter.

Quigley and Leo had just finished discussing the contents of the file when the chief returned. He told Quigley that Christos Petropoulos had just telephoned and arranged to meet him at the chief's office at two o'clock. Quigley asked the chief for permission to use the telephone to make several calls and to confirm his preplanned flight to Paris the following day. The chief showed his two visitors into a small adjoining office where Quigley could make his phone calls in private.

He first telephoned TWA's 800 number to see if there were earlier flights out of Athens and into Paris that evening. When he found there were none, he confirmed his already-booked flight scheduled for the following morning. Before telephoning Kelly to report his findings, he decided to try reaching Henri's parents so he could report the outcome of his efforts to locate them.

As he placed the call to Paris, he considered the possibility that the parents too were dead. Or, they may have moved, he thought as he heard the ring at the other end. But that wouldn't prove a problem, for they could easily be found, if alive.

He was relieved that the elderly gentleman who answered spoke English. After identifying himself, Quigley learned the man was Henri's father, Paul LaPierre. The Frenchman told him Marie LaPierre's health had deteriorated after her son's death and had died in 1975. Paul LaPierre now lived alone and was in relative fair health for his age. Quigley informed him he was due to land at the DeGaulle International Airport outside Paris not later than mid-afternoon the next day. The elder LaPierre had no objection to meeting with him.

When he hung up, he contacted Kelly to inform him of Henri's death and his planned meeting with his father the next day.

He and Leo left the police department after making arrangements with the chief to meet Christos Petropoulos that afternoon. Leo then took Quigley to his agency's headquarters, where he introduced him to his supervisor and colleagues.

Learning that Quigley had visited Athens only on a quick trip once before, Leo gave him an abbreviated tour. They ate a late lunch at a small restaurant.

Afterward, they returned to the chief's office to meet Christos Petropoulos. The retired detective was pleasant. He insisted being called just "Chris." Quigley, Leo, and Chris left almost immediately in Leo's car.

As the three men headed out of Athens through its suburbs and into the rural area, Quigley quizzed Chris about his part in the investigation of Henri's death. Chris, who explained he had reviewed the file to refresh his memory, confirmed the persons who killed Henri had been searching for something important to them. He described the many wounds that could still be detected in the burnt body. The autopsy concluded Henri was already dead when the fire was started. He didn't die from smoke inhalation or asphyxiation, but from blows delivered to the body with strong force. Finally, Chris revealed that a crude torture device was found near the body.

It took them forty-five minutes to reach the spot where Henri had met his death. The walls of the burnt dwelling were still standing. Chris led them through the ruins, pointing out the layout of the dwelling's various rooms. The debris, crumbling walls and flooring, and roof timber that created a safety hazard had been removed long ago. Chris noted the general area where Henri's body had been found. He also pointed out the location of items of furniture that convinced him someone searched and ransacked the dwelling before setting it afire.

As the three men walked away from the ruins, Quigley asked Chris if he had ever discovered or suspected what the killers had been searching for.

Chris shook his head, smiled, then asked Quigley, "Have you?"

The question took Quigley by surprise. "Pardon?" he asked.

"You've come a long way in search of someone who's been dead almost thirty years. I was curious if your interest in coming here had anything to do with what the ones who set fire to this place were searching for."

He smiled. "I can only speculate we're searching for the same thing they were back then."

They drove back to the police department, where they visited for a few minutes with the chief. Quigley thanked him and Chris for their courtesies and assistance.

The next morning, Leo picked him up early and drove him to the airport. They had time to eat a light breakfast at one of the airport restaurants.

Once again, Leo proved his adeptness in helping Quigley avoid the usual delays at the overcrowded air terminal. Security was tight this morning, they discovered, because several bomb threats had been made by phone the night before. The airport had in operation three separate security areas, all operated by the KYP and the airport police. Leo took Quigley into the security office, where he arranged for Quigley to be escorted to his gate without delay. Quigley thanked Leo for his help, and the two men parted.

That evening, the cab carrying Quigley meandered through the Paris outskirts in search of Paul LaPierre's residence. He had called Paul LaPierre soon after he checked into a modest hotel near the airport. He asked if it would be a good time to meet. When Mr. LaPierre told him that it was, he didn't bother unpacking and called for a cab.

Paul LaPierre's home was set on a small hill a few feet away from the narrow paved street. The area was an upper class neighborhood just outside the municipal boundaries of Paris. The homes here were large, and the yards were spacious and filled with colorful flower gardens, neatly-trimmed shrubs, and huge trees that appeared to be over a hundred years old. A sweet aroma of the blooming flowers filled the cool evening air.

As he exited the cab, Quigley paid the cab driver but asked him to wait while he verified they had found the residence. A short, stout woman in her mid-fifties, the care giver/housekeeper for the elder LaPierre, answered the doorbell. She didn't speak English, Quigley found out when she had answered the phone earlier. Nonetheless, he identified himself to her in English. He surmised Paul LaPierre had alerted her of his arrival.

The woman smiled at him, then said something in French he didn't comprehend except for *monsieur*. She opened the door wide and gestured for him to enter. He waved on the cab driver.

The woman ushered him into a narrow but large study. There, Quigley found his host seated in a lounging chair reading a newspaper near a large coffee table and an unlit fireplace. A tea setting and tray were set on the coffee table. Although a floor lamp lit the room, little natural light entered through the two narrow windows found along the room's far wall.

The elder LaPierre stood up slowly as his housekeeper approached from across the room with Quigley following. Using a cane, the Frenchman took a few unsteady steps forward. "*Monsieur* Quigley," he said, extending his hand. "I am truly sorry for not greeting you at the door."

Quigley took Paul LaPierre's hand and shook it gently. "Please don't apologize," he said. "It's unnecessary. I'm happy you've agreed to see me."

The woman said something to Mr. LaPierre in French, he said a few words in reply, and she disappeared from the room. Mr. LaPierre asked him to sit in a chair on the other side of the coffee table and offered him a cup of tea. He noticed the extra cup setting on the table and accepted the welcoming gesture.

As Mr. LaPierre poured the tea, Quigley noticed his host seemed much older and frail than his 81 years. Before flying into Paris, he had requested a *bio sketch* on Paul LaPierre. From the sketch, the agent learned his age, the date his wife had died, where he had worked, and other data compiled from various intelligence sources.

Mr. LaPierre poured the tea from the silver server with great care but with an unsteady hand. He wore a cream-colored beret that seemed too large for his small head. The cap and the elderly man's white hair seemed to make his skin appear pale, causing him to look almost anemic in the darkened room. His face was extremely wrinkled. That and his small stature were what made him appear frail.

"The ravages of old age," he said as he sat back in his chair. "I used to feel in my prime there was nothing I couldn't do." He motioned toward the tea server. "Now, even pouring a guest a cup of tea appears to be more than I can handle."

Quigley smiled. "I thought you did that quite well," he lied.

Mr. LaPierre picked up his cup. "Thank you, *Monsieur* Quigley." He sighed, then held his cup up in a toast. "Welcome to Paris and to my home."

"Thank you." He returned the toast. "You're most gracious."

Mr. LaPierre put his cup down. "My limitations appear to have accelerated during the last few years. Michelle, my housekeeper, now does for me what I can't do for myself." He looked around the room. "I should have sold this big house long ago after Marie passed away, but I couldn't bear the thought of leaving the home she and I shared for so long. Things changed drastically for me after she died, but with the grace of God, I've managed this far." He sat there silently for a moment.

"I'm sorry about the loss of your wife," Quigley said, trying to avoid an awkward silence. "And, of course, for the tragic loss of your son, Henri."

Mr. LaPierre said nothing for a long while. "Thank you, *monsieur*. Somehow my wife was never the same after Henri's untimely death. She had been in poor health, and when we heard about Henri—the horrible way he died—that proved too much for her."

He now felt uncomfortable, as if he had invaded a grieving man's privacy. "I believe it took great courage on your part," he said awkwardly, "to overcome both your son's and wife's deaths so near to each other." He paused. "I know my visit has brought up these sad memories for you, Mr. LaPierre. As I said on the phone, I wouldn't have bothered you unless it was important."

"There isn't a day that goes by that I don't think of both of them. So you're coming here has made no difference in that respect." He stood up and walked the few steps to a small desk. He took a two-picture frame setting on the desk and handed it to Quigley. "That's Henri and his beloved mother. My memories of them, which in reality are all I have that I treasure, are still an important part of my daily life."

Quigley studied the photographs of Marie LaPierre and her son, Henri, then handed the frame back to Mr. LaPierre. The elderly man took the frame and gazed at the images of his wife and son. A faint smile appeared for a moment on his gaunt face.

"God rest their souls," he said as he set the frame down on top of the coffee table. "Henri was but 36 years old when he died. That's the pity of it." He sighed. "Which brings us, I suppose, *Monsieur* Quigley, to the purpose of your visit."

"Yes," Quigley said. "About your son. We were trying to find him in Athens when we learned of his death." He studied the elder LaPierre's face. "I was informed you knew the circumstances of his death."

"I suppose you're referring to the fact the police concluded the fire had been deliberately set. Yes, we knew that. That's one reason why his death proved difficult for his mother to accept."

"I can imagine what it was like for both of you." Mr. LaPierre hadn't said *murder* nor anything about his son's suspected torture during the final minutes of his life. He decided there was no need to go into any of the gory details, in the event the man hadn't already been informed of them. He changed the discussion to the CIA's interest in the story Henri had been working on before his murder. "I'm sure you have an idea about the CIA's function in international affairs."

"Yes, yes, but of course. And in 'espionage,' you might add, *monsieur*, since it's an intelligence-gathering organization."

"Unfortunately, much of what we do is cloaked in secrecy. For that reason, as well as for your own safety, I can't divulge certain information that might help you comprehend why—"

"Please, *Monsieur* Quigley, I understand fully the nature of your agency's work, so let me assure you that you won't have to compromise your task. But there is one thing puzzling me—one thing only—that I would like for you to explain."

"And what is that?"

"Why you're interested in my son after so many years." He drank what was left of his tea. "That is, if you can do so without divulging anything you believe is inappropriate."

"You're entitled to know, of course." He leaned forward, his hands clasped together and his elbows resting on his knees. "First of all, let me assure you our interest in your son has nothing to do with any improper conduct on his part. We're merely interested in information he may have come across before he died; information collected in connection with his work."

"What exactly was this information? Can you reveal that much?"

"Well, that's where it might get into this sensitive area we talked about." He paused. "Let me put it this way. We believe your son was working on a story that may have implicated others in significant wrongdoing. He never got around to having the story published. We've also learned he believed his life was in danger because of the sensitive information he possessed."

"What of his death? Do you suppose that was connected to what you're telling me?"

Quigley nodded. "I think I'd be safe telling you the cause of your son's death goes beyond mere suspicion on our part. My agency has good reason to believe his death came about as a result of the story he was working on. Someone wanted this information. We've narrowed the field and have a good idea who these persons are."

"I'm not going to ask you to reveal who you suspect and jeopardize your work, *Monsieur* Quigley. If and when the time comes, I'm certain you'd let me know. For the time being, I'm the one who should thank you. After all, with what little you've told me, you've shed more light on my son's death than anyone else ever has." He sat there, as if contemplating what Quigley had told him. "What you've said also explains why Henri seemed upset—tense—before he returned to Athens."

"Was he, now?"

"Yes. Both his mother and I tried to find out what was the matter. I remember his mother suggesting he might be having girlfriend difficulties

247

he wouldn't have wanted to talk about." He had been looking downward as he spoke. He now raised his head and looked straight at Quigley. "But tell me, *monsieur*, why has all of this now surfaced after almost thirty years?"

Quigley gave his host a brief explanation of his and Kelly's work on the case, including the information they had obtained, without revealing names and much of the detail. "We're concerned for the safety of one particular individual who knew your son in Vietnam—John Garcia. He was a lieutenant in the United States Army when he met Henri. He now lives in the United States with his wife and two children. We believe their lives may be in danger and that the information your son possessed might help us—"

Mr. LaPierre gestured with his hand to interrupt Quigley. "Pardon me, *Monsieur* Quigley!" he said, standing up. "Please give me a moment." He paused. "Yes, I'm certain that's the name. You mentioned a John Garcia?

"Yes."

"Why that's the name on the envelope Henri gave to his mother and me for safekeeping before he left Paris. I told you a moment ago how nervous he seemed to us at the time."

"Yes."

"Well, before he left, he entrusted us with a sealed envelope. He didn't tell us what it contained, but he had written on the face of it the name of a 'First Lieutenant John Garcia.'"

Things were starting to make sense, Quigley thought. "What did he say to do with it?"

"He explained to me he had sought a friend he knew in Vietnam, Lieutenant Garcia. He was going to continue searching and should he succeed, he instructed us to give it to the lieutenant once he contacted us."

Quigley couldn't hide his excitement. "What did you do with the envelope?"

"I placed it in a safety deposit box at our bank. It's there today."

"We're in touch with Mr. Garcia. I'll deliver it to him."

"I would like to cooperate, *monsieur*. But I must insist on honoring my son's last request—that it be delivered only to *Monsieur* Garcia and no one else. Besides, I don't believe it would do any good to deliver the envelope in the United States."

"Why is that?"

"It was a thin, manila envelope, so it couldn't have had much in it, except for what I suspected were instructions."

"Why did you suspect that?"

"Because I could feel what was in it. A key."

"A key?"

"Yes. I assume it opens a safety deposit box or some other locked compartment. Most likely somewhere here in Paris. And so I suspect, *Monsieur* Quigley, that you'd only find yourself returning here should you take the envelope to *Monsieur* Garcia. And I would like to honor my son's wishes. You'll appreciate my insistence, I'm sure."

"But of course," Quigley said. "I'll see whether Mr. Garcia can join me soon."

"I knew you'd understand, *monsieur*. Then I'll hear from you again, I suppose."

"Definitely."

CHAPTER 21

THE Soliz trial was scheduled to resume Monday morning, about the time Quigley was returning from the scene of Henri's death outside Athens. That past Saturday, however, John had learned Leroy's funeral services were scheduled for mid-morning Monday. He contacted Keith and Judge Walker at their homes to arrange postponing the trial until sometime after lunch. Keith didn't object, and Judge Walker granted the request.

John and Demi caught an early morning flight into Farmington, then drove on to the small church in Shiprock. The services were followed by the burial at a cemetery just outside the village. It was a military funeral, with color guard and all the military flourishes, an appropriate manner in which to bid a final farewell to a military comrade.

At the cemetery, John introduced Demi and himself to Leroy's relatives. He explained his renewed friendship with Leroy and their tour together in Vietnam. He couldn't help feeling guilty that he didn't divulge what he knew of the events leading to Leroy's death. Kelly stated that the cause of death was going to be listed as a hit-and-run accident

251

officially, in order to keep the CIA and FBI's involvement under wraps. For the time being, Leroy's family would have to stay under the impression he had been a hit-and-run victim.

After the services, the family invited John and Demi to a reception at the local Elks Club. They explained their flight out of Farmington would prevent them from attending.

The return flight arrived in Albuquerque a few minutes before one. That gave John barely enough time to pick up his file at the office before the start of the trial at one thirty.

His plan that afternoon was to call Bernardo's sister, Carmen, and his parents to the stand. Afterward, he intended to have Bernardo testify sometime mid-afternoon. He estimated Bernardo's testimony, including Keith's cross-examination, would carry over into most of the next morning.

After establishing that Carmen was married, had two children, and that she and her husband worked, John elicited from her that she visited her mother almost every week day. She happened to be there Saturday morning, two days after the attack on Patty, when Morales arrived to question Bernardo. The warrant for his arrest wasn't issued until the following Monday afternoon. Monday morning, however, Morales had again gone to the Soliz home, and Carmen was also there.

It was then, according to Carmen, that an angry Morales questioned her mother, Ramona, about Bernardo's whereabouts. When her mother asked the detective why he wanted to question her son, he refused to tell her, accusing her of not cooperating. Carmen testified Morales told her mother in Spanish that if he were to come upon Bernardo somewhere, and Bernardo made the slightest move to flee, he, Morales, would kill him. Morales' threat had caused her mother to shed tears, Carmen said. It was Morales' temper, not her mother's lack of cooperation, she testified, that had caused bad feelings between her mother and Morales, to which she claimed the detective had testified falsely. Bernardo's sister also verified that Monday afternoon, when Morales had returned with an arrest warrant, her mother was distrustful of him and that was why he may have testified she was angry and uncooperative.

John then moved backward in time to the previous Thursday evening to establish Bernardo's alibi. Carmen testified she remembered that evening because she worked three days a week, Tuesday through Thursday, and she got paid on Thursday. She owed her mother money for having baby-sat her children, so she had gone to pay her. She and her mother had gone to the store to buy the ingredients to make red cheese enchiladas.

Carmen's testimony laid the important time sequence. She, her parents, her two children, Bernardo, and Bernardo's wife were present. They began eating at around seven o'clock and finished about seven twenty. She then stayed, after helping her mother with the dishes, waiting for her husband to get off work. She watched TV with the others. Her husband didn't show up until eight thirty, and they both left ten minutes afterward. She testified Bernardo had been on the couch the entire time watching TV since having eaten dinner, with the exception of a few minutes sometime after eight o'clock. At about that time, he stepped out to the shed.

To stress to the jury why she remembered so well the evening in question, John asked her several times what she had been doing at seven o'clock on various dates he picked at random. She didn't know, she replied. How, then, could she remember so well the particular night when Patty had been stabbed? Because, she explained, the day after Bernardo was arrested, the P. D. questioned her when her memory was fresh. The lawyer had suggested she form a mental imprint in her mind about that particular evening because she was going to be called upon to recall it.

In response to Keith's cross-examination, she recited the channel the family was watching and the programs that had appeared from seven until she left sometime after eight thirty. Keith also questioned her concerning the time Bernardo had gone outside into the backyard. Could that have been longer than a few minutes? No, she insisted. Could Bernardo have stepped out prior to eight and not after that time, as she had claimed? No, she testified.

Reinaldo Soliz, who testified in Spanish through a court interpreter, buttressed his daughter's testimony on the alibi. But his testimony was important for other reasons. First, John wanted the jury to know about the lawyer-client relationship he and Reinaldo had shared many years before when he had represented him in the workers' compensation claim. He considered that an important backdrop to explain why the Solizes had sought out his help. Second, he wanted to establish he was representing Bernardo pro bono and that the elder Soliz couldn't afford to pay him otherwise. Third, he considered it important to establish that Reinaldo's love for his son wasn't the reason he was claiming Bernardo had been at home when the attack on Patty took place. The reason he was making the claim, he persisted, was because it was the truth—he knew his son was innocent of the criminal charge wrongly filed against him.

During his cross-examination, Keith attempted to show that Bernardo had gotten a haircut the weekend after the assault on Patty and before photos of him were taken. The prosecutor wanted to support Patty's and Carol's insistence that Bernardo had attempted to change his appearance by combing his hair in a different way. Keith was unsuccessful, for Reinaldo denied knowing anything about a haircut.

Ramona Soliz was an important witness, second to Bernardo. As expected, she joined her daughter and husband in providing an alibi. Through her testimony, however, John also hoped to gain sympathy for her and her family. The jury, of course, would be instructed at the end of the testimony that it wasn't to base its decision on sympathy but on the facts heard in evidence and the law as instructed by the court. But that technicality never kept a seasoned attorney from trying to gain sympathy nonetheless. With Ramona on the stand, John thought, this sympathy could come about in two ways. Not only was she a humble, caring mother, but he felt that Morales had to be discredited for his disrespectful treatment of the Soliz family at their home. John hoped Bernardo's mother could do that by giving her own version of the conversation with Morales the day he went searching for Bernardo at her home.

Ramona too testified in Spanish. She stated that on Saturday morning, the detective had spoken to Bernardo about his whereabouts the prior Thursday evening. Bernardo's mother thought that conversation with her son, which took place after she had invited Morales into her house, had taken care of the matter. That's the reason she was alarmed, she explained, when he reappeared Monday morning again looking for her son. She became so worried then that, as soon as the detective left, she attempted contacting an attorney. In the presence of a lawyer, she thought Morales would be more forthright about the reasons he wanted to talk to Bernardo.

"That Monday morning," John said, "when he came to your home a second time looking for Bernardo, did you know where he was at the time?"

"No, sir, I didn't," Ramona replied.

"Were you afraid when the detective approached you?"

"Yes, I was."

"Why were you afraid, Ms. Soliz?" He spoke with considerable sympathy.

"Because I was concerned for my son!" Ramona cried out. She took out a handkerchief and wiped the tears from her eyes. "Then there were the guards they posted around our house since that morning. We found that frightening. Of course, Mr. Morales wasn't helpful in telling us what he wanted with Bernardo. He was angry with me because my son wasn't there. I tried explaining that wasn't my fault, but he wouldn't listen." New tears appeared. She stopped to wipe her nose with her handkerchief, then continued. "Instead, he got angrier and began shouting at me. That's when he made the threat, which scared me even more."

"What threat was that, Ms. Soliz?"

"The one against Bernardo."

"Please tell us exactly what Detective Morales told you."

More tears came, which she tried wiping away. "He was pointing his finger at me, and shouted in anger, '*Si por casualidad, por cualquier razón me encuentro con su hijo, Bernardo, y hace una movida, lo voy a matar! Eso le prometo!* If by chance, and for whatever reason, I happen to see your son, Bernardo, and he makes one move, I'll kill him! That, I promise you!'"

"Had you said anything to Detective Morales to get him angry enough to say that to you?"

"No—nothing. As I said, I think he got angry because Bernardo wasn't there." She dabbed at her eyes.

"Did you feel you were cooperating with him under the circumstances? He said here in this courtroom the other day that you weren't only uncooperative but hostile."

"The man was lying if he said that!"

He paused for a moment to let the response linger in the minds of the jurors. "Now, let's move on to later that day, when Detective Morales returned, this time with an arrest warrant. When he arrived with a warrant for Bernardo's arrest, were you still feeling the ill effects from your talk with him that morning?"

"Yes, very much so. And I'm ashamed to admit it, but I myself was angry for his having treated us as he did that morning."

"Were you still worried about the threat he had made against Bernardo?"

"Oh, yes."

"What did you tell him, if anything, when he told you he had an arrest warrant for Bernardo?"

Ramona's tears began to flow again. "I—I—I told him—" She paused to gain her composure. "*Así se lo dije. Ni muerto, ni vivo; nunca te voy ha entregar mi hijo!* This is the way I told him. Neither dead nor alive; never will I deliver my son to you!"

In his cross-examination of Ramona, Keith took special pains not to appear intimidating. Yet, his questions were firm. John could tell Keith sensed John had been successful in gaining some sympathy from the jury, and the prosecutor didn't want to add to that sympathy by being perceived as overbearing or threatening to the witness. He asked Ramona one question after another concerning Bernardo's whereabouts on particular days. Instead of claiming ignorance, she insisted that her son had been at home during those times. The prosecutor's purpose was not only to confuse her but to show that, as Bernardo's mother, she was willing to say just about anything to protect her son.

For that reason, when Keith had completed his cross-examination, John decided to ask a few more questions to rehabilitate her.

"Mrs. Soliz," he began, "do you consider yourself close to your son, Bernardo?"

"Yes, I do," she answered.

"Do you feel you have the love of a mother for him?"

"Of course."

"By virtue of that love, are you interested in whether he is found guilty of this crime?"

"Yes."

"Does that fact affect your testimony in this case?"

"Yes, it affects me," she said, appearing a little confused.

"I realize the charges brought against your son affect you, Mrs. Soliz. What I meant was this—concerning your testimony about Bernardo's whereabouts in the evening when Ms. Gregory was assaulted. Are you testifying as you have because of your love for your son?"

"I'm saying it because it's the truth!" she said, again fighting back tears.

"And there's no doubt in your mind Bernardo was in your home that evening."

"No doubt at all. So help me, God, he was there!"

"Except for the time he stepped out back?"

"Yes, except for then. He was gone for several minutes."

John walked back to his seat and addressed Judge Walker. "I have no further questions of this witness, your honor."

He next called Bernardo. Before Bernardo took the stand, John asked the court reporter to swear in Bernardo as a witness. John had purposely not had his client join the other witnesses when they were sworn in as a group at the start. If Bernardo had been sworn in then and later not testified, the jurors might wonder why he hadn't. John didn't want them to expect his client's testimony.

In a criminal case, a defendant couldn't be compelled to testify. Some defense attorneys, however, often felt uneasy that some jurors expected a defendant to testify if he was innocent. Jurors were instructed not to consider the fact that a defendant didn't take the stand. Human nature being what it was, however, lawyers often wondered if some jurors found it difficult to follow that instruction. For these reasons, John wanted to keep his option open not to put Bernardo on the stand, depending on what happened during the course of the trial that might change his mind.

He began his direct examination by asking Bernardo questions concerning his physical characteristics. Bernardo testified he weighed 109 pounds, had brown eyes, and black hair. John asked him if his hair had always been black, and Bernardo confirmed he had never changed his hair color. John thought it important to emphasize this fact because Patty had insisted Bernardo's hair color was dark brown and not black. He would let the jurors judge for themselves what color Bernardo's hair was. But he wanted them to know that the color of hair they saw as Bernardo sat there was the same color it was on the day of the assault.

Again, he laid the groundwork for the alibi. The P. D., when he first interviewed Bernardo, had gone over his whereabouts at the time of the stabbing. The P. D. had insisted Bernardo *vividly imprint* his own actions of that evening in his memory. He'd later be called upon at trial to account for where he was at the exact time Patty was fighting for her life. Now on the stand, Bernardo insisted he had been at his parents' house the evening of the attack. He remembered in detail the various TV programs he had watched throughout the evening and recounted them for the jury's benefit.

John next moved on to the period of time of some thirty to forty minutes when Bernardo had left the living room. No one could account for him then. Before trial, Bernardo had told John he had left his family in the living room about ten after eight.

As John saw it, there were several potential problems with this period. First, Bernardo's parents and sister claimed Bernardo was absent a *few*

257

minutes. This short time didn't by any stretch of the imagination translate to thirty or forty minutes, which was the time Bernardo himself had committed to. John had raised the difference in estimates to Bernardo, who said his family had been mistaken. When John first questioned the family members, they committed themselves to the *few minutes* they estimated Bernardo had disappeared into the shed. After he had learned from Bernardo that he himself estimated the time lapse to be closer to thirty or forty minutes, John confronted the family with the time disparity. It was then they had insisted Bernardo was the one who was mistaken.

Of course, Bernardo and his family agreed on one important aspect of his absence. Whatever its length, they all agreed it had occurred a few minutes after eight, the latter being the time the assault took place.

John wasn't too concerned about the absence itself for an important reason. Even if one assumed Bernardo's estimate was correct, thirty to forty minutes wasn't enough time to commit the crime. He would have had to travel to the Gregory residence, have the first conversation with Patty, leave, return, stab Patty, flee to the park, and then backtrack to his parent's house.

Addressing the time difference was important for several other reasons. First, Keith could use the disparity to suggest it showed bias on the part of Bernardo's family. He could argue that it suggested the family was trying to help him by cutting down the time of his absence. Second, he might argue that Bernardo was mistaken or lying about the thirty to forty minute period. Third, both Bernardo and his family could have been mistaken about when the absence took place. It might have occurred before eight o'clock, not after, as they insisted.

If so, and if Bernardo was mistaken about the time, it wouldn't have been impossible for him to be at the Gregory residence to do his dastardly deed. Such an argument, if believed, could wipe out the alibi defense.

For these reasons, John made certain during his questioning that there wasn't any doubt his client had left the living room ten minutes after eight and not before the hour. In questioning his client, he also thought it would be a good strategy for the defense to point out the disparity to the jury. This tactic might prevent the jury from later speculating on its own. Bringing it out in the open would lessen its negative impact.

Bernardo was candid in answering John's questions, conceding that either he or his family was mistaken. But, he insisted, there was no question that his absence from the room had begun at least ten minutes after the assault had taken place. Bernardo also testified that even a forty-minute period wasn't long enough for him to have committed the crime. He estimated it would have taken at least an hour to have traveled the distance, committed the act, and returned to his parents' home.

It was a few minutes after five that afternoon when Judge Walker brought a halt to Bernardo's testimony. The jurist instructed the jury to return at eight thirty the next morning, for the testimony would resume at nine.

Bernardo took the stand the next day at precisely nine. Having spent most of the afternoon the day before on Bernardo's alibi, John's plan now was to move on to questions intended to further discredit Morales' testimony. He wanted to show that the detective's approach not only failed to meet the standards of reliable police work, but was downright sloppy. He first elicited from Bernardo that he hadn't gotten a haircut after the attack on Patty, thus refuting Keith's theory that he had tried to alter his appearance. He then wanted to emphasize Bernardo had turned himself in to the metro court judge on Tuesday morning, after having learned late Monday that Morales had a warrant for his arrest.

"Did you enter a plea of not guilty," John asked Bernardo, "when you turned yourself in to the metro court judge?"

"No, sir," Bernardo replied. "The judge told me he would appoint a public defender to represent me. I entered a not guilty plea the following day after the public defender spoke to me."

"Were you taken directly to the Bernalillo County Detention Center from the metro court?"

"No, sir. Detective Morales first took me to the police department, where they took some photographs of me."

"Were your fingerprints also taken at that time?"

"Yes, sir."

"Is that where he got the information concerning your height and weight?"

"Yes."

"Were you present when he was entering the information on the arrest report?"

"Yes."

"Did he ask you how much you weighed?"

"Yes. I told him I weighed 109 pounds."

"What did he say in response."

"He said, 'No, you weigh more than that—at least 135 to 140.'"

"He told you that?"

"Yes. Then he put it down in the arrest report."

"Did they measure your height at that time also?"

"More or less. He just asked this other person to move me closer to these measurements on the wall, and he put down my height as 5-5 to 5-6. I wasn't even near the wall."

"Didn't they have you stand with your head against the wall?"

"No, sir. He just estimated it 'cause I was several feet away."

"After they finished doing that at the police department, were you then booked at the detention center?"

"Yes, sir."

"And you remained there until when?"

"Several weeks ago, when you made arrangements for my release on bail."

"So you were in jail for about three months, is that correct?"

"Yes, sir," Bernardo said.

"Let's move on to the lineup, Bernardo." He thought it a good tactic to address one's client by his given name rather than formally. The idea was to convey to the jury that a closeness—a bond—existed between the attorney and his client. In this way, he hoped the jury would get the impression he was vouching for Bernardo's veracity or at least believed in his innocence.

An implication of Keith's earlier attempt to show Bernardo's different hair style was that he had intentionally changed it. In part, this could explain Carol's confusion. The motive for such deception, Keith could argue, was that Bernardo had indeed committed the crime and was attempting to lead the witnesses astray. John thought it important to address that point and neutralize the inference of a deception.

"Did you get ready for the lineup in any way?" he continued.

"No, I didn't," Bernardo said, "because I didn't know when it was going to be. When they went to get me at the jail, I had just taken a shower."

"What time did they pick you up at the detention center?"

"I don't know. Sometime in the afternoon."

"And you had just taken a shower?"

"Yes, sir."

"Your hair was wet, then?"

"Yes, sir."

"Did you get the chance to comb it?"

"Yes."

"Bernardo, let me show you what's been marked as State Exhibit 16." He picked up the photograph Keith had used to question Bernardo's family about the way Bernardo parted his hair. He approached the witness stand and handed the photograph to Bernardo. "Did you comb your hair differently when that picture was taken than when you wash your hair?"

"No, sir. I always comb it like that until it dries. Then I comb it back when it's dry so it'll stay flat."

"Is your hair hard to manage or part in any way?"

"Yes, it is."

"Compared to your hair today, was your hair that Thursday evening when Ms. Gregory was stabbed shorter or longer than it is now?"

"I'd say it was longer then because it went over my ears."

"What about on top?"

"On top, it was barely longer than it is now, I think."

"Let me ask you pointedly—did you attempt to comb your hair any different for the lineup?"

"No, sir. It's always like that every time I take a shower. Like I said, I didn't know I was going to the lineup."

"What about when you arrived at the police department. Was there anytime there when you may have been alone and had the opportunity to change the way you combed your hair?"

"No, sir. I was never left alone there."

John next returned to asking a few questions intended to clear up some of the facts concerning Bernardo's alibi defense. He ended his examination of Bernardo with pointed questions meant to convey Bernardo's unconditional denial that he stabbed Patty.

"Bernardo, let me ask you a direct question to which I want your direct answer." He left the podium and approached his client. He leaned on the railing, making sure he didn't block the jury's view of Bernardo's face. "Did you at any time, on the day Ms. Gregory was stabbed, go to her residence on Amherst Drive?"

Bernardo's face took on a solemn, almost sullen expression. "No, sir. I did not." His voice broke, betraying his emotions.

"Please look at the jury, Bernardo, when you answer my next questions." He gestured to the jurors with a movement of his head. "Do

261

you deny ever going to Ms. Gregory's residence, as she testified that you did?"

Bernardo turned his somber eyes toward the jury. "I deny it, sir!" he said, as if addressing a drill sergeant's interrogation. His eyes never left the jurors.

"Do you deny that you stabbed Ms. Gregory three times on that day?"

"I deny it." He kept looking into the eyes of the jurors.

"Can you explain, then, why she has testified that you were the one who stabbed her?"

"No, sir, for the love of God, I can't." He paused in thought. "Except to say that she has mistaken me for the person who did it."

"But it wasn't you."

"It wasn't me, sir."

"No further questions, your honor," he said as he walked away from Bernardo and returned to his chair. He turned to Keith. "Your witness." He sat down.

Keith stood up with his note pad in hand and went to the podium.

"Are you left handed, Mr. Soliz?" he asked.

"Yes, sir," Bernardo replied.

"You heard Ms. Gregory testify she believed the person who attacked her was left-handed, didn't you?"

"Yes, sir."

"The day you were arrested, when was the last time—"

"Objection, your honor," John said, standing up. "The evidence doesn't show Mr. Soliz was arrested. He turned himself in."

Before the judge had an opportunity to respond, Keith corrected himself. "Pardon me, your honor, Mr. Garcia's correct." He addressed Bernardo once again. "On the day you turned yourself in, Mr. Soliz, when was the last time before then that you had washed your hair?"

"Since I was arrested," Bernardo said, obviously confused.

"No—before. Did you wash your hair on the day you went to metro court and turned yourself in?"

"I don't recall."

"Well, you recall having your picture taken at the police department on that day, don't you?"

"Yes, sir."

Keith walked to the reporter's table and picked up the photograph taken of Bernardo on the day he was booked. He handed it to him. "And that exhibit is that picture, isn't it?"

Bernardo glanced at the photograph. "Yes."

"And you testified earlier that your hair was over your ears then, isn't that right?"

"Yes, sir."

"But it isn't over your ears in that picture, is it?"

"No, sir."

"And that picture was taken on the day you turned yourself in, when you had said your hair was over your ears."

"I didn't have it combed when I went to metro court to turn myself in."

"Why not?"

"I didn't have time."

"Why didn't you have the time?"

"Because I had heard they had an arrest warrant for me, and I was in a hurry to get to court. I didn't want to be arrested."

After asking more questions concerning Bernardo's hair style and overall appearance before and after the lineup, Keith moved on to his alibi, asking question after question.

"And so a moment ago, when you were reciting to Mr. Garcia the programs you watched on TV that evening when you claim you were at your parents' house, you left out *Have Gun, Will Travel*, didn't you?"

"Yes, sir."

"You watched it in fact?"

"That's correct, sir."

"You must have forgotten to mention it, I guess," Keith said with a bit of sarcasm. "Have you discussed this," he went on, "with your parents and your sister? What you were watching that night, I mean."

"No, sir," Bernardo said with a slight tone of hostility. "I didn't need to discuss it. I know what I was doing that night and didn't have to discuss it with anyone."

John realized he had made a mistake in not going over this fine point with Bernardo. It was obvious the young man was now becoming a little defensive with Keith's questions because he must have thought Keith was suggesting he and his family had gotten together to make up the alibi story. John now wished he had emphasized to Bernardo there wasn't anything wrong with the family members comparing notes. Because there was nothing wrong in doing that, he needn't have reacted as he did. As a result, John now sensed Keith would take advantage of Bernardo's misunderstanding.

"Let me get this straight, Mr. Soliz," Keith said. "You haven't discussed it with them?"

"No, sir, I haven't," Bernardo answered.

"Have you talked to them?"

"I've talked to them, but not about that."

"You've never talked to your parents and your sister about what you were doing that night?"

"No, sir."

"Have you talked to Mr. Garcia about it?"

"Yes, I told *him*."

"But you've never talked with any member of your family about what went on that evening?"

"I didn't need to. I know what I did that night because I was there. I'm not just telling you what I did because that's what they said. I'm saying it because it's the truth!"

"Speaking of the truth, let's go over the time when you stepped out into the shed." Keith paused to review his notes. "Could you be mistaken about the length of time you were gone?"

"No, sir, I'm not."

"How can you be so sure about that, Mr. Soliz?"

"Because I remember leaving about ten minutes after eight and returning to the living room about twenty minutes before nine, that's why. Carmen and her husband were still there when I went back into the house."

"What time did your sister and her husband leave your parents' house that night?"

"I remember she testified her husband arrived at eight thirty and they left a few minutes later. That sounds about right."

"If she was mistaken about that, and left closer to nine, that means you may not have returned until sometime closer to nine, isn't that correct?"

"But she wasn't mistaken because I remember what time I returned, and she and her husband left only a couple of minutes after I got back."

Keith hesitated, appearing as if wanting to continue this line of questioning but instead moved on to the time disparity. "Your parents and sister said you were gone a few minutes, and you told Mr. Garcia they were mistaken about that, didn't you?"

"Yes, 'cause I actually looked at the clock and they're just estimating the time, I think."

"Why did you go out to the shed, anyway?"

"We have an extra bathroom back there. Besides, I lost interest in the TV program I was watching, and I thought it was a good time to go."

"It took you thirty minutes to do that?" Keith asked.

"No, but I laid down on the bed to rest for a minute 'cause I didn't want to watch the rest of the program until the movie came on at nine."

"But you returned to the living room earlier than that, didn't you? About twenty of nine?"

"Yes, sir."

"You said your parents and sister were mistaken in guessing you were gone for a few minutes."

"Objection, your honor," John said. "Mr. Keith is mis-characterizing the testimony of the witness. He said he believed they were *estimating*, not *guessing*."

"I'll rephrase the question, your honor," Keith said, not waiting for a ruling from the judge. "Let me ask you, Mr. Soliz—could your parents and sister also be mistaken about the fact that you left the room after eight o'clock and not before?"

"No, sir."

"Why not?"

"Because I looked at the clock, and it was about ten after eight, that's why I know they aren't mistaken." Bernardo paused. "Besides, even if it had been before eight, the time I was gone wouldn't have given me enough time to go that distance and stab Ms. Gregory and then return to the house."

"Unless you, yourself, are mistaken about the length of time you were gone, isn't that right?"

"But I'm not mistaken!"

"Are you sure about that, Mr. Soliz?" Keith asked.

"Yes, I'm positive," Bernardo said with emphasis.

Keith next moved on to other areas John had covered on direct examination to clarify some points. When the prosecutor completed his examination, John asked only a few brief questions to correct several impressions he himself thought Keith's questions might have left with the jury. Some of John's questions were intended to convince the jury that despite Bernardo's defensiveness when replying to Keith's questions, he was a credible witness. John hoped the jury would realize that if innocent, any person fighting for his life might act defensively.

With his last questions of Bernardo, John rested his defense. It was already eleven forty. Judge Walker excused the jurors for lunch, asking them to return by one fifteen so the trial could continue at one thirty. Before recessing, the jurist allowed John to make a record on his renewed motions for dismissal and for a directed verdict. Such motions were rarely granted, but they were necessary to preserve certain errors in the event an appeal was taken. Again, as John expected, the judge denied his motions. He then asked John and Keith to return by one o'clock, when they would review the instructions to be given to the jury.

Later that afternoon, Judge Walker instructed the jury on the law of the case. After the judge finished reading the instructions, Keith began his closing argument, outlining his version of the evidence presented during the trial. He spoke for about forty minutes, leaving twenty minutes of the one hour he had been allotted for rebuttal. Because the state in a criminal case had the burden of proving a defendant's guilt beyond a reasonable doubt, the prosecutor was permitted the opportunity to argue last before the jury. John's closing argument took a little over an hour and was followed by Keith's final pitch to the jury.

The jury began its deliberations a few minutes before four o'clock. At six, Judge Walker returned the jurors to the courtroom and arranged for the bailiff and a sheriff's deputy to accompany them to dinner at a local restaurant. They returned at seven thirty to continue their deliberations. At about nine thirty, they sent a written request to Judge Walker that they wanted to review parts of Patty's direct examination. The judge reconvened the jury in the courtroom, and the court reporter read from her notes the portions of Patty's testimony the jury had requested. The testimony dealt with Patty's descriptions of her assailant and her later ID testimony involving Bernardo's photographs and the lineup.

When the court reporter completed reading the testimony, Judge Walker informed the jury he was considering dismissing it for the night. The jurors could then continue their deliberations the next morning when they would be rested, the judge told them. In response, they asked to be permitted to go on with their deliberations that night. The jurist polled Keith and John to find out their preference. Both opted to go along with the jurors' desires.

At eleven forty five, when no word had been heard from the jurors, Judge Walker informed John and Keith that he wanted to reconvene the jurors in the courtroom to poll them. When the jurors were seated, the judge requested that they report where the total voting among them stood, without revealing if the vote was for conviction or for acquittal or how each juror had voted. A middle-aged man had been selected foreman. He reported the jury was deadlocked seven to five. The judge then questioned the jurors individually to find out if they thought they could reach a verdict that night. They assured the jurist that they wanted to try.

Before releasing the jury, Judge Walker asked them to wait in the courtroom while he and counsel discussed a matter of procedure in his chambers. There, the judge informed John and Keith that he believed the length of time the jury had taken to deliberate warranted the giving of what has been termed in court parlance as the "shotgun" instruction. John voiced his objection, expressing his belief that the instruction was unduly coercive, forcing the jury to rush to a decision. He reminded the judge that a state bar committee, under the direction of the New Mexico Supreme Court, was considering abolishing the instruction precisely because it had been questioned as coercive, thus generating needless issues on appeal. The judge, believing the instruction would benefit the jury's deliberations, overruled John's objection.

Besides the legal basis for his objection to the instruction, John had strategic reasons as well to argue against the giving of the instruction. He reasoned that, if the juror's vote remained deadlocked, thus resulting in a "hung" jury, the jury would be dismissed and a new trial held at a later date. This was because the verdict had to be unanimous for conviction or acquittal. In a criminal case, a hung jury was usually viewed as a victory for a defendant because it was considered proof that the defense had been successful in creating the existence of reasonable doubt in the jurors' minds. Forcing the state to retry a defendant often led to the state reevaluating the strength of its case and a consideration of an outright dismissal or plea bargain.

Returning to the courtroom, Judge Walker began addressing the jury. If the jury later returned a guilty verdict, John thought, as the judge was about to read the shotgun instruction, the jurist was providing an excellent ground for appeal. But he hoped it wouldn't come to that.

"Ladies and gentlemen of the jury," the jurist began. "Ordinarily I would have excused you for the night long ago so you could go home to rest and then proceed with your deliberations tomorrow. However, you've shown a desire to deliberate tonight, and I've allowed you to because counsel for the state and the defendant haven't objected. Now that you've shown your willingness to continue, the court believes it's necessary to give you an additional instruction to consider." He picked up the single sheet on which the shotgun instruction had been typed by the court reporter.

"It is your duty, as jurors," Judge Walker continued, "to consult with one another and to deliberate with a view of reaching an agreement, if you can do so without violence to your individual judgment. Each of you must decide the case for yourself but should do so only after a consideration of the case with your fellow jurors, and you should not hesitate to change an opinion when convinced that it is wrong. However, you should not be influenced to vote on any question by the single fact that a majority of the jurors favor such a decision.

"In other words, you shouldn't surrender your honest convictions concerning the effect or weight of the evidence for the mere purpose of returning a verdict, or solely because of the opinion of the other jurors. I hope that after further deliberations you may be able to agree on a verdict. That is why we try cases, to try to dispose of them and to reach a common conclusion, if you can do so, consistent with the conscience of the individual members of the jury. The court suggests that in deliberating, you each recognize you are fallible, that you hear the opinion of the other jurors, and that you do it conscientiously with a view of reaching a common conclusion, if you can."

After the instruction was read, the jury returned to the jury room.

It was one o'clock in the morning when an exhausted jury returned with a unanimous verdict. The jurors found Bernardo guilty of attempted murder in the second degree but recommended clemency. The fact that clemency was recommended suggested the jurors who had been holding out for acquittal, when the vote had been seven to five, had compromised. In return for their *guilty* vote, John surmised, the majority had promised the minority to vote for clemency.

Before the jury had begun its deliberations, during Judge Walker's review of the instructions, the jurist ordered that the clemency instruction would be given. John had objected to it because he believed it worked against a criminal defendant. It did so by giving jurors who had held out before by voting for acquittal the false impression they were giving the defendant a break by recommending clemency, if they changed their vote. On sentencing a defendant, trial judges hardly ever paid attention to such recommendations but relied instead on the pre-sentence report prepared by a probation officer. For these reasons, John thought the clemency instruction provided another basis for appeal.

CHAPTER 22

IT was almost two in the afternoon when John returned from the interview in Santa Fe. He forced himself to divert his thoughts from the meeting with the Appellate Nominating Commission, even though he thought it had gone well. The Commission, made up mostly of lawyers and judges, had met in the Supreme Court's ornate courtroom to interview nine candidates for the court vacancy.

As he approached the garage entrance of the Hyatt Office Tower, he had Demi on his mind and the concerns she had shared with him during the past weeks. They were now his concerns too, and he felt the need to tell her. Besides, she had asked him to call when he returned from the interview to let her know how it had gone.

He had finally approached her about her moodiness. She had been feeling much better when they had talked, and it surprised him that she spoke openly of her doldrums. She told him of an emotional change she thought their relationship was undergoing, describing hers as utter confusion and a desperate feeling of being overwhelmed by it all. Everything was happening so fast, she feared. Yet, she felt good about one

271

thing—his interest in the Supreme Court vacancy. In her heart, she felt that was a good move on his part. For that reason, he found himself wanting the job now more than ever, and he wanted to share that with her.

He hadn't been to her office in months. The urge to surprise her came as he was about to turn into the garage. He found himself passing it, headed instead for the intersection ahead, where he turned on the narrow street that would lead him to Herman Weingarten's offices.

Within minutes, he arrived at the offices, a converted Victorian house off Broadway near Lead Avenue. He was disappointed to find Demi had left for the day around one o'clock, which puzzled him. Herman invited him into his private office.

"Tell me, John," Herman said as he offered John a chair, "I heard you put in for that Supreme Court vacancy. How's that going?" They both sat down.

"Yeah, I decided to give it a shot," John replied. "In fact, I just returned from the interview."

"Oh. How did it go?"

"Fine, I think. You never know about those things."

"I'd be surprised if you didn't make the list. Won't the commission announce its recommendation before the end of the day?"

"Yes, but I decided not to go through the agony of waiting there. An acquaintance of mine on the commission said he'd call me when the results are made public this evening."

Herman nodded. "I wish you luck."

As he sat there listening to Herman chatter away, he found himself enjoying the unrushed pace of the office. There appeared a tranquil simplicity in Herman's sole practice that he welcomed. It was the old furniture and the antiques Herman had collected through the years as well as the hardwood floors that he found inviting.

Herman asked if he'd mind his pipe smoke. He said he wouldn't, and Herman relit a pipe setting on his desk. The tobacco's sweet aroma filled the air, which seemed to add to the warmth of the spacious room.

Herman rested his lean, angular figure against the high back of his chair. With one hand, he brushed his thick, white hair back, as he held the pipe to his mouth with the other. He wasn't wearing a coat, but wore a heavily starched, white shirt that was still neatly pressed, as if he had just put it on. He had loosened his tie and unbuttoned his collar.

"You're a busy man," Herman continued. "Demi told me a couple of weeks ago you had undertaken that criminal trial. I've kept up with it in the papers and read this morning of the conviction."

"Yes, it was disappointing." He briefed Herman on the events that had unfolded during the past week and the night before.

"Sounds to me as if you took on quite a challenge representing that young man. But really, that's just the thing that makes law practice exciting, isn't it?"

"I suppose so." John felt an uneasiness as he once again feared his dealings with the CIA and FBI might have affected his defense of Bernardo. He wondered if Herman sensed his discomfort.

He didn't get the chance to dwell on that, for Herman spoke. "It appears as if you had an uphill battle countering the victim's ironclad ID."

"It was tough going, but I gave it my best shot." Had he, though?

"That's all anyone can expect from us, of course—to do our very best." He paused to place his pipe on an ashtray. "Have you come to regret having taken on the case?"

"Not at all," he said without hesitation. He had been slouching on the chair and now straightened up. "Having taken on this case has made me realize there's more to law practice then what I've been doing the past several years. That's one reason I decided to put in for the vacancy on the Supreme Court."

"Yes. Demi mentioned that the other day." He picked up his pipe and placed it in his mouth without relighting it. "It's strange, isn't it, how we go treading along—no matter in what field, but especially the practice of law, I think—without considering changing the way we go about doing our work. We get so wrapped up in it without asking ourselves if there's a better way."

"That's the way I'm feeling about my practice at the moment—that it could have been different. I suppose I never took the time to think about it before. My work load has added to my doubts. That's because it's affecting our time as a family. It's straining our marriage, according to Demi, and I hate to say it, but it's just now dawning on me. She's worried and has been for quite some time without my knowing the extent of her worry."

"I've found that most persons whose marriage partners are lawyers come to understand that law practice indeed is a 'jealous mistress,' even more so when they're lawyers too. I've noticed, though, that Demi hasn't quite been herself lately. She seems preoccupied."

John felt a sinking sensation at the pit of his stomach. Herman had noticed. This was the second time since this ordeal began that he was seeing Demi through the eyes of someone else.

"Of course," Herman went on, "I wouldn't get too worked up over how you feel, if I were you. I've always admired you for your professionalism and drive. Yet, I've known many attorneys who have experienced doubts similar to what you're referring to. 'Burnout' I think some call it nowadays, a phenomenon shared by other pursuits." He relit his pipe, making a slight sucking noise. "But, I must say, the legal profession especially lends itself to such burnout."

He paused. "Do you remember Atticus Finch?" he said.

John pondered the query. "Wasn't he a character in a novel?"

"Yes, he's the protagonist in Harper Lee's classic novel about a sole practitioner. It's set in the Deep South sometime after the depression and was first published in '59 or '60, I believe. *To Kill a Mockingbird.*"

"I remember reading it," he said. "Saw the movie too. Gregory Peck played the lawyer."

"That's right. Gave a magnificent performance, I thought." He swivelled in his chair and took a small book from a shelf behind his desk. "Here's something you might find interesting reading." He handed the book to him.

"*In Search of Atticus Finch*," John read the title. He read the description in the cover. "Hmmm—a motivational book for lawyers." He smiled. "Is that what you think I need, Herman—a burst of motivation?"

Herman laughed. "No, not really. Actually, I was disappointed in the book. It lacked substance, I thought. But the author makes a good point concerning the issue you appear to be dealing with. That's the reason I recommend it." He smiled. "Why don't you take it and read it? I think you'll find you're not alone in experiencing those self doubts. According to the book, you've got plenty of company."

It was two thirty when he headed back to his office to check for messages and review the Soliz case. Judge Walker had scheduled a hearing mid-morning of the next day to consider several matters, including whether to continue Bernardo's bail as an appeal bond. Keith had telephoned John that morning before he left for Santa Fe to inform him of the judge's desire to hold the hearing. Before leaving for the interview, John had asked Lynda to call Bernardo and his parents to let them know of the hearing and to schedule an appointment with them at the office before the hearing.

Stopped at a traffic light on Central Avenue near *La Posada de Albuquerque*, a small hotel, John spotted Demi exiting the hotel's side entrance. She was followed by Dick Dunn. Stopping a few feet away from the hotel entrance, they exchanged a few words. They embraced, and Dick kissed Demi on what appeared to be the side of her neck. It happened so fast that John found it hard to register what was going on. Yet, he felt the immediate surge of adrenalin through his body, and for a moment, he thought he might pass out.

As Dick and Demi went their separate ways, he apparently to his office and Demi toward the corner where John waited for the green light, the driver of the car behind him honked. The light had turned. Demi hadn't seen him. As he drove, he saw Demi's car parked at the curb. He went almost a block before finding an empty parking space. He pulled into it, slammed on the brakes, and got out of the vehicle. As he hurried to meet Demi at her car, he noticed he was hyperventilating and that his hands were shaking. *Regain control*, he said to himself. There's got to be a sensible explanation. Demi deserves a chance to explain. Explain what, though—exiting a hotel, embracing, and an intimate kiss? It didn't look good, and he prepared himself for the worst.

She opened the door to her car when he was still a few yards away.

"Demi!" he called out.

She looked up. He noticed the shocked expression on her face. Right away, he felt a heavy, sinking weight inside his body, believing her look said it all. Words couldn't be more effective in confirming in his mind what he had seen with his eyes.

"John, you're back!" she said. "How did it go?" She closed the door without entering.

When he couldn't find the words, he brought his shaking hand to his forehead and looked down. Before he knew it, he lost what control he had so far managed to hang on to. "What the fuck's going on with you and Dick?" he blurted out. "I can't believe you'd—"

"Hold on, John! You've got this all wrong so let me explain—"

"What's there to explain. It's written all over your face."

"But we were just—"

"You were just what? Getting a quickie with Dick before he went back to his office and you went home to our kids. Is that what you fucking want to explain?"

Her face flushed, and she jerked the door open. "Fuck you, John. I don't have to listen to this crap! Don't even bother coming home unless you decide to cool off." She started the car.

Angrier now, he tried to open the door, but it had locked automatically when she turned on the ignition.

"Demi, wait!" he shouted through the closed window.

"Get your sorry ass out of my way," he heard her say as she stepped on the gas pedal.

He felt nauseous when he returned to his car and for a moment thought he'd throw up. Then another upsurge of anger overcame him, and he felt compelled to confront Dick. He found him in his private office, not remembering how he got there.

"Hi, John," Dick began as John stormed in, "how did it go with the—"

"I saw you and Demi coming out of the hotel together," John interrupted.

"Hold it a sec', John. Did you talk to Demi?"

"I didn't need to. Her guilt was all over her face and I—"

"Calm down. You're mistaken about this. We were just having a late lunch and a drink at the hotel's restaurant."

"You expect me to swallow that. Since when did you and Demi start having lunch together?"

"Sit down and listen, for Pete's sake. Demi called and said she needed to talk to me."

"About what?" Feeling weak, he sat down.

"About you, as it turned out. She wouldn't tell me when she called but insisted we not meet here. She was concerned it'd raise questions among the staff, and I agreed."

Dick went on to explain Demi's concern that John's work was creating problems for them. She had wanted to know Dick's opinion on how John was managing at the office. He had insisted to her everything was fine, but she was growing worried he wasn't being objective in assessing his ability to handle his work.

"How do I know you're not just trying to cover your ass?"

"You know, John, I'm starting to see what Demi was getting at. A part of me is wanting to tell you to get the hell out of my office because I don't give a rat's ass what you think of me. What's keeping me from doing that is I think you're being utterly unfair to Demi at a time she's worried about you and cares about your marriage. That's the fucking irony of all this."

"Why the secrecy? She and I already have an ongoing dialogue about this."

"Would you stop letting your paranoia get the best of you and come to your senses! Look at this from her point of view for a moment, not yours. You damn well know you wouldn't have understood if she told you she was coming to see me. She got desperate and wanted someone else's opinion; someone like me who has his hands on what's going on in this firm. Can't you see? She was just seeking information and another perspective to deal with what's going on between you. Besides, I got the distinct impression she planned telling you about our visit as soon as she could sort things out." He sighed.

"If you made the mistake of confronting Demi a while ago," he continued, "you owe her a big apology. So I suggest you get your butt on home and work your way out of this one."

A minute ago, he couldn't have imagined feeling any worse, but he did now. "I owe you an apology, too, Dick," he said. "I've handled this poorly and feel like an asshole."

"It's forgotten, as far as I'm concerned. But go on home to Demi and forget about me."

"I think I will." He stood up.

"Listen, one last thing, though, before you get away. Your jumping to conclusions like this tells me you're really stressed out."

"I won't argue the point. So?"

"Demi made a vague reference to something other than your work that might be eating at you. I thought she was referring to your decision to go for the court vacancy, but she said that wasn't it. I didn't pursue it because she seemed hesitant to discuss it. Is there something else going on?"

He nodded. "Yeah, but it's not anything you can help with. Demi's right, though. I'm beginning to think it's affecting me more than I thought at first." He took a deep breath. "Again, Dick, I'm sorry this happened."

Dick placed his hand on his shoulder and followed him to the door. "You needn't add this to your worries, so don't." He half-smiled.

John went straight home. The children were in their rooms doing their homework, and he spent a few minutes with them. He found Demi alone in the sitting room just off their bedroom. She had been crying, he could tell. She didn't ask him to leave. He asked her to forgive him for being such a jerk. She didn't respond at first, but then told him she needed time to think about their future. She didn't plan to leave him, she said, but thought a trial separation might give both of them time and space to think and to help calm things down. It was then he decided to reveal to her the true nature of the CIA's interest in him and of the agency's theory that their lives were in danger. Neither his confession nor his explanation that he had kept the truth from her because he didn't want her to worry did anything to quell her renewed anger.

"How could you, John?" she cried after he explained details of all he had learned from Kelly and Quigley. "After what you pulled this afternoon, and now this, how can I ever trust you?"

"I admit I was wrong, Demi," he answered. "What happened this afternoon made me realize just how much everything's been affecting the way I deal with issues. And I honestly felt Kelly was wrong; that the CIA was making much ado about nothing. That's why I didn't think you needed to know. I thought it'd blow over. I turned out to be wrong."

"Oh, John, that's so lame. Leave me alone. I want to be by myself. Please."

He felt he didn't deserve to utter another word, and so he acceded to her wish and left. After he undressed and put on some warm ups, the call from Santa Fe came. He and two other candidates had made the list. He tried acting relieved and happy about the news with the caller and thought he succeeded in doing that. But in reality, his making the cut did little to lift his spirits.

He went into his study and stayed there most of the evening, except for going into Crystal's and Johnny's bedrooms to say goodnight and making a sandwich for himself in the kitchen, which he took upstairs to the study. Much later, when he heard Demi getting ready for bed, he walked into the bedroom and told her of the call from Santa Fe.

"Congratulations," she said with little emotion as she went into the bathroom and closed the door.

Never before had he felt such loneliness—emptiness—despite the good news. Even Demi didn't seem to care.

CHAPTER 23

THE meeting with the Solizes was scheduled at nine. Judge Walker had set the hearing at ten thirty, so John had plenty of time to talk to the Solizes before the hearing.

He arrived at the office earlier than usual. Although he and Demi had been civil to each other as the children got ready for school, he felt awkward, for he sensed she didn't want him around. He had been tempted to force the issue with her but decided it'd be better if he waited. He had learned through the years that she needed more time than he did to cool off when they had an argument. Without doubt, he had blown it the day before and would now have to suffer the consequences. Even though he still felt a sickening emptiness when he got to the office, he managed to put the matter of his screw up aside so he could get to his tasks.

Some of his time was spent accepting congratulations from the staff. Dick Dunn and Edmund Runyan popped into his office to offer their congratulations, as did other colleagues. Dick didn't bring up their discussion of the day before.

One of the last things he did before meeting with the Solizes was to talk to Guy, who called to congratulate him.

"I heard from a reliable source in the Governor's office," Guy said, "that the Governor's going to move fast on this appointment. As soon as next week, matter of fact."

"You've got to be kidding," John said. "That quick?"

"That's my understanding. You'll probably get a call soon setting up an interview sometime next week."

"This is moving a lot faster than I expected."

"You better get ready to make the move. One of the candidates is a Republican, so you know he doesn't stand a chance with this governor. That leaves you and the other fellow, and from what I hear, he doesn't have the right kind of support. So in my book you're a cinch to get the nod. This couldn't have worked out better if I had orchestrated it myself."

"Now that you got me into this, Guy, I've got a big favor to ask of you."

"Just name it, bro'."

"Should this appointment come through, I'd like for you to consider taking on the Soliz appeal. I feel strongly Bernardo's got a better than 50-50 chance of reversal. I'm planning to file a motion for a new trial soon. I'll barely be getting into it when someone else will have to take over. I can't think of a better lawyer to handle this kind of case than you."

"Have you talked to the kid about this?"

"I'm meeting with him and his parents later this morning. I plan to fill them in on what's happening with the appointment."

"Well, break it to them and if they feel comfortable with my talking to them about representing the kid, I'll do it."

"Good. Thanks. I'm going to recommend you, just in case the appointment comes through."

"It's going to happen, I tell you."

"Well, we'll see. If it doesn't, I'm prepared to go forward with the appeal. If it does, I'll be owing you a big favor."

"You won't owe me a thing. Besides, as a Supreme Court Justice, you don't want to be owing lawyers any favors."

He managed to laugh. "I've got to run, Guy. Thanks for being a good friend. I'll touch base with you later."

"*Adios, amigo.*"

"See you."

A few minutes later, he met a sullen Bernardo and his parents in the reception room. He escorted them into his office and offered them coffee. Reinaldo accepted, and John asked Lynda to bring two cups of coffee, one for himself.

As John sat at his desk, he noticed Bernardo appeared nervous, as well as depressed. That his client seemed to be down didn't necessarily surprise him. The nervousness, however, puzzled him. He knew of nothing imminent to explain it.

"I realize," he began in Spanish, "this wasn't the ending we were hoping for. I know too this ordeal hasn't been easy for any of you. And now, you face a continuation of that with post-trial motions and the upcoming appeal." He sighed. "I tried my best, and I want you to know that." But had he been at his best, he wondered as he studied their faces. Had his occupation with the LaPierre case diminished his effectiveness?

He next went on to alert them of his candidacy for the Supreme Court appointment. He took several minutes to explain his increasing interest in the position, the selection process, and lastly the fact that his name was being submitted to the Governor for the eventual appointment, which could take place anywhere from a week to a month. In the event he was selected, he told them, he wouldn't be able to handle Bernardo's appeal. They had been listening with grave interest.

"What's gonna happen to my case?" Bernardo asked when he had finished.

"If I get the appointment, it'll be a few weeks before I could take office because I'd have to wind up or reassign the cases I'm handling to other lawyers. I'll have just enough time to prepare some of the paperwork for the hearing on the motion I intend to file for you."

"But after that? Who's gonna represent me?"

He explained his talk with Guy and Guy's willingness to handle the appeal, as well as the post-trial hearing he planned to ask for on the motion for a new trial.

There was an awkward moment of silence when he finished. Reinaldo spoke first.

"We're satisfied, Mr. Garcia," he said, "that you did all you could to help. My wife is angry at the jurors for convicting our son, but I myself don't blame them. As you yourself reminded us many times—the evidence against Bernardo was strong." He sighed. "But as far as this new turn of events, although it catches us by surprise, it can't be helped. You have your own life and career, and we wish you well with this position you're seeking. There are some things we can't control."

John noticed Ramona's reaction to her husband's reference—her anger toward the jury. He could tell she was on the verge of tears. Bernardo, who was sitting next to her, had his downcast eyes gazing at the floor. In an attempt to console her, he turned to her and placed his hand on hers, which was resting on her lap. She appeared tiny sitting there, almost lost in the big arm chair.

"It's natural for you to be angry," John said to Ramona, not knowing what else to say. "After all, you believed in your son's innocence. And, in finding him guilty, the jury essentially rejected your testimony."

Ramona lost the control she had managed to retain and broke out crying. John's words had uncovered a sensitive nerve. Reinaldo took out a handkerchief and gave it to his wife.

"*Bendito sea Dios!*" Ramona cried out through her tears. "Blessed be God! How could they do such a thing to my son? And now you'll be leaving the case." John could hardly make out her words, but her comment about his leaving the case didn't escape him since it followed her reference to what *the jury had done to her son.*

Bernardo placed his hand on his mother to console her. "Please don't cry, *Mama,*" he mumbled over her sobs, choking on his own words. "I don't like seeing you like this." He himself was ready to cry.

Reinaldo too seemed to find his wife's cries of despair too much to bear. He held his hands up to his eyes to remove his own tears, then looked up at John. "It's the *madre* in her that can't comprehend how this could happen to her own son," he said in an apparent attempt to explain the obvious. "She doesn't respect a system of justice that would do this to him. Please understand that, Mr. Garcia."

"I do," John replied. "I understand perfectly." At least, he thought, the possibility he might have to drop the case didn't appear to be as much a concern to them as was the fact that the reality of the conviction was apparently sinking in. Yet, his leaving the case might have added to their desperation; their hopelessness. He fixed his attention once again on Ramona, wondering what he could possibly say to make her feel better. "You should cry if you feel like it, *Señora* Soliz," he finally said. "It'll help you deal with what's happened, I think."

No one said anything for a long moment as Ramona cried into her hands. It was a difficult and long moment for him, for he pondered the strength of a loving mother's concern for her child. Especially one who faced imprisonment for a crime she believed he didn't commit. He thought of Crystal and Johnny. They were still in their tender years, but how would he react—how would he feel—if one of them was threatened by the same system later in life?

He felt an anger come over him. He was angry he hadn't succeeded in swaying the jury. What could he have done differently? Not only to avoid a conviction but to prevent the agony he witnessed in this poor woman? He had wanted to help so desperately.

Finally, Ramona's cries subsided. "*Perdóname, Señor Garcia,*" she said through her now softened sobs, "*pero nadie sabe como me siento cuando he perdido mi fe en la justicia.* "Pardon me, Mr. Garcia, but no one knows how I feel when I've lost my faith in justice. But I want to add to my husband's words. We appreciate your willingness to help. You have a good heart, and God will always bless you for that."

"You needn't apologize, Ms. Soliz," he said. "I too feel bad for what's happened. I've tried to help your family any way I can, and I'm sorry I may not be able to continue."

"We're grateful for what you've done already. We have faith in your trust that Mr. Zanotelli can help Bernardo. Please go on with what you wanted to say to us."

"As difficult as this may be for all of you, it's important you don't give up. We must try doing everything we can to overturn Bernardo's conviction. I want all of you to know Mr. Zanotelli is prepared to do that if I have to step out of the case. That is, if you agree to have him represent Bernardo."

"Of course we do," Reinaldo broke in. "I realize you yourself took on representing Bernardo without us paying you a cent, but I want to change that with Mr. Zanotelli. We'll try to raise whatever money it will take to—"

"No, Mr. Soliz," he interrupted, "that won't be necessary. Guy Zanotelli's willing to continue handling this case without pay. You needn't worry about the money."

Bernardo broke his silence. "We feel bad we've taken up weeks of your time." He didn't meet John's gaze. "As you said, I had hoped this would have ended with the trial. Now that it hasn't, my family would feel better if we paid Mr. Zanotelli something."

"He wouldn't hear of it, Bernardo. He knew I was representing you pro bono. He's willing to do that too."

"But I was hoping it'd end with the trial. Maybe we should end it right now and not appeal." Bernardo still wasn't making eye contact.

John was taken aback. Bernardo had changed the conversation from a willingness to pay for Guy's services to a suggestion that an appeal not be filed.

"Why would it even enter your mind not to appeal, Bernardo. I happen to believe you stand a good chance of getting a new trial."

"I just don't feel good relying on your help anymore or Mr. Zanotelli's help without paying for it, that's all," Bernardo said, not sounding convincing.

"But you can't afford to pay, Bernardo."

"We could try raising some money."

He didn't address Bernardo's comment. Instead, he said, "Besides, what does payment of a fee have to do with whether you appeal or not, if either I or Mr. Zanotelli represent you at no cost?"

"Nothing, I guess."

"Well, I suggest we don't mix them up."

Again, he noticed Bernardo seemed nervous, but he now also appeared to be afraid. It wasn't shame or embarrassment that his family couldn't pay for an appeal that he detected in Bernardo's demeanor. It was something else. What fear could Bernardo possibly have in his continuing to represent him if he didn't get the appointment? Had the boy lost faith in his ability to handle the appeal? John hadn't detected that lack of confidence. He had noted such misgivings in clients before, and he sensed that wasn't what was bothering Bernardo. Instead, it was an apprehension he sensed. He decided to get to the bottom of it, realizing it could be his own insecurity that was causing his suspicions.

"Bernardo, let me ask you a pointed question," he said, looking at him straight in the eye. "Are you content with the way I represented you? I'd like for you to think hard before answering."

"I don't need to think about it, Mr. Garcia," Bernardo replied. "I don't understand why you would ask that." He appeared uncomfortable about the turn the discussion had taken.

"Just answer the question."

Bernardo glanced over at his parents, then turned to John. He appeared embarrassed now. "Sure, I'm satisfied. Even before you told us, I knew it was going to be an uphill battle." He looked downward, then returned his gaze at John. "What have I said that's made you think I'm not satisfied?"

"It's not what you've said. But I get the impression you're concerned about something. Are you afraid of appealing?"

"No." Bernardo hesitated. "But I'm afraid for my parents and my wife—of giving them false hope. And I'm concerned about the time you or Mr. Zanotelli would spend on the case for nothing if we were to lose. Maybe we should let the judge sentence me now instead of waiting on an appeal just to postpone my jail time. If I appealed, maybe he would give me a stiffer sentence." He frowned, as if not appreciating the prospect. "Wouldn't he?"

"I doubt it. Judge Walker is a fair man. He realizes there are legitimate grounds for an appeal. And, I might add, there are valid grounds for the motion I intend filing."

"Why don't you explain what you think is going to happen on that?"

"I'll do that, Bernardo, but I'd like to continue our conversation concerning how you feel about appealing. I'd like to see you alone on that sometime next week. Why don't you call Lynda Monday morning so she can schedule an appointment for you?"

"All right."

John then went on to explain the basis for the motion he intended to file. He summarized the grounds for the motion, as well as for the appeal, should the motion be denied. Generally, there were four basic issues John intended to argue.

First was the suggestive nature of the photographs used by Morales. Second was the possible tainting of the lineup identification from the use of the suggestive photos. The third issue was the shotgun instruction given to the jury. The "clemency" instruction was the fourth basis.

It was ten o'clock when the Solizes left. John told them he'd meet them at the courthouse in twenty minutes.

As was his custom when conferring with clients in his office, John had asked Lynda to hold all telephone calls during his meeting with Bernardo and his parents. One of the calls was from Kelly. Earlier, the agent had spoken to him about Quigley's trips to Athens and Paris. Kelly told him of the envelope the elder LaPierre had in safekeeping. At least two known deaths now could be attributed to Henri's mystifying story—one a few days ago, and the other almost thirty years before.

Kelly had wanted to know if John had time to fly to Paris to retrieve the envelope. Anxious to discover what was in the mysterious envelope, John suggested Kelly have someone look into possible flights later that day. He would then have Lynda reschedule his work week to allow for the trip.

He telephoned Kelly. The agent had just learned of his possible court appointment and wished him well. Then he got down to business. He had found a flight out of Albuquerque that would get John into LaGuardia in New York late that night. The transatlantic flight was to leave for Paris in the wee small hours of the morning. Quigley would meet him at the Paris airport Friday morning. The agent had already arranged a meeting with Paul LaPierre at the Frenchman's home around noon that same day. A return flight already booked out of Paris the following day could be changed if it turned out they needed to stay longer.

At the hearing a few minutes later, Judge Walker asked if John intended representing Bernardo through the sentencing phase. John confirmed that had been his intent but explained he might not be able to in the event he was chosen to fill the vacancy on the Supreme Court. If that were to happen, John told the jurist, Guy Zanotelli would most likely enter an appearance in the case. Judge Walker said he understood and congratulated John. He had heard the news on TV the night before. The judge then asked about the likelihood of an appeal. John explained he had discussed it with the Solizes, and it was likely the conviction would be appealed. Guy Zanotelli might handle that as well.

Judge Walker allowed the property bond to continue. That meant Bernardo wouldn't be incarcerated during the sentencing phase and the appeal. The judge then directed the probation officer to meet with Bernardo and gather information for the pre-sentence report. Before adjourning, he scheduled the sentencing hearing the fourth week in October.

When John returned to the office, he telephoned Demi to explain the whirlwind events of the morning and his sudden flight to Paris. Although she appeared stunned, he could still detect an indifference in her tone. She agreed to meet him at the 4th *Street Café* for a quick lunch. He didn't expect the lunch would be without tension, but he wanted to see her before he left. Being apart for a few days might be a good thing under the circumstances. Before leaving the office to meet her at the restaurant, he met with Lynda to rearrange his schedule for the rest of the week.

"What's going on, John?" Lynda asked when he gave a cryptic explanation of the unexpected trip. "Is anything the matter?"

He forced a smile. "No," he lied. "Just a quick trip on some personal business," he added when he realized how arcane his trip must have seemed. In the past, she had always booked his flights. He realized his change of plans, along with the lack of specifics, gave her good reason to be concerned. "A friend booked the flight," he explained, "if you're wondering. I'm doing him a favor."

Lynda seemed as perplexed as ever. "I'm not trying to meddle," she said, "but I hope you understand why I'm worried. You haven't been your usual self during the past couple of weeks, and I didn't know if it was the Soliz case or something in your personal life you'd rather not talk about."

"Neither," he lied again. He felt guilty, for he thought Lynda, who had always been loyal to him, deserved a more direct answer. "Well, that's not quite true," he added. "Let's just say I've been doing a lot of thinking about my life. I've got a feeling I'll be explaining it all to you sometime soon, and it'll make sense then. Meanwhile, I don't want you to worry."

Before he left to meet Demi, he got a call from the Governor's appointment secretary, who wanted to know if he was available for an interview Monday morning the following week. Lynda confirmed that he was, and so he told the Governor's assistant he could make the interview. She was still attempting to coordinate and confirm the availability of the two other candidates, the assistant told him, so she would call later to confirm the time. John suggested she talk to Lynda, for he was leaving town.

After lunch, he said goodbye to Demi outside the restaurant. He could tell she was apprehensive about his trip, even though it was apparent she hadn't forgiven him. He went home to pack, where Kelly showed up later with the plane tickets. Kelly drove him to the airport.

His plane landed at DeGaulle International Airport a few minutes before noon the following day. He managed only a couple of hours of sleep but was surprised when he walked off the plane he wasn't tired from jet lag. He assumed it was because of his anticipation of meeting Paul LaPierre. Quigley met him in a rented car. The two men grabbed a quick lunch at a small diner they wandered upon by accident.

During the hurried lunch, Quigley mentioned Kelly had told him of the potential court appointment, and he wished John luck. He then gave him a quick rundown on what he had uncovered in Athens and his visit with Paul LaPierre. It was from Quigley that he learned of the key.

"A key?" John exclaimed. He was intrigued by the turn of events, as well as by the thought that unknown events occurring long ago were revealing themselves now. "What could it be to?"

"Mr. LaPierre thought maybe a safety deposit box," Quigley responded, "or some other locked compartment somewhere in Paris."

"Are you thinking what I'm thinking?"

"Possibly. What are you thinking?"

"That whatever the key opens contains something connected to Henri's project?"

The agent smiled. "I'd say chances are good that it does. And I'd be willing to bet it contains more than a mere copy of his story."

"Are you suggesting some sort of documentation?"

Quigley nodded.

They left the diner and continued their journey to the LaPierre residence. Quigley rubbed his eyes, and for the first time, John noticed he looked tired.

"You must be beat," he said. "I bet you've had an exhausting week."

Quigley nodded. "But I'm used to this sort of thing." He grinned. "You'll be beat too before the week's over."

"I suppose. I didn't get much sleep on the plane." He yawned. "Incidentally, where has Mr. LaPierre kept this envelope all these years?"

"In his own safety deposit box. When I called to tell him you were arriving today, he told me he planned to retrieve it."

John found Paul LaPierre to be a pleasant individual. Michelle, his housekeeper, had just brewed some hot tea, Mr. LaPierre told his two visitors. He insisted they join him in the library to have some. The rotund housekeeper soon appeared with the tea server and cups on a serving tray, left the tray on the coffee table, and quietly left the room.

Quigley and John sat on the sofa to enjoy the tea with their host, exchanging pleasantries as they sipped the tea. Mr. LaPierre showed considerable interest in John's career, asking especially about John's law practice. John obliged the Frenchman by recounting his short military career, his practice, and his family life. The man listened intently.

As he spoke of his work and his life since leaving Vietnam, he experienced an odd sensation. It was brought about, he thought, by the wonders of jet-age transportation. Here he was, a guest in the home of Henri LaPierre's father, whom he had never met before, thousands of miles from his home and over a quarter century after having met his host's son.

There were many events that were predictable—expected—in the course of one's life. But what of a defense litigator who just completed a criminal trial three days ago? What if he found himself transposed into a different world? Into the home of this elderly Frenchman, for example. That wasn't predictable. What other unforeseen events lay in store for him as a result of this intriguing new chapter in his life? He sensed he'd be better off not knowing.

"So you knew my son in Vietnam?" Paul LaPierre asked him finally.

"Yes," John answered. "But not as well as I would have liked."

"Obviously, *Monsieur* Garcia, well enough that he would entrust you with something he must have considered of utmost importance."

"I suppose so." As he spoke, he realized he wasn't hiding the fact he was a little dumbfounded Henri would entrust him with such material. "I assume, Mr. LaPierre, you're referring to the envelope you've kept all these years."

"Yes, but of course." A faint smile appeared on the man's face. "Strange, isn't it, how life has its many surprises. I've held on to that envelope for all these years. Most of the time, it was forgotten, except when I had occasion to open my safety deposit box. Every time my eyes came upon the envelope, I wondered, *Monsieur* Garcia, who you were that Henri should want you to have what was in it. I even found myself wondering what you looked like, if you can imagine that."

He smiled again and continued. "Of course, I've never attempted to find you, for I've followed my son's wishes implicitly. His express instructions were that I was to turn it over to you only if you yourself contacted me. I assumed from that, possibly wrongly, that you were to have both knowledge and possession of the envelope's contents on one condition—only if you should learn of it through some direct communication from my son." He turned to Quigley. "A few days ago, I learned from *Monsieur* Quigley the circumstances under which you discovered Henri's wish that you receive certain information. I presume he was referring to the contents of that envelope."

"Yes," John said, "we too concluded as much."

"Oh, well, the envelope, then." He stood up, went to the small desk setting near the wall, opened a drawer, and took out a discolored manila envelope. "I suppose you gentlemen wish to carry on with the business you came here to do." He returned to his chair, reached over, and handed the envelope to John.

He then drank what was left of his tea and stood up. "Let me leave you gentlemen alone so you can open it in private. I'll go into the parlor. It's down the hallway there to the right. You can come fetch me if you should need me. I'm at your service while you are guests in my house."

He walked slowly, even with a cane, and disappeared into the hallway.

John looked at Quigley and gestured to the envelope in his hand. "You want to do the honors, Quigley?"

"Of course not," the agent replied. "Like Mr. LaPierre said, let's honor his son's request. It's addressed to you, so go ahead and open it."

Carefully, he tore open the envelope. He looked into it and saw the key. He took it out and gave it to Quigley, while he pulled out the envelope's other contents—a two-page letter. Once again he recognized Henri's handwriting but noticed the letter appeared to have been written in a hurry. He read it to himself.

July, 1973

Dear John,

If you're reading this letter, it will mean that either our mutual friend, Leroy Etcitty, or I was successful in reaching you to request you contact my parents in Paris, France. I've tried reaching you, to no avail, and finally wrote to Leroy, hoping he might know how to get in touch with you. I've left explicit instructions with my parents that they safeguard the envelope containing this letter and key and to release it only to you and no one else. They will know that, should you contact them, I will have succeeded in reaching you so you could have access to the material I entrust to you and you alone.

I realize only too well that I'm imposing upon you, but I didn't know where else to turn at a time when I'm fearing for my life. I'm writing to you from my parents' home in Paris, having returned to see them for what may be the last time.

I'm entrusting certain documents to you, including my completed story I intended to publish before I left Vietnam. I leave it to your discretion to make effective use of the sensitive information I possess. I know you'll use your good judgment in getting it to the right persons. I'm returning to Athens, where I've been living (in hiding, to be truthful) for the past year. There, I plan to dispose of another copy of my story, other documents, and duplicate notes. I had planned publication of the material but have run out of time. At this moment, my life's in danger, and I must deal with that first.

The key inside this envelope is to a storage locker you'll find at a railway station in the outskirts east of Paris. The locker contains a suitcase in which I've placed the material I want you to have. Once again, I apologize for the inconvenience this may cause you. I realize my request may place even your own life in danger. Unfortunately, I don't know what else to do, for you are the only person I can trust to get this important information to the proper authorities. I'm afraid I have little time left.

Kindest regards, John, and God bless you.
Your friend always, Henri

When he finished reading the letter, he passed it on to Quigley.

Quigley took the letter and gave him the key. "The key's got a number on it," he said as he turned his attention to the letter.

"I'll ask Mr. LaPierre to join us," he said when he finished reading it. "We'll need his help in finding that railway station." He returned the letter to John.

Quigley disappeared into the hallway and soon reappeared with Paul LaPierre by his side.

"Why don't you let Mr. LaPierre read it?" the agent said.

John handed the letter to Mr. LaPierre. Paul LaPierre sat, put on a pair of reading glasses setting on top of an end table, and began reading. When he finished, he first glanced at John, then turned to Quigley. John thought he noticed teary eyes behind the glasses.

"Oh, Henri, my son," Mr. LaPierre said in a half whisper. "If I had known then what he was going through, possibly, just possibly, I could have done something to help him." He kept looking at the letter held tightly in his gnarled hands.

John was moved by the man's sentiments. He handed him the key. "Would you happen to know which train station Henri was referring to?" he asked.

Mr. LaPierre examined the key and nodded. "There's only one it could be. But I'm afraid it burnt down about twenty years ago and has been abandoned ever since. A new one was constructed several miles further down the railroad line."

"That's not good news," Quigley said. "Do you think the storage lockers are still there, Mr. LaPierre?"

"I can't say. As I recall, they were in the main part of the terminal, which wasn't terribly damaged by the fire." His attention returned to the letter, and he reread it.

After thanking Paul LaPierre for his help and bidding him farewell, John and Quigley followed the Frenchman's directions and drove to the abandoned railway station.

They were relieved to find the main building intact. The outside walls were still standing, and the roof in the central portion of the building appeared not to have been damaged much by the fire. They parked on the side of the building.

The station was in an area isolated from the beaten path of present-day foot and vehicular traffic. For this reason, Quigley told John, there was a good chance the lockers hadn't been ransacked or destroyed. But had they been removed, John wondered.

They entered the building through a side entrance.

This particular part of the structure was full of debris. Parts of the roof, rotted with age, had fallen into the building through the years. Large pieces of roof timber and roof tile covered the floor. As the two men entered the central or terminal part of the large building, Quigley spotted the lockers against a far wall.

"There they are," he said in a tone revealing his excitement. He took out the key to verify the locker's number, even though they were still a few yards from the lockers.

"Well, a good number of them are still here," John said as they moved across the debris.

"Let's hope the one we're looking for is one of them." Quigley shook his head. "You know—we're very lucky. Your friend, Henri, never expected this suitcase to be found so many years after he hid it."

"You're right. Besides, I suppose he thought he'd find me before anything happened to him."

"Precisely." Quigley moved carefully through the cluttered area.

"It's a good thing the fire didn't reach into this part of the building or we'd find nothing but ashes inside the locker."

Close to two hundred lockers spanned the width of the wall. Near the middle of them, they found the one they were looking for. Quigley took the key from his pocket and inserted it into the lock. He found it difficult to get the key to go in all the way. Through the years, a thick layer of dust, sand, and grime had accumulated in the rusty lock.

After considerable effort, the key went in all the way, and Quigley turned it. But even after he rotated the key, the door wouldn't budge. John left Quigley there struggling with it to look for a piece of metal they could use as a lever. He soon returned with a long bar, which they used to pry the door open. After several frustrating minutes, the door gave way.

John breathed a sigh of relief when he spotted the leather suitcase. Through the years, the container had peeled and was covered with a thick layer of soot and dust. It appeared intact and undisturbed, however, since that time long ago when Henri had placed it there. Quigley gently pulled the suitcase out, as if it were delicate.

The agent took out his handkerchief and began wiping the thick layer covering the suitcase.

John began looking around for a place to set the suitcase on to open it. On the far wall, he spotted a long counter. "We can open it there," he said, pointing.

"As anxious as we both may be to see what's in it," Quigley said, "I suggest going back to the hotel room to open it."

"Why?"

"I'd hate to be found here by someone of authority and have to explain our presence; especially, what we're doing with this suitcase. Not that we'd be doing anything wrong, but I'd rather not risk having a lot of explaining to do."

"You've got a point. Let's move, then. You've just given me reason to be nervous."

Back in the hotel room, Quigley laid the old suitcase on the bed and opened it. It was jam packed with papers—Henri's handwritten notes, typewritten memos, copies of official documents, and brittle and yellowed writing tablets and newspaper clippings. The suitcase also contained various copies of military memoranda detailing procurement information involving many requisitions and shipments of supplies.

Quigley began gleaning the contents of the documents as he delicately pulled each one out of the suitcase. John picked up each document or set of documents to inspect as Quigley laid them aside. As he reviewed them, he tried absorbing as much information as possible. He realized he and Quigley were witnessing the work product of Henri's time-consuming investigation spanning more than a year of his short life.

As they sifted through the suitcase's contents, the thrust of their importance began to emerge. After all, Henri had given his life to protect what was in the container. The names of military personnel, as well as Vietnamese and Chinese officials, were repeated in many of the documents. The one that surfaced most was that of Colonel Emory M. Condon.

The final document Quigley pulled out of the container was the original manuscript of Henri's story. It was at the bottom of the pile of papers. As Quigley read each page of the manuscript, he passed it on to John and continued with the next page. In that manner, they spent the next hour reading accusatory documentation confirming the CIA's suspicions. Condon, as an officer in charge of procurement during his final tour, was involved in criminal activity.

The illegality included the embezzlement of millions upon millions of dollars worth of assorted supplies. In addition to implicating Condon of making hundreds of false entries in vouchers and requisitions, Henri provided proof he had accepted an unknown quantity of U. S. currency from unidentified sources. Receipt of the currency was payment for the diversion of supplies to the Chinese Communists. Although the story divulged the names of other U. S. military and Vietnamese officials, Condon was the highest ranking military officer involved in the illicit activity. The schemes had spanned a two-year period, the length of Condon's second tour in Southeast Asia.

The final pages noted that Henri believed he had only uncovered the tip of the iceberg. Losses in funds and supplies could well reach into the billions of dollars, he suspected. The People's Republic had been a major benefactor.

The article appeared well documented, for the many memos the journalist had included in the material verified his accusations and amounts. Condon's signatures appeared in many of the requisition documents. There was a paper trail following Condon's rerouting of supplies that later disappeared into the hands of various North Vietnamese and Chinese officers, as well as principals of various black markets in Saigon.

When they finished reading the manuscript, they spent another hour sifting once again through the material. They did so to comprehend the importance of what the Frenchman had uncovered.

"What do we do with all of this now?" John said as he dropped the final document on the bed. He was sitting on the bed, reclining his head against the headboard.

"For starters," Quigley said, "we'll go to the U. S. Embassy, where we'll make duplicate copies of these documents, as well as Henri's story."

"Why is that necessary?"

"You and I will take back the originals. The copies, we'll have returned to the U. S. by diplomatic courier. On occasion, our embassies throughout the world, as a favor or inter-agency courtesy, transport sensitive documents for us if we consider it essential to our national security. In that manner, we're assured at least one full set will arrive at CIA Headquarters."

"You're talking of a possible plane crash here, aren't you?"

"That's right. It's simply a precaution we've learned to take, after being burnt by lost originals in the past. It's become not only routine but an agency directive. If I failed to follow it, I'd be out of a job in no time flat."

"I see. Looks as if we hit the mother lode here, didn't we?"

"I'd say so."

"There's one thing that still puzzles me," John commented. "Even after going through this paper arsenal."

"What?"

"I realize these contents appear to implicate the Chinese Nationalists in the illicit activity. But why would they be interested in what we found after so many years after the fact? That doesn't make sense."

"I think Kelly was right—something's happened to renew their interest."

"What we found here doesn't explain that."

"Not that I can see."

They had made inroads, but there were still questions for which they had no answers.

"Are you calling Kelly?" John asked.

"I'll wait until we get to the embassy. They've got equipment there that'll scramble the voice signal. Now that we've verified what we've suspected all along, and have the documents to prove it, we're going to treat this information with the sensitivity that it deserves."

"Do you think Condon's aware of any of this?"

"I've no idea. But if he isn't, he's going to be in for the biggest surprise of his career."

"How will this be used against him?"

"I'm not prepared to say. Much of it will depend on decisions to be made by our director. I suppose the Attorney General, and possibly even the President himself, will become involved. There are so many implications that it'd be hard to say what's going to happen as a result of what we've uncovered."

"How do you think Henri would want us to act on this?"

"That's hard to say. But one thing's for sure."

"What's that?"

"He wanted what he had uncovered to be exposed. And that, he left up to you."

CHAPTER 24

THE following week, John telephoned Dan's office and spoke to Susan. He was disappointed to learn Dan was away for a few days and asked if the senator was expected in New Mexico anytime soon. She explained the senator was out of the country and referred him to Stella Chavez.

Dan was in Mexico City with a congressional delegation, Stella told him, and wasn't due back until Friday night. He had no immediate plans to travel to New Mexico. John explained it was urgent he meet with him. She informed him Dan planned to come into the office Saturday morning to catch up on the week's work. She could schedule an appointment then. Once he learned if he could book a flight, he told her, he'd be back in touch.

He asked Lynda to check on available flights. She confirmed he could catch one into National Airport early Saturday morning, arriving in Washington after lunch. He asked her to make reservations and set up the appointment.

The prior Friday, he had spoken by phone to Kelly from the U. S. Embassy in Paris. He wanted to know what his role should be concerning Henri's indictment against Condon. Should he play a part in any action to be taken against the senator? Would he feel he'd be carrying out Henri's wishes if he participated further, Kelly asked. John told him he would, but only if he could do so without compromising the CIA's efforts.

Soon after that conversation, Kelly had traveled to CIA Headquarters in Langley, Virginia. There, he briefed his immediate supervisor on the discovery of the LaPierre documents. Kelly's supervisor considered the discovery important enough to include Herbert Welch, the CIA Director, in the briefing, so the director was asked to attend. After the meeting, Director Welch instructed Kelly to continue the limited surveillance of John and his family.

But he directed Kelly to have another talk with John now that the LaPierre documents had confirmed China's involvement in the illicit activities. Possibly, the turn of events would convince him that he and his family were in need of added protection. This might be especially the case since the agency's intelligence indicated the Chinese weren't yet aware the CIA had already uncovered the LaPierre documents.

Even if the Chinese soon learned the agency already had its hands on the documents, the director believed, their contents could still benefit China significantly. Just in case John changed his mind, Director Welch directed Kelly's superior to arrange with the FBI to have the required number of specially trained agents ready to travel to New Mexico to provide the expanded surveillance on forty eight-hour notice. If Kelly succeeded in persuading John, he authorized Kelly's supervisor to triple the number of agents supporting the FBI.

The discovery of the LaPierre documents was important enough to warrant its inclusion in the briefing Director Welch held every week with President Henning. The director, however, was departing for an undisclosed destination the following weekend, and the briefing hadn't been scheduled for the coming week. It was then that Kelly told the director of John's desire to be involved in conveying the sensitive information to the White House. Kelly explained John felt Henri LaPierre would have wanted him to. Senator Conniff of New Mexico, Kelly told the director, was John's personal friend and had direct contact with the counsel's office in the White House. For that reason, John also wanted to involve the senator from his home state.

The director acceded to Kelly's request because he deemed the intelligence gathered as incomplete. The LaPierre documents provided sufficient basis to implicate Condon in crimes he committed years ago. That was enough to destroy the senator politically. But that wasn't the agency's purpose, the director told Kelly. So there was more work to be done.

The director wanted the investigation into Condon's activities to search for what he termed *present-day relevance*. If the senator had benefitted from the embezzlement and diversion of millions of dollars worth of supplies, as Henri had accused him of, what had the senator done with the money? Did he now have access to the funds, and if so, where? If the investigation uncovered solid evidence that funds of such high amounts existed, Condon would have a difficult time explaining their source. Were there tax consequences? Equally important, had he used the funds illegally in the past? Did he have plans to do so in the future? If so, what were they? The director wanted answers.

Later that morning, John left for the interview with the Governor in Santa Fe. He had met the Governor on numerous social and political occasions but didn't know him well enough to call him a friend. Guy had telephoned John Sunday afternoon to tell him several of John's supporters who were close to the Governor had already spoken to him about John's candidacy. The Governor had been impressed with John's credentials and had given those who spoke to him the impression he favored him.

John reflected on that conversation with Guy as he sat in the Governor's ceremonial office. Although the Governor did in fact ask him a few initial questions concerning the Supreme Court's role and John's qualifications, for most of the forty-minute interview, the two of them spoke of politics in general and the Governor's long range plans if he was reelected. Possibly, John thought as he listened to the Governor's political philosophy, he had already made up his mind, and the interview was a mere formality.

Late in the afternoon, as John wrapped up his work for the day, the call came from the Governor's office. The Governor himself was calling to tell him he was selected to fill the vacancy. A half hour later, calls began to come in, for the press releases had reached the news media. As soon as the celebration in the law firm's offices died down, John called Demi to tell her the good news. She had warmed up to him somewhat that weekend on his return from Paris. Yet, they had only conversed in small talk, and no mention was made by either of what had to be resolved at some point. He sensed she was seeking the illusive *right time*. But now that he was telling her of his selection, she sounded both relieved and genuinely happy for him. He too was relieved, more so because of her positive reaction than because of his appointment.

He got home early, which surprised Demi. A few more congratulatory calls came before the family sat down for dinner. They let the answering machine record any messages while they ate. Demi had told Crystal and Johnny of their father's appointment, and they appeared happier than usual. As they giggled and laughed, they toasted their father with their milk; they seemed proud of him. After dinner, John offered to help with the dishes, but Demi suggested she could finish cleaning the kitchen quicker if he wasn't around to get in her way. She was probably correct, he concluded, and although not offended, he suspected she considered his offer a trifle way of making amends.

As Demi began cleaning up in the kitchen, he joined Crystal and Johnny in the family room, where they were watching TV. He had enjoyed his conversation with the children during dinner. But he knew he hadn't made up for lost time that had passed him by. He wanted to take advantage of this rare opportunity before they went into their rooms to do their homework.

Crystal and Johnny were engrossed in one of their favorite programs. John decided not to interrupt their concentration. That kind of parental involvement, they wouldn't appreciate. Instead, he sat quietly next to Crystal. She glanced up at him and smiled. He returned the smile but didn't say a word. After all, he had entered their turf, and he'd have to respect their TV time, which was limited by Demi.

Johnny sat on the carpet. At the first commercial break, he was on his feet. "I'm getting a Fudgsicle," he said to no one in particular. "Mommy said I could have one." He disappeared into the kitchen.

John turned to his daughter. "How's school, Pumpkin?"

"Fine, Daddy," Crystal said. "We have no school after tomorrow!"

"Really? How come?"

Johnny hurried back into the room, the fudge bar in his hand.

"There's a teacher's convention. We have those days off every year."

"Oh, yeah, I remember."

Johnny got back down on the floor, slurping his Fudgsicle. "Are you gonna go with us to Santa Fe, Daddy?" he asked.

Crystal gave her brother a dirty look.

His son's remark surprised him, and he didn't hide it. "I don't think so, son. When is your mother taking you?"

"Wednesday morning," Crystal replied. "You think you can join us this weekend, Daddy?"

"I don't think so, Pumpkin. I'm leaving for D. C. early Saturday."

"We're gonna stay with Grandma Lupe," Johnny said.

"That's great, son. I wish I could go."

"Mommy was going to tell you about our going," Crystal said.

He had suspected the children sensed there had been some sort of disagreement. It was almost impossible to hide that from them when it happened. "I haven't even told her about my going out of town," he replied. "I planned telling her tonight."

"So was Mommy, I think."

He only nodded, for the commercial ended. The children's attention returned to the program. Silence returned to the room except for the sound coming from the TV. He just sat there and eventually became interested in the program, watching it to the end.

It was eight o'clock when Demi entered the room during the commercial break. She reminded the children it was time for their homework. Crystal complied, but Johnny put up a bit of a fuss. Demi joined John on the sofa.

"The kids were just telling me you're taking them to Tesuque Wednesday," he said. He muted the TV with the remote control.

"Yes," she said, "I was going to tell you tonight. I told Crystal that; I'm surprised she mentioned it to you."

"It was *Johnny* who spilled the beans."

"I didn't realize there were any 'beans to spill.'" She seemed defensive. "Maybe you can join us Friday. The Santa Fe Fiesta starts then. We could take the children on Saturday."

He knew she needed more time to herself but seemed willing to make an exception if it meant doing something together as a family. She had opened the door only to find out he'd be unavailable. He told her of the trip he had scheduled that morning. She was pissed, he could tell, and there was an awkward silence. Well, at least they were talking, he thought.

"When did you decide on the trip?" he finally asked.

"This morning. I talked to my mother after you left for work."

"How long will you be gone?"

"I've made arrangements for the kids to be out of school a couple of days next week and arranged for their make-up assignments. So we'll be back late Tuesday afternoon."

"I wish you'd have given me more advance notice so I could have planned—"

"Would it really have made a difference even if I had said something a week or so ago?"

"It might have."

"Give me a break. Be honest, for God's sake." She sighed, and he could tell she was annoyed. "The way your schedule's been lately, it's a wonder you even found time to go see Dan this weekend. And that's going to keep you from your kids, that's for sure."

He thought it best not to address her remark about the children. "Well, that trip wasn't on my schedule until this morning. So—"

"That's what I mean. Next week, something else will come up that wasn't on your schedule, but you'll find a way to make room for it."

"You don't need to get so upset over it, Demi." He placed his hand on her lap.

She quickly removed it. "This LaPierre thing is getting out of hand, and it's enough to upset anyone. Including you! That's why you lost it last week with your accusation."

"I hope there'll come a time when we can move on from that. I've apologized for being such a jerk."

"Well, that's just not enough at the moment."

"Demi, I've never believed you were capable of doing what I accused you of. But I knew you've been upset and unhappy, so I took a blind leap. It was a terrible blunder, and I regret it."

"I'm starting to think you wouldn't have done it if you yourself weren't feeling the pressure we've been under."

"I've come to the same conclusion." He took a deep breath. "Getting back to your visit to your mother's, I'm truly disappointed I can't join you and the kids there."

"Well, to tell you the truth, John, maybe it's for the best." She looked into his eyes. "Frankly, I think we could use the extra time away from each other to sort things out. That's why I decided to go visit her in the first place. Our lives are turning topsy-turvy on us. What's going to happen if things don't change?"

"I hope, Demi," he said with a look of concern, "you're not thinking of a separation."

302

"No, I'm trying to prevent one! I don't want us to grow apart."

"I'm concerned if you and the children go to your mother's," he said.

"Why?" she asked.

"Kelly had a long talk with me this morning. He suggests we agree to have our house bugged and also to expanded protection for you and the kids."

"Why would that be necessary?"

"They've got reason to believe someone else may be after the documents we discovered."

"That's something else I've been pissed off about—your lying to me about this situation with Kelly and Quigley."

"I didn't lie. I just didn't tell you everything."

"It's the same thing, for heaven's sake, and you know it damn well. You deceived me."

"Because I didn't want you to—"

"I know, I know—that lame excuse about your not wanting me to worry. Well, that's backfired on you."

"How well I know it." He couldn't resist smiling.

"John, please don't do that. You know I dislike your trying to inject humor into something as serious as this."

"I know. I'm sorry."

"Actually, I knew Kelly had some of his agents following me and the kids. I suspected as much ever since Quigley showed up with that FBI agent in Santa Fe. It's just that I thought they were being extra cautious, so I didn't say anything to you. I didn't realize they thought our lives were in danger. And I resent your keeping that from me."

"Then you'll agree to the expanded surveillance?"

"I didn't say that. Let me think about it."

"Why?"

"I need the time. What they're doing right now will have to do. I haven't gotten the kids or my mother prepared for this. Besides, you didn't agree to it, so why should I?"

"Because the reason for my not agreeing to it no longer exists—you now know everything."

"I said I'd think about it, okay?"

"Fine."

Even though he didn't care for the tenor of their conversation, he was grateful that they were at least talking. That was far better than her silent treatment over the past weekend. He took her hand in his. This time she didn't push it away.

"Even if I had to go to D. C. on Saturday," he continued, "I wish I had the weekdays free. I could go on Wednesday and spend some time with you and the children until Friday night. But the Soliz case and other business will keep me here. The fact is, I've got a full week."

"What's going to happen on Bernardo's motion hearing and his appeal now that you got the appointment?"

"Guy's going to take over the case. The Solizes have agreed to have him represent Bernardo."

"So what's happening on the case?"

"I've got to do some work on the motion for a new trial before meeting with Guy later this week. Tomorrow, I'm meeting with Bernardo."

"What about?"

He was glad she was again taking an interest in his work. "Last week, when I met with him and his parents, he seemed a little up tight about the appeal."

"That's not surprising, is it? After all, the guy's been convicted and is facing the prospect of a few years in the slammer."

He let out a short laugh. "It's true that fact would give anyone reason to worry, but that's not what I mean. There's something else going on that I can't quite put my finger on. It's been bothering me ever since I spoke to him last week." He paused for a long moment, as if in a trance.

"Hello, anyone in there?" she said finally, waving her hand in his face.

"Sorry," he said, coming out of his pensiveness. "Got lost in my thoughts."

"So I noticed. Anyway, tell me what's bothering you about Bernardo?"

"I got the distinct impression he's worried about my appealing the conviction. I think he's even more nervous about my filing the motion I intend to file."

"Like I said, maybe he's just got the usual post-trial jitters—afraid of going to jail."

"I think he's got those. As you noted, he's facing the possibility of a few years behind bars. But that's not what I'm referring to. He seemed afraid."

"Really? Are you sure he wasn't just nervous? Aside from prison, what's there to be afraid of?"

He shrugged. "That's what I don't understand. I even asked him if he was satisfied with my representation. I thought maybe he might have felt I didn't do a good job and wouldn't do any better with the appeal."

"What did he say?"

"He said he was surprised I even asked the question."

"I am too." She paused. "Seriously, you aren't having doubts about the job you did for him, are you?"

"To be honest, I've wondered if I wasn't too wrapped up with what's been going on in our lives to represent him well."

"That's the first time I've known you to doubt the quality of your work in the courtroom. I think you're being too hard on yourself. I'm convinced you did your best for that boy."

He shrugged. "I wouldn't be feeling this way if he had been acquitted."

"Well, I think you came close to getting that acquittal. To be honest, I've always thought you had an uphill battle. Did you really believe all along he didn't do it?"

"I believed him, yes."

"I've never been too sure about that myself."

Her trip to her mother's was still on his mind, and he decided to get back to that. "I wish I could join you in Santa Fe."

"What's with you. That's the second or third time you've mentioned that. I didn't mean for you to feel guilty about it."

"Maybe I am."

"Well, please don't be. Besides, like I said, maybe it'll be good for us to be away from each other for a while."

He nodded. "You were right. Our lives seem to have turned upside down all of a sudden."

"It's not 'all of a sudden.' It's been happening for quite some time now. You just haven't noticed."

"You think so?" He was perplexed by her statement.

"No, I don't just think so. I *know* so."

He moved closer to her and held her by the shoulders.

"I don't like this happening to us, Demi."

"I know. Neither do I." He hugged her, then kissed her on the cheek. She looked at her watch and stood up. "I've got to get to that work I brought home."

"Oh? That rarely happens."

"I've got a brief due by the end of next week, and I can't finish it tomorrow. If I'm taking off, that'll leave little time to complete it."

"If you're going to work on that brief, it might be a good time to go visit my mother and tell her the good news."

"Good idea. But I bet she's already heard about it. Give her my love."

"I'll do that."

His mother was happy to see him. She had heard of his appointment on the six o'clock news and gave him a big *abrazo* as she congratulated him and told him how proud she was. He had told her of his interest in the position a day or so after filing his application. She was glad he had come to share his celebration.

He almost missed her, she told him, for she had just returned from a rosary. She invited him into the small living room, where she spent many hours in her comfortable chair watching TV.

She offered him a cup of coffee or a soft drink, but he declined. She asked about Demi and the children.

He was pleased to find his mother in a good mood and was glad he decided to visit her. Her eyes appeared to sparkle, even in the dim light of the room. She seemed calmer than he had found her several weeks ago when he had paid her the surprise visit on his way to work.

He wondered if she could detect he was a bit uptight at a time when she would expect him to be joyous. Demi and the children's trip to her mother's saddened him, he now realized. He couldn't quite figure out why, except possibly that it reinforced Demi's belief he had become so wrapped up in his work that he couldn't take a brief trip with his family. The thought depressed him, and it probably showed. His mother confirmed that when she spoke.

"You seem worried, *mi'jo*," she said in Spanish, a look of concern in her eyes. "Is anything the matter?"

He thought of saying nothing was wrong. But his mother would see through the lie. He had come to believe that most women, especially mothers, had a "sixth" sense about such things.

"Now I *know* there's something wrong," she said when he didn't answer. "What's bothering you, son?"

He forced himself to smile. "I was thinking, *Mamita*," he began in Spanish, "that you were always able to know if something was bothering one of us when we were growing up. You haven't lost that touch, have you?"

She gave out a short laugh. "I guess not." She paused. "So tell me, what's happening?"

"Not anything I'd want you to be concerned about." He sighed. "It's true there are some things going on for me at the moment. Nothing that can't be resolved, though."

She smiled once again. "I'd worry more if you decided not to tell me anything. Besides, it does one good to talk about it."

"There are several things." He pondered his concerns. He thought of the LaPierre matter, especially of the added danger now that Henri's documents had surfaced. For certain, he intended to keep that from her. He saw no need to have her worry over something she had no control of. And he had no intention of telling her the particulars involving his and Demi's recent problems. "My worries have to do with my work. I'm afraid it's gotten a little out of hand, and Demi's concerned it's affecting us as a family."

"And I wouldn't blame her. A mother's concern is always for her children. She feels responsible for their welfare, and so she reacts when she sees anything that threatens them. Believe me, I know, for I raised you and your sisters. I know firsthand what it is to worry about one's children."

"You were always there for us. There was no doubt about that, and I thank you for it."

Her face lit up with gratitude, but she didn't acknowledge his adulation with words. "And I still worry about all of you. I suppose I'll always worry until my dying days."

"I hope that doesn't make you unhappy."

"Don't be silly. It doesn't do that."

"I'm glad."

"Please go on, son."

"I used to enjoy my work. I never questioned what I was doing because I thrived on it. It's taken me a long time, I'm afraid, to realize my work has kept me from Crystal and Johnny at a time when they'd benefit most from having a father around. And I'm not even enjoying my work like I used to. It bothers me that Demi had to be the one to point that out to me."

"I understand what you're saying, *mi'jo*. But don't make the mistake of being too hard on yourself." She sighed. "That too isn't a good thing."

She had touched a sensitive nerve, and he felt the tears form in his eyes. Unexpectedly, he became confused about what was going on for him. He had come to pay a pleasant visit to his mother and to celebrate with her. Instead, he found himself wanting to pour out his soul to her. Could it be that this was what he came here to do? How long had it been since he shed a tear? A long time.

He thought of the events of the past weeks and of his and Demi's many talks about the marriage, his work, and of her concerns. Most likely, she would have welcomed his tears, for it'd be a sign to her that he cared. He wondered what it was that had brought out his emotional side in his mother's presence.

"What in God's name are you thinking, *mi'jo?*" Juanita said. She got up from her chair and sat down on the sofa beside him. She placed one hand on his lap and the other on his shoulder.

The tears in his eyes got heavier, and he took his handkerchief to brush them away. "I was just thinking I haven't cried in front of Demi in a long time." He dabbed at his eyes again. "I haven't cared enough to cry."

"But of course you care, *mi'jo*. At this moment, you're showing you care." Tears started flowing from her own eyes. "Why do you men always find it so difficult to cry in front of others? Including those you love. It's a natural thing that flows from hurting. And you can't tell me that men don't hurt once in a while."

"I suppose we show it in other ways, *Mamita*."

"I don't believe that for one moment. You show anger or toughness, or some other manly reaction, but only to *hide* the hurt you feel, not to *show* it. That isn't such a healthy thing, son, and I think you know it."

He nodded. "You're absolutely right." The tears kept coming, and he wiped his eyes again. "What now hurts the most is that I've been obsessed with doing well in my practice and making a lot of money." He shook his head. "I've come to realize now I'm kidding myself that I'm doing it for Demi and the kids. What's it all worth if I'm ignoring the ones I'm supposedly working so hard for?"

"Many make that mistake." She paused, as if in a trance. "Even more so in today's crazy world. God forbid if your father were living today. He'd get caught up in it too!" She sighed. "But now you needn't worry.

You've got this new position, and that's why you said you wanted it, right?"

He nodded. "I shouldn't be burdening you with this."

"It's not a burden, son. I'm glad you're sharing your hurt." She wiped the tears from her eyes. "Please tell me more."

"You know, *Mamita*, I've been involved in this new case—a criminal charge against this boy. You know, his mother reminds me of you. Not the way she looks, so much, but her mannerisms." He stopped crying and grew excited as he spoke.

"This new case," he went on, "—well, it's made me think a lot about the course I've been headed in my law practice—representing big companies—people with lots of money." He looked at his mother with sad eyes. "I've forgotten what it's like to represent flesh and blood clients. People I used to identify with; my roots. I've abandoned them. Until this one case came along." He paused to wipe his nose.

The last time he had cried in front of his mother, the tears had been shed because of *her* pain. Tonight, they were being shed for *his*.

"You know, *mi'jo*," Juanita said, "when you decided to go to law school and become an attorney, I was so proud of you—and happy for you, too."

He nodded.

"But I confess to you now that at the same time, I was afraid for you."

"Why?"

"Because I knew you well, even then when you were much younger. I saw how determined you were—your drive, your ambition. You were going to right every wrong, fight every battle, win every war. I could tell you had a heart even then. A big one—one that could help you help others. But at the same time, one that could cause you much pain. I also sensed your obsession for doing the right thing and in exactly the right way—your way."

She started crying again. "And so I knew then that you would someday have this problem. I didn't know how it would come about, or when, but I knew you would have to deal with it. You've become like *Don Quixote*, I'd say, fighting at windmills—what you now seem to believe are lost causes."

She wiped her wet eyes with a tissue she took out of her pocket. "That seems to me to be at the root of what I see as your dissatisfaction with your work." She corrected herself. "Or should I say your awareness of it?"

"The latter, I think, *Mamita*. You may be right about the past. But this criminal case changed all that. It motivated me. Even though the boy

309

was convicted last week, I'm hoping the lawyer that will soon be representing him can win it on appeal."

"I know about the case, son."

"You do?"

"A neighbor showed me the newspaper when the boy was convicted last week." She stopped to wipe her nose. "I hope your friend does win it, son. For your sake as well as for the boy. For I know how you take on responsibility."

John's eyes showed his excitement. "Representing this boy revitalized me. I've never wanted to help someone so much in my life. Now that he's convicted, I was ready to fight harder than I've ever fought a case before. Much of what I felt had to do with his parents—in helping him, I'd also be helping them." He paused. "God only knows, I hadn't felt like that in a long time."

The sparkle that had disappeared when the tears had come returned to Juanita's eyes. She smiled at him. "I'm proud of you, *mi'jo!* I hope this boy wins his case in the end. You deserve that satisfaction, especially if you believe it's changed the way you feel about your work."

He returned her warm smile.

"And something tells me you've got this matter about your family almost licked too. I know in my heart you and Demi will work it out. It seems to me you've become aware of what you yourself consider your failings. As for me, I don't see them as failings. I've always considered it a manly thing that men do. From what you've said, I gather you'll find out soon how to manage it."

He realized she didn't know exactly the nature of his and Demi's problems. But did that matter, or was it her faith in their ability to work things out that did? "I'm sure I will," he replied. "Thanks for being such a good listener, *Mamita*."

"Thanks for being such a fine son!"

CHAPTER 25

A morose Bernardo sat in John's office. John hoped his client would be less withdrawn than when he had seen him the week before. But at the beginning of their discussions, he could hardly get Bernardo to talk. Bernardo was meeting with Guy later in the week, and John wanted Guy to start with a client willing to cooperate. Again, he tried to find out how Bernardo felt about appealing the case. Obviously depressed, Bernardo uttered only a few words. He had heard the news on TV the night before, he volunteered, reporting John's appointment to the Supreme Court. He congratulated him.

Within a couple of minutes, John became convinced he wouldn't get his client, who was now slumping in the chair, to open up. Finally, he showed a flicker of emotion when John questioned him concerning his satisfaction with John's representation. He told Bernardo he was convinced his parents were sincere when they themselves had said they were satisfied he had done everything he could for Bernardo.

That comment triggered a sensitive nerve, and he noticed his client's first tears began to trickle down his cheeks. He was relieved the young man was now reacting in some way. It was the first time he had seen this side of him.

"Why are you crying?" he asked when Bernardo's silence continued despite his tears.

Bernardo still didn't answer. Instead, he took out his handkerchief, brought it to his eyes, and covered them with both hands.

"If you're really being sincere, Bernardo," John persisted, "when you say you want the appeal to go forward with Mr. Zanotelli representing you, I think you owe me the courtesy of a response. I'm beginning to think you're not being honest with me."

Bernardo took the handkerchief away from his eyes, and, looking downward, finally spoke. "I'm being honest with you, Mr. Garcia," he uttered. "I feel bad I've made you think I'm not." But he didn't stop crying.

"For God's sake, what then is the problem?" He was trying hard not to lose his patience. "I know you've been through a lot of shit, but something tells me that's not what's bothering you."

From his slumped position, Bernardo sat up straight. "My parents and I," he said, "are thankful for what you've done." He hesitated. "That's why I feel guilty about Carmen."

"What about your sister?"

"I feel bad about this, Mr. Garcia. I really do."

"Go on. What's Carmen got to do with this?"

"She's angry—upset. She's telling us you didn't do a good job; that you could have worked harder to convince the jury." He wiped his eyes. "I'm ashamed 'cause I don't think you deserve her thinking that. My parents don't agree with her either."

"It's too bad she feels that way, but it's not the first time someone didn't think I had done my job well. After practicing law for as long as I have, one gets used to it. I've learned I can't possibly please everyone."

"Please don't hold it against her. She believed in my innocence. She's angry, that's all, so she's looking for someone to blame. Like everyone else in my family, she thinks I didn't do it."

"That's understandable. I know it means a lot to you to have your family's support." Pondering the cryptic manner in which Bernardo had referred to Carmen's blind loyalty, he wondered how to respond. "I don't blame her for thinking you got a bum rap. I happen to think you did too.

312

Our system's not perfect, but it's what we've got. Sometimes, the innocent get convicted, despite our efforts to prevent it."

He noticed Bernardo shudder, and he knew without a doubt he had hit another soft spot. The youngster then leaned forward in his chair, burying his face in his hands. He began sobbing uncontrollably, covering his face with the handkerchief. The sobbing turned into a desperate cry of anguish. John sat there without saying a word, shocked at the sight of one who seemed to be losing it right before his eyes. For a moment, he didn't know what to do or say, and then decided it was best to let Bernardo have his cry. He sat there for several, uncomfortable minutes, waiting until the boy's sobs subsided.

When he stopped crying, Bernardo just sat there, his face still hidden in the handkerchief now soaked in tears. He wiped his eyes on the wet handkerchief, then blew his nose. Finally, he lifted his head, and, for the first time since he had entered the office, looked straight into John's eyes.

"I'm not innocent," he mumbled. Despite what he had said, which made no sense to John, Bernardo now appeared in touch with his surroundings. It was as if a great weight had been lifted off him, and he appeared to have snapped out of his depression.

John looked at him in disbelief, then sat up straight in his chair. He changed his mind about his impressions. The boy had indeed flipped out. He wasn't in touch, but out of touch, with reality.

"What are you saying, Bernardo?" John managed to say.

Bernardo sat up straight. "I'm saying I did it! I stabbed Ms. Gregory." New tears came to his eyes. "I lied to you, Mr. Garcia." He paused. "Please forgive me."

John sat there stunned. How could he have misjudged the youngster? If Bernardo was telling the truth, why hadn't he been able to see through the big lie all along?

He felt a mounting anger. Although he was unsure what to say, he finally spoke. "Bernardo," he said, "you didn't just lie to me! You lied to the court and to the jury." He paused. "And worse yet, you lied to your family."

Again, there was an awkward pause as Bernardo wept.

After a long while, he stammered, "I-I'm s-sorry." He appeared to gain control of his emotions. "I should never have lied to you. But I was scared!"

John looked down at his hands; they were trembling. "Let's calm down," he said, more for his own benefit than the boy's. "I'd like to take a minute to collect my thoughts. You've got some explaining to do."

The office felt stuffy, and he couldn't breathe. He sat there bewildered, finding it hard to believe what Bernardo had told him. Not knowing what else to say, he decided to tell his client exactly that. "I don't believe you, Bernardo. I can't accept what you're telling me."

Bernardo looked down to the floor, seemingly unable to meet John's gaze. "*I-I'm* t-the one who let you down, not you."

"This can't be! Your family—they swore you were with them."

"They were telling the truth. Don't blame them."

"But if they were telling the truth, how could you have had time to commit the crime?"

"Like I said before, they were mistaken about the time I was gone. It must have seemed like a few minutes to them." Bernardo spoke louder now, and he at last appeared his normal self. "I was gone longer than the thirty to forty minutes I told the jury."

"It's hard to believe your entire family was mistaken by that much time."

Bernardo shrugged. "Maybe they were stretching the truth to help me out."

"Are you telling me they were lying?"

"I can't say that. But they're only human. I hope you're not disappointed in them."

John ignored the suggestion, for, at the moment, he didn't care to consider the possibility that anyone else had lied to the jury. Instead, he focused on the boy's admitted actions.

"My God, Bernardo," he said, "you lied throughout your testimony! You perjured yourself." He stopped for a moment, trying hard to stay calm. "Tell me about the time you were gone. First of all, explain to me why you left the house! Surely you had no intentions of hurting Patty Gregory."

"It wasn't like that," Bernardo answered. "I needed to get away from my family and decided to go for a walk. But I never intended to stay gone so long. I was confused about my life—my wife's and my future. At the house, I felt suffocated and needed time to myself."

"Okay, I'll buy that. But what does that have to do with what happened to Patty Gregory? How does she fit into the picture?"

"I was roaming the streets, going nowhere in particular. It was just by chance I happened to go by there and spotted her washing her car."

Bernardo's words began weaving a story that now sounded believable. For the first time since he started working on the case, John began to understand the bits and pieces of the case that hadn't made sense. The stabbing, for one thing, appeared quite senseless—no apparent motive. Not that Bernardo had just now given him one. But at least his surprising confession fit the piece of the puzzle that had given John the most trouble. Why, he had asked himself time and again, in the face of Bernardo's unequivocal denial that he had stabbed Patty, was she so adamant in saying otherwise?

"I stopped to ask about the house across the street, like she said," Bernardo continued. "Even though I didn't have a job, the thought of looking for a place of our own to rent made me feel good. We couldn't afford it, but I was like—fantasizing."

"But why return to stab her? What in God's name was that all about?"

The boy appeared to ponder the question. "I don't know," he said, shaking his head. "It was a crazy thing I found myself doing. I couldn't believe it was happening. To this day, I can't explain why I did it." He stopped to clear his throat. "But it's what happened. And I lied about it."

Even now, after hearing Bernardo's admission, John found it hard to believe him. Yet, why would he confess to a crime he didn't commit? Although John hadn't handled a case where that had happened, he had heard of such confessions. He recalled documented cases in which an accused had confessed for many different reasons. Notoriety, for instance, had been one of them, as bizarre as that sounded. What would Bernardo's reason be? There were two possibilities. Either he committed the act, had lied about it, but was now telling the truth. Or he hadn't committed the act but was now confessing for some unknown reason. John wondered if he was questioning the admission only because he didn't *want* to believe his client had committed the act. He'd have to find out. One way to do that was to search for facts corroborating his confession. The key was to ask questions to which only the true offender knew the answers.

He thought of the knife. It was never found. Only the assailant would know where it was—what he had done with it. Could Bernardo produce it?

"The knife!" he blurted out. "What did you do with it?"

315

Bernardo seemed taken by surprise. He took his eyes off John for a few seconds, then returned John's stare. "Why is that important?"

"Just answer the question!"

Bernardo appeared to hold back. "I threw it over a fence in the alley."

"The police searched all over that alley. They didn't find a thing."

"I threw it over this metal shed close to the wooden fence. I remember it hit the roof because it made a sound, but I think it fell over on the other side of the shed. That's why they didn't find it."

He asked Bernardo a few more questions to satisfy himself his client wasn't holding back. He was hardly paying attention to the responses. Instead, one question kept racing through his mind—how could he have been duped by Bernardo's claim of innocence when he visited with him that first day at the detention center. He couldn't believe his defense had been based on a lie. Without knowing it, he had played a role in the deception. He felt guilty for having misled the jury.

Bernardo wanted to know if John was going to cancel his appointment with Guy Zanotelli. John confirmed that he was. What about the motion for a new trial and the appeal, Bernardo asked. There would be no motion filed and no appeal, John replied. The confession changed everything. Bernardo seemed relieved. John also explained he felt obligated to review the code of ethics to learn if he had to tell Judge Walker and the prosecutor's office of the perjury.

Before the youngster left, John suggested he go home and tell his family the truth. He was ashamed to tell them, Bernardo answered. Could John tell them, instead? John explained the code of ethics, which prohibited him from divulging such information, unless he had his client's permission. He had his permission, Bernardo implored him. No, John said, it was important for Bernardo himself to confess his wrong. Bernardo then pleaded for John to be with him when he told his family. John declined, insisting Bernardo was on his own.

That afternoon, Carmen visited John unannounced. When Lynda informed him that she insisted seeing him, he assumed Bernardo had confessed. He discovered otherwise the moment Carmen spoke her first words.

"My brother's told us he now wants to drop the appeal!" she said. She appeared distraught. "He said he decided to do that after you spoke to him this morning. You must have advised him against it. Why would you do such a thing?"

"That's not what happened, Carmen," he started to explain. "What else—"

"He told us you didn't intend to file the motion for a new trial and that you were going to cancel his appointment with Mr. Zanotelli. Is that true?" She didn't hold back her emotional venom, pointedly directed at him.

"Carmen, I'm going to ask you to calm down if we're to continue this conversation. Otherwise, I'll have to ask you to leave."

"I'm upset, but I have a right to be." She paused, as if to slow the adrenaline pumping through her. "I want to know what you said to Bernardo. Is that asking too much?"

"No, it's not. But let me ask you a question to help me understand where you're coming from."

"But why did you decide not to file the motion? That's the first good thing you've done for my brother since you started representing him."

It was hard to take the insult without losing his cool, but he fought the temptation. "I regret you feel that way. Bernardo warned me this morning you were trying to turn your family against me." He reflected on Bernardo's insistence that he was indeed satisfied with his representation. "I can understand your anger at the conviction. You're free to think what you want about how good or how badly I did my job. Even so, your opinion doesn't mean a thing to me. Not as long as I feel you're just trying to find someone to blame."

"I admit I'm upset," she cried out. "But I'm trying to calm down."

"I can see that, but try not to be insulting." From the way Carmen was acting, John sensed Bernardo hadn't confessed, but he wanted to be sure. "Besides Bernardo telling you I wasn't planning to request a hearing on our motion and of his decision not to appeal, did he say anything else?"

She appeared confused. "No, that's all he told us." She hesitated. "What was he supposed to tell us?"

"I'll get to that in a moment. Tell me this, Carmen—how was your brother acting when he talked to you?"

"He wasn't acting himself. I thought he was keeping something from us. That's why I decided to come see you."

He stood up. "I thought so. He *was* keeping something from you." He walked around the desk. "I'd like for you to come with me. We're going to pay your brother a visit. Is he home?"

317

"He was when I left."

John asked Lynda to reschedule his appointments that afternoon. He suggested to Carmen that she leave her car there; they'd go in his.

They drove to the Soliz residence, where they found Bernardo in the shed out back. His wife and mother had just gone to the grocery store, he said. He showed no surprise and John could tell he knew why he was there. There were no chairs in the room. Bernardo was sitting on the edge of the bed, and Carmen sat beside him. John remained standing. He explained Carmen's visit and her version of what Bernardo had told his family.

"You didn't do what I asked you to, Bernardo," he continued, not hiding his disappointment. "Why didn't you?"

Bernardo said nothing. John waited for an answer.

"I don't know," Bernardo finally mumbled.

"Well, that doesn't matter now." He sighed. "I want you to tell your sister the real reason why you're not appealing the case."

The boy remained mute, looking down at the floor.

"I'm asking you to tell her," John repeated. "You owe her that, and you owe me!" He waited another moment, but Bernardo didn't respond. "Tell Carmen why you don't want to appeal the case, damn it!"

There was another long wait.

Carmen appeared both confused and anxious. "Please answer the question, Bernardo," she pled. "Tell me, for heaven's sake!"

Bernardo looked at his sister with desolate eyes. He then turned away. "I don't want to appeal," he stuttered, "'cause—'cause—I–I did it. I stabbed that woman."

Once having found the words, his eyes filled with tears of apparent agony. He threw himself on his sister and wept.

Early Friday evening, Demi sat sipping a cocktail at the *Pink Adobe*, a well-known restaurant in Santa Fe. She had heard it was Robert Redford's favorite restaurant in town. John had called earlier to tell her he wanted to see her before he left for Washington. They arranged to meet for dinner, although she wondered if it was a good idea, for she truly believed time away from each other was important. Because he wasn't certain how long a hearing scheduled for that afternoon would last, she told him she'd be at the restaurant at six. He was to join her as soon as he could.

She and the children had arrived at Lupe Flynn's house mid-morning on Wednesday. Lupe seemed happy to see her daughter and two grandchildren, and the children were elated to see their Grandma Lupe. Lourdes dropped by Wednesday afternoon after work, and the reunited family enjoyed Lupe's home cooking.

Although Demi had enjoyed her visit with her mother during the past few days, she had missed John. This was so even though she had reconciled herself to the fact that the separation would help her sort out what they could do to help their strained relationship. It saddened her that they were having problems, but she hadn't lost hope they would work them out. It lightened her sadness to know she missed him. On more than one occasion recently, she had found herself questioning her feelings for him.

When she had spoken to him a few weeks ago of her fear that they were growing apart, she felt then that they had been taking each other for granted. When they had talked on the phone, however, she sensed not only that she played an important part in his life but that he knew it and was beginning to appreciate that fact. The upshot was that she didn't feel insecure about his feelings for her. Yet, until now, she had never questioned *her* feelings toward him. During the first years of their marriage, she couldn't conceive of a life without him. Their need for each other was mutual then, and she never doubted their love for one another.

What of her doubts now about her love for him? Did they have anything to do with her resenting what she perceived as his avoidance of responsibility toward her and the children? It made sense, she thought, that if she blamed him for shunning his familial responsibility, it could trigger that resentment. Wouldn't this in turn cause her to question her feelings toward him? It relieved her to believe that could be the explanation for what she had interpreted as doubts of her feelings for him. That was because he now seemed aware of the problem and was willing to do something about it. If he succeeded doing that, there would be no basis for her resentment. Was it that simple? She hoped so.

He arrived at the restaurant about half past six, as she was about to order another drink.

"I was just about to order a drink," she said as he approached. "Would you like one?"

"Yeah, I could use one," he replied as he sat down. "We can get 'snockered' together."

He leaned over and planted a sustained kiss on her mouth. It surprised her, for she had learned long ago that he was easily embarrassed to show emotion in public.

The waitress appeared, and they each ordered a drink.

"I'm surprised you're here so early," Demi said.

He grinned. "You would have been proud of me. I spent only five or ten minutes at the office after the hearing before heading home to change."

"Good for you. Don't do that too often, though. You might get into a good habit you won't be able to break." She gazed at him in such a way as to make clear there was a mini-lecture in her humorous but cynical remark.

The waitress brought their cocktails. As they sipped their drinks, he spoke of his appointment to the Supreme Court and how he was looking forward to the new job. He hoped it would bring about the changes in their marriage they had talked about. There was a certain, renewed excitement building within him, he explained. He told her he was convinced his representing Bernardo was what had motivated him in the end to consider doing something entirely different than what he had grown accustomed to through the years.

"You know, I'm surprised Bernardo's case has had such an effect on me. On the way I felt about my work. The other night, when I went to visit my mother, I found myself talking to her about the case and how it changed the way I viewed my practice."

"What did she say?"

"Something I didn't expect. She wasn't surprised to find out about the soul searching I was going through."

"I've always felt that, next to me, your mother knows you well."

"I found myself opening up to her. I spilled my guts out and got emotional about it."

"What's wrong with that?"

"Nothing, I suppose, except that I don't often find myself doing that. The other night, with her, I seemed confused and showed it by letting out my feelings."

She snickered. "You men find it so hard to do that. You're afraid to. Instead, you end up putting up a big facade to hide the way you feel. You have to act tough—macho."

"And you're suggesting women are different?"

"Of course. That's something men should have learned long ago. The expression of feelings happens to be one of the differences. It's all in that best-seller, *Men Are From Mars, Women Are From Venus*. But the concept's nothing new."

"It's that simple, huh?"

"Well, not exactly." She paused. "Anyway, I'm glad you opened up with your mother. I bet you felt better afterward."

"As a matter of fact, I did. Seeing what I'm going through from her perspective helped me understand much of what you've been telling me."

"You don't know how relieved I am to hear you say that."

"I thought you'd feel that way. Now, of course, I'm concerned about how my telling Bernardo and his parents I could no longer represent him may have affected him."

"I don't understand."

"Well, as I explained to Guy the other day when I told him of Bernardo's confession, I can't help wondering if Bernardo feels I let him down; abandoned him."

"Really? How could that be? He confessed to hurting Patty Gregory. He admitted he had lied to you all along and perjured himself as well. What did he leave for you to abandon?"

"But I surprised him with the news I could no longer represent him before he confessed."

"What difference does that make? The fact is, once he admitted having stabbed the woman, there wasn't anything to appeal."

"I realize that, but I still feel I disappointed him. Right or wrong, I can't help thinking that may have helped trigger his decision to confess. It's hard to explain. It's probably just me. I keep thinking there were valid grounds to win the appeal."

"Well, his confession changed all that, so you shouldn't feel as if you abandoned him. What did Guy say about it."

"Essentially the same thing you did."

"Well?"

He shrugged. "Maybe you're right. Let's leave it for now. What do you say we get down to the business of eating. I'm starving."

"I'm absolutely famished."

It relieved her to know he seemed aware changes were necessary and that he was excited about the judicial career he'd soon take on. At the same time, though, she was a little annoyed at him. Possibly even irritated. Her irritation arose, she guessed, because it had taken him so long to realize he was losing touch with his family. Why had he been so oblivious to what was happening in the first place? She feared she might even be a little resentful he had first expressed his true feelings to his mother and not to her.

Reflecting on these negative feelings, which she'd rather not have, she soon realized she should be happy he had taken the plunge. It was time to count one's blessings and not dwell on *what ifs*, she reminded herself.

After dinner, they walked the short distance to the plaza to join the throngs of people participating in the city's celebration of the Santa Fe Fiesta.

The fiesta commemorated the conquest of the Pueblo Indians and the reoccupation of Santa Fe by the Spaniards in 1692-93, a dozen years after the Pueblo Indian Revolt of 1680. Legend had it that Don Diego De Vargas, the captain general who led the resettlement, held a nine-day prayer or vigil to *La Conquistadora*, literally translated as "the lady conqueror." De Vargas was said to have promised *La Conquistadora* that if the conquest was successful, he would hold a fiesta in her honor. And so had begun the first celebration of *La Fiesta*, an event that was to continue for over 300 years.

After an hour of fighting the heavy crowd in the plaza, they squeezed their way through the maze of people toward Fort Marcy Park, where they witnessed the burning of Zozobra, also known as "Old Man Gloom," a forty-foot tall puppet made out of a large wood frame covered with hundreds of yards of muslin. Its burning was supposed to rid the participants and merrymakers of their worries and ills from the past year. After their own turmoil of the past few weeks, Demi saw the symbolism clearer than ever.

She tried hard to be festive and to warm up to him, but he had hurt her, and so she found herself holding back. On the way to the park, he had held her hand, but she reacted somewhat indifferently and thought he had sensed it, for he released her hand after a short while.

Afterward, as the flames died down and all that was left were the smoking skeletal remains of Zozobra's carcass, the crowd began to disperse. John and Demi began moving with the slow pace of the crowd toward the plaza activities.

It was almost eleven when she reminded him of his early flight in the morning. He insisted following her in his car to her mother's house.

"I'm glad you agreed to see me," he said at the house's side entrance.

"Don't be silly," she said. "You're my husband and are leaving in the morning."

"Just the same. I knew you had mixed feelings about my coming up here when you haven't gotten over my hurting you."

She had to admit he knew that part of her well. "Even so, that doesn't mean you shouldn't have come, and that's why it was fine with me. I'm actually glad you came and that we got to say goodbye."

"I feel better having seen you tonight. Even if it's not the best of circumstances."

"Give it time, John."

"It's hard."

In the dim moonlight, she could see the sadness in his eyes. He placed his hands on her shoulders.

They embraced, then he kissed her, softly at first, then passionately. She responded, returning the kiss, and she could tell he became sexually stimulated for she felt him harden. As he kissed her neck, he began to fondle her breasts under the loose blouse she wore.

"Please don't, John," she half whispered. "This isn't the place—the children and my mother might hear us."

"We can go somewhere else." He didn't stop.

"No, you've got an early flight, and it's late. It's just not the time nor the place. So please stop before you lose control."

"I already have." He was now biting her shoulder tenderly, and his hands had found her bare back and were trying to unhook her bra."

"Don't!"

He ignored her. "I want you—need you." He began lifting her skirt and held her with her back against the wall.

"You're going to wake up the kids!" She spoke louder. "Stop it, please."

As he wrestled to lift her skirt, he nibbled at her neck and shoulder. "You're the one who's going to wake them up by resisting."

The *animal* in him had taken over, she thought. "John, I'm asking you to stop." She panicked, realizing there was no stopping him now.

"I'm hungry for you, Demi. Please understand."

She soon understood the only way to put an end to it was to make a scene, an ugly one, which she didn't want. So she stopped fighting. Without passion on her part, she allowed him to penetrate her. For a brief moment, as he plunged himself into her, she felt sensually aroused, but it was gone the instant she saw the occurrence for what it was—a betrayal of trust. She could tell he noticed she wasn't responding emotionally or even carnally when he stopped kissing her on the mouth and concentrated instead on her neck and shoulder until he ejaculated.

He stood there against her motionless body for what seemed a long time, even though it must have been only a few seconds. He pulled away and began to straighten first her clothing, then his.

"I needed to make love to you," he said, sounding apologetic. "I thought you'd respond, but I guess I was wrong."

At first, she didn't say anything. Instead, she smoothed out her blouse and skirt underneath her jacket. "Yes," she finally said, "you certainly were."

There had been times when they had made love in the past that one of them hadn't been connected emotionally. That was bound to happen, she believed, and it hadn't bothered her. But tonight was different. If she hadn't given in, she feared, he would have for certain taken her by force—raped her. Yet, she understood the nature of all men's sexuality and bravado, and so she knew she'd eventually forgive him. But at the moment, the fact it had happened made her sad.

"I'd have stopped if I had known you weren't going to respond," he said with obvious guilt.

She only nodded.

"What's going to happen to us, Demi?" he said, sounding bewildered.

His question saddened her even more, for she herself didn't have an answer. "I don't know," she said. "I wish I did, but I really don't." She opened the door and stepped inside. "Have a safe trip," she said without turning back.

He hesitated. "Goodnight."

"Goodnight." She closed the door.

324

CHAPTER 26

JOHN sat in a heavily cushioned chair in Dan's office enjoying the view through the large window. It was a warm and pleasant Fall day in the nation's capital. He listened as Dan gave an account of his recent trip to Mexico City. Dan was seated on a small sofa with his back to the window.

Minutes before, he had fixed John a scotch and soda. He himself was drinking a glass of plain grapefruit juice. He had plenty of work that afternoon, he explained, and so he wanted to be clearheaded. John felt anxious, and he thought the scotch would relax him.

For the next half hour, he related his extraordinary tale culminating in the discovery of the LaPierre documents. Dan listened patiently, captivated by John's narrative. John told every detail, going over each event as it unfolded.

Finally, he gave an account of his trip to France and the discovery of Henri's papers. He described Henri's indictment of Condon as a principal player in the drama of the in-depth, but unpublished article.

"What you're telling me is incredible," Dan said. "It's amazing that all of this has been happening to you." He paused in an obvious attempt to collect his thoughts. "How's Demi holding out through all this?"

"She's doing quite well, considering," John answered. "She went to Tesuque this week to visit her mother."

"Is that a safe thing to be doing at a time like this?"

"I've been asking myself the same question. Kelly's been wanting to increase the FBI's surveillance since we found the LaPierre documents. But until a few days ago, I hadn't shared the full extent of the problem with Demi. I was concerned she'd worry needlessly. I'm reassessing my resistance to Kelly's suggestion. Demi's pissed off for my keeping her in the dark for so long. Kelly maintains these fellows who are after me will surface soon. That's what the CIA wants."

"I can appreciate your concern for Demi. What about your kids? Do they know anything?"

John shook his head. "So far, we've managed to keep it from them."

"Now that Demi's aware of the need for increased surveillance, perhaps you should let the CIA do what it wants."

"Yeah, I'm thinking of doing just that."

"You seem to have put a lot of trust in Kelly. At a time when the world as you've known it has turned wild."

"You could say that."

"Damn it, John, I wish you had told me about this earlier."

"I wanted to say something last time we visited. It was hard not to. But Kelly insisted we keep it under wraps and tell anyone only on a need-to-know basis. Now, of course, things have changed, and some action has to be taken. That's why I'm here today."

"You've certainly given me a lot to digest. I've got several questions but don't quite know where to begin." He picked up the glass of grapefruit juice, drank what was left, and set the empty glass back on the coffee table. "For starters, how certain is Kelly that it's the Chinese who are after you?"

"Kelly and Quigley suspected early, even before they made contact with me, that China was somehow involved." He finished off his glass of scotch in one final gulp. "Once the CIA learned that members of Tong were involved," he went on, "Kelly's suspicions became stronger. At least, he felt comfortable making assumptions in working the case."

"I suppose the documents you found strengthened the CIA's theory on China's involvement."

"They sure do."

"Does Kelly now think those documents are what the Chinese were looking for when they focused on you?"

"Exactly." John went on to explain Kelly's original theory about why the Chinese were interested in the LaPierre documents. "Kelly believes China's interest now has something to do with relations between the U. S. and The People's Republic—possibly even Condon. It's just an educated guess on his part, I think, and he has nothing concrete. Now let me get to why I'm telling you all this."

"I've been wondering about that. I didn't think you made a special trip all the way up here just to get this off your chest."

"I'll get to it in a minute, but we've gotten sidetracked. Let me tell you what's happened since I returned from France." He picked up his empty glass and drank the water that had melted off the ice cubes. Dan gestured if he wanted a refill, and John shook his head.

He set the glass back down on the table. "Since Quigley and I got back from Paris, the CIA's uncovered additional evidence against your colleague."

"There's more? It seems the LaPierre documents alone provide sufficient evidence to convict Emory in any federal or military court."

"Possibly. But there's nothing wrong with a little corroboration. It seems our senator from South Carolina has opened not one, but several Swiss bank accounts with substantial deposits."

Dan's face turned pale, but he managed a faint smile. "I've always known Emory was well off but never thought he'd have reason to hide his wealth. How much money are we talking about?"

"Upwards of $30,000,000.00, if you can believe that!"

"You've got to be joking! How reliable is the CIA's source?"

"Extremely reliable. According to Kelly, Condon has used fake names for the accounts through an elaborate scheme of dummy organizations he's created."

"Can the CIA tie him to these accounts?"

John nodded. "Through independent sources, the agency has now confirmed that Condon, since his tour in Vietnam, has set up skeleton corporations that technically own the deposits. But he himself controls them."

"This is hard to believe! I suppose the next thing you're going to tell me is that the money in these dummy accounts is traceable to what Emory accumulated from his illicit activities."

"Kelly thinks so. The senator's earned a lot of interest on the original sums he deposited at various times long ago. With deposits the size that he made, he could accumulate a lot of interest in almost thirty years. Fantastic earnings, really." He thought for a moment. "Getting back to your question, the circumstantial evidence is all there. Several of the original accounts were first set up during the early seventies, at the time Condon was serving his second tour in Vietnam. Quite some evidence, wouldn't you say?"

"I'd say so."

"There's more."

"Nothing else would surprise me."

"The CIA just learned, Kelly informed me yesterday, that the senator's immediate plans are to funnel a good portion of the Swiss funds to his presidential campaign effort next year."

Dan sat there dumbfounded. "The fellow's been building a political war chest! Evidently waiting for the right time to use it. And what better way to spend it than in seeking the office of President of the United States. Never in my wildest dreams would I have imagined you were going to floor me with something like this."

"I knew it would shock you."

"That's an understatement." He let out a short laugh. "I've got a few quick questions. Why are you telling me this? What is it you want me to do?"

"We'd like for you to arrange a meeting with someone at the White House who's close to President Henning. I thought that, since you knew Chris Dunlevy there well, that would be a start. Maybe he could set up a quick appointment, even with the President himself."

"I'll be glad to help. I could try contacting Chris this afternoon to see if we could set up a meeting today or tomorrow."

"I'm flying out of here tomorrow, but I could postpone my flight. I'd appreciate your trying to schedule it this afternoon. The sooner this information reaches the President, the better."

"As I said, I'm willing to help. But tell me—why go through me on something this sensitive? The CIA has its direct channels to the President."

John explained Kelly's visit with CIA Director Welch. He then spent the next five or ten minutes answering Dan's remaining questions.

After their discussion, John said he needed to go to the hotel to register and unpack. He'd wait there for Dan's call after he talked to Chris. Learning that John didn't have any plans for the evening, Dan invited him to join Candace and him for dinner, and John accepted.

Right after John left, Dan picked up the phone and dialed Chris' office. He had a direct number to Chris' secretary, but not into Chris' private office. The phone rang several times. He was just about to conclude Chris' staff wasn't working this afternoon when Margaret, Chris' secretary, picked up the phone. He breathed a sigh of relief.

He explained the urgency of talking to her boss. Was he in? Yes, she said. Within a matter of seconds, he heard Chris' voice.

"Dan," Chris said, "are you calling from Mexico?"

"No," Dan answered. "I'm back at the office. How did you know I was in Mexico?"

"The two daily newspapers are required reading here at the White House. You must have just gotten back?"

"Got in late last night. So I'm back at the office catching up on stuff that can't wait."

"I'm impressed. What gives?"

"You remember my friend, John Garcia?"

"Of course. Did he decide on that judgeship?"

Dan let out a slight laugh. "Well, we haven't talked about that recently. But he's soon to be a Supreme Court justice in New Mexico."

"Really. When did that happen?"

"The Governor appointed him to a vacancy just a few days ago."

"He hasn't decided against the federal judgeship, has he?"

"I don't think so. We thought it wouldn't hurt if he got some state judicial experience should he decide to go for the judgeship next year."

"Of course. Excellent idea."

Dan took a deep breath. "He left my office a few minutes ago. There's a matter of great importance we'd like to talk to you about. In my opinion, it has both national and international security implications. Could we see you this afternoon? I wouldn't be asking on such short notice if it weren't important."

"I know that. Can you give me some idea what this is about?"

"I'd rather not over the phone. Though I believe it's something that needs to get to the President soon."

"It's that sensitive, huh?"

"Yeah. You think you might be able to arrange it so he can get the information by tonight?"

"Unfortunately, President Henning's at Camp David this weekend. So is his high-echelon staff. It'd be impossible to arrange an appointment even with the President's Chief of Staff or his deputies. They're all with the President, and they're not due back until Monday morning."

"Maybe you can set up a meeting with someone else?"

"Look, why don't you come on down here as soon as you can. I plan to be here all afternoon and into the evening. Use the southwest gate, which is closer to my office. I'll have Margaret notify security there so they'll let you in."

"We'll be there as soon as possible."

An hour or so later, John and Dan sat in Chris' office in the west wing.

"It's nice seeing you again," Chris said to John.

"Thanks," John said. "Likewise. I appreciate your agreeing to see us."

"No problem."

"Listen, Chris," Dan began, you've got a load of work to do, I'm sure, so we'll get right down to the point." Dan turned to John. "Why don't you tell Chris what you told me."

John then told his story again. He could tell Chris was intrigued because he spoke without interruption. Chris had a few questions, which John answered.

Chris sat there for a long moment, as if contemplating what John had told him. "It's ironic, John," he said, "that you should end up playing a role in this drama."

"How's that?" John said.

"I recall the last time we talked, we spoke of the presidential race coming up next year, and Condon's name came up."

"That's right. That made me feel rather weird at the time, his name popping up like that."

"Why was that?" Dan asked.

"Well, let me put it in perspective. That luncheon meeting of ours came a few days after I learned about the CIA's surveillance. Kelly had just asked me to draw on my memory banks to try remembering persons I had known in Southeast Asia. Then Condon's name surfaced during our discussions."

"You're right," Chris said. "Who'd have predicted then that we'd be discussing Condon once again in a context in which you yourself were involved?"

"Now we know how Emory's planning to fund his campaign," Dan added. "Discovery of the LaPierre documents, though, is definitely going to destroy his political plans."

Chris smiled. "It'll destroy not only his plans for next year but his entire political future."

"I was wondering what's going to happen with the information," John said. "What I mean is—how will these incriminating documents be used against him."

"Well, there are several possibilities. What's important, I think, is that it has more far-reaching implications than just affecting Condon's presidential aspirations. It may also involve other individuals. Just as important, once the intelligence goes public, other countries or groups that may have been involved in the illegalities will probably feel some heat. Certainly, China will."

"Once President Henning's informed of the documents, do you think he'll take his time deciding how to use the information?"

"I don't think so. My sense would be that he'd act quickly."

"I've been wondering what effect the documents would have on those implicated today as compared to when Henri hid them. In a curious way, their disclosure will have a greater impact today, especially on Condon, than they would have if I had gotten my hands on them back then."

"And you would have found the documents long ago, John," Dan added," if Etcitty had informed you then of Henri's interest in finding you.

"There's a bit of irony in that. Although I didn't have the documents in my possession and didn't even know of their existence, I managed to get my hands on them. What's ironic is that wouldn't have happened but for the Chinese coming after me in the first place. Everything that's happened to lead me to the documents seems to have fallen into place from that point forward."

"Getting back to the Chinese's sudden interest," Chris pondered, "it won't be the first time they've shown a strong interest in this country's affairs, if that's what they're after. John, I think your CIA friend, Kelly, is correct that some recent event has rekindled their interest in the documents."

"Do you think that interest might have something to do with Emory?" Dan asked.

"That's hard to say, but at the moment, I'd say if that was the case, it'd be an interesting coincidence."

"So how's the best way to get this material to President Henning?"

"How long will you be in town, John?"

"I've got a flight tomorrow morning," John replied.

"That means I'd have to set up something this afternoon, then." He paused for a moment. "Well, the Vice-President didn't go to Camp David. It's standard policy that he stays here if President Henning's out of town. Possibly, I could set up a meeting with him later today."

Chris was referring to Vice-President Charles Melvin Hirsch, whom President Henning was considering not choosing as his running mate in the following year's primaries. Rumors of the President dumping Hirsch in favor of another candidate had already surfaced in Washington's political circles. President Henning, however, when approached on the question, always managed to avoid answering it by claiming Vice-President Hirsch was doing a fine job. To political analysts in the know, however, that wasn't the same as saying the Vice-President would be the President's running mate next year.

"What do you think, John?" Dan asked.

"That's fine." John said. "It'll at least start the ball rolling, and we can follow it up later."

Later that evening, John and Dan were greeted by Vice-President Hirsch in his suite of offices located in the west wing.

The Vice-President was tall but not lanky. He was rather stocky, possessing broad shoulders and a heavy bone structure. He met his two visitors in his spacious office and ushered them into an adjacent conference room. John thought the switch a bit odd but assumed the Vice-President had a good reason for it. The man towered above the six-foot heights of John and Dan as he asked them to sit at the conference table. He sat at the head of the table. They exchanged pleasantries. John sensed a cool reception by their host, which made him uncomfortable.

Vice-President Hirsch also seemed a bit impatient and aloof, even though he used kind, even gentle words as he spoke to his visitors.

John dismissed the aloofness as the trait of a person in such high office. He had never met the Vice-President before, having known him only by his TV image. He seemed friendly enough on TV, but that obviously wasn't the case today in this private meeting.

Despite the Vice-President's cool demeanor, John couldn't help being awed by the experience. Discussing a matter of such importance with a man of his stature wasn't an everyday event.

For the next half hour, Dan and John briefed Vice-President Hirsch on the LaPierre documents. John had asked Dan beforehand to do most of the talking, and Dan had agreed. Although he went into considerable detail concerning the documents themselves, he only summarized the events leading up to John's involvement.

Although the Vice-President appeared mesmerized as Dan related the information, his impatience soon appeared to have been replaced by a slight anxiety. It manifested itself by the man's inability to remain seated without moving around.

"This is rather shocking news, indeed," he said in a deep voice when Dan had finished. "I'll inform the President of our meeting as soon as possible after his return from Camp David. I'm certain he'll be eager to learn of this interesting bit of intelligence you've provided me with, Senator Conniff. I'm much obliged to both of you."

To John, the man seemed a bit edgy now.

"Will someone be getting in touch with us soon, Mr. Vice-President?" Dan asked, using expected protocol.

"I would assume the President's Chief of Staff, if not the President himself, will be back in touch with you, Senator Conniff, after they've been briefed. I intend to speak to the President directly. Possibly as early as tomorrow afternoon, when I expect to talk to him by telephone."

Without in the slightest hiding his impatience, the Vice-President turned to gaze at the wall clock. It was a clear sign that he had other important matters to attend to and now considered the meeting at an end.

John and Dan took the hint. They thanked Vice-President Hirsch for taking the time to see them. Dan expressed his regrets for imposing on his busy schedule. The Vice-President escorted his visitors through his private office and into the broad hallway that would lead them to the northwest gate. There, the Vice-President bid them farewell.

After the meeting, Dan went home to shower and to pick up Candace. John returned to his hotel room. Before parting, they made plans for dinner at the *Potomack Landing*, a restaurant specializing in seafood.

They traveled to the restaurant in separate cars. It was located at the Washington Sailing Marina on Daingerfield Island, along the west bank of the Potomac. The island was on the Arlington, Virginia side, just off the George Washington Memorial Parkway. It was a mile or so south of the Parkway's exit to the terminal at Washington National Airport.

At night, across the Potomac to the northeast, diners at the restaurant had a beautiful view of the glistening lights in the nation's capital. The brightly-lit, white marble of the Capitol on the Hill and of the Washington Monument stood starkly against the blackness of the night sky.

As they dined, John and Dan were careful not to mention their meetings with Chris and Vice-President Hirsch. Instead, they spoke of politics back home and of Dan's political future.

The conversation moved on to John's judicial appointment. John told them of his growing eagerness to wind down his affairs at the firm and to start his work in Santa Fe. It was an exciting time for Demi and him, he said, and he hoped Dan and Candace could attend his swearing in and reception just days away. The staff at the office had already begun coordinating their plans with court officials for the ceremonies. Dan and Candace promised they'd be there.

CHAPTER 27

AFTER dinner, they ordered after-dinner drinks. Much to Candace's amusement, John and Dan wrangled over who was going to pay the check. John, the more insistent, won the round and ended up paying the tab.

As they left the restaurant, Dan suggested they stop for a nightcap at his and Candace's favorite night spot in Georgetown. John declined the invitation, explaining he was tired and preferred returning to his hotel room to rest. They took a detour to their cars, walking part way along a dirt path between the restaurant and the Potomac River. At the end of the path, they walked through the sailing marina onto the parking lot, enjoying the cool breeze that blew across the water.

John kissed Candace on the cheek before she entered the car. Before leaving, Dan told him he'd contact Kelly as soon as he heard any word from the White House.

A few miles after entering the Parkway, John veered right to take Interstate 395 North, which crossed over what was known as the 14th Street Bridge. The bridge had been named the Arland D. Williams Jr.

Bridge, but its more common name stuck with the natives. From there, John would cross the Potomac into D. C., where he would have easy access to his hotel.

As he came onto the bridge, he noticed the bright headlights of a car approaching fast from the rear. Realizing something wasn't quite right, he kept his eye on the car through the rearview mirror and began to accelerate. He could see the car had two occupants, the driver and another person seated in front. The car was following at close range, and he grew apprehensive. In a moment, he felt the beat of his heart as the adrenalin pumped through him.

The car began to accelerate. Before he could register what was happening, the vehicle was traveling alongside him on the inside lane. At this time of night, there was little traffic on the bridge's three eastbound lanes. Both cars were midway across the bridge by now, traveling at a high rate of speed. He wondered if Kelly had arranged for an FBI surveillance team tonight. If the agents were around, he thought, they'd be right on top of them by now.

His heart pounded faster as he realized the mystery car wasn't going to pass him by. The unknown driver accelerated again until the front of his car was a few feet ahead of John's. He then began edging his way into John's lane. John swerved to the right, thinking he had plenty of space to maneuver. But the concrete wall running along the edge of the bridge prevented him from maneuvering further right.

He thought of applying his brakes and slowing down but realized that wouldn't cut it. The other car would only slow down to match his speed. Besides, through the rearview mirror, he noticed the headlights of other cars in the distance. Stopping or even slowing down could prove dangerous.

Again, the car swerved to the right, crowding him even more. He veered to avoid a collision, inches away from the embankment. The other vehicle now occupied half of his lane. If the driver swerved a third time, John had little room to maneuver before sideswiping the bridge's concrete edge. The two vehicles approached the end of the bridge. The inside lanes led to Route 1 and 14th Street, which passed through downtown, while the outside lanes continued on to Interstate 395.

John began having difficulty keeping a firm grip on the steering wheel and noticed why. His hands were sweating.

Ahead, at a point after the bridge ended and Interstate 395 veered to the right, he noticed an exit ramp. The ramp, he recalled, led into East

Potomac Park, which at this time of night was barren of activity. It wasn't the place to end up.

If the mysterious car swerved toward him further as they approached the exit ramp leading into the park, John would have plenty of space to veer to the right to avoid a collision. But unless he pulled into the exit ramp, he risked colliding head on with the embankment separating the bridge lane from the ramp. He soon realized that's what the driver was attempting to do—force him onto the ramp. He was unsure whether the ramp would lead him past the park. But he had no choice.

As he had anticipated, when he cleared the embankment edge and came upon the ramp entrance, the car swerved one last time onto his path. He veered inches to the right, hoping to avoid a collision. In an instant, he looked up and saw he was headed into the embankment dividing the ramp from his lane. He turned the steering wheel to enter the ramp. As he did, the driver turned his wheels and followed him down the ramp.

The ramp veered to the right in a half-circle. As John approached its end, he grew confused by a number of detour and road repair signs. He maneuvered around a maze of barricades and, for the first time, recognized the road. He was underneath the bridge, crossing to the west into West Potomac Park. Driving fast past the temporary barricades, he wasn't sure which way to go. Several times, he turned into several temporary, unpaved roads that seemed to lead him nowhere outside the immediate area.

The unknown driver hadn't let up on the chase. His blinding headlights kept at high beam, he was close behind. Fortunately for John, in the confusion, the driver made a wrong turn, running into a road barricade from which there was no exit. The car lost time in backtracking. As a result, John managed to increase the distance between them by 100 yards.

Ahead, he noticed new barricades, leaving only one way out—a narrow, circular path. He missed one of the barricades as he turned the steering wheel, causing the car's wheels to lose traction as he maneuvered the sharp turn to the right. He then found himself on a circular road bearing right. Without warning, he came upon a wide barricade blocking his path. He had no place to go except for turning around and heading back the same road. Panicking, he brought the car to a stop. Now what?

His eyes soon registered his surroundings. To his left was the Tidal Basin, to the right, the Jefferson Memorial. He had three choices. The basin wasn't a real option. His second alternative was to take off running down the concrete path or sidewalk around the Tidal Basin, scampering into the fields of vegetation surrounding it. In the darkness, if he was lucky, he'd lose his pursuers in the heavy brush. He opted for the final choice, which he thought his best—run up the steps into the memorial to seek help.

Lit by the many flood lights focused on its stark white marble, the colossal memorial stood above him. At the top of the wide marbled steps, he spotted a National Park Service guide standing forward of the front entrance. The front of the structure where he had brought the car to a halt was closed to vehicular traffic because of the extensive road construction in the area. Apparently, the guide had noticed John's car, for the area he had entered, John noticed, was prohibited to vehicular traffic.

Behind the park guide, he saw several tourists near the front entrance to the memorial. He hoped there was some kind of armed security in the memorial, possibly even a patrolman from the National Park Police.

He had visited the Jefferson Memorial in the past and remembered it had a gift and souvenir shop. Would his pursuers harm him in front of a dozen or so onlookers? Besides, if there was a phone there, he could call for help.

He leaped from the vehicle. He had run around the front of the car when he noticed the approaching headlights from behind. He ran to the steps and began climbing them two and three at a time. Even at a run in the dim light, he saw the surprised look on the park guide's face. The guide's eyes moved from John to the car that had just pulled up, then to John again. The two men exited the vehicle.

Obviously realizing something was wrong, the guide hurried down the steps to meet up with John. John tried waving him back when he heard the sound of running footsteps behind him. He didn't dare turn around for fear he'd lose his footing. His plan hadn't worked, he thought, for they had chosen to follow him after all, undeterred by the presence of the park guide and what few tourists walked around the memorial.

On the verge of panic, he sensed he had to do more than just try running away from his pursuers. He shouted at the park guide, who was now a few yards away from him, to summon help. The young man appeared confused. Again, John yelled to call the police. He was about to warn the guide that the men were dangerous when he heard the sound of a gun blast behind him. A second shot rang out, then a third.

The park guide toppled forward onto the marble steps. One of the shots had hit its mark. John began running faster now and didn't bother stopping to see if the fallen guide had a weapon. When he ran past the guide, he heard him groaning. Thank God, he thought, at least the man's alive.

For a split second, the thought of stopping and facing his pursuers swept through his mind. Would they be bold enough to take him by force in front of others? Did they want to interrogate him? He knew what they were after.

Yet, these men were killers. They had killed Leroy. They'd stop at nothing, and John's life, absent the LaPierre documents, meant nothing to them. No, he said under his breath, he wouldn't give up without a fight.

He reached the floor of the memorial and spotted the small groups of tourists there. They were running for cover, for they either had heard the shots or had seen the park guide gunned down. John hoped he'd spot a policeman or another guide but saw no one he thought would come to his aid.

He was on his own and had to find a place to hide. That was his only hope.

There were two wide copper-toned metal doors on each side of the entrance. Before him was the towering bronze figure of Thomas Jefferson, its penetrating eyes looking above the Tidal Basin and toward the White House. His only chance not to be taken hostage was to enter through one of the two doors, hoping he'd find either someone who could help or a place to hide.

He entered the door on the left, which was closest to him. The door, he recalled, was to a lobby leading into the gift and souvenir shop. In the gift shop, there were several tourists browsing through souvenirs. An elderly gentleman minding the shop stood behind the glass counter. John thought of entering the shop but rejected the idea, for he wasn't sure what lay beyond.

He tried a closed metal door to his left. It was heavy, but it opened. A stairway led downward below the monument. He decided against going down the stairs. His gut instinct told him it too led to a dead end. He was close to panic—most likely, his pursuers had reached the floor of the monument. There was one other choice—a middle door. It too was unlocked. Without hesitation, he entered and closed the door behind him.

He found himself in a darkened room. There wasn't even a hint of light coming from an exit or window. Outside, he heard the hurried footsteps of the men, first on the monument floor, then in the lobby. The door leading to the stairway opened, and he heard the sound of steps running down the stairs into the basement and whatever lay beyond. He wasn't certain both men had gone down the steps. One might still be in the lobby area.

He was tempted to open the door and peek out. If the two men had gone down the stairs, the coast would be clear to run down to his car and drive away before they realized what had happened. But the risk was too great—if he was spotted, he'd be a goner.

His eyes began to adjust to the pitch darkness of the room. He tried to find a light switch by feeling the wall nearest him with the palms of his hands but couldn't. His pupils had dilated, and he now could see beyond the darkness of the room and detect the outline of shelving and the room's fixtures. He also saw the outline of boxes piled up high. The room was a storage area.

It dawned on him that, in order for him to see the stack of boxes, some light had to be entering the room from somewhere. He hurried to the middle of the room, making sure he didn't stumble on a box or piece of furniture.

He looked around to see if he could spot a doorway or opening from which even a sliver of light was coming through. At first, he saw nothing. Then he glanced up to the ceiling.

There, near the far wall, he saw what appeared to be some kind of opening. He walked toward the wall. The opening turned out to be the beginning of a tall shaft leading upward twenty feet or so above the room's ceiling. At the top, there appeared to be some kind of door. That was where the light was filtering into the room. Adjusting to the dark even more, he spotted the metal ladder bolted parallel to the wall, reaching all the way up the shaft to the opening.

Outside, he heard footsteps coming up the stairway. He wouldn't have time to look for another exit. Climbing the ladder was now his sole option. He hurried up the ladder as fast as he could. When he reached the top, it occurred to him that the cover might be locked. He spotted the latch and turned it. There was no lock—it opened. He pushed the cover upward, and it moved. Through the crack, he glimpsed a sliver of the night sky. He was on the roof. He let the cover back down.

If the men should come into the room below and discover the ladder, he had nowhere else to go but onto the roof. Was there another way down? If they spotted him and came up the ladder after him, would he be trapped on the roof? He tried not to think of that eventuality, for it was possible the men might not even enter the room. Or they might not find the ladder. There was even a chance they would decide to abandon their efforts and leave. Fat chance, he mumbled to himself.

He decided to remain there and not climb onto the roof. Yet, he might find another door on the roof leading below. As he pondered those thoughts, what he had dreaded happened—he heard the sound of the door opening below. He felt weak from fear.

The chase had caused a surge of adrenalin so that he hadn't taken time to reflect on his next move. But now, after some quiet moments of reflection, the thought that he could elude his pursuers or that they would abandon their chase had been a real possibility. That evaporated when the men entered the room. He was now confronted once again with the risk of being discovered and captured.

As he looked up at the metal cover above him, he soon saw light coming from below. His first thought was that the men had found the light switch. He looked downward. There was definitely some light in the room, but it wasn't bright enough to come from a ceiling light.

When he saw the light move and cast shadows, he recognized its source. One of the men had a small flashlight. The light kept getting brighter, which meant to him the two men were nearing the shaft. The light got stronger until a beam of light fell at the bottom of the ladder. In another second, he spotted them—they were looking up. One was shining the flashlight on him.

He pushed the cover open and climbed onto the roof. As soon as he closed the cover, he heard the men climbing up the ladder. He examined the cover to see if it could be locked from the outside, but it couldn't. He looked around to see where on the roof he was.

The roof had different levels. He was on the lowest level. In the center, lit by the large floodlights located on the grounds surrounding the monument, was the structure's dome. Below it was a circular parapet, followed by the middle level roof. This second level was surrounded by a curved wall that hid the roof level from him.

It occurred to him that the mid-level might provide another way out. He attempted scaling the high wall without success. On the outside rim of the roof level he was on, there was a circular parapet about five feet high that formed the outer rim or ledge. Anyone looking up toward the massive dome would be able to see him from the shoulders up. He might be able to signal someone for help.

He rushed to the outer ledge and looked down. He was on the east side of the monument, the Capitol on the Hill shining to the northeast. He looked north, toward the White House, which he could see even in the pitch darkness surrounding it. He ran to the outside ledge on the north end, the front of the monument. It overlooked the marble steps he had run up a few moments ago. There was no one below he could yell down to.

He moved counterclockwise along the circular roof, hoping he would stumble upon another door cover, but he found nothing. Panic again set in, for he realized there was no place to go. He was trapped. Behind him, he heard the sound of the metal door closing. The two men were on the roof. In one last, desperate attempt, he jumped up as high as he could against the inside circular wall that separated him from the middle roof level. Again, he was unable to scale the wall. He was now at the monument's south end.

He waited for the inevitable to happen. Would he be tortured? Would he end up like Henri, a pile of ashes? Matters could be far worse, he tried to convince himself, for he was alone, and Demi and the children were back home safe. Tong could have made its move when he and Demi had been together, or worse yet, when Crystal and Johnny were around. That in a sense was some consolation. Was there an FBI surveillance team covering him? If so, had it been eliminated before his encounter on the bridge? Were these men on the roof Tong operatives? He'd soon find out.

Within seconds, he heard footsteps on the gravel roof approaching from his left. Seconds later, he heard the same sound coming from the other side. Soon, he'd have the satisfaction of seeing the faces of his tormentors. He wouldn't even be able to put up much of a fight. They probably had guns; he didn't.

The two men soon appeared to each side of him, seconds apart. Both had their handguns drawn as they rounded the edges of the circular wall. He could see their faces from the light reflecting off the dome above. Their Asian features couldn't be mistaken. He noticed a slight smirk on

342

the face of one of them. The other looked at him almost without expression. Neither of them said a word. John himself, afraid to speak out, remained frozen in place. At that moment, he could have sworn he heard, not just felt, the heavy pounding of his heart.

Events moved fast from then on. He first heard the low roar of what sounded like an aircraft nearby. The sound seemed to have no particular direction but was all around him. The sound became louder and began to reverberate at a high pitch. It was a whirling-like sound, and its vibration filled the night sky.

He looked up, searching for whatever it was that was making the loud roar. He then recognized the pulsating, reverberating sound—the rotary blades of a helicopter. Where was it? It had to be close, for the sound had become ear-deafening. The two Tong operatives too began searching the sky.

Without warning, the swirl of the high-velocity air came down on the three men, and the helicopter appeared above the monument dome. Hovering above them, the aircraft shined an intense, blinding spotlight down on the roof. Because of the whirlwind thrust caused by the rotary blades, it became difficult for the three men to maintain their balance. They held their hands and arms up in a futile effort to protect themselves from the intense light. Tong reinforcements, John guessed, coming to help in his eventual abduction.

Before he could even begin to realize what was taking place, the two men began running for cover. Without looking up, the would-be abductors began firing their weapons into the sky in the direction of the aircraft. John hit the roof floor to protect himself from the gunfire that now came from the helicopter. Someone in there was firing a rapid-fire weapon. But he soon realized the fire was directed at his would-be captors.

Within seconds, the two men were gunned down as they attempted to flee. Riddled by bullets, they fell onto the gravel. John stood up, protecting himself from the whirlwind force of the aircraft's blades. He braced himself against the inside marble wall.

The intense light then disappeared, and the rotating blades of the aircraft changed their pitch as the helicopter pulled away. He stood there stunned, attempting to comprehend what had happened within a matter of seconds. Leaving no trace except its fallen prey and, for him, a vivid memory of its ear-deafening sound, the aircraft disappeared into the blackness of the night sky.

For what seemed an eternity, he stood there motionless, trying to make sense out of what had occurred. Were those FBI or CIA agents in the helicopter? If not, who in hell were they? He had no idea how long he remained standing there when he heard the wailing sounds of sirens approaching.

When he returned below, he wasn't surprised to find considerable panic among the tourists and several employees. The few tourists who were still on the floor of the monument moved about full of nervous energy. He learned from one of them that the wounded park guide had been carried by his co-workers into one of the offices inside the monument.

Down below, at the foot of the steps leading down to where John had abandoned his car, several National Park policemen were interrogating another group of tourists. One of them was pointing to John's car and the vehicle left there by the Tong agents.

From one of the park guides, John found out where the injured guide had been taken. He walked through the doorway at the opposite end of the monument. There, inside a small office, he found the wounded man lying on a portable cot. He was conscious, which relieved John. A National Park policeman was interrogating him. As soon as the guide spotted John, he identified him to the policeman as the man being chased by the men who shot him. The policeman asked John to wait outside; he wanted to talk to him. John left and waited for the policeman to appear.

Soon, two paramedics arrived with a stretcher. They moved the injured park guide onto it and took him down the steps to the waiting ambulance. After inquiring of John whether he was hurt, the policeman asked him a few questions in an attempt to piece together what had occurred. John pled ignorance to the officer's main question—why was he being chased? He explained his encounter on the bridge and the chase leading to the monument. He informed the policeman of the two dead men on the monument's roof and showed him how to get there.

After he had finished questioning John, the policeman used his cellular phone to call his headquarters. The officer made arrangements for John to meet with park investigators later at park police headquarters. He was to wait at the memorial until he received further instructions.

At the police station later, his statement was audio recorded during an interrogation that lasted half an hour. He wasn't sure how much information he should provide to the investigators. He knew Kelly didn't want him to divulge information concerning the CIA and FBI's involvement.

Over and over again, he explained what had happened on the 14th Street Bridge. He told his interrogators of the chase into the monument grounds, his decision to seek help at the memorial, and how he ended up climbing the ladder onto the roof. He spoke of the mysterious helicopter that had appeared out of nowhere. More than that, he preferred not telling them.

Even though he thought he had satisfied their interest for more information, they continued with their questions. They wanted to know the identity of the two men and the reason for the chase. Did he know why they might want to hurt him, they asked. He told them he had no idea, but he could tell they didn't believe him.

They persisted, and he merely rephrased his responses so they appeared to add new pieces of information here and there, without providing anything new. He hoped doing so would quench their thirst for information, but it didn't work. Even if he were to mention the CIA or FBI's involvement in the case, he sensed his interrogators wouldn't be satisfied with a part of the story.

After a few minutes, several FBI and CIA agents arrived. He was relieved to see them, for the park police were beginning to get impatient. The interrogators were puzzled by the appearance of the agents. It took little time for the agents to exert their authority, and John was soon whisked away to FBI headquarters.

There, he felt more at ease answering questions, for he could speak without being concerned about what he divulged. In fact, he had a few questions of his own. He learned that two FBI agents had indeed been assigned to tail him that night but were attacked, presumably by the two men later gunned down. They had been intercepted in the parking lot of the *Potomack Landing*. The two agents were alive, the CIA/FBI team said, but were injured as a result of several bullet wounds and taken to Georgetown University Medical Center.

The interrogators also confirmed that the two men who had tried to abduct John were Tong operatives. The helicopter, however, was a mystery. They had no idea whom it belonged to, who had been operating it, or where it had come from. They hoped he might shed some light. Had he noticed any identifying marks on the aircraft, they wanted to know. Not a chance, he said, explaining the intensity of the light shining down on the monument roof, which prevented him from seeing the aircraft, much less markings.

Did he even have a vague idea who was in the helicopter, they asked. He thought for a moment. Who, other than the FBI or CIA, had an interest in protecting him? Who else might want to make sure the Tong operatives didn't harm or kidnap him?

It didn't take long, once he put his mind to it, to come up with a possibility. Could it have been Guy Zanotelli? It made sense. Guy hadn't trusted the CIA. He had made that fact clear to him. He remembered Guy had been insistent in offering help. It wouldn't hurt, he had told him, to have backup protection.

John was about to relate his suspicions to his interrogators when the telephone rang. It was Kelly on the line. The investigators postponed their interrogation to permit John to take the call.

Kelly had learned what happened within a half hour after the two agents tailing John had failed to report into headquarters. Was John all right, he wanted to know. John assured him that he was.

"That helicopter saved my fucking ass," he whispered to Kelly. "These fellows here insist it wasn't theirs. Can you confirm that?"

"Affirmative," Kelly replied. "Our agency knew nothing about it. But I've got my suspicions. I think your lawyer friend, Zanotelli, was involved."

"Yeah, I was thinking the same thing and was just about to tell these guys when you called."

"Let me handle it. I'll give him a call as soon as we hang up. Contact me tomorrow when you get ready to leave; I'll let you know what he said."

"I'll do that."

Kelly paused. "Meanwhile, John, I'm getting a lot of heat from my boss due to your close call. He's insisting we end our clandestine surveillance and instead provide full-time, round-the-clock protection. Face it. You and your family are in danger, now more than ever."

He didn't hesitate. "The last thing I need is a lecture, Kelly. I'm already pissed at myself for letting it get this far. Do it, damn it! I want my family protected to the fullest. But do me a favor—don't let Demi know what happened tonight. I'll tell her at the right time."

"Fair enough. I'll get on it right away. But for the time being, we'll have to use our local agents to cover your family."

"So?"

346

"Exceptionally skilled agents that are trained for this specialized surveillance will have to be flown in from elsewhere. Until they're in place, we'll do the best we can with what we've got."

"I understand." He cursed to himself; he had no one else to blame for this predicament. "But whatever you do, please don't get Demi and the kids alarmed."

"We'll do our very best."

"When can you start?"

"First thing in the morning. I'll get in touch with Demi myself."

Before hanging up, Kelly confirmed he'd be at the airport to meet him the next day.

CHAPTER 28

ON a beautiful, sunny Sunday afternoon, Demi and Lourdes sat in the outdoor patio of the *Mañana Restaurant & Bar* in Santa Fe. An early afternoon breeze felt crisp and was filled with the sweet odor of piñon firewood lingering from nearby fireplaces burning through the night.

The restaurant occupied a stucco-adobe building alongside the diminutive Santa Fe River. Wrought iron tables and wooden director's chairs furnished the patio. Bright green and orange umbrellas covering the tables provided the patio with a gay atmosphere. The floor was inlaid with large flagstone pieces on the outer edges and terrazzo tile in the center.

Demi had met Lourdes earlier at St. Francis Cathedral a few blocks down the street, where they had attended eleven o'clock mass. They walked the short distance from the cathedral to the restaurant to eat a light brunch.

The two women had just ordered. Lourdes was sipping a cup of coffee, and Demi was drinking a glass of orange juice. The last day of the Santa Fe Fiesta was in full swing. The activities down on the plaza had lured the curious tourists away from their usual eating places. Demi was glad, for she found the less-crowded dining area refreshing.

The previous night, Lourdes suggested she could stop by their mother's house in Tesuque to pick up Demi for church. Demi resisted the idea and insisted she'd meet her sister at the church. Her reason for not wanting Lourdes to pick her up at Lupe Flynn's house was a good one.

The FBI, Kelly had explained, made some last-minute changes to their surveillance. He had called Demi that morning to tell her it had become necessary to tighten security measures, thus requiring changes. The surveillance teams were instructed to cease their undercover work and to come out in the open so that closer protection could be provided. Kelly wanted his agents to be present at Lupe Flynn's house. What about John, Demi wanted to know. Had Kelly spoken to him about the changes? John was aware of them, Kelly replied, and had given his approval.

Demi became alarmed, wondering what had prompted the change. Kelly offered no explanation, however, other than that the agency had reason to believe the threat to her and the children's safety was now more immediate, thus warranting the added precaution.

She'd have to seek permission from Lupe Flynn to allow the intrusion into her home. Even so, Kelly instructed Demi not to divulge to her mother or sister more than needed to permit the agents in her house.

Demi didn't want her sister to know of the FBI protection, for fear of getting her involved and thus be put at risk. As it was, she was reluctant to tell her mother much concerning the FBI/CIA effort for the same reason. But she knew that couldn't be helped. She was surprised her mother had asked few questions concerning the men in her house. That was typical of Lupe Flynn—trusting when it came to her daughters.

As Lourdes brought Demi up to date on the recent romances in her life, she called the waiter to order two glasses of wine before their brunch order arrived.

Demi's sister was much smaller than Demi, but a little broader at the waist, a fact that she often reminded Demi of. She'd tell Demi often that she'd give anything to have her slim waist. Yet, Lourdes resembled Demi in her facial features, including the same straight, well-structured nose. She wore her hair shorter. This morning, she also wore small, rimless glasses, which Demi had never seen before.

"To you and your love life," Demi said when Lourdes finished telling her of her most recent involvement. "May you soon sort things out and live a life of bliss forever after. Believe me, you'll know in your heart when the right man comes along."

They each picked up their glasses and brought them together.

"Speaking of bliss," Lourdes said, "let's move on to your life. You've seemed a little stressed the last few days. You can't hide it from your sister, you know. What gives?"

"I admit I've been uptight," Demi answered. "Quite a lot is going on in our lives right now. It's not a serious problem—yet." She knew she was lying and paused, wondering how much to divulge. She decided she'd minimize what she definitely considered a major problem. "That's why I decided to get away. Give us some breathing room."

"Shit, Demi, sounds serious to me. What's the problem?"

"John's work at the office has been getting out of hand. It's gotten grueling and demanding for him. As a result, he's found himself under a tremendous amount of pressure. And, as you might expect, it's stressing us out, to put it mildly."

Demi thought of the LaPierre affair and of what she considered the CIA and FBI's unwanted entry into her family's lives. She glanced to the far corner of the patio, where an FBI agent sat drinking a cup of coffee and reading a newspaper. He had been assigned to provide protection this morning and had followed her to church from her mother's house and then on to the restaurant. Had Lourdes noticed him following a half block behind after they exited St. Francis Cathedral, she wondered. And this was only the beginning, Kelly had explained. Specialized agents were on their way to provide what he termed *intensive* surveillance.

She was tempted to tell Lourdes all she knew of the LaPierre matter. It'd be a relief to tell someone. If she were to reveal it to anyone at all, for sure it would be to her own sister. But why involve her in this mess? What could she do, other than act as a sounding board? Talking to her might help relieve some of the pressure, but it could place her in danger. Even if it didn't do that, why give her reason to worry?

The waiter brought their food order. By then, they had finished their glass of wine, and Lourdes convinced Demi they should order another one with their brunch.

As they enjoyed the food, instead of telling Lourdes about the LaPierre matter, Demi explained the basis for her earlier comments. John's behavior Friday night flashed through her mind, but she managed to block it out. She told Lourdes how John's demanding work at the office had placed a strain in their marriage. She spoke of his lack of involvement as a result of his being consumed with work.

"I could tell something was wrong," Lourdes said when Demi finished.

"I've been wondering if it was beginning to show," Demi said. "It's been hard."

Demi wasn't much of a drinker, and so she felt relaxed with the second glass of wine. She now realized she had blamed most of her stress on John's law practice. In fact, the LaPierre case was also responsible.

"I shouldn't place all the blame on John's work," she found herself saying.

"What do you mean?"

"Well, let's just say there's something else that's come up."

"Like what, Demi?" Lourdes paused to drink some wine. "There isn't another person involved romantically with John, is there? Or with you?"

Demi forced a laugh. "Of course not. Nothing like that." Her sister's question brought to mind the incident with Dick Dunn.

"What are you referring to, then?"

"I shouldn't have brought it up. But since I have, let me just say I'm not going to involve you because I don't want you getting hurt."

"Demi, you're scaring me!" Lourdes put her fork and knife down and pushed her plate away. "What's going on? Tell me, for God's sake. I'm your sister."

"I can't, Lourdes." She was angry at herself for opening the door. "I didn't mean to give you reason to worry." She placed a hand on her sister's hand. "But it's got nothing to do with John's or my fidelity. It's something that's arisen involving John's past, and it's causing a bit of a problem. But we're hoping it'll get resolved soon."

Lourdes pled with her to confide in her, but she refused to revisit the subject.

As the two sisters brunched at the *Mañana Restaurant*, a few miles north of Santa Fe, in the outlying area of Tesuque, Lupe Flynn sat in the covered patio of her adobe home.

Its floors inlaid in flagstone, the patio ran across the entire length of the house's back wall. Large redwood trellises covered the courtyard. They were tied together and laying horizontal on top of vertical, decorative posts anchored into the ground along the edges. The trellises allowed the vivid blue sky to be seen overhead. Overgrown shrubs planted along the patio's edges and at its center made the patio appear smaller than it was.

Vertical trellises filled with vines lined the patio's edges. The side facing the backyard was open, however, permitting a clear view of the land lying beyond Lupe's property line.

Lupe was a petite woman in her mid-seventies. Despite her age, she was a person full of vigor and an appreciation and love for life. Her salt and pepper hair was rather long, and this sunny afternoon, she had fixed it in a bun at the back, held together with a large hair pin. She possessed striking green eyes, which were watching her two grandchildren play in a large, portable pool.

Lupe had enjoyed Demi's and her grandchildren's stay. She loved them with all her heart and invited them into her home with open arms. In the past, she made certain they knew they were always welcome. Ever since Wednesday morning, when her daughter and the children arrived, Lupe's hours were filled with happiness.

This morning, however, her sullen eyes betrayed her thoughts. Her mind was occupied with impressions of the reason behind her daughter's visit. Demi said nothing to her, not even providing the slightest hint. Lupe, herself, was careful not to appear as meddling by making inquiries.

What worried her was her instinct that Demi was using the trip to get away from something bothering her. And she seemed edgy. Although she hadn't lost her smile and her sense of humor, at times Lupe had noticed the frowned brow or forlorn eyes betraying her gaiety.

For that reason, she suspected Demi and John might be experiencing hard times. She resolved herself to ask Demi if she was feeling well. That kind of inquiry would only show her concern for her daughter's welfare, not an intent to meddle in her affairs.

There was a more immediate reason for her concern as she sat in her favorite rocking chair watching Crystal and Johnny splash water on each other. It had to do with the two men who had earlier that morning imposed themselves in her home. Who were they? What in God's name were they doing here? Government agents of some sort, Demi had said to her when Demi asked her permission for the men to stay at her home. They were there to protect them, Demi explained. In heaven's name, why, Lupe asked, alarmed that her daughter and grandchildren needed protection.

Demi was more than a little vague when she explained the needed protection had something to do with John's military background. It had to do with events that occurred when John had served with the armed forces in Vietnam. Had he done something wrong, Lupe wanted to know. Demi assured her he hadn't.

If Demi said the two men's presence was necessary for the protection of her family, why should Lupe argue otherwise? She'd honor her daughter's request. Yet, she was uneasy all morning and would remain so until she learned more. She was determined to seek answers from her. While she delved into that, she decided, she'd ask if that was the source of Demi's seeming unhappiness.

Lupe sat facing the backyard, keeping an eye on her grandchildren. At the moment, Crystal and Johnny were getting out of the pool. They ran the few feet to the spot on the lawn where they had placed their beach towels earlier. The two of them lay down on their stomachs to soak in the warmth of the afternoon sun.

Lupe's attentive watch over her grandchildren was interrupted when she noticed movement along the side of the house. She turned and saw one of the government agents as he sat under some shade at the far end. He positioned the chair so he could see toward the front of the house and at the same time keep an eye on the two youngsters basking in the sun. Although the afternoon was warm, the FBI agent hadn't bothered taking off his suit coat. The coat, Lupe surmised, hid the weapon he carried so as not to upset the children. Lupe had caught a glimpse of it earlier that morning.

The other man, as far as Lupe knew, remained inside the house. Throughout the morning, the two men apparently alternated assignments with each other. A third man had been there earlier but disappeared after Demi left to meet Lourdes. Lupe guessed the man was assigned to follow Demi and would be gone until she returned.

No sooner had Lupe returned her eyes to her grandchildren when she heard the FBI agent inside the house call out to the one at the far corner of the patio. She returned her attention to the man at the edge of the house.

"Leonard," the agent inside shouted. "Come in here a minute!"

Several doors led out of the house and into the backyard. The ones used most often were the French doors near the middle of the house. The agent's voice inside the house, however, had come from the far side, near the door a few feet away from the man sitting outside. That door led into the kitchen. Lupe had kept the door open all morning to cool off the house. An unlocked screen door covered the doorway.

The man in the chair stood up. "What's the problem?" he shouted back.

"No problem; just wanted to show you something."

The agent opened the screen door and walked inside the house. Lupe returned her attention to the children. Crystal was still lying down on the towel, but Johnny had gotten up and wandered off. He was now at the far corner of Lupe's property, near the barbed wire fence separating the property from an open field. He acted as if he had become restless and now appeared to be exploring that part of the large yard.

Lupe became startled by the sound of loud voices, then shouting, coming from inside the house. The shouts were followed by the sharp sound of furniture being moved, as if a scuffle had ensued.

Within seconds, three strangers appeared through the French doors, armed with handguns. They wore black hoods that covered their heads, necks, and faces except for the holes cut out for their eyes and mouths. One of them ran to Lupe; the others toward the children. Afraid, she stood up and screamed. She ran toward the children but took only a few steps before the man in the hood grabbed her around the neck and shoved her to the ground. She continued screaming to the children as her assailant turned her over on her stomach, pinning her arms behind her back. Kicking, she turned her head so she could see Crystal and Johnny.

"Crystal, Johnny, run!" she shouted as hard as she could to make sure the children appreciated the danger of what was taking place. She panicked, not out of fear for what might happen to her but for the children's safety. A bullet from one of the weapons for certain would silence her any second, she feared, but the children must escape.

"Run, Johnny! Run, Crystal! Oh, my God, don't let them get you." She cried in agony as she saw Crystal and Johnny terrified and confused by the unexpected intrusion and the screams of their Grandma Lupe.

Crystal finally noticed the two men running to her and Johnny. Even from where she lay on the ground, Lupe couldn't mistake the look of fear in Crystal's eyes as she too began screaming. The young girl ran toward Johnny.

"Run, Johnny!" Crystal screamed at the top of her lungs. "They've got guns. Don't let them catch you!"

Johnny crossed the barbed wire fence and ran as fast as he could. The two men split off. The nearer of the two went after Crystal, the other after

Johnny. When he reached Crystal, the first one put his gun away and picked her up.

"Get away from here, Johnny!" she yelled. "Run as fast as you can."

The man placed a cloth to her mouth. He then took a small glass tube from his pocket and crushed it. Covering it with his hand, he placed it over Crystal's nose. In seconds, Crystal went limp in his arms.

Although unable to comprehend all that was happening, Lupe realized well what the man had done. He had given her granddaughter chloroform or some other kind of anesthetic that made her lose consciousness. Lupe screamed when she realized her granddaughter was about to be kidnaped.

"*No, no, madre de Dios, no puede ser!*" she cried. "Mother of God, this can't be!"

Johnny, who had gotten a good start on the third stranger running after him, was now far off in the distance. Although small, he was fast. He disappeared behind a hill, where Lupe was hoping he could lose himself in the thick brush of the foothills. She watched as the man too disappeared behind the hill. In another minute or so, Lupe saw the man reappear at the brim of the hill. Thank God, Johnny had escaped, she said to herself, wishing her arms were loose so she could make the *Sign of the Cross*.

Meanwhile, the man who carried Crystal walked back toward the house. As he passed by, he spoke to the man holding Lupe on the ground, but Lupe didn't understand what he said.

"I beg you," Lupe cried at the stranger carrying an unconscious Crystal. "For the love of God, please don't hurt her, whatever you do. I beg you!" She began sobbing, thinking the worst that could happen to her granddaughter. She couldn't comprehend why any of this was happening.

Out of breath, the other man returned from searching for Johnny. He rushed inside the house without saying a word. The man keeping a firm hold on Lupe released his grip. He stood up, and he too walked back into the house.

She remained lying there, not moving an inch. They might return, and the thought of running in the direction Johnny had disappeared crossed her mind. But she was too frightened to get up. She thought too of going inside the house and pleading with these terrible men not to hurt Crystal. But she knew they would ignore her pleas, intent in their purpose.

After what seemed an eternity, she heard the front door slam. Afterward, she heard the screeching of tires on the dirt shoulder of the road.

She waited another couple of minutes before she recovered her courage to stand up. Getting up, she noticed her hands were trembling. She sensed a desperate need to run crying onto the road to seek help. With it came a sense she might get hysterical. But she convinced herself it was important to stay calm and not lose control.

She hurried into the house. In the kitchen, she found the two federal agents on the floor. Thank God, there was no blood. She felt for a pulse. They were alive. She supposed they too had been given the same quick-acting anesthetic the abductors had used to immobilize Crystal.

She picked up the phone and dialed 911. Surprised that she had regained her composure, she reported the incident. After hanging up, she rushed outside in search of Johnny.

After finishing their meal, Demi and Lourdes each ordered cappuccino. They were waiting for their hot drink to arrive when a waiter they hadn't seen before approached them. He had entered the dining area not from inside the restaurant but from a side entrance leading into the back parking lot. He stopped at their table. The other waiters serving in the patio were rather trim and young—probably no more than thirty. This waiter wasn't only stockier but much older. To Demi, he seemed out of place.

In white costume and headdress, two Seiks sat at the next table. Seiks were members of a worldwide religious sect headquartered in Española, a small town north of Santa Fe. The two men in white clothing, clearly Asian, got up from the table and stood behind the stocky waiter. Demi couldn't help noticing the three men encroaching on their space. The two women exchanged puzzled looks.

From the corner of her eye, Demi noticed a busboy approach an unaware FBI agent at the far corner of the patio. It took her a split second to realize something was wrong. The worst she had dreaded these past weeks was about to happen. She panicked and bolted.

"Lourdes, get—" she managed to shout before the waiter lunged at her. He covered her mouth with a tight grip.

As a shocked Lourdes stood up, one of the Seiks grabbed her arms and pushed her face down on the floor. He immobilized her by placing his knee against the back of her legs. She began to scream.

Across the courtyard, the FBI agent looked up from his newspaper. The busboy reached from behind to restrict the agent's movement with a body grip. In another quick second, an anesthetic brought from the busboy's pocket knocked the agent unconscious.

Demi struggled with all her might as the Seik and waiter attempted to restrain her. The waiter brought the chloroform capsule to Demi's nose. Within moments, she lost consciousness, going limp in her assailants' arms.

Until now, the other patrons in the patio sat there paralyzed by the turn of events that had interrupted their quiet meal. Now, however, they sensed the danger of what was occurring, and so they began emptying the courtyard.

Two of the assailants, carrying an unconscious Demi, hurried through the wrought iron gate abutting the street. By now, the busboy too had disappeared. Outside the gate, he entered the driver's side of a car parked alongside the curb, the engine running. The Seik restraining Lourdes released his grip on her. He then followed the others through the gate leading to the street sidewalk. Lourdes, in pain and weak from her struggle, continued lying down. Managing to turn on her side, she caught a final glimpse through the open gate of Demi's limp body being placed in the car by her abductors.

The Seik who had subdued Lourdes opened the front door of the car, and the other abductors scurried in. The car disappeared around the corner, headed south away from the business district.

In the patio, a customer and two restaurant employees rushed to where a stunned Lourdes lay on the floor. She hid her face and began to weep.

CHAPTER 29

THE plane John boarded at National Airport arrived mid-afternoon in Albuquerque, a few hours after the abductions.

Before boarding, John had talked to Kelly by phone. The agent confirmed Guy's involvement the night before. Guy had admitted that *special friends* of his had arranged for the countermeasures made necessary by the turn of events.

Kelly displayed some concern that John's lawyer friend might be getting too involved in the case. Guy's involvement, he said, could interfere with the FBI/CIA's operation. John didn't hide his sarcasm when he reminded Kelly that, if it hadn't been for Guy, he would at this moment be in the hands of Tong. Kelly conceded the point.

When John hung up, he had fifteen minutes before having to board the plane. He decided to call Guy at home.

"I owe you my life," was all he said when Guy answered.

"John!" Guy said with considerable joy, recognizing John's voice. "Are you all right?"

"I'm doing fine, Guy, thanks to you. I just got off the phone with Kelly. That was quite a coup you pulled."

"Don't mention it. I love you like a brother; you know that. And I've always said I'd do anything for you."

"Yes, but gunning down two of these goons like that. Tell me about it. Did you know beforehand something was going to happen?"

"Yeah, as a matter of fact. And your CIA pals could have too, had they been on the ball."

"How did you find out?"

"Well, I told you I'd have someone keep an eye on this situation from the start. My New York contacts have powerful resources. I won't bore you with details, but through reliable channels, they got wind early yesterday that something was going down."

"But how could you have planned for this so fast? And the helicopter—who's idea was that?"

"My friends ran by me what they knew and laid out a great plan. They placed a transmitting device on your car to keep track of you. The chopper was my idea, and it went along beautifully with what they had in mind. A buddy of mine owes me a few favors. He's got an aircraft service just across the Potomac in Alexandria. He provided the chopper, and my contacts arranged for a skilled weapons team to be on stand-by. As soon as they got word you were in trouble, they were airborne. The rest you know."

"They scared the shit out of me, but it worked. That's what counts, right?"

"Fucking-A! Other than shitting in your pants at the time, are you okay now?"

"I'm fine." He sighed. "Now it's Demi and my kids I'm worried about."

"I'm going to level with you. That's an angle we haven't covered. So the fucking CIA better be alert on that one. I can make arrangements, though. Just say the word."

"No, Guy, you've done enough. Besides, I already gave Kelly the go-ahead to arrange the added protection." He recalled the agent saying it was temporary until specialized teams arrived. It wouldn't be a bad idea to consider other options, he thought. "Just in case, when could you have your people in place?"

"I'd guess sometime tomorrow evening. You want me to give the signal?"

John hesitated. "No, that won't be necessary. Kelly's already upset you've gotten involved. Listen, though, I owe you one."

"You don't owe me a thing, bro'."

"I don't care what you say. I owe you plenty." He glanced at his watch. "Listen, I've got to board my plane. I'll talk to you later."

"Have a safe trip back, my friend. So long."

"So long, Guy." As he hung up, he heard an announcement over the PA that his flight had been delayed fifteen minutes.

He'd have plenty of time to call Demi at her mother's. She had been on his mind throughout his stay in D. C. but especially since the incident the prior night. His close call had reinforced his need to hear her voice. He knew full well the source of that need—his having forced himself upon her. What had possessed him to act in such an ungodly manner? How could she ever forgive him? Never before had he treated her that way. His recollection of the weak excuses he had mouthed off after he had hurt her added to his shame.

He placed the call. Thank God she answered, he thought when he heard Demi's voice.

"Hi, it's me," he said.

She seemed surprised. "Hi," she replied, then paused. "Is anything wrong?"

"No. I just wanted to hear your voice."

"Oh." Silence.

"I'm about to board my plane."

She didn't say anything.

"Actually," he continued, "I wanted to ask your forgiveness for what I did Friday night. I feel terrible about it, especially because—" He stopped, realizing he shouldn't even hint at what had taken place the night before.

"Because why?" she said. "Has something happened?"

Her sixth sense at work again, he marveled. He mustn't alarm her. "No," he lied. "I meant to say that if something happened to me, I wouldn't want the other night to be the last time I remembered spending with you."

"Don't be silly. Nothing's going to happen. You're speaking of a plane crash, right?"

"Yeah. One never knows." He felt anxious and took a deep breath. "I just want to feel close to you, and I haven't since Friday night. Will you please forgive me?"

"I know in my heart that I will, John, but you'll have to give me a little time." She paused, but he didn't respond. "You've always been good to me—and respected me. I consider what happened the other night an aberration of what you are as a person. I love you for who you are—the whole person that you are—and I'd rather not dwell on that one isolated incident."

"Thank you for saying that. I needed to hear it."

"Hurry home so we can be together with the children. They miss you." She paused. "And I miss you."

"I miss you too. I want you to know I didn't expect you to forgive me right away. But I wanted to ask."

"I'm glad you said that."

The voice over the PA announced the boarding of his flight.

"They've just announced we're boarding," he said. "Otherwise, I'd talk to Crystal and Johnny."

"Don't worry. They're doing fine. I'll tell them you said 'hello' and give them a big hug for you."

"Please tell them I love them."

"I'll do that. Have a safe trip home."

"I will. I love you."

"I love you, John.

As he approached the gate to board the plane, an FBI agent introduced himself. The agent was assigned to accompany him on the plane, he explained, taking a seat a few rows behind him.

When his plane landed, Kelly was at the gate to greet him. The FBI agent accompanied John off the airplane. Kelly smiled when John spotted him in the crowd. The smile seemed forced. John dismissed it, thinking it was a sign Kelly was embarrassed over the confrontation at the Jefferson Memorial.

It was at the baggage claim area that John discovered the reason for Kelly's somber appearance. While the three men waited for the luggage to come down the baggage chute onto the carousel, a still sullen Kelly pulled John aside, away from the crowd.

"I'm afraid I've got bad news," Kelly said in a low voice. "I'd give anything not to be the one to tell you what's happened since you got on the plane."

John's heart sank. God, don't let it be about Demi or the children, he thought. He found himself getting angry, not at Kelly particularly but at this entire experience. Not only wasn't it going away but kept getting worse.

"What in God's name has happened?" he asked, agonizing Kelly's response would confirm the worst.

The agent's face became expressionless. "I'll come straight to the crux of it." He paused, as if gathering the strength to continue. "Demi and Crystal have been kidnaped," he uttered.

"Oh, my God," John cried out. "How could your people let something like that happen? I was counting on you, for God's sake!" Tears came to his eyes, and he turned away from the crowd. He bowed his head and brought his hand up to cover his eyes. Without looking at Kelly, he said, "Please tell me they're alive." He wiped his tears with his bare fingers, then looked up, waiting, yet dreading Kelly's reply.

"We have reason to believe they're not only alive but doing fair, John." He spoke with apparent confidence. "Their abductors won't be hurting them anytime soon."

"How can you be sure?"

"For one, because of the methods used. From the accounts we have, neither Demi nor Crystal was hurt when taken. They were knocked unconscious by a strong dosage of chloroform, a volatile anesthetic that knocks out a person within seconds."

"How do you know that?"

"We found traces of it at the scenes."

John shook his head in disbelief. "You said 'scenes.' Weren't Demi and the children together?"

"No. Demi was at a restaurant having lunch with her sister. The children were with their grandmother in Tesuque."

"When did this happen?"

"The incidents occurred within a half hour of each other—a few minutes before one."

"What about Johnny? And Demi's mother and sister?"

"I'm glad to say Johnny managed to get away. Lupe Flynn was badly shaken by what happened, of course, but was unhurt. She complained of breathing problems, but a checkup at the hospital revealed she was just suffering from a bad case of anxiety. They gave her a sedative to calm her down. Demi's sister wasn't hurt either."

"Is Johnny all right, though?"

"He's doing remarkably well."

"Where is he?"

"He's at your mother-in-law's house. And we've got them guarded very well, so I don't want you to worry about a repeat."

"You don't think they'd try again?"

"I doubt it. They've got the one they were after—Demi, primarily. Taking the children was merely to give you an added incentive to cooperate."

"Their holding Demi is enough incentive."

"Of course." He shook his head. "I'm sorry this happened."

John stared at Kelly with a look showing his anguish had turned to anger. "I'm upset over this, Kelly." He emphasized every word. "What happened last night, happened to *me*. I can live with that. But what's happening now is happening to my family, and that's unacceptable!"

"I don't blame you for feeling that way." He sounded apologetic but then looked away. "I'll take full responsibility for what's happened." He returned John's gaze.

John shook his head. "I can't hold you personally responsible. The FBI's calling the shots. Besides, if anyone's to blame, I'm the guy that screwed up by not going along with your suggestions in the first place."

"Don't be too hard on yourself."

"No two ways about it, Kelly, I blew it!"

Kelly took him by the arm. "Listen, that's water under the bridge. What's important is that we work together. We need to keep our cool. I realize that's more difficult for you than for us."

For a long moment, John was silent. He spotted his luggage on the baggage claim carousel and walked over to pick it up. The FBI agent had already retrieved his bag. The three of them left the baggage claim area and walked the short distance to the parking garage.

"I'd like to see Johnny soon," John said as they got into Kelly's car.

"Sure," Kelly said. "We can arrange it." He started the car and drove off.

"You're positive he's doing okay?"

"He's doing fine. We thought the best place for him would be at his grandmother's. She's understandably distraught. So she was glad we decided to leave him with her."

"I'll trust your judgment, Kelly, despite what I said a while ago. I shouldn't assign blame for what's happened. You warned me they might pull something like this."

"I understand you're upset. But I promise you—the same thing won't be repeated on your son. The FBI's got four local agents at your mother-in-law's house right now, and we plan to keep them there round the clock. But now that you've given the go-ahead, we've got agents flying in that are experts at this because it's what they do every day."

Kelly picked up his cellular phone and dialed headquarters to report in. He informed the person who answered that John had arrived, then asked about developments at the command post in Santa Fe. Before hanging up, he reported he was dropping off the FBI agent at the hotel where all the nonresident agents were staying. From there, he said, he planned to drop off John at his home before driving to the command post.

"If you don't mind," John said when Kelly hung up, "I'd like to go with you."

"You sure you wouldn't rather rest?" Kelly said. "One of my men can pick you up later."

"I was tired when I got off the plane, but this has got me pumped up. Rather than getting restless at home, I'd like to go. Besides, I want to see Johnny."

Kelly nodded. "I hear you."

Kelly dropped off the agent at the hotel, then headed north toward the City Different. John sat without saying a word for the first few minutes of the drive up the Interstate, his mind attempting to sort out the events of the last twenty-four hours. The meeting with the Vice-President yesterday afternoon seemed as if it had taken place long ago. Countless questions kept running through his mind. He decided he'd better start getting some answers.

"Tell me what's going on in Santa Fe," he said.

"Well, first of all," Kelly replied, "we've set up our command post at the Emergency Management Center, a facility operated by the Department of Public Safety."

"Is that a fancy way of saying 'the state police'?"

"The state police office is an arm of the department. They've offered their help, so they're involved in the operation. Both that agency and their parent department have been very cooperative."

"I guess that means this thing's out of the bag now. Will that make a difference?"

"Not really. Actually, it's not true that our involvement is 'out of the bag.' We've got a coordinated effort in full swing among the various law enforcement agencies in the Santa Fe area. We felt we had to involve them. In addition to the state police, we've got the Santa Fe Municipal Police and the Santa Fe County Sheriff's Office involved."

"Won't that make finding Demi and Crystal a little unwieldy?"

"Not at all. Getting them involved assures us we won't hit any snags."

"How so?"

"If these agencies didn't know we were working a case in the area, we'd be taking a big risk they'd take some action that might impede our operation plan. It'd be impossible to carry out an 'op' plan without their help or knowledge. Setting up roadblocks, for example, would be impossible without getting them in the picture."

"What about the press? It seems to me that with so much activity going on, the media's bound to find out about it."

"That's true. The news media scan law enforcement frequencies, and they're likely to pick up on the increased radio activity. That's why we've designated a media representative. All news media inquiries will be channeled to our media 'rep.' It'll be his job to come up with bogus reasons for the increased activity."

"What would he tell them?"

"He'll deny any crime is being investigated and claim the activity is part of a training exercise. The state prison, for example, is a couple of miles from our command post. Local law enforcement agencies often go through coordinated training exercises to prepare for a prison riot. Media reps are good at what they do. We wouldn't run an op plan without one."

"Who's heading the operation?"

"The kidnapings are within the FBI's jurisdiction, so the head of that agency's Santa Fe office was placed in charge. You'll get to meet him when we get to the command post."

"But won't these local agencies need to know what this is all about?"

"Not necessarily. There have been two abductions—that's all they need to know. Both state and federal laws have been broken, so involvement of both state and federal agencies isn't unusual. The local agencies have learned our agency's involved, so we've informed them the kidnaping's tied in to our foreign activities, thus explaining our involvement. In short, we'll tell them everything they'll need to know to help us, but that still leaves a lot of information out of the picture. For example, they don't know Tong is involved."

"How certain are you that Demi and Crystal were kidnaped by Tong operatives?"

"We'd be surprised if it were otherwise. As you know, we've confirmed that the fellows gunned down at the Jefferson Memorial were working for Tong. We've also come across new intelligence that Tong operatives were responsible for Leroy Etcitty's death. And we now know for certain that Tong is working for the Chinese Communists."

"What is this cooperative effort by all of these agencies going to do? And what's this op plan you mentioned?"

"Well, for one thing, we've set up a dragnet throughout Santa Fe and roadblocks in the surrounding area, hoping to come up with some clues where the kidnappers are holding Demi and Crystal. An operation or op plan is what the name implies. It's a plan prepared to achieve our mission, which in this case is rescuing Demi and Crystal."

"How sure are you they're being held in the vicinity? Isn't it likely they'd be hundreds of miles from here by now?"

"I doubt it. We've set up roadblocks on every road leading out of Santa Fe County. We've also kept track of planes leaving airports in the vicinity. An operation like this requires coordinated manpower. The local agencies provide that. If we find Demi and Crystal, our plan calls for using their SWAT Teams and Tactical or TACT Teams."

"How can you be sure the assholes didn't get past those roadblocks?"

"We're pretty certain. Besides, it wouldn't make sense for them to go elsewhere. They're holding Demi and Crystal as hostages, not for a monetary ransom but for information they now know you possess. They'd stay in the area because it's what *you've* got that they want. Abducting Demi and Crystal was their way of getting to the LaPierre documents. I expect you'll be contacted soon by phone with some demands."

"If that's the case, shouldn't I be at home?"

"That's probably where they'll first try reaching you." Kelly pulled out a small cellular phone from his coat pocket. It was a different one than the one he had used earlier to call the agency's headquarters. He handed it to John. "I took the liberty of having your home phone hooked up by relay to this cellular. If someone tries reaching you at home, with that you can answer the call from within a one-hundred mile radius."

John inspected the phone, then placed it in his coat pocket. "You said the Tong organization now knows I have the documents. How did they learn that?"

"Not Tong, necessarily, but the Chinese themselves. Remember that the Tong operatives are merely working for The People's Republic in a limited capacity—to get the LaPierre documents. As we noted before, the Chinese have an intricate intelligence network. I'd suspect they learned you came upon the documents soon after you and Quigley found them in that abandoned railroad station."

"But why would they want them now? They know not only of your involvement but that you too possess Henri's papers."

Kelly nodded. "That's true, but that probably doesn't make a difference to them. There's a definite advantage under the circumstances, I think, for them to know what we know. The fact that they kidnaped your wife and daughter proves that. I believe, though, there's another reason why they want the documents. Although I don't know for certain what that might be, I've got an idea."

"You think it involves Condon?"

"I'd be willing to bet on it."

Now that Kelly had placed the events in context, the kidnapings took on a reality that frightened John. Even if he turned over the documents, what assurance was there that Demi and Crystal would be released unharmed? Obviously, none. Even Kelly couldn't promise him that. It occurred to him he didn't know how cooperative Kelly wanted him to be with the abductors if and when they contacted him.

"What if they should contact me?" he asked. "Am I to agree to their demands? More to the point, will the CIA go along with my releasing the documents?"

"You're ahead of me," Kelly said. "We'll fill you in later on what to say when they make contact. But let me assure you that our immediate interest is to get Demi and Crystal back to you unharmed. We're hoping we can do that without having to exchange the LaPierre documents for their safe return. But to relieve you of any anxiety, we wouldn't hold out giving them the documents to secure their safety. That's the bottom line."

John nodded. "I'm going to hold you to that, Kelly." He met Kelly's stare. "Yet, I want them back not only alive, but unhurt. And the sooner, the better." Tears appeared. "And if either Demi or Crystal is hurt, I swear I'll kill those fucking assholes with my bare hands!"

A minute or so passed without either saying a word. John turned and looked at the road ahead. He then spoke. "I just don't know how much more of this I can take. "I'd rather have been kidnaped last night than to have Demi and Crystal go through this ordeal. I pray to God they're doing okay."

Kelly didn't reply right away. He slowed the car due to heavy traffic that had piled up ahead. He moved the car over to the inside lane and began to accelerate, avoiding the slower traffic on the right. Ahead, they came upon one of the roadblocks Kelly had mentioned. This one blocked the southbound traffic along the Interstate. Cars were backed up for a half mile or so. It had even caused the northbound traffic to slow down a bit.

"Tong intended to kidnap all three of you," Kelly said finally. "You last night, and Demi and Crystal today. That way, they'd have been in a better bargaining position to negotiate a deal. Let's be thankful they didn't succeed in abducting you, or we'd be worse off."

"I'm not sure it would make a difference to me," John said. "Either way, they could put pressure on me." He had been eyeing the backed-up traffic ahead. He turned to face Kelly. "Right now, they've got my wife and daughter. That's all that matters to me."

"Well, if it's any consolation, keep in mind that as long as they don't have you or the LaPierre documents, Demi and Crystal will be safe."

"I hope you're right." Their talk had calmed him down. "Thanks for leveling with me."

"I wish there was more I could do."

"Let's change the subject, if you don't mind. Have you heard from Dan Conniff or anyone else concerning our meeting with Vice-President Hirsch?"

When he had spoken to Kelly by phone late Saturday night, he had barely touched on the meeting with the Vice-President.

Kelly wavered. "No, I haven't. Why don't you tell me about your meeting with Hirsch?"

John briefed him. "At first, he seemed almost mesmerized by our story," he said when he finished. "But near the end, he seemed abrupt and a bit edgy."

"That wouldn't surprise me. He didn't want to hear what you were telling him."

"Why do you say that?"

"Oh, just a hunch." He glanced at John, then returned his eyes to the highway. "By way of explanation, and in fairness to Hirsch, let me first tell you that I don't care for him. I care for him less as Vice-President."

"I didn't realize you knew him."

"Well, I've met him a couple of times. I didn't care for the way he carried on. He seemed rather pompous to me."

"I got the same impression. Although I must admit I was excited about the prospect of discussing such a sensitive matter with the Vice-President, I came down from Cloud Nine when he began treating us somewhat shabbily."

"All in all, though, did you get the feeling he was going to get right on it and speak to President Henning?"

"He told us he was."

"Did he seem interested in what you had to say?"

He frowned as he considered Kelly's question. "I don't know how to answer that. I guess my answer would be 'yes and no.' As I think about it, I'd say he was more shocked than interested in what we had to say. It was as if our revealing Condon's activities in Vietnam hadn't surprised him, but the fact that we knew about it intimidated him. Does that make any sense?"

"I think so." He paused, as if contemplating what to say next. "I should tell you, John, that I have reservations about how fast Hirsch will act on the information you gave him on Condon."

"What makes you say that?"

"For one thing, I think he's chummier with Condon than the President would like him to be."

"You don't say. I don't think Dan knew that. He certainly didn't express any reservations about talking to Hirsch."

"His closeness with Condon is one of the reasons I heard through the bureaucratic pipeline in Washington that President Henning won't be picking him as his running mate next go-around." Kelly paused as he concentrated on passing a slower-moving vehicle. "But that's just one of the reasons why I don't think Hirsch can be trusted. I've got other reasons to suspect he'll be less than eager to tell the President about your meeting with him."

"Like what?"

"I'll explain later, when we've gathered more information."

"Good God, Kelly, are you investigating the Vice-President?"

The agent gave out a short laugh. "I'm tempted to give you a 'no, we're not' answer, but I'd rather wait to respond. I'm going to ask you to trust me on this for the time being." He gave John a pensive look.

"Meanwhile, let's concentrate on what we're going to do to get Demi and Crystal back to you. That's something we've got a plan for."

"Fine with me."

They had cleared *La Bajada* Pass and were now approaching the outskirts of Santa Fe. Neither of them said anything more for the few minutes remaining before Kelly would exit the Interstate to get to the command post.

John used the time to reflect on Demi and Crystal. His face showed his deep concern. He hoped Kelly was right—that the Tong operatives wouldn't hurt them. Because he blamed himself for their predicament, he felt he wouldn't be able to forgive himself if they were hurt in any way.

To his surprise, he now began to view what happened to them as an omen that he had to make other major decisions. How had it come to this? Was he somehow being punished for his failure to change his ways when it came to matters involving family? Did he have to get knocked over the head with a sledgehammer before making these changes?

More than anything, he realized now that, without family, the other things he thought mattered in his life—in his work—were insignificant. Even meaningless. If he should lose either Demi or Crystal, he saw no way at the moment how he would garner the strength to overcome his grief or to move on with his life. At the same time, he realized that many others, having lost loved ones, had picked up the pieces and managed to do exactly that.

What had already happened to Demi and Crystal was bad enough. But he couldn't bear the thought of their having to suffer through something worse. He found himself begging God that the abductors would soon call, and Demi and Crystal would remain unharmed in the meantime. Yet, at this moment, he'd have given anything to trade places with them.

CHAPTER 30

KELLY took the *La Cienega* exit from the Interstate and drove along the frontage road for about a mile before turning south into the Emergency Management Center.

The EMC, as the facility was known in law enforcement circles, consisted of an assortment of buildings scattered throughout a five-acre tract. The property bordered the frontage road on one side; the other sides bordered open fields of sagebrush, buffalo grass, and piñon trees.

It was an unimpressive structure built in traditional New Mexico territorial architecture. Bricks in a shade of red, offset along the top of the walls, formed the outer roof line a few inches above the building's flat roof. Most state buildings were beige in color, but the principal building at the EMC was stuccoed white, which had discolored through the years.

The facilities stood alone in the rolling hills of piñon, except for the prison facilities a mile or so to the southeast and the Santa Fe Downs race track on the north side of the Interstate.

John accompanied Kelly through a narrow, dungeon-like corridor into a large conference room. Double doors led into another room. The

Department of Public Safety had offered use of two rooms to the FBI/CIA team. Already, furniture had been rearranged to accommodate the operation.

A large number of individuals were milling around. Most were dressed in lightweight, navy-blue jackets with yellow lettering on the front and back identifying them as FBI agents. Kelly introduced John to a group of agents standing near the room entrance.

"Has the FBI taken over your case?" John said to Kelly.

Kelly smiled at the snide remark. "Remember, this is now a kidnaping case," he explained. "They have the specialists to work such a case. They're versed in police technics, such as search and seizure. We're not." He placed his hand on John's shoulder, as if to reassure him. "But to answer your question, our agency's still very much involved."

"It's just that I've gotten used to working with you and Quigley. I'd feel more secure if you were heading the operation."

"Thanks for saying that." He grinned. "Don't worry, we won't abandon you."

As he mentioned Quigley's name, John spotted him at the far end of the room. While Kelly spoke to the FBI agents standing at the entrance, he walked over to greet Quigley. The two men chatted for a moment. Quigley asked about his close call the night before.

How about the FBI agents who had been assigned to tail him in Washington, John asked. Were they doing okay, he wanted to know. Quigley told him they were expected to be released from the hospital in a day or two.

Kelly soon joined them. He took John to the adjoining room, which was crowded with technical equipment. Several technicians were busy putting the system together. Kelly began to explain the different pieces of equipment. Just then, the special agent in charge of the Santa Fe FBI office approached from the other side of the room. Kelly introduced him to John as "Chips." His full name was Charles Bratton, but he insisted on being referred to as Chips.

"I promise we'll do everything we can to get your wife and daughter back safely," Chips assured John.

"Thanks," John said. "I'm impressed by how you fellows have this operation up and running."

"We hope to have all of the equipment here ready to go in another hour or so. It requires considerable work, as you can see."

John gave a perplexed look at Kelly, then at the special agent. "I'm confused," he said. "Kelly handed me a cellular phone a while ago that's been tied in to my home phone. If I got the call, how's this equipment going to pick it up?"

"They use a patching device," Kelly explained. He turned to the special agent. "Chips, why don't you explain it to John while I make a couple of phone calls?"

"I'll be glad to," the special agent said.

Kelly disappeared into the conference room. Chips began showing John the equipment. He explained the idea behind the system as rather simple, despite the fact that sophisticated equipment was necessary for the concept to work.

"Any call to your home," Chips explained, "can be tapped into and then patched over at the telephone company's mainframe computer. From there, the call can be transferred and even intercepted anywhere. The cellular phone you've been provided with has been set up the same way. When a call comes in on your phone line at home, the call will be transferred not only to your cellular phone but to the equipment we're setting up here."

"Isn't there an easier way?" John asked.

"Actually, there is," Chips said, nodding. "With today's technology, we can have one of our agents at the telephone company's mainframe. Anytime a call is made, the company has the capability of visually picking up the number from where the call originated."

"Why then do you need the equipment you're setting up here?"

"It's a backup system, using older, but reliable methods. We're concerned the fellows we're dealing with might have a piece of equipment that's capable of blocking the signal. If they do, the telephone company won't be able to find out the number the easy way. If that should happen, we'll need the backup we've installed here. So we'll try getting the number the easier and faster way, but if we're stumped, we'll get it by using this more time-consuming technology."

Kelly approached as Chips finished giving John the quick tour. He told Chips he was wanted on the phone. Chips excused himself and disappeared into the conference room.

"Chips just finished explaining the equipment," John said. "Does it work like Caller-ID?"

"Not really," Kelly said. "They'll think of a way to block that, even if the call comes in from a phone booth." He gestured toward the equipment. "No, it'll take this sophisticated equipment to use the older tracing methods. That'll give us the caller's location."

"Chips said there's a faster way of finding out the number at the telephone company's mainframe."

"That's true. By the way, that sort of works on the same principle as Caller-ID. But did he explain they might have equipment that'll block that?"

"Yeah. So what happens when you trace the phone call, if it's made? Then what?"

"Oh, they'll make it, all right. By now, I'm sure they know you're back." His eyes scanned the equipment. "I'm just hoping this will be up and working when the call comes in."

"Won't they know you fellows are monitoring the call?"

"Most likely, but that's par for the course, I'm afraid. They've probably thought of that and have some plan to overcome our monitoring. Whatever their overall plan is, it's intended to do one thing—isolate you from us in some fashion so they can deal with you alone—one on one. They don't want us around. By tracing the call, we hope to be one up on them."

"What do you mean?"

"What you see here is only part of our plan." Kelly smiled. "It's the FBI's plan, so I better give credit where it's due. I've already told you that this is their specialty."

John grinned. "Of course, this is a concerted effort, correct?"

Kelly nodded and smiled. "The plan is to have four helicopters in place, preferably airborne when the call comes in. We've divided Santa Fe and the surrounding area into quadrants and assigned each of these to one aircraft. If the call is placed within a ten-mile radius of the city, the op plan calls for the designated helicopter to fly to the location where the call's been traced to."

"So you trace the call to a particular number at a particular location. You wouldn't need a helicopter hovering over the area to find the person or persons making the call. You could get there by car, if you needed to. How is that going to help you find where Demi and Crystal are being held? Besides, you'll know the location from where the call was made but that wouldn't mean Demi and Crystal are going to be there."

"That's right. Tong operatives aren't too smart, but it doesn't take a rocket scientist to know the phone company doesn't assign a phone number without a name and address to go along with it. As you noted, even if a phone assigned to a particular location were used, chances are unlikely that the call would originate from where Demi and Crystal are being held."

"You think the phone call will be made away from there?"

"I'd be willing to bet on it. Most likely from a pay phone. That's what we're hoping for. In fact, this operation is banking on it. If we can isolate the call to a public phone, our pilot will hone in on that location. We're hoping the person making the call will lead the chopper to where Demi and Crystal are being held."

"But won't the helicopter be spotted?"

"That's always a possibility. The pilots we're getting are highly trained, and they'll be flying at a high altitude."

"Won't they have to get low enough to spot the caller?"

"Sure, but the pilots know how to maneuver the chopper to avoid being seen." Kelly paused, a worried look on his face. "There's another minor concern I have with our plan. For that reason, I'm hoping we can trace the call the quick way and bypass the equipment we've installed here."

"Why?"

"Because we'll need *lead time* for the aircraft to get to where the call originates. When the call comes in, I suspect these fellows won't stay connected long. You'll have to try keeping them on the line as long as you can."

"But why, if you're bypassing the equipment here and getting the number at the mainframe? I thought the number could be picked off almost right away."

"It can. But we still need that lead time for the pilot. Even if we pick off the number, we want to make sure the chopper gets to the area before the caller leaves the phone. Time is critical."

"I see what you mean."

"There's still another minor hurdle. It takes a pilot about three to four minutes to get a helicopter off the ground. That's from the word 'go' when he's told to take off. It's got something to do with the temperature of the engine getting to a certain level before it can become airborne. So he can't take off right away."

"How's that a problem?"

"It's important to have some idea when the call will come in. That way, we'll have the aircraft ready to get airborne so it can reach the location in a hurry. Otherwise, the caller will be long gone."

One of the technicians setting up a piece of electronic equipment began using a drill that made it hard for John and Kelly to continue their talk. They walked out of the room into the conference room, and Kelly halfway closed the double doors.

John shook his head. "I don't know, Kelly. This plan seems awfully 'iffy' and sounds even risky to me."

"I'll admit it's not failsafe, but no plan is in this business. If it doesn't work, we've got other irons in the fire. But, at the moment, for the short span of time that's passed since the kidnapings, this is the plan we feel will get us quickest to your wife and daughter. None of us wants this thing to drag on."

"You've got that right." He spoke with emphasis. "Are the helicopters in place?"

Kelly shook his head. "We're hoping they will be when we need them."

"But what if the call were to come in now?"

"We've made arrangements to get the aircraft in place within another couple of hours. Besides, as I said a moment ago, the first phone call won't be more than to make initial contact and instruct you to await another call with more specific instructions."

As Kelly finished explaining the plan, John became startled by the buzzing sound of the cell phone in his pocket. Kelly reacted with surprise. The phone buzzed again. The room, which had been filled with the loud murmur of voices seconds before, became dead quiet. Everyone's attention was drawn to the phone in John's pocket.

"Holy shit!" Kelly whispered. "I didn't expect it'd come this early. It's a damn good thing you came along!"

John stood there frozen in place. "What should I do?" he said. "Is it too soon for your equipment to pick up the signal?" He dug into his pocket and took out the phone.

"Go ahead and answer the call, John," a voice said from across the room. It was Chips.

John glanced at Kelly, who nodded.

Kelly held the double door ajar and glanced into the other room. He signaled to one of the technicians to let him know John was about to answer the call. The technician closest to him gestured with his forefinger that they hadn't completed installation. The other technician gave a *thumbs up* to Kelly, suggesting he'd attempt to trace the call with what equipment was in place. Kelly returned his attention to John. In the sudden quietness, no one else in the room moved.

"They're going to try," Kelly whispered. "Pick up the call, and we'll see where it gets us. Try staying calm."

John pushed the Talk button and placed the phone to his ear. "Hello," he almost whispered at first, then cleared his throat. He was trembling. "Hello," he repeated, this time a little louder, but his voice still quivering.

"Good day, Mr. Garcia," the male caller said at the other end in a formal tone. "I'm certain you've been expecting our call."

John nodded at no one in particular, signifying it was the expected call. "Yes." He hesitated. "Yes, I've been told you'd call." He cleared his throat again. "I'm listening."

"We know the FBI and the CIA have been protecting you, Mr. Garcia. We also have good reason to believe this call is being monitored. For that reason, my message to you will be brief, so please listen closely."

Kelly once again glanced into the other room. The technician nodded; the call was being processed. The agent picked up a notepad from the desk behind him and scribbled a note. He held the pad up in front of John. It read: *Keep him on the line as long as you can!*

John nodded.

"I want to know about my wife and daughter," John demanded, almost choking on his words.

"They're doing fine," the phantom voice said, "and will continue to do so as long as you cooperate and don't try anything foolish."

"Please let me talk to them."

"That won't be possible. You'll have to trust me they'll remain unharmed. Listen! You will be receiving another call tomorrow, between the hours of one and four in the afternoon. We will choose later what time we will place the call. I suggest you make yourself available during that time if you're truly interested in your wife's and daughter's welfare."

Kelly peeked into the next room again. One of the technicians rotated his hand in the air, as if winding a spool. They needed more time.

"One final warning, Mr. Garcia," the voice threatened. "Keep the CIA and FBI away from you when we make contact. You'll receive express instructions tomorrow to use another phone at a location unknown to you at this time. A telephone that cannot be monitored. For the sake of your family, Mr. Garcia, I suggest you follow these instructions."

Kelly held the pad up again in front of John.

"I'd like to know if—" John said into the receiver.

It was too late. The caller had hung up. All that the technicians were able to detect during the call's short duration was that it had originated from a pay phone.

Before leaving Santa Fe, John, Quigley, and the two FBI agents who had been flown in to protect John drove the short distance to Lupe's house. They were met at the door by a member of the new surveillance team assigned to protect Lupe and Johnny. The two agents accompanying Quigley and John remained outside as Quigley joined John inside.

John found Lupe in the kitchen, where she greeted him with open arms. She began crying the instant he embraced her. He held on to her for a long time and let her cry.

"Oh, my God, John!" Lupe cried as she pulled away from him. "What have they done with our Demi and poor little Crystal?"

He grimaced when he saw the tortured look on her face. "They're going to be fine, Lupe. The FBI will be doing everything it can. They're working to get Demi and Crystal back to us." He fought hard to sound convincing.

Lupe raised her head and looked up at him. "What in the name of God is going on? I don't understand any of this."

"It would take too long to explain, Lupe. Besides, it doesn't matter now. What matters is for us to get Demi and Crystal back unharmed. Let's pray for that."

"I haven't stopped praying. I've got several candles lit in my bedroom where I said a novena last night and a rosary this morning."

"God bless you, Lupe." He kissed her on the forehead. "I'm glad you still have your faith."

"I am too." She wiped the tears from her eyes. "Little Johnny is in the TV room out back. He's been asking for you."

John walked into the TV room.

"Daddy, Daddy!" Johnny screamed. He ran to him and hugged him around the legs.

John bent over, caressing his son's head. Johnny held on to his legs for a long time. After a while, John took him by the shoulders, pulled him away, then knelt down in front of him. He looked into his son's teary eyes and wiped away the tears.

"They took Mommy and Crystal, Daddy," the boy said. "I got away from those awful men."

John smiled. "I know you did, son," he said. "That was a brave thing you did. I'm proud of you." He gave him a big squeeze.

"Those men aren't gonna hurt Mommy and Crystal, Daddy, are they?"

"Of course not. We're not going to let them. Okay?"

"That's right, Daddy. We won't let them!"

The pure faith of a child in his parent, John thought as he looked into his son's eyes. The youngster was smiling at him, as if, without question, his father was soon going to get his mother and sister back to them. Oh, God, he thought, was there anything that parents couldn't fix or make right for their children?

In the wide corridor leading to Vice-President Hirsch's ceremonial office, Condon walked at a fast pace. He was running late for his appointment with Charles Melvin Hirsch.

The office was on the second floor of the senate wing in the Capitol, just off what was called the Senate Reception Room and not far from the Minority Leader's office. The senator, however, was coming from his suite of offices in the Russell Senate Office Building, by way of the underground tram. The second floor wing, which led into the floor of the senate's chambers, was a busy place while the senate was conducting its business. At this late hour, however, the senate wasn't meeting. For that reason, the floor was without activity, except for a couple of Capitol police officers here and there. There wasn't even a tourist in sight when the senator exited the elevator.

He walked into the Senate Reception Room and then through the wide entry into the waiting room outside the Vice-President's private office. Four secret service agents crowded the room.

Condon wasn't his usual self today. For one thing, he felt tired, as he hadn't gotten enough sleep during the last several nights. From the manner of his walk this late evening, he could tell he wasn't himself. He felt sluggish, and it seemed his feet dragged a little.

Usually, he prided himself in walking with an air of confidence—even a bit of sophistication. He had earned a reputation as a legislator who pulled no punches and possessed an exhilarated drive to accomplish any task. He was well respected for the energy with which he conducted the business of the senate as Minority Leader. He was also known for his uncanny ability to spend many hours into the night absorbing the hundreds of legislative bills and many committee reports that filled his offices. But today, he didn't feel a bit exhilarated, and he didn't have the drive for which he was known.

During the past week, he had even found himself lacking the usual pride in his manner of dress. Even now, he was aware his wool suit hung from his tired torso. Was it his imagination, he wondered. Had he lost weight? He wasn't old enough yet, he thought, to begin feeling this way about his appearance. So why was his body giving up on him?

But it wasn't only his body, he realized. His mind too hadn't been the same since that day a week or so ago when he had that disgusting and unpleasant conversation with Charles Hirsch. He felt lacking in his concentration, and he was forever finding himself barking back at his office staff. He displayed such irritability with staff members that he became convinced they were avoiding him.

During his senatorial tenure, he had known some grumpy, cynical legislators who were up there in years and had been around Capitol Hill much too long. He made no bones about it when, as a younger man, he avoided these codgers like the plague. Was he becoming like them, now in his final years he hoped would be the golden age of his political life?

God, don't let that be, he muttered to himself as he walked up to the middle-aged secretary seated at the desk just outside the Vice-President's office. A tall agent stood guarding the door.

Although the office was known as a ceremonial office, and other vice-presidents before him rarely used it, Vice-President Hirsch used it often as a working office. He found it convenient to be close to the senators when they were conducting business on the senate floor.

The Vice-President's secretary, the woman with "the baggy eyes," as Condon sometimes referred to her, pounded away on her computer keyboard. She guarded the door behind her with considerable zeal. Finally, she noticed him towering over her and stood up. She glanced at her wristwatch.

"The Vice-President has been expecting you, Mr. Minority Leader," she said. "I'll let him know you've arrived."

"Thank you, please do," he said, forcing a smile as he sat in a chair. "—you old goat," he completed his salutation under his breath so that the agent wouldn't hear him.

Reflecting again on Charles Hirsch's phone call earlier that day, he began to worry. He didn't want a confrontation. That was the last thing the two of them needed at a time when their cooperation was critical. The dilemma was enough to concern him about the nature of the unanticipated meeting that evening. It didn't help matters that the Vice-President wasn't going to find him in a good mood.

Besides, Hirsch himself hadn't sounded too amiable on the phone when Condon had suggested they postpone the meeting until the following day. The business he needed to discuss with him couldn't wait, the Vice-President insisted. They would have to meet in the late evening in the event Condon found himself unable to get away before then, the Vice-President said. And so there was a question in his mind whether the meeting would prove beneficial. In some ways, he thought, it might even turn out to be counterproductive.

The *old goat* with the baggy eyes reappeared at the double doors leading into Hirsch's office. With a somber face, she gestured to Condon. "Vice-President Hirsch will see you now, Mr. Minority Leader," she said in a dull voice. The agent stepped aside.

A smiling Charles Hirsch greeted him at the door. "Emory, my good man," he said in a tone conveying genuine gladness to see him.

Forcing a smile, he took the Vice-President's hand and shook it.

The Vice-President's smile disappeared as soon as *old baggy eyes* closed the door behind her. In its place Condon saw a somber, worried expression. It was possible, he thought, that his host was suffering from the same malady with which he seemed afflicted. *Two grumpy old men*, the thought came to his mind, like Walter Matthau and Jack Lemmon in that movie he had once seen, just didn't cut it for a meeting of such importance.

"Have a seat, Emory," the Vice-President said in a cold tone as he walked behind a highly-polished antique desk made of a dark wood. He sat in the large arm chair.

The office had decorative arches on all four sides of the room that reached high up onto a vaulted ceiling. A fireplace occupied the space between two high windows. It was surrounded by a decorative marbled mantle with pillars to each side. A large, gilded mirror filled the space above the mantle.

Little light came through the windows at this time of day, and so the room wasn't well lit, despite the large chandelier up above. The floor was made of inlaid square tile pieces forming a colorful, circular design symmetrical to the rounded ceiling.

Condon sat in one of the upholstered, wooden chairs in front of the desk.

"It appears, Charles," he began, "that you too are tired this evening. I don't feel well, either. So perhaps we may be doing each other a favor if—"

"Please, Emory," the Vice-President interrupted. "What I have to say to you simply can't wait. I would have spoken to you on Saturday if your office had gotten hold of you in South Carolina, where I understand you went for the weekend."

"Yes, I received your message saying it was urgent but only upon my return this morning."

The Vice-President waved the excuse away. "It doesn't matter now."

"Well, tell me, since you're so determined to have this meeting, what has got you so agitated?"

Hirsch's face remained melancholy. "I was paid an interesting visit this past Saturday by one of your colleagues, Senator Conniff. He was accompanied by a constituent who happens to be a close friend of his. A gentleman by the name of John Garcia. Do you know him?"

Condon wrinkled his brow. "At the moment, I can't say that I do."

"Think hard, Emory, because he knows *you*. Or let me say he knew you back in Vietnam when both of you were in the military. He was an army lieutenant back then."

He thought hard. "Yes, yes, I do recall him now." He managed a smile. "That was a long time ago. You've made my task for the day— jogging my long-term memory like that. It's good to know it hasn't abandoned me."

"Well, it's not going to make your day when I tell you what my unanticipated visitors had to say about you."

Condon's face again displayed the worry that was with him before he entered the office. Hirsch was going to unload another barrage on top of the one he had unloaded at their last meeting.

He now became convinced this meeting was about the leaked information he had dismissed before so nonchalantly in Hirsch's presence but that secretly had given him cause for concern. He realized that was the real reason he had wanted to avoid this meeting, not because he felt tired. The inevitable was happening. A part of his dreadful past, which he'd rather leave unstirred, was coming back to haunt him.

"I suspect what you're going to tell me is the continuing saga of our last discussion."

"Precisely. How did you know?"

"I suppose because those dreadful things never go away, do they? They stick to us like molasses. As career politicians, you and I know that by now."

"Believe me, Emory, there is no way this thing's going 'away.' Not by a long shot."

"Go on. Tell me the bad news."

Hirsch cleared his throat. "I'll summarize this new *saga*, as you aptly termed it." He proceeded to tell Condon of the uncovered LaPierre documents. "These documents implicate you, Emory, in this criminal activity." His voice grew louder. "Just a few days ago, when I confronted you with what little I knew about you as a target of a CIA investigation, you denied any involvement. You even termed it a 'witch hunt' or something of the sort." He shook his head in apparent disgust. "And now this new, incriminating evidence surfaces!"

Condon just sat there, bewildered at the revelation. He then became angry. "And I deny it now!" He spoke with defiance, slamming his fist on the desk.

"But they insist these documents exist, Emory. Some of them had your signature as a military officer in charge of procurement."

"I deny it, I tell you! And you must believe me, if our plan is to succeed." He was now fuming. "I signed many documents in Vietnam. What in blazes does that prove? Nothing, I'm telling you! Absolutely nothing!"

"I may as well tell you, Emory, that since Senator Conniff and Mr. Garcia came to see me, I've done a bit of digging on my own. I've uncovered additional incriminating information. I can keep this information to myself. But it will be next to impossible to keep the information provided by my visitors from the President much longer. They'll grow suspicious the longer I delay getting this intelligence to Henning. All I can hope for is to delay the inevitable until after we carry out our plan. By then, it'll be too late for them to do anything about it."

"Whether credible or not, this new information can cause us a lot of damage. So delaying its impact becomes imperative." He was breathing hard now. "And exactly what is this new information you yourself have uncovered?"

"My own sources reveal the CIA has just learned you have millions of dollars stashed away in Swiss banks. The sources implicate you in a conspiracy with various corrupt South Vietnamese officials, the Viet Cong, and the North Vietnamese, who were benefactors or recipients of embezzled supplies. But in addition to those groups, many of the supplies fell into the hands of the Chinese Communists."

"The People's Republic? Impossible!"

"Please, Emory, keep your voice down." He glanced at the door. "Yes, China. It appears the Chinese too now want to get their hands on the information for two reasons. First, they don't want it to leak out now because they feel it would have a profound and negative impact not only on its present ties with Hanoi and the Vietnamese Communists, but with other world powers.

"That would come at a time when they want to raise their country's credibility in the international arena as a world power. The Chinese don't want to suffer the embarrassment that it was taking millions of dollars in supplies for its own benefit. This occurred at a time when it was offering military and other financial aid to North Vietnam under the table during the war. Especially when those supplies were meant for the Viet Cong and North Vietnam."

The Vice-President paused, as if to collect his thoughts.

"What's the second reason?" Condon said.

"I was coming to that. This one pertains to the office you now hold. It seems that this reason is as important to the Chinese, if not more so, than the first. Apparently, China is interested in finding out if the LaPierre documents implicate you in criminal activity."

"And why would that be important to the Chinese?"

"Because, you fool," Hirsch barked, slamming his open hand on the desk, "they could use it against you! By holding this incriminatory matter over your head, they could try to influence you. They'd have you under their control concerning this country's legislative matters and international policies. Political blackmail! The World Trade Organization, comes to my mind. China's been wanting to become a member for a long time, and it knows Congress is very much against it. We can assume the Chinese are well aware of your influence in such matters."

Condon sat there stunned by Hirsch's revelations. For a long while, he said nothing. He gazed instead beyond the figure of the Vice-President. After a long moment, he spoke.

"These are all lies, I tell you. Nothing but lies!"

"You had better be correct on that score," Hirsch retorted. "Otherwise, our plan will fail before it even begins." He paused. "Frankly, Emory, I'm tempted to pull out of our joint venture. I'm dreading that my part in it will be discovered and my reputation ruined in the process."

Condon stood up. "Come, let's not get cold feet about our deal." He didn't sound convincing. "Try not to worry too much over this unfortunate turn of events." It surprised him that he had managed to calm down. Yet, he felt mesmerized by what he had heard. "It merely throws a ripple in our plan, that's all. It's not a tidal wave. You'll see soon enough." He had been looking down at the floor. He now lifted his head and gazed into Hirsch's eyes. "Meanwhile, I'm going to ask you to delay further getting this volatile information to the President. The more time you can buy us, the better the chances our plan will succeed. Will you do that for me?"

"I'll try, Emory."

"Good." He shuffled his feet toward the door. "I bid you farewell, Charles. Have a good evening."

"Good evening. I hope you sleep well tonight."

Despite the open display of spirit in the Vice-President's presence, Condon hobbled back to his office. He felt more tired than ever.

He knew what was behind his dejection; his depression. It was the revelation that, long ago, the Chinese Communists all along had their fingers in the till, and he, now a distinguished United States Senator, a loyalist to free enterprise, a true patriot, hadn't known about it. He had been duped. If these facts leaked out, he'd be thrown in with the scum. There was no doubt in his mind. The scandal would make him appear as if he had conspired with the enemy—the communists. He couldn't stomach the thought of that perception.

And now, to add insult to injury, the filthy communist bastards were trying to learn of his own involvement. The thought of what they were trying to do angered him to the point of making him nauseous. He fumed once again. The emotion appeared to invigorate him—to give him nervous energy.

Blackmail him? How dare those impudent fools entertain such thoughts. It angered him that this bleak turn of events was happening at what could be the most important turning point in his life. He seethed even more. There had to be a way to stop this new threat to his career. Otherwise, he would end up in ruins. All that he had ever worked for would be lost.

CHAPTER 31

AS promised, the call came late in the afternoon the following day. John was at the command post when the call was made. At the time, the conference room was buzzing with activity as the various law enforcement agencies prepared to coordinate their assigned tasks under the op plan's rescue mission. The plan depended on Demi and Crystal's whereabouts soon being discovered.

The Santa Fe Police Department had provided a twelve-man contingency that would be split into two six-member Special Weapons and Tactics Teams, known as SWAT Teams. In addition, two Tactical or TACT Teams from the state police were assigned a backup position in the second wave of the rescue. The SWAT Teams were armed with rapid-fire rifles and dressed in black uniforms with the white letters *SWAT* imprinted in back and on the right sleeve. The state police's TACT Teams were also dressed in black but without markings. They too were equipped with lightweight, automatic rifles. These four teams had spent the entire morning being briefed by Chips and simulating their assignments.

Even now, the teams were outside a hundred yards or so from the command post, rehearsing their assigned tasks. Under the circumstances of the operation, going through a mock rescue proved difficult. Having a mock-up of the actual target site and layout proved helpful. In this instance, however, because it wasn't yet known where Demi and Crystal were being held, it wasn't possible to create a mock-up of the terrain and structures surrounding the target. The rehearsals were necessary nonetheless.

If and when the expected phone call was traced and the target site found, the tactical teams would have to move without delay to the deployment area to launch the attack. Actual deployment planning would take place during last-minute briefings held there. In such an event, no mock-rehearsal could take place. The actual teams being used in the operation today, however, were trained to work under such a scenario.

It was four o'clock when the call came. As John's cellular phone buzzed, Chips held his hands up, gesturing for everyone to quiet down. The roomful of agents became still by the time John picked up the phone.

This time, he didn't hesitate. "Hello," he said into the receiver. "This is John Garcia." His hands trembled as he held the cellular phone close to his ear to make sure he heard every word. He sounded tentative, even though he had prepared himself for this moment.

"Good afternoon, Mr. Garcia," a deep, clear voice said through the receiver.

John could tell it wasn't the same voice he had heard yesterday. He didn't reply.

"Listen carefully," the voice continued, "because what I have to say won't be repeated. You are to follow my instructions to the letter, and we expect you to cooperate."

"I'm listening," John said, his voice quivering.

"Good. It's important that you do."

That morning, Chips and Kelly performed their job well drilling him why the length of the phone call was important.

"You claim to be holding my wife and daughter hostage," John said, remembering the admonishment. "I'd like to ask whom I'm talking to. Whom do you represent?"

Quigley had been in the adjacent equipment room when John answered the phone. He now popped his head through the doorway and signaled to Kelly. With his thumb and forefinger, he formed a circle in the air, indicating the caller's number had been picked up at the mainframe. He eased the door closed as he returned to the equipment room.

"That's irrelevant, Mr. Garcia," the voice responded. "What is rele—"

"I have the right to know! If you want my cooperation, I'd think that you'd—"

"Mr. Garcia, we insist on your cooperation! Let's not forget our roles here. *We're* holding your wife and daughter hostage. I'd think that would be enough incentive for you to cooperate."

"Believe me, it is. It's just that—"

"Then don't stall this conversation again! Allow me to give you our instructions. I'm tempted to hang up, for I suspect attempts are being made to trace this call. But time is important to us. So listen up! Don't force me to warn you again."

"Go ahead," John said, giving Kelly and Chips a disappointing look. "I'm listening."

"And without interruption, I should add." There was a slight pause. "Please take notes if you have to. At exactly seven this evening, you are to be waiting for another phone call from us at the corner of *Paseo del Norte* and Tramway Boulevard in Albuquerque. You are to be there precisely at that time. There, you will find a pay telephone to the south. When you pick up the receiver, you are to identify yourself by stating your first and last name and then say nothing else. You—"

"What if I'm—" John interrupted, risking the caller's ire."

"If you interrupt me one more time, Mr. Garcia, I will hang up! Do you understand?"

"Yes. I understand." He sighed. "Please go on. I won't repeat that."

"You will wear a light blue, long-sleeve dress shirt and a pair of dark slacks—no coat or jacket. If you don't own such clothing, you are to purchase it beforehand." The caller spoke at a slower pace. "You are to go there alone. You must park at least a block away from the telephone booth, then walk there. If you're not there by seven, you will miss our call." The caller paused to catch his breath.

"You'll find a cell phone hidden underneath the seat inside the booth. We'll be keeping an eye on you and the booth to make certain no one tampers with the phone we've provided. We'll also make sure you won't be followed. There, you'll get additional instructions to go to another location, where we'll make arrangements to meet you. You are to take the cellular phone with you for that purpose. These instructions, I trust, are clear to you."

"They're clear. And I'll follow them."

"Fine. Have a good day, Mr. Garcia."

John heard a click, followed by the dial tone.

The door leading from the equipment room opened, and Quigley hurried into the conference room.

"We're in luck!" he said. "The phone company gave us the address location within seconds."

"Great," Kelly said.

"Fortunately, the chopper assigned to the southwest quadrant was in the air when the call came. So the pilot should have time to fly to the target."

"Where was the call made from?" Chips asked.

"A pay phone on the corner of St. Francis and Sawmill Road," Quigley replied.

John knew the area well. It was a busy intersection just off Interstate 25 within the municipal limits of Santa Fe.

As John listened to the explicit instructions from the caller, high above and to the southwest of the intersection of Sawmill Road and St. Francis Drive, the helicopter pilot descended from a high altitude. The pilot eased the controls with skill, flying to a lower altitude above an area just south of, and approaching the Giant Food Store on the corner. The copilot was on the radio. Just seconds before, he had received instructions to go to the location of the store.

"Roger, Headquarters," the copilot said into the small portable microphone connected to his headset. "Is the caller still on the line? We're descending but need more time. Approaching the target fast as I speak. Over."

"Affirmative," came the reply at the other end. "But we can't guarantee how much longer. So hurry there, pronto! Over."

"Almost there now. Continuing to descend to a safe altitude. If the caller's still on the line when we get low enough, I'll bet you a cold beer we'll track him. Over."

"Negative, you'd better—the caller has hung up! You're out of time. Over."

"Easy. We're there."

The chopper approached the location from a direction so that the afternoon sun would make it difficult to spot the aircraft from the ground. A prevailing and somewhat gusty wind blowing from the northwest would likewise make it difficult to hear the sound of the aircraft from the area surrounding the convenience store.

"Hold her steady," the copilot said to the pilot.

"Roger," the pilot replied. "Got it."

With a pair of binoculars, the copilot looked down to the area where he had spotted the public phones. He next saw the man hurrying out of the phone booth and into the driver's side of a mid-size, four-door sedan. He was dressed in a light suit but no tie, and he appeared to be alone. The copilot wasn't certain, for he couldn't see into the vehicle.

The automobile exited the store's parking lot and headed south on St. Francis Drive. As the copilot kept his eye on the car through his binoculars, he reported into the microphone, giving his headquarters a detailed account of the vehicle's route.

John hung up the phone. The formality of the voice both surprised and angered him. He supposed he was angry because the caller's confident attitude reminded him the man and his confederates appeared very much in control. That wasn't a good sign, he realized. He hoped the tracing efforts would lessen or even neutralize that control.

Kelly and Chips had been listening to the conversation on separate earphones wired to the equipment in the next room.

"So what now?" John asked Chips.

"We keep our fingers crossed," Chips replied. He instructed the technicians in the other room to patch the chopper's radio communication through the speakers installed in the conference room. "In a few seconds, we'll be patched in to the helicopter pilot's radio frequency. We'll soon know if he succeeded in making visual contact. If he has, we should hear him give the location and heading of the vehicle. From that point, it's a question of whether the caller will lead us to where your wife and daughter are."

John took out his handkerchief and wiped his hands, which felt clammy. "As you can tell, I'm nervous."

"You've got every reason to be," Kelly remarked.

"I'll venture to make an educated guess," Chips said to John in an obvious attempt to calm him down. "If you were to be at that pay phone this evening, they'd instruct you to go to some isolated area outside of Albuquerque. What do you think, Kelly?"

"That would be my guess. In a sparsely-populated area, they'd be sure we wouldn't be anywhere around for as far as the eye could see." He turned to Chips. "I'd guess too, Chips, that they'll use a helicopter to pick up John and take him to another location. Somewhere near the *Sandias*, maybe. What do you think?"

"Yes, that's my take of—"

He was interrupted by the copilot's voice coming through the speakers. The command post became dead quiet as its occupants listened to the crackling voice. Loud shouts rang through the room as it became obvious from the copilot's transmission that visual contact had been made.

The vehicle entered onto Interstate 25, the copilot reported. It was now traveling east away from Santa Fe. After a few minutes on the Interstate, the car exited the highway, continuing south on U. S. Highway 285. Several miles down the paved road, the vehicle veered to the right onto State Road 41, again heading south. The helicopter pilot continued following behind at an altitude that would make it difficult for the driver to hear or see the aircraft. The copilot continued reporting the speeding car's location on the radio, as well as its direction of travel.

A few minutes later, when the driver reached the small village of Galisteo, he turned east past several horse corrals onto a gravel road. In another minute, he stopped at a small, stuccoed-adobe house, isolated from the village. The copilot estimated the dwelling was about three-quarters of a mile from the turnoff the car had taken in Galisteo. He described the residence as secluded from the graveled roadway by a heavy patchwork of large trees and thick shrubbery surrounding the dwelling. The copilot next gave out the house's approximate coordinates, then reported the man exiting the vehicle alone and entering the house through a side door. The copilot's final report before the chopper left the area was the aircraft's own coordinates and directions of how to reach the dwelling from Galisteo by vehicle.

At the command post a few minutes later, Chips described the location of the dwelling in Galisteo. The SWAT and TACT Teams, together with the state police and FBI/CIA agents who had been designated to help in the rescue effort, paid close attention. Using a military map of the target area, Chips explained to the rescue team the best way to get into the area without being detected. He pointed out a dirt back road that would take the tactical teams to within a few yards of the dwelling.

The chosen deployment area was a small clearing surrounded by a grouping of trees, from where the teams would coordinate their assigned tasks and receive last-minute instructions for launching the attack. There were few questions asked when Chips completed the briefing. The four teams left the facility at once. Outside, they hurried into four vans. Within a matter of seconds, the vans sped away toward the small village.

After the SWAT and TACT Teams went on their way, Chips gave last-minute instructions to the FBI agents and the state police officers who had their own special assignments while the rescue was in progress. Four state police patrol units were assigned the task of creating two roadblocks along the paved road that passed through Galisteo, one north of the village and the other to the south. Two units were to be stationed at each of the roadblocks. Three of Kelly's CIA agents, as well as Kelly and Quigley, were assigned to join the rescue teams at the target sight as part of a special backup team, but they had no specific assignments.

When Chips finished his instructions, the remaining members of the rescue and support teams, with the exception of Chips, Kelly, Quigley, and John, hurried into two additional vans that had pulled up to the command post. The vans left as the last man boarded the vehicles. Chips, Kelly, Quigley, and John rushed to a concrete pad on the far end of the EMC compound, where they boarded a waiting helicopter. The chopper lifted off the pad and flew the four men to the outskirts of Galisteo, about three quarters of a mile from the target residence. Wind direction had been taken into account in selecting the landing site to prevent the chopper from being heard. From there, they walked to the deployment area, where they awaited arrival of the rescue teams.

Some twenty minutes later, the four vans carrying the SWAT and TACT Teams arrived at the selected deployment area. It was protected by trees and a good amount of other wild growth, providing sufficient seclusion and cover to begin the attack. It was no more than fifty yards from the target site. The remaining FBI/CIA agents and state policemen arrived a few minutes later. Everything but the final execution appeared in place. What now remained was the coordinated deployment of the teams and specific, last-minute instructions to specific teams members who were to enter the residence first.

The rescue party couldn't be certain Demi and Crystal would be found in the dwelling. But it was a reasonable assumption, given the circumstances, and they had no choice but to act on that assumption.

John stood at the edge of the clearing, a few feet away from where Chips was giving his last-minute instructions to the rescue teams. He was nervous, and it showed. Yet he became more anxious as he heard Chips' explicit instructions on the use of firearms.

He walked over to Kelly, who was standing on the other side of the clearing. "I suppose you realize I'm getting very uptight," he said.

"I can see that," Kelly said. "This has got to be tough on you. But bear with us. The raid will take place soon."

"The waiting is what gets to me. I gave some thought this morning to not even coming. But I concluded I'd be more of a wreck if I stayed behind."

"You're probably right. It was Chip's talk about gunfire that got you nervous, wasn't it?"

"I'm afraid so."

"Leaving you back there wouldn't have been the right thing to do. You belong here."

He nodded. "I'm worried, though, that Demi and Crystal might get hurt if there's a lot of gunfire. I'd guess that weapons will more likely be fired than not."

"I wish I could say you're wrong. Chances are these fellows inside the house are armed. So I'd be lying if I told you I didn't think there'd be gunfire. But, even though Demi and Crystal could be hurt during an exchange, we've got plans to reduce that possibility."

"You hadn't said anything about that before."

"I know. But our discussions focused on tracing the call. We never talked about specifics of the rescue."

"We weren't even sure there would be a rescue attempt."

"Right. Anyway, let me tell you what we've got planned to lessen the risk to Demi and Crystal. In a minute or so, we'll be getting a visual report from a helicopter that's flying above us as we speak."

John looked up at the sky. The sun was hidden behind large billowing rain clouds that had blown in from the northwest. There was still plenty of light left in the late afternoon, despite the overcast skies.

"I doubt you'd be able to see the chopper, even if it were broad daylight and the skies were clear. It's flying at a high altitude."

"And just what is it going to be doing up there?" John said.

"The aircraft contains technical equipment that emits infra-red rays. I know a little behind the principle of the technique. They've made some major advances with the technology in recent years, and it's accurate enough to do the job. Anyway, the infra-red emissions or sensors are sensitive to body heat. They're used to detect even slight variances or differentials in ambient temperatures.

"The plan is to lock the sensors to the house and take temperature measurements. We then use a downlink microwave transmission that's picked up by a receiver installed in one of the vans we left back there behind the trees. One of the men with Chips is carrying a laptop. That's tied in by cellular modem to the monitor in the van. It'll show us images picked up by the infra-red sensors installed in the chopper. We're hoping the pictures will tell us how many persons are in the house, their specific location, and more importantly, which ones are Demi and Crystal."

"How can the pictures tell you that?"

Before Kelly could answer, Chips approached them. "We've got to get in place," he told Kelly. "I've just given the teams final instructions to deploy into our final position. Let's go!" Chips turned around to follow the waves of the rescue team that now crept toward the dwelling.

Kelly turned to John. "We've run out of time. I'll answer your question as we get the video from the chopper. For now, let me just say that we're taking every precaution to reduce the possibility that Demi and Crystal will be hurt. That risk is real, no matter what we do. Unfortunately, it'd be risky and even foolish, I think, to wait until there might be another, safer approach. The quicker we act, the better will be their chances of coming out of this unharmed."

Kelly turned to follow Chips, who was closing in on the dwelling. "Let's go. We've got to hurry, though, because we've got to be in place when we began receiving the images from the chopper."

The waves of teams separated into smaller groups as they closed in on the house. John remembered Chips had instructed them to perform surveillance near the house before receiving last-minute instructions. The groups scattered before regrouping for their final instructions in the final seconds before the surprise rescue raid began.

CHAPTER 32

TO familiarize themselves with the immediate area, the SWAT and TACT Teams conducted the quick surveillance along a wide perimeter of the secluded dwelling. They returned to the clearing to await the first visual report from the helicopter.

Chips held the laptop in front of him, the computer screen displaying a deep blue background. A portable printer was hooked up to it.

"Here goes," Chips said, watching the screen.

The color monitor began showing the first images. Chips inserted a single sheet into the printer and entered an instruction on the keyboard to print the image. The printer whirled into action. As it printed the first color picture, Chips explained the images on the screen.

Kelly whispered to John, "Listen closely. I think Chips' explanation will answer the question you asked a moment ago."

John nodded and studied the screen as Chips spoke.

The dwelling's contour had been graphically superimposed on the infra red images. The interior of the house was shown in black, except for five circular markings that were a bright orange with a tinge of red in the center. There was actually a split screen showing two images of the house.

"These reddish-orange images," Chips whispered, pointing, "show the places inside the house where the infra-red sensors in the chopper have detected a slight variation in ambient temperature. With the software we're using, we have the capability of changing the screen colors. To better see the images we're interested in, which are these reddish-orange spots you see here, we've shown the house interior black in color and superimposed these white lines to designate the outline of the house. Otherwise, we'd see the interior of the house in a pale orange, compared with the exterior. That's because the temperature inside the house is higher than the temperature outside.

"By doing that, the picture brings out any persons or objects emitting heat with more contrast. We've programmed the equipment to detect body heat."

He pointed to the screen again. "So we know that these five bright, circular markings here represent the locations in the house occupied by five individuals. These fellows in there must be cold-natured. This darkest red spot here suggests they've had the furnace going sometime during the day, which reaches a much higher temperature than the human body."

He turned to John. "We're going to assume that two of them are your wife and daughter."

"Why are there two pictures?" John asked.

"The picture on the left is in real-time. It's showing what's being picked up at this instant as it's happening. And it's continuous. In contrast, the picture on the right is a still image that changes at thirty-second intervals. It shows the location of images thirty seconds apart. We can compare the images to detect movement within a certain time."

He pointed to the real-time picture. "Look here. If you compare this with the still picture, you'll notice that, at least for two of the five circular images, they're shown as having moved. If you'll notice, those two images here were in a different location thirty seconds ago. Although the other three show little if no movement, I'd venture to say that these two bright spots right here represent your wife and daughter." He pointed again.

"How could you even begin to guess something like that?" John asked.

Chips glanced at Kelly. "Would you like to take a shot in answering that question, Kelly?"

"I'd say it's because those two particular spots," Kelly answered, "are in close proximity of each other, compared with the other three."

"Right. Instead of separating your wife and daughter, which happens quite often in a double-kidnaping, I'd say these *dudes* have permitted them to stay together. That's because of your daughter's age. I'd guess your wife and daughter are sitting here, likely on a couch. I say that because the images are so close together in this picture. This third image here close to your wife and daughter, I'd say, is the fellow keeping an eye on them."

"Why print the images?" John asked.

"The hard copy that's printed is nothing more than a still picture of what you see on the screen at the time the software sends the print command to the printer. I'm printing hard copies so the teams can take them along with them. It'll give them one last chance to study the relative locations of the images just before the attack."

Chips now spoke faster. "I'll be assigning specific team members to each individual inside the house, once they enter—three SWAT Team members per kidnaper. When we launch the raid, each member will then know where that individual is in the house moments before the attack. Within a certain margin of error, of course, due to the time delay from image creation on the hard copy to the actual time of the raid. Those team members remaining, I'll assign to locations along the perimeter for possible backup and to guard the exterior in case our 'friends' inside the house manage to escape to the outside."

The grouping of trees where the briefing was taking place wasn't far from the front of the house. The sound of the front door opening caught their attention, and they froze in place. One of the kidnapers had come out of the house. The man walked to one of two cars parked in front. He got into the car and drove off.

"That should make your job a little easier," Kelly said to Chips.

"For sure," Chips agreed. He turned to one of his agents. "Hurry back to where we left the vans," he instructed the agent. "Use your cellular to alert the four state police units at the blockades. Instruct them to intercept that 'turkey' who just left."

The agent disappeared into the brush.

Chips began to print the next batch of hard copy images. As they printed, he walked to where the teams awaited their final instructions. There, he went on with his briefing. When the hard copies had printed, Kelly took them to Chips. John and Quigley tagged along.

"Imprint these images in your mind, men," Chips said to the team. He gave several hard copies to the team leaders and kept one. "Okay, I've made the necessary adjustments on your assignments due to one of these fellows having left the house. We're a bit lucky because things will get a little less confusing with just two of them inside. Maybe that's a good omen." He pointed to a hard copy. "Now, to summarize what we know. I think we can assume that our two hostages are here. You're to do everything possible to keep your weapons pointed away from them.

"This *dude* close to them is probably armed. For the three of you assigned to him, you can't let him draw or fire his weapon, so don't delay your fire. From the surveillance reported to me when you inspected the perimeter, I'd assume this other fellow here is in the kitchen, maybe preparing something to eat. You might catch him off guard." He glanced around the team members. "You should know what to do, so there better not be any questions." He paused for questions, but there were none. "Okay, then, let's get on with it! Good luck."

The teams separated for the last time to converge on the three entrances into the house. Chips went off with the support groups to their assigned area. This area was on the side of the house without a door or window. Kelly, Quigley, and John crept along the brush as close to the front of the house as they could without being seen. Only the dirt road separated them from the house.

Demi sat on the small sofa in the living room. It was a small house, making the living room seem cramped. Crystal was sleeping beside her, stretched out on the sofa, her head resting on Demi's lap. She had a bad night, hardly sleeping at all. Late this afternoon, Demi managed to calm her enough to get her to lie down on the couch to rest. Crystal complied with a fuss but, within minutes, had fallen fast asleep. Demi too hadn't slept well the night before. Crystal was terrified most of the night, and Demi spent some of the time trying to calm her. Once in a while, the youngster managed to doze off, only to reawaken from a bad dream.

Where had these men brought them, Demi wondered. They had been brought here separately. Demi arrived at the house before Crystal. She was glad for that part of the ordeal because she was able to calm her hysterical daughter when she arrived a half hour or so later.

She learned that Crystal had remained unconscious during the entire time she was driven from Tesuque to the house. She woke up right before the men dragged her into the house. As a result, she had little opportunity to realize she had been kidnaped. Demi surmised Crystal's long period of unconsciousness was due to the strong dosage of chloroform her abductors had given her, considering her body weight. Apparently realizing what had happened as she was led into the house, the youngster began to cry. Upon entering the living room, her eyes came upon her mother sitting on the sofa, and she rushed to her, crying uncontrollably.

When Demi herself first regained consciousness, the vehicle was traveling at a high rate of speed. She was lying in the back seat, blindfolded, so she couldn't see at all. One of the kidnapers was sitting next to her. He had one hand on her shoulder. On several occasions, she attempted to sit up, but the unseen man forced her back down.

As the car continued on, she decided to lie still and concentrate on movements and turns the car made. She might get some idea where she was being taken but wasn't sure that would matter. Yet it might turn out to be important in case she later got an opportunity to call for help.

Because of the speed at which the car was moving and the absence of any sharp turns, she guessed they were traveling along Interstate 25. But in what direction? South toward Albuquerque or northeast toward Colorado? Wherever they were taking her, she thought, it wouldn't be too far from Santa Fe. Otherwise, they'd risk being stopped at a roadblock. She hoped someone at the restaurant had reported the kidnaping and prayed Lourdes hadn't been hurt.

By the time the car exited the roadway she had guessed was the Interstate, she lost all sense of direction. The additional turns the vehicle made did nothing to reorient her.

Once inside the house, the blindfold was taken off. Through the tiny windows, she caught glimpses of the area surrounding the small residence, but it didn't help her get a feel for where she was. The dwelling appeared to be somewhere out in the country. But various trees and shrubs in the immediate area around the house blocked the view, making the surroundings she could see unrecognizable.

Several times since they had been brought here yesterday, she pled with the three men to let Crystal go. They would still have her to bargain with, she explained, and didn't need her daughter, an innocent child. But they refused her pleas with little comment.

This morning, when she realized they had no intention of releasing either of them before getting what they wanted from John, she lost control.

"Listen, you creep!" she lashed out at the one keeping an eye on her and Crystal. "There's no way—no way in hell—my husband is ever going to cooperate with you if you should hurt us in any way." Her voice became louder, and she found herself spitting out her words. She took a few steps forward, her face inches away from the victim of her wrath. "Is that clear, you spineless worm?"

Crystal sat frozen in place next to Demi, witnessing her mother's sudden rage.

Although seething with a fury that surprised her, Demi was also frightened. It was the fear, she thought, that triggered such venom in her words. She didn't know quite what reaction to expect from her abductor, but she could sense his own anger as he stood there glaring at her. But he said nothing. Without wavering, she looked straight into his eyes.

She began focusing on Crystal, who was now trembling. Demi wasn't even aware her daughter had been squeezing her hand with her tiny hands. She looked into her daughter's eyes. When she saw the terror in them, she wanted to cry.

The man brought up his clenched hand to strike her. He then held back, as if realizing hurting her in this way wouldn't be accepted by those over him.

Crystal screamed. "Mommy, Mommy!" she cried, terrified. "Please don't make him angry."

The man put his hand down, apparently angry at himself for losing control.

"We're not here to hurt you," he spoke with what she detected as a slight embarrassment. "Now back off before you make me do something I'll regret!"

Placing both hands on Demi's shoulders, he said, "Now take care of your daughter." He shoved her.

She fell on the sofa. Crystal went down with her, for she was still hanging on.

"Mommy," Crystal cried, "don't let him hurt us!"

"I'm not going to hurt you, you little brat!" the man yelled down at Crystal. "Now quit that bawling, or I'll have to gag you. You want me to muzzle you like a dog?" He leaned a few inches of the child's face.

Still afraid, Crystal quieted her cries down to a whimper. Demi held on to her to calm her.

When Crystal had stopped sobbing, Demi looked up at the man towering over her. "If you so much as touch her in any way," she said, unafraid, even though she was trembling with fear, "I'll kill you myself!"

She could see the scorn in the man's eyes.

He leaned down, holding his face inches from hers. "Listen, you bitch!" he mouthed off. "No one's going to hurt you or your daughter. What we're after, your husband's got. Meanwhile, we expect you and your daughter to cooperate." Catching his breath, he paused. "And your threats are empty!" He pointed to himself. *We*, not you, hold the strings here, lady. Despite your gallant words." He turned around and walked away.

She comprehended the man was right—she couldn't carry out her threat. These men could do anything they wanted; she and Crystal were helpless. The thought of any of them violating or even as much as touching her daughter repelled her.

She convinced herself her angry words had served a purpose. The reason behind the abductions was to get John to turn over the LaPierre documents. That was what Crystal's and her presence here was all about. She believed it was important for her to impress upon her abductors that if they expected John to cooperate, they'd better not hurt his daughter. To protect Crystal, she wanted to make that point. She prayed she had succeeded.

Now, as she sat on the sofa, reflecting on the confrontation that occurred earlier, she wasn't sorry she lost control. Crystal still slept on her lap. The man she exchanged words with was no longer watching over them. Instead, one of the others, to prevent a recurrence, took over the watch. He now sat on the cushioned chair in front of the sofa, a gun setting within reach on the small end table.

Crystal began to stir. Oh, God, please don't let her wake up now, Demi thought. She needed the sleep. To her surprise, her daughter had been eating well, and Demi was glad for that. They couldn't complain about that part of their ordeal, for the kidnapers had provided them with enough food. Demi, whose appetite was poor, had eaten little in the twenty-eight or so hours since their abductions. Now, sitting on the couch, she felt weak from not having eaten.

Her thoughts turned to John. Where was he this moment, she wondered. She had prayed her captors would let her speak to him. Yesterday, she pleaded with them to let her call him, but they refused. It wouldn't serve their purpose, she was told by the man she had exchanged words with. She renewed her request with his replacement this afternoon, but he too had said no. They had strict rules to hold them incommunicado, he explained.

On the occasions when she had been permitted to visit the bathroom, she made it a point to see if she could spot a telephone as she was accompanied down the hallway. But she saw none. The abductors each had a cellular phone, but they kept the phones close to them, never leaving them laying around. Not that she could have made the call, even if she had gotten her hands on one, for the men watched her like a hawk.

The problems she and John had spoken of during the past few weeks now seemed small and insignificant. Even the regrettable, emotional upheavals and misunderstandings of recent days seemed unimportant. With what they had together, they could rise above the bad times she'd rather forget. Now more than ever, she knew she loved him and that he loved her. She was also convinced they both cared enough about each other that they'd do anything to preserve what they had, which she thought priceless. Never before had that fact been clearer than now, when she faced the unknown. And, she was certain John felt the same way.

He too was a victim of this ordeal. She knew he'd give anything to trade places with them. She had prayed last night he was coping well with the knowledge his wife and daughter were being held hostage by these thugs. Was he with the FBI or CIA at this moment, waiting to be contacted? By now, the FBI might be planning some kind of action—counter-measures. Didn't the agency usually play a big role in kidnapings of this sort? Was it planning a rescue attempt? But to do that, the agents would have to know where she and Crystal were being held. What were the chances of their whereabouts being discovered? Not good, she concluded. Yet, she kept her hopes up there would soon be a rescue.

Yesterday, she suspected one of the men had placed a call to John. Earlier this afternoon, she sensed one of them, the one who had just returned to the house, had again telephoned John. But she wasn't certain because the three men never discussed anything within earshot of her. But she trusted John to do the right thing.

She wondered if her thoughts of a possible rescue were her mind's way of permitting her to deal with a hopeless situation. Were her hopes a coping mechanism triggered by the mind's need to relieve the stress of being held captive? Yet, sitting there stroking Crystal's hair, she experienced an odd sensation. She felt her body tingle in anticipation of an unknown but impending event. Something *was* going to happen. She was sure of it. She didn't know what, but the feeling became stronger as she concentrated on the thought. What she sensed was something positive—almost a premonition that something good was about to occur.

A loud noise startled her. It was loud enough to wake up Crystal, who sat up. She seemed confused.

Three members of the SWAT Team crashed through the front door. In another instant, several other team members sprang through the side entrance. There was another crash out back as the outside door there was broken down.

Startled, Demi and Crystal looked around them, unable to absorb or comprehend the event. Heavy shouting filled the room as countless men in black uniform ran through. Loud shouting and a heavy shuffling of feet could be heard in the back of the house. For Demi and Crystal, it was utter chaos.

Crystal began crying. "Mommy, Mommy, what's happening?" she screamed.

In the confusion of the moment, Demi wanted to comfort her daughter. But she found herself unable to speak—the words just wouldn't come. So she did the next best thing. She threw herself on her daughter and held her against her own body. Crystal clung to her mother for dear life.

In the living room, the man seated in the chair stood up, the gun in his hand ready to fire. He never got the chance.

Exploding gunfire filled the room. The man slumped to the floor. Demi and Crystal screamed.

Elsewhere, earsplitting shots rang out in the smoke-filled house. In the kitchen, the man who had been preparing something to eat was shot twice by the teams members bolting through the rear door. Wounded, the man rushed into the hallway, running toward a back bedroom.

Demi hadn't yet registered what was occurring—the rescue she had hoped for a moment ago was taking place.

It was bedlam. The house had filled with other men in black. Four of them rushed to the couch where Demi and Crystal clung to each other.

407

The men surrounded them, forming a human shield to protect them from the gunfire in the hallway.

Three members of the SWAT Team ran into the hallway in pursuit of the wounded abductor. Entering the bedroom, the man slammed the door shut. Once inside the room, he pulled his own weapon out of his jacket, placed it in his mouth, and pulled the trigger.

CHAPTER 33

JOHN'S family celebrated their reunion in the living room of their home. Crystal and Johnny sat on the carpet in front of their parents. Johnny had his head down near his mother's legs, enjoying her soft touch as she stroked his hair. Crystal's hands and arms rested on her father's lap, as he told the family of his near abduction. The children listened in awe.

"You feel better, now, Pumpkin?" he said to Crystal when he finished. He touched her cheek with the back of his hand.

"Yes, Daddy," she said, "much better." She smiled and squeezed his legs. "And I'm happy we're all home again."

John returned her smile, then turned to Demi. He sighed. "That was quite an ordeal you and your mother went through." He took Demi's hand and squeezed it. "You just don't know what a relief it is to have you both back."

"I'm glad that nightmare's over," Demi said. "I'm still having a hard time believing it happened. I don't even want to think about having to spend another day with those men."

"Well, thank God you don't have to think about it because you're both here in one piece." He leaned over and planted a kiss on her cheek.

Four FBI agents had been assigned to the house to spend the night and the remainder of the week. One of them was now in the next room, allowing the family some privacy. Another one was somewhere else in the house. The other two were outside in the front and back yards. In addition, six state police patrolmen had been assigned to provide outside surveillance throughout the neighborhood during the night hours.

Chips, Kelly and Quigley had just left the residence, after assuring themselves John and his family were doing fine.

After Demi and Crystal had been airlifted from Galisteo, Chips and Kelly insisted they be taken to the ambulatory unit of St. Vincent Hospital in Santa Fe. An examination by an internist there confirmed that both Demi and Crystal were doing remarkably well, with a few minor exceptions. Demi was slightly dehydrated, and she complained of feeling weak, which the internist believed was from being malnourished. She was placed on an IV for an hour or so before being released. Crystal was still anxious from the trauma. The internist injected a mild sedative to the youngster.

Johnny too showed considerable relief the family was back together. Earlier, at the hospital, when he was reunited with his family, he wouldn't let go of his mother, even when the doctor was trying to examine her.

A van brought the entire family back home from St. Vincent Hospital. On the trip into Albuquerque, Johnny wanted to know why his mother and sister were taken away by those *bad persons*. The abductions had made clear to the children the CIA and FBI's involvement in their lives. For that reason, John believed the time had come to explain to both children why *these terrible things* were happening, as Crystal had phrased it.

John and Demi had talked often in the recent past about how they were going to handle this scenario if it ever arose. It seemed only a matter of time before the children realized something unusual was going on. And when that time came, how much of the story should they reveal?

Demi agreed that the kidnapings and John's near abduction justified giving their children some explanation. The two of them spent the next fifteen or twenty minutes answering the youngsters' queries. They didn't tell them about Henri's and Leroy's deaths, nor did they go into any great detail in explaining the LaPierre documents. At the end, they assured Crystal and Johnny that all of them would be protected from now on and that they needn't worry they'd be hurt again. The children appeared satisfied with the explanations.

John accompanied the two children upstairs to their rooms and tucked them in their beds for the night.

A few minutes later, before going upstairs with Demi, John peeked into the family room. There, he found both FBI agents. He told them the family was going to bed and said goodnight.

John and Demi walked into the bedroom and closed the door. In the privacy of their room, they embraced for a long moment.

"God, I worried about the two of you," he whispered into her ear. "I don't know what I would have done if you had been hurt by those goons."

Demi squeezed him. "Well, we weren't," she said, "and that's what's important." She kissed him on the cheek. They parted.

She saw he was teary. "You're crying," she said. She raised her hand and wiped away the tears.

He grinned. "I may be from 'Mars,'" he joked, "but these are tears of joy." He kissed her on the forehead. "I want to make a vow to you tonight."

"About?"

"About us."

"I'm listening."

"I promise you'll never have to worry about us growing apart. I'll try hard as hell not to let what happened between us ever happen again. Whatever it takes, I'll do it."

"Thanks for saying that." She kissed him on the lips. "You don't know how happy it makes me to hear you say that."

The phone rang. He walked over to the night stand, picked up the cordless phone, and answered the call. It was Dan, he told her.

"I'll take it in the study," he said as he walked to the door.

Struggling to take off her dress, she just nodded. She walked into the bathroom, and he disappeared out the bedroom door.

"I just arrived into town an hour or so ago," Dan explained at the other end as John walked into the study. "I didn't hear until noon today what happened to you in D. C." He spoke faster than usual. "And I heard just a few minutes ago about Demi and Crystal. How are they doing?" He seemed concerned.

"They're going to be fine, Dan," John said. "Thanks for asking."

John was surprised Dan knew about his close call, much less about the abductions. Kelly explained to him earlier that, for now, the news agencies wouldn't be informed of the abductions or of the Jefferson Memorial incident. The law enforcement agencies participating in the rescue operation were sworn to secrecy. Chips and Kelly reemphasized to the agencies that the case involved the country's national security. Kelly considered it important that no information be released until an extensive investigation revealed and confirmed the parties responsible for the kidnapings. The agencies were told the matter was being handled by federal authorities because it involved national security. They were asked to defer to these authorities until the FBI investigation was completed.

The local agencies vowed their cooperation. The usual, routine reports these agencies ordinarily generated were to be kept sealed until approval was given by the FBI and CIA. Finally, the agencies were instructed that all inquiries by anyone, including the news media, were to be referred to the media rep appointed for the rescue operation.

"How did you find out what happened?" John asked Dan as he closed the door to the study.

"I learned about the Memorial incident from a confidential source in Washington," Dan explained. "What happened there, of course, has been kept under wraps, and the news media hasn't gotten wind of it."

"At least not yet. Kelly told me it'd be kept from the public. Who's your source?"

"I've got a friend over at the National Security Agency in Maryland." Dan laughed. "That agency makes it a point to know almost everything that goes on in Washington. They're no different from Kelly's agency in that respect. Anyway, getting back to my source, he heard of the incident through normal channels. When he found out Candace and I had dinner with you Saturday night, he telephoned and told me what happened. Are you all right, John?"

"It was a frightening experience, but it's over. Demi and Crystal being taken hostage—that was an ordeal I wouldn't want to live through again. How did you learn of the kidnapings? Those too were supposed to be kept under wraps."

"Kelly told me about that tonight when I called him from the airport. I told him I was going to call you to set up a meeting for in the morning."

"A meeting? What's going on?"

"I'd rather not talk about it over the phone after what happened to Demi and Crystal. This thing is getting too wild for me. But it's important that we talk *pronto*. Can you meet me at my office first thing tomorrow?"

"Have you already set this up with Kelly?"

"Yes, a minute ago. As a matter of fact, I called his cellular and reached him as he was driving away from your house. So he asked me to call you to see if you could join us at eight. Can you?"

"Sure."

"Good. I'll call Kelly right back to confirm the time."

"See you tomorrow, then. Bye."

"Have a good night, John. Again, I feel bad about what happened. Please give my best to Demi and the children."

"I will, Dan. Thanks again."

The next morning, John arrived at Dan's Albuquerque suite of offices a few minutes before eight. He was ushered into Dan's private office by the receptionist, where Dan and Kelly were waiting for him.

John glanced at his watch. "Am I running late?" he said to no one in particular.

Kelly responded. "No, I was just early," he said, grinning.

"Please have a seat, John," Dan said, gesturing to an empty chair. "Kelly was just filling me in on what happened in Galisteo yesterday. Sounds like quite a remarkable feat the rescue team pulled off."

"I'll forever be grateful to them," John said. He sat and turned to Kelly. "And, again, Kelly, thanks for your support through all this."

"You're welcome, John," Kelly said. Just part of the job." He smiled. "How are Demi and the children this morning?"

"The kids were still asleep when I left the house. Demi's doing fine. She seemed rested, even though we've both been up since five."

"That's early. I hope both of you slept well."

"We slept like babies. I may have awakened then because I knew it was going to be a long day for me. I got to the office a few minutes after seven because I wanted to get the top of my desk somewhat organized before starting my work day. I've been out of pocket the past two days, and some things there needed my attention."

"You should have taken a few more days off," Dan suggested. "What would another couple of days hurt?"

"I wish I could have, but this is my last week at the office. Winding down one's practice isn't easy. And it's time consuming. I might be able to finish soon and not go back Friday and Saturday."

"Now you're talking."

"I bet Demi's wishing you had stayed home," Kelly said.

"She understood," John replied. "Actually I'm quite proud of her. I'm surprised she's doing so well. I was afraid there would be some long-term effects from all this."

"She's stable. I too was surprised yesterday when we were bringing your family home. She appeared as if she had gone through a typical day."

"You think Crystal and Johnny are going to be all right?" Dan asked.

"Considering what they've been through, especially Crystal," John said, "I think they're doing well. Demi's planning to let them stay home from school the rest of the week just to keep an eye on them. We had a good talk with them last night. Demi and I tried explaining without too much detail why all of these crazy events were taking place."

"It'd be tough, I'd think, explaining something like that to your kids in a way they'd understand."

"I hope Demi feels comfortable that the surveillance teams will be able to protect Crystal and Johnny from here on out," Kelly said. He seemed defensive.

John smiled. "Of course. Listen, she and I are grateful for all you've done. And we know the FBI's doing everything it can to protect us. As I confessed before, I'm the one who screwed up. In keeping the children out of school, I think Demi's doing the natural thing—being a mother. She's apprehensive, of course, but who wouldn't be under the circumstances."

Dan shook his head and smiled in apparent admiration. "I have a high regard for you and your family, John," he said. "You've been through living hell the past few weeks. I hope Demi and your kids will continue to do well in dealing with this."

"Demi told me Crystal got quite shook up while held hostage. But if the way she was feeling last night is any sign, I think she's going to come out of this just fine."

"I'm glad to hear you say that." Dan paused. "Listen, I know both of you need to get back to your work, so I'll get to why I asked you here. Just before I left D. C. yesterday, I received a phone call from Chris Dunlevy. It appears that, although Vice-President Hirsch met with President Henning yesterday morning, he said not a word of our meeting with him last Saturday. Chris and I thought that odd."

"It sure was," John said. "Though there might be a good reason why he didn't. Maybe the President curtailed his time."

"That's possible, of course, but considering the nature and sensitivity of the information we passed on to him, I think it's unlikely. This information's important. Hirsch should have insisted President Henning hear him out, even assuming the President's schedule was tight."

Kelly, who had been listening to every word, finally spoke. "How did Chris find out Hirsch didn't pass on the information to the President?"

"Pure coincidence. It just so happened he was passing by the Oval Office when his immediate supervisor, Aaron Riley, ran into him. It seems Aaron, the President's Chief Counsel, had just been to see President Henning. Aaron told Chris that he point blank asked the President about Hirsch's visit with him earlier that morning."

"From what you've said," John broke in, "I'm assuming Chris had told Aaron about our meeting with the Vice-President."

"That's right. Chris briefed him first thing yesterday morning when Aaron returned from Camp David. Those are matters that Chris wouldn't keep to himself."

"I'm a little curious why Aaron Riley found it necessary to even ask about Hirsch's visit with President Henning."

"I have no idea. Chris didn't either, and Riley didn't tell him anything. But Chris and I think that Hirsch is biding his time and just sitting on the information you and I provided him with, for a reason known only to him."

"I might be able to shed some light on your question, John," Kelly volunteered. He turned to Dan. "Dan, may I?"

"Go ahead," Dan said. "Please enlighten us."

"Your suspicion," Kelly began, "that Hirsch is biding time with the information you two gave him is quite legitimate. First of all, I happen to believe he's trying to protect himself. Equally important, however, he's also stalling because he's trying to protect someone else as long as he can."

"Who?"

"Your colleague. Senator Condon."

John became confused but said nothing, deciding not to interrupt.

"Are we talking some kind of conspiracy here?" Dan asked.

Kelly nodded.

"How do you know this?"

Kelly turned to John. "You'll recall that when you and I were driving to Santa Fe Sunday, I touched on this. I told you I didn't think Hirsch would be eager to tell the President of your visit."

415

"Yes, I recall," John said. "But you wouldn't tell me why."

"Well, I'm going to tell you and Dan now." Kelly cleared his throat. "I told you the other day that Hirsch and Condon were buddies—I may have said they were 'chummy'—I don't recall. Well, we think it's more than just a recent friendship that's developed between them. You already know we've had Condon under scrutiny for quite a while now. What you didn't know was that we've also kept tabs, on a more limited scale, on Hirsch. We're now aware of several meetings between the two during the past three weeks."

"What kind of meetings?" Dan said. "I mentioned *conspiracy* a while ago. Is that what you think is going on?"

"We're still trying to figure it out. And we will in time. But this much I can tell you—something suspicious appears to be going on between the two." He glanced at John, then turned back to Dan. "What we do know is that Condon now appears to be aware our agency's investigating him."

"You have any idea how he found out?"

Kelly nodded. "Yes. We suspect Hirsch told him."

"That's incredible! The information we fed him, he divulges to Emory but not to the President, for whom it was intended."

"We suspect Hirsch had already gotten bits and pieces of our investigation of Condon from his own sources. The two of you not only confirmed it for him, but provided additional intelligence he didn't yet have his hands on." Kelly turned to John. "When you told me about your visit with Hirsch, I became interested to learn how long he'd keep the information from the President and how soon he'd get it to Condon. Your visit with him helped us confirm our suspicions."

"I bet the President's going to have a field day with this!"

Kelly nodded. "We're going to have to step up our investigation efforts on Hirsch. That'll require President Henning's approval. When are you due back in Washington, Dan?"

"Tomorrow around noon."

"Sometime today, could you contact Chris to try scheduling a meeting with President Henning as soon as possible after you get back there?"

"Sure. Who'd be attending?"

"That'll depend on the President's wishes. But I have in mind you, my boss, Director Welch, and possibly Chris or his boss, Riley. Director Welch should be back in town tomorrow afternoon. You could schedule the meeting either tomorrow evening or sometime Thursday, depending, of course, on the President's schedule."

"Would you be attending, Kelly?"

"I'd like to, but only if the Director wants me to. I'm calling him this evening to brief him." He paused. "I haven't yet gotten a chance to tell him the good news about Demi and Crystal's rescue. He'll be happy to hear about it, I'm sure."

"What about you, John? Would you like to attend?"

John grinned. "I'd be lying to you," he replied, "if I said I wouldn't look forward to meeting with the President on something this important. But I think the time's come for me to drop out of the picture and let you and Kelly go on with this. There's no reason for me to tag along." He looked at Kelly. "This go-around, I'd prefer to stay at home with my family. Besides, I'm wrapping things up at the office, remember?"

Kelly grinned. "I had an inkling that's the way you'd feel about it."

"I'm depending on you, Kelly, to wrap this case up as soon as possible so Demi and I can move on with our lives."

"And move on to the Supreme Court and next year, the federal judgeship," Dan added, smiling.

John laughed. "Well, the Supreme Court, next week for sure. As for the other, if it's in the cards, that too."

CHAPTER 34

IN the reception room outside the Oval Office, Kelly and Dan awaited the arrival of Herbert Welch, Director of the Central Intelligence Agency. A minor emergency at CIA Headquarters in Langley had delayed his arrival.

It was late afternoon, and President Henning was spending the rest of the day alone in his smaller, working office near the Oval Office, catching up on his legislative paper work. He was to be notified the minute Director Welch arrived.

The meeting this afternoon had been coordinated between Chris Dunlevy, Irving Klein, the President's Deputy Chief of Staff, and Herbert Welch's office. Dan telephoned Chris to arrange the conference on his return to Washington.

Although Kelly had devoted almost thirty years of his life to the CIA, never had his work brought him to the White House. In a few minutes, he'd be entering the office where many private conversations among world leaders had taken place under the helm of many presidents. He too would soon be one of an elite group that had spoken privately with the President of the United States. But, alas, he had never married, and so he had no children or grandchildren to tell the story to.

He had been nervous when he and Dan had entered the White House grounds. But as he sat in the receiving room waiting for Director Hirsch, his nervousness subsided. Now, he looked forward to meeting with the President, feeling quite eager to get on with the business at hand.

He now felt his ordinary self, as he normally did when handling a sensitive case. It didn't matter that President Henning was involved. The President was just another player in the action, although he'd be the one calling the shots. Kelly's job was to provide him with the information on which to act. That was his task in every case—to gather the intelligence so that important decisions could be made by those empowered to make them.

As Kelly and Dan waited, Kelly brought Dan up to date on the case since they had met in Albuquerque.

"I talked to John this morning," Dan said to Kelly after the agent summarized his tentative plans. "I told him about this meeting. He was glad to hear you'd be here."

Kelly smiled. "Yeah, me too," he said. "The Director insisted."

"It makes sense. What about the FBI?"

"They're involved, of course. Bill Pierce, the FBI's deputy director, was supposed to be here but couldn't make it at the last minute. Director Welch will brief him later. The FBI's going to be handling the additional surveillance we've got planned."

"You're referring to the clandestine investigation of Hirsch?"

Kelly nodded. "I've gotten the okay from my director to ask President Henning for approval to conduct the in-depth surveillance."

"I think it'll be a touchy subject. But I'd think that, considering the circumstantial evidence you've already accumulated against the Vice-President, President Henning would approve your going ahead with it. Don't you?"

"I suppose that would depend how successful I am in convincing him it's necessary. I think you're right—it'll be a sensitive issue for him. The President having his VP tailed *and* bugged. How would that look to the news media if it leaked out?"

"Could prove quite embarrassing to the President, I'd imagine. If it later proved to be justified, though, it wouldn't be as bad if the media learned about it then."

"Yeah, the old 'end justifying the means' argument, right?"

420

"Right. The President would then be perceived as having done the right thing."

Director Welch entered the room. Kelly and Dan stood up to greet him. After shaking hands with the two men, Herbert Welch sat down.

He was a man of small stature who looked younger than his sixty-five years, despite his thinning hair. He wore tailor-made suits that fit him to a T, for he was a person who was meticulous and conscious of his appearance.

He was appointed by President Henning as head of the CIA at the beginning of the President's term of office. Previous to that, he had served the President's predecessor as an assistant Secretary of Defense. While serving as assistant Secretary at the Department of Defense, he and President Henning, who was then a member of the United States Senate, became close friends. They golfed and played tennis together.

"I'll notify the President's secretary you've arrived, Herb," Dan said, walking toward the door leading into the next room. He opened the door and walked out.

Within half a minute, he was back. He sat back down. "She's gone in to tell the President you're here, Herb."

"Good," Welch said. "I apologize to you gentlemen that I couldn't get here sooner. I hope the President didn't mind."

"His secretary said he had scheduled the second half of the afternoon as a work day in his private office, so I think it worked out well for him."

The President's personal secretary, a woman in her late fifties, soon entered the receiving area and told the three visitors the President was ready to see them. She ushered them through her office and into the Oval Office.

President Henning sat behind his large desk. He stood up to greet them.

"Gentlemen," he said with a wide smile, "it's good to see you."

Kelly had heard before that the President was a gracious host. The man's greeting showed that, he thought.

Kelly and Dan allowed Welch to take the lead and remained a few feet behind him. Welch and President Henning shook hands.

"Herb," President Henning said, "it seems as if we haven't seen each other in ages."

"We'll need to get in a game of golf soon," Welch said. "*That*, for sure, we haven't done in ages." He grinned, then turned his attention to

Kelly and Dan. "You know Dan, of course." He paused to permit the President to greet Dan.

"Dan, it's nice seeing you again," President Henning said, shaking Dan's hand. "I understand the delegation had a successful trip to Mexico."

"We certainly did, Mr. President," Dan said.

"Mr. President, I don't believe you've met Special Agent John Kelly," Welch said. "He's been with our agency for almost thirty years."

Kelly smiled. "Mr. President, it's a pleasure to meet you, sir," he said, extending his hand. He was getting nervous again.

The President returned the smile. "Agent Kelly, it's *my* pleasure," he said and shook hands.

The President gestured to the two sofas facing each other near the fireplace, separated by a massive coffee table. "Please sit, gentlemen. May we get you something to drink?" He glanced at his secretary, who had been standing to one side, waiting to be excused.

The three visitors declined the offer, and the secretary excused herself and left the room. The visitors sat on the couches, and President Henning joined them, moving a chair closer to the sofas.

The President's hair was jet black, except for the sides, which had grayed in recent years, thus adding to his stately appearance. Radiating a powerful presence, even in the privacy of the Oval Office, he possessed striking blue eyes that seemed warm and gentle, giving one in his presence a feeling of acceptance.

"Mr. President," Director Welch began, "I've asked Special Agent Kelly to join us because he's been working this case for several weeks. He's familiar with the details."

"Fine, fine," President Henning said. "So what is this case, Herb, which I've been informed involves a matter of considerable importance to our national security?"

"If you don't mind, Mr. President, I'd like to have Agent Kelly brief you on the case first from its inception. It'd help, I think, for you to have an understanding of the case's history and progression to appreciate it in the present day's context. With your permission, then, if Agent Kelly may do that before we discuss what we're here to ask of you."

"Not a problem." He spoke with emphasis. "I'm listening."

Welch turned to Kelly. "Kelly, would you please brief the President?"

422

Kelly cleared his throat. "I'll be happy to," he replied. The President's warm manner had put him at ease. It would help with his presentation, he thought.

He began by telling the President of the intelligence the agency had gathered bit by bit, culminating in the discovery of the LaPierre documents. He explained John Garcia's involvement, noting the tribulations the Garcia family had undergone, including the attempted abduction of John himself and finally, the kidnaping of Demi and Crystal and their eventual rescue. President Henning appeared moved by the traumatic events.

The agent then laid the groundwork leading to John and Dan's meeting with Vice-President Hirsch the week before. He made it clear the evidence his agency and the FBI had uncovered implicated the Vice-President in what he theorized as a possible conspiracy with Condon.

"A conspiracy to do what?" President Henning asked. He gestured with his hand. "Before you explain, let me first say that I'm astounded by these events the CIA's uncovered. Especially by the accusation you make against the Vice-President."

"I appreciate how you feel about that, Mr. President," Welch volunteered. "To respond to your question, we don't know at this point what the conspiracy is. All we know is that the Vice-President has been acting a bit peculiar in his dealings with Senator Condon. His meetings with the senator, for example, when he knows well the senator may be the Republican's presidential nominee next year. They're suspicious, I hope you'll agree."

The President nodded. "I grant you that much, Herb. More on point, however, I also agree that Charles better have a reasonable explanation why he hasn't told me about his meeting with you, Dan. But I'm not certain that alone warrants the conclusion there's some kind of conspiracy between him and Emory Condon." He paused. "I definitely plan talking to him about it."

"If I may, Mr. President," Kelly jumped in, a look of concern evident on his face. "I would respectfully request that you not confront the Vice-President with the information at this time."

"And why not, Agent Kelly?" President Henning said, showing surprise.

"Our agency and the FBI need more time, Mr. President."

"More time to do what?"

423

Kelly glanced at Herbert Welch. The Director nodded, giving Kelly the go-ahead to reveal their planned surveillance.

"To come straight to the point, Mr. President, we're here to ask for your permission to investigate the Vice-President," Kelly said.

"Investigate the Vice-President?" President Henning said, raising his eyebrows.

"Sir, the FBI wants to conduct an in-depth surveillance of Vice-President Hirsch. This would involve placing bugging devices in his office here at the White House and in his office at the Capitol. If you approve the plan, it would also entail direct clandestine surveillance of the Vice-President's every move. We fully realize, Mr. President, that our plan is rather intrusive. But we wouldn't be recommending it unless we felt it was necessary."

"This is a very unusual request, gentlemen. And risky." He turned to Welch. "Herb, what have you got to say about this? Do you realize your agency and the FBI would be treading on thin ice if I gave my approval?"

"We're well aware of the risks involved, Mr. President," Welch answered. "But we've weighed these risks as well as the political implications in the event the surveillance should leak out to the news media."

"That's for sure. With the eve of the elections upon us, they'd have a field day with this one. Especially if your suspicions turned out to be wrong."

"If I may suggest, Mr. President," Kelly broke in, feeling nervous again, "the risks of the alternative—not doing anything at all—would also be high. And dangerous too."

"In what way dangerous, Agent Kelly?"

"I believe the Vice-President is trying to protect Senator Condon, as I already noted, but I think he's also trying to protect himself."

"From what?"

"That's where our conspiracy theory kicks in. We don't think the Vice-President would go through the trouble of not telling you about our investigation of Condon just to protect the senator. He wouldn't risk the implications of keeping it from you for that reason alone. There's got to be something more. Our agency thinks he's buying time."

"Time to do what?"

"That, I'm afraid, only Vice-President Hirsch knows. That's why it's important to conduct the additional surveillance. We must rule out the possibility that our national security will be compromised, or worse yet, that even your own safety, Mr. President, may be at risk."

President Henning said nothing for a long time as he appeared to ponder Kelly's comments. He then turned to Welch. "Herb," he said, "I assume you've considered Agent Kelly's proposal and approve it."

Welch nodded. "I sure do, Mr. President. I echo his concern that the risk must be taken to rule out any potential danger to this country or direct danger to you."

The President said nothing for a moment, as if considering the Director's remarks. "All right, Herb—Agent Kelly. You have my approval to go ahead with the surveillance." He shook his head, showing his obvious reluctance. "What part, if any, do I play in this plan of yours?"

Kelly spoke. "First, Mr. President, it's important you not confront Mr. Hirsch about his failure to divulge his meeting with Senator Conniff and Mr. Garcia. You shouldn't say anything that might make him suspect you know he's keeping information from you."

"That'll be easy enough. Go on."

"Second, should the Vice-President himself approach you on the subject in any way, you should pretend to know nothing about it. Third, of course, the FBI will need your direct approval to conduct the surveillance and to install the electronic devices. We realize your time's important, Mr. President, but we ask that you make yourself available when Mr. Pierce, Deputy Director of the FBI, contacts your deputy Chief of Staff. That'll require some coordination with your office. And secrecy, of course, on the part of your staff."

The President nodded, then stood up. "All right, gentlemen," he said, displaying a dismayed look. "Is there anything else?"

Welch spoke out. "No, Mr. President," he said. "I believe that's all we've got at the moment. Thank you for meeting with us." He stood up.

Dan and Kelly took their cue from Welch and stood up also. The President accompanied them to the door.

"Herb," he said, "I'm relying on your good judgment, but I want you to know I'll be holding you personally responsible if anything goes wrong and this plan of yours should backfire on us. We just can't afford the embarrassment."

"I understand, Mr. President," Welch said. "I assure you both Bill Pierce and I comprehend the political implications of what we're doing."

President Henning opened the door. "Good, I'll make sure I tell Bill Pierce the same thing when he contacts this office. Meanwhile, Herb, I'd like a daily report from you on the ongoing investigation."

"I'll make sure you get one, Mr. President."

The President escorted them into the broad hallway outside the reception room, where he bid them farewell.

Without delay, the necessary arrangements were made for the surveillance to begin the next day. Late that night and in the early morning hours of the next day, listening devices were installed in several locations. They included the Vice-President's limousine, his offices at the White House and at the Capitol, and Condon's office at the Capitol and in the Russell Senate Office Building. Micro transmitters capable of emitting a strong signal were also placed in the Vice-President's and the senator's motor vehicles to keep track of their every move and even of whispered conversations. These devices prevented the need of having the two men tailed when in their cars. The small transmitters were sensitive and could thus be picked up by the FBI's receivers.

By the end of that week alone, Hirsch and Condon met alone on three occasions, twice in the Vice-President's ceremonial office in the Capitol and once in Condon's offices in the same building. On those occasions, the two men's conversations revealed nothing substantive or incriminating, but only information the FBI/CIA team already possessed. For the most part, these discussions related to the agencies' investigation into the senator's activities in Vietnam, which was non-incriminating.

On two other occasions the following day, however, the two men spoke of *our plan* and the need to carry it out before the Vietnam information on the senator became public. That public disclosure, both men agreed, might affect, if not destroy their plan. One fact became clear—Condon continued to insist he had nothing to hide about his tours in Vietnam. He continued to maintain his innocence of any wrongdoing, calling the investigation a witch hunt intended to hurt his chances for his party's nomination and later in the presidential election. The Vice-President seemed to believe the senator.

Their last meeting, however, took place in neither the Vice-President's nor senator's offices but outdoors near the reflecting pool along the Mall. During the conversation of the two men on that particular occasion, a special listening device picked up the most serious and incriminating information thus far. But a malfunction of the equipment midway through the conversation caused a part not to be picked up. That part, unfortunately, revealed the serious nature of the two men's alliance—a conspiracy of major proportions.

On the day of that meeting, Hirsch had telephoned Condon from his offices at the White House to invite the senator to lunch. The two men agreed to meet at *The Monocle*, a well-known restaurant located on Capitol Hill. The small restaurant was frequented by many legislators and lobbyists during the noon hour. Hirsch made arrangements to pick up Condon in the Vice-President's limousine outside the Capitol to travel the short distance to the restaurant.

After the two men finished their lunch, Condon noted he had a meeting at the State Department at two o'clock. When Hirsch learned that the senator was planning to take a cab to his scheduled meeting, he offered to give him a lift in his limousine. The State Department building was a few blocks from the White House.

"I need to speak to you, anyway," Hirsch said as the two of them walked out of the restaurant. "But not here or in the limo. We'll go some place where we can talk in private."

"Has this thing got you paranoid, Charles?" Condon asked just before entering the limousine.

Inside, the Vice-President eased back in his seat. "It always pays to be cautious, Emory," he said. He instructed his chauffeur to detour from his usual route to the White House along Constitution Avenue. He explained that he and the senator would be taking a short walk near the reflecting pool before driving the senator to his meeting.

Near the Lincoln Memorial, the chauffeur jumped the curb of the curved street. He pulled the limousine onto a grassy knoll. Within a matter of minutes, Hirsch and Condon strolled on the broad sidewalk alongside the reflecting pool, away from the chauffeur and the secret service detail assigned to the Vice-President, who trailed thirty or so feet behind. The two men walked east toward the Capitol. The Vietnam Wall Memorial, with dozens of onlookers and tourists milling about, stood out in the background.

Kelly's agency and the FBI were prepared for such an eventuality. Equipped with ultra-sensitive listening equipment, the FBI/CIA team had set up a van several hundred feet away from where the two men were taking their jaunt. The device installed in the van had the capability of narrowing in on a confined or narrow area to pick up sounds. The equipment was sensitive enough to pick up whispers half a mile away.

Unaware their conversation was being monitored and recorded, they spoke with no restraints.

"It's foolproof, I tell you," Condon said as the listening device picked up every word. "Soon, you won't have to worry about this witch hunt."

"How certain are you of these persons you've involved in this?" Hirsch asked.

"They're reliable, I assure you, Charles. I've paid considerable sums to hire the very best. These individuals are professionals. They know what they're doing. And they're paid top dollar for this sort of thing."

"I realize that." Hirsch rubbed his hands together. "Not that aspect. I mean technically. How versed are they with the equipment they'll be using?"

"They've tested it again and again. It's been put to the test and worked every time. What are you worried about?"

"That it hasn't been put to the ultimate test," Hirsch said. "That's what."

It was at this precise moment that a signal interference of unknown origin caused the listening device to fail for a few seconds. It emitted static and faint, garbled sounds during that brief period. It was then that the technicians failed to pick up the incriminating nature of what followed.

"It's not every day," Hirsch said without being monitored, "that one attempts to kill the President of the United States. So this plan of yours better be foolproof!"

"And I'm telling you that it is!" Condon retorted. "Don't worry, it's going to work. President Henning will soon be history, just like President Kennedy during his third year in office. I assure you—this president too will not complete his third year. And that'll open the door for you, Charles. The office will be yours!"

"What I would like to know, Emory, is when and where will the assassination take place."

"That, I've left up to the ones doing the dirty work."

As quickly as it had appeared, the interference went away, and the conspirators' last words were heard again by the technicians.

"Surely, Emory, you must have some idea," the Vice-President said, sounding annoyed.

"I must admit I know the time and place. I dislike being so secretive, but I think you'll agree that the least number of persons who know of our plan, the better the chances it'll succeed." He paused. "Stop worrying. It's going to happen soon!"

CHAPTER 35

THE formal swearing-in ceremony took place late Monday afternoon the following week in the banquet room of the *El Dorado Hotel* in Santa Fe. It was followed by a crowded reception in the hotel's large dining room-lounge. Although the Simms law firm was the main sponsor of the event, other firms had contributed to the event's costs. Kelly hadn't returned from D. C., but Quigley joined in the festivities. Dan and Candace Conniff had flown in to be there.

The FBI/CIA Team had arranged for additional agents to move among the heavy crowd, at all times staying within a few feet of John and Demi as they greeted the guests. John and Demi spotted them right off, but to others, the agents were lost in the crowd mingling as guests. Crystal and Johnny too had been assigned several agents who never let them out of their sight. The children too knew they were being watched. Ever since the abductions, they followed their parents' instructions without question. As a result, they never wandered off into other parts of the hotel, but instead stayed close to their parents.

The past weekend, Quigley had explained the logistics in providing security and surveillance once John began work in Santa Fe. Although he and Demi would work in their offices without agents present there, surveillance teams would be in place outside. From there, they'd follow John and Demi wherever their day-to-day tasks took them. The operatives had strict instructions, Quigley assured John, not to reveal themselves unless there were signs of impending danger. In addition, transmitting devices had been installed in the family vehicles and at the residence. John and Demi were instructed to go about their activities as usual without in any way alerting those around them to the agents' presence.

After the reception, John and Demi joined Guy, Dan and Candace, and a few other friends at the hotel's restaurant for dinner. The children were escorted back to Albuquerque by four FBI agents, where their sitter, Eloise, waited for them at home.

John had actually been sworn in at a private ceremony in Chief Justice Walter Bentson's chambers that morning. That brief event was attended by Demi and the two children, as well as John's and Demi's mothers and sisters. John began work that morning. He put in a full day's work the following day, as well, when Chief Justice Bentson invited him to lunch to offer welcomed advice and suggestions.

On his way home at the end of the day, John stopped at a supermarket just off the Interstate to buy a few groceries Demi had asked him to get. As he gathered the items into the basket, he mused that even Supreme Court justices were subject to such domestic orders and directives. He had no problem with that. But already, he could tell it'd be easy for some to let the job go to their head. Demi, he was sure, wouldn't allow that. She'd kill him first.

As he went through the check-out counter, he was surprised to bump into Carmen Fresquez. He hadn't seen her since that day when she confronted him; the day Bernardo confessed to her. She had apologized to him when John drove her back to his office.

Walking out of the store with John, she brought up her behavior of that day. "Would you please forgive me?" she asked as they walked toward the parking lanes.

"You were understandably upset then," John replied, "and I was willing to forget what was nothing more than a misunderstanding. You'll recall I accepted your apology. It isn't necessary to apologize again."

"But I want to. It's just that I haven't seen you, and I told myself the next time I saw you, I'd tell you how sorry I was."

He smiled. "Well, if it's important to you, I'll accept your apology once more."

"Thanks."

She continued walking with him to his car, and John used the time to ask about Bernardo and her parents. They were fine, she told him. Bernardo's wife, Beverly, was pregnant. Both she and Beverly had visited Bernardo at the penitentiary in Santa Fe several times. "He looks sad most of the time," she added.

"I can understand that. Guy Zanotelli told me after the sentencing that he thought Judge Walker had been lenient in suspending part of the sentence."

"Yes, we were happy he didn't give Bernardo the maximum. Mr. Zanotelli did a good job, and my parents and Bernardo liked him. I actually planned to telephone him the other day. I even thought of calling you."

"Oh, really? What about?"

"I came to realize after that day at your office that if my parents and I were wrong about the amount of time Bernardo was gone from the house, he could very well have done what he was accused of."

"That's the conclusion I drew after he claimed all of you were mistaken."

"I know. But I think he was lying, Mr. Garcia."

"Why do you—"

"He didn't do that horrible thing!"

John noticed their *private* talk had caught several shoppers' attention. "Carmen, why don't we continue this conversation at the Village Inn across the street. Let me buy you coffee or a soft drink. Are you in a hurry? I'd like to hear what you have to say."

"No, I'm not rushed."

"Good. Why don't you put your groceries in your car and meet me there."

"Great. I'll see you in a minute."

Once they were seated, John ordered coffee. Carmen ordered a Coke. He had half an hour before Demi would start to wonder where he was, so he decided to move the discussion along.

"In these circumstances, it's natural to be defensive of one's brother, Carmen," he said as the waitress left. "You refused to believe it, even though he told you he did it. I didn't want to believe it either."

"I thought you might think I was just sticking up for him." She took a deep breath. "But I feel he wasn't telling us the truth. I felt that way ever since the day he confessed but especially since I've visited him in prison."

"Why do you feel that?"

The waitress delivered their drinks. Carmen took a drink of her Coke, then continued.

"For two reasons. First, there's the question of time. Believe me, Mr. Garcia. I realize we said he was gone only a few minutes. That's what it seemed to us, probably because we were watching TV." She paused to catch her breath. "But he couldn't have been gone as long as he kept insisting after he confessed."

"Why not?"

"Because I'm sure of one thing—he left at ten minutes after eight, give or take a couple of minutes. My husband and I left about fifteen minutes before nine. I remember Bernardo returned just before we left, so the most he could have been gone was forty minutes. You yourself said he couldn't have done all they claimed he did in that time."

"That's true. The way you've explained the outer time limits, you make a valid point. What's the other reason you think he's lying?"

"That's the one that bothers me the most." She seemed anxious. "It's more convincing to me because I know my brother."

"How is it more convincing?"

"When he was a little boy, because I was much older, I used to take care of him if my parents were gone. He used to do things he wasn't supposed to—you know, mischievous stuff—I could always tell when he was lying." She gulped down the rest of her Coke.

He gestured to her empty glass. "Would you like a refill? You drink fast."

She let out a short, nervous laugh. "No, thanks."

As he listened, John thought Carmen was still in denial by relying on some sort of sixth sense. The time issue she had brought up impressed him—it always had. But he hadn't thought of it since the confession. Her explanation of an *intuitive feeling* that Bernardo was lying didn't.

He decided to pursue that point. "How could you tell he was lying?" he asked.

"Because, whenever he used to lie to me—when he was just a kid—he'd avoid my eyes. Anytime I would catch him lying, he'd always do that—look away instead of looking right at me."

434

"And I suppose you're going to say he did that since his confession a couple of weeks ago?"

"Yes—he wouldn't look me in the eye when I've asked him about it."

"When have you asked him?"

"At the penitentiary, when I visited him."

"On more than one occasion?"

"Yes. Several times. And even before then."

"Let's be sensible, Carmen. Even if your gut instinct is correct, why in the world would he confess to something he didn't do?"

"I don't know." She appeared more distraught than ever now. "Maybe he's protecting someone."

"Why would he risk imprisonment to do that?"

She shook her head. "I don't know that either." She stared at him. "Please, Mr. Garcia, maybe you or Mr. Zanotelli can confront him. I just know he's not telling the truth!"

He looked at his watch. It was almost six. "Listen, Carmen, I've got to go. Let me think about it. I'll talk to Guy Zanotelli and tell him what you've told me. Maybe he can pay Bernardo a visit."

"Please; you go talk to him. He respects you. He'll listen to what you have to say."

"I can't do that, Carmen. I've withdrawn from the case. Mr. Zanotelli's his attorney now."

"But just go see him. He's in the penitentiary in Santa Fe, where you work."

"Yes, and that's why I can't see him. I'm on the Supreme Court now and have no business doing that."

"Even if you were his attorney at the trial?" She seemed disappointed.

"Yes, that doesn't matter now. You understand, don't you?"

She hesitated. "I guess so. But you'll at least talk to Mr. Zanotelli and see if he'll go visit Bernardo?"

"I'll do that much." He stood up and picked up the tab.

"Thanks, Mr. Garcia. We'd appreciate your and Mr. Zanotelli's help."

As he drove home, he couldn't stop thinking about what Carmen had said. For certain, his visit with her raised questions in his own mind. Some of these he had noted soon after Bernardo's confession, but he hadn't explored them. First, there was the matter of the anonymous phone call. The tip had been the reason Morales had suspected Bernardo in the first place.

From the beginning, that phone call had bothered him. Had there been an accomplice? Even if Bernardo had committed the crime, who else would know about it? Had an unknown person witnessed the attack? The only way that witness could have pointed the finger at Bernardo would have been if he had known Bernardo beforehand. Otherwise, the witness' observations would be no different from Patty's or Carol's.

That brought to mind the question of the discrepancies. From trying the case, the clear picture John had was that the attacker was stocky. Bernardo was small and thin. Even taking into account Patty's and Carol's explanations of how they could have been mistaken, he had nevertheless been bothered by the differences. Had someone else committed the crime? Someone Bernardo was now protecting? It seemed absurd he'd pull something like that and risk being punished.

Then there was the knife. It had never been found. The assailant would be the one person who knew what had happened to it. It was for that reason he had asked Bernardo what he had done with it. He threw it over the wooden fence along the alley, he had explained.

As he thought of the knife, it dawned on him he wasn't far from the area where the stabbing had taken place. The temptation was too hard to resist. He decided to visit the alley.

He parked his car on the east end of the park, the one closest to the alley. He soon spotted the metal shed. Bernardo had told him the knife hit the roof of the shed and that it may have fallen on the shed's opposite side. He climbed the fence and searched the ground near the shed. He even climbed onto a wall next to the shed from where he could inspect its roof. There was a narrow space between the shed and the house to which it belonged. It was wide enough for him to enter, and he searched there also.

He went over the same ground a second and then a third time, combing the weeds and wild grass with his feet and hands. He made it a point not to look for a reflection from the blade. By now, the blade would have lost its glimmer. He gave up the search. Bernardo would have a bit of explaining to do if Guy decided to question him.

The next morning, as John drove along the Interstate on his way to work, he spotted the state penitentiary silhouetted against the southeastern horizon. Bernardo was somewhere behind those walls, he thought. He couldn't stop thinking about his visit to the alley. Again, the temptation was too great. He had already passed the exit leading to the

436

correctional facility and so he got off at the next exit to reverse course on the frontage road leading to the facility. He knew one of the administrators there, who he felt certain could arrange for him to see Bernardo.

Half an hour later, he was visiting with his acquaintance in his office when Bernardo, dressed in the facility's light blue jumpsuit, came in through the open doorway, escorted by a guard. Bernardo's face turned almost ashen when he spotted John. A big smile soon lit up his face, and he greeted John with a bear hug. It was plain he was happy to see him.

The administrator left the two of them alone and gestured to the guard to wait for Bernardo outside the office. He asked John to knock on the door when he was through and explained the guard would take Bernardo back to his cellblock. He'd send someone to escort John to the main exit.

John spent over half an hour talking with an excited Bernardo. At the beginning, he let the boy do most of it. When Bernardo had unwound, John asked him questions intended to find out how he was adjusting to prison life. Bernardo talked several minutes without stopping. He felt lonely, he emphasized several times, and missed his family and especially his wife; he found that to be the hardest adjustment and always looked forward to their visits.

At last, John got a chance to explain why he was there. He told him of Carmen's strong belief that he was lying when he confessed. Carmen insisted he hadn't had the time to commit the crime. Was he holding back something he wanted to get off his chest, John asked.

Bernardo denied he was lying or holding back. He insisted his sister was exaggerating that she could tell when he was deceptive as a child. John mentioned the knife and asked him if he'd be willing to go to the alley near the park to search for the knife if Guy Zanotelli obtained a court order directing his transport outside the prison. Bernardo expressed surprise he'd be allowed outside the prison walls. John explained it could be done to assist Guy Zanotelli in filing a motion for a new trial on the basis of newly-discovered evidence. Bernardo hesitated at first but finally agreed.

Early that afternoon, John called Guy to tell him of his talk with Carmen.

"That was a bit risky," Guy said when John finished explaining his unanticipated visit with Bernardo. "You know as well as I do that there are limits to what you can and cannot do now that you're a justice."

"You're right, I know that very well," he answered, "but I felt I owed it to the Solizes to explore Carmen's theory. I was willing to take the risk, Guy, so please skip the lecture."

"Whatever you say, Justice." Guy sighed. "I'm fairly certain I can get the order allowing the kid's transport later today. But I'm leaving late this afternoon for a deposition in Grants and won't return to the office until tomorrow afternoon. So I can't accompany the boy until then."

"Do me a favor and put my name down to act on your behalf. I'll take the order down in the morning. I want this over and done with."

"What's the hurry? Why don't you wait and I'll—"

"Just do it, will you? I've already done whatever damage there's to be done. One more visit's not going to make a difference."

"All right, have it your way. Against my better judgment, I'll do it."

The next morning, in the alley, Bernardo pointed out the area where he had thrown the knife. It was the exact location John had searched two days before. They crossed the fence and began the search. Two sheriff's deputies had met John at the penitentiary earlier and had transported a shackled Bernardo to the park. John had followed in his own car. The deputies had removed Bernardo's handcuffs and leg shackles so he could assist John in the search. But they stood close by, armed, never letting Bernardo out of their sight.

After John and Bernardo had twice combed every square inch for half an hour, John spoke. "Are you sure this is the place?" he asked. "Think carefully. You were running fast and probably nervous."

Bernardo continued to search the ground and barely glanced up at John to answer. "I'm sure."

"How positive are you?"

Bernardo looked into John's eyes. "As positive as I can be."

"Then where's the knife?"

"Someone must have taken it."

"That's unlikely. This spot isn't accessible to the public. And the owner of this place would have turned it over to the police, unless he doesn't read the newspapers." He walked toward the fence. "Let's return to the vehicles. If we haven't found it by now, we're not going to."

They walked back to where John and the deputies had parked their cars. He explained to the deputies he wanted to speak with Bernardo some more and asked for their permission to let Bernardo get into his car so they could talk in private. The officers honored the request.

As soon as Bernardo got into the car, John confronted him. "Carmen thinks you're lying to protect someone, Bernardo." He related what Carmen had told him.

His eyes on the floorboard, Bernardo didn't look up. He shook his head, appearing disappointed his sister had spoken to John. "She's the one who's trying to protect me. Can't you see that?"

"If she's right about the time, Bernardo, she's got me convinced."

Bernardo kept looking down. "What do you mean?"

"Just that you've insisted all along you left the house at ten after eight, give or take a few minutes. You yourself said you returned before Carmen and her husband left. If she's correct that they left at fifteen of nine, and she insists that she is, that gave you less than thirty-five minutes to commit the crime."

"So?"

"So we've already established you wouldn't have had enough time to do it even in forty minutes, much less in thirty-five. Even you told Keith that on the stand. Right?"

Bernardo nodded, refusing to look up.

"Now we've got this added mystery of the knife," John added.

Still Bernardo said nothing.

"I'm beginning to believe Carmen's right. You're trying to protect someone, aren't you?" He tried to sound convincing, even though he didn't have the slightest idea where he was going with this.

Bernardo remained silent, but John thought he noticed him shiver.

"Whom are you protecting?" John paused to give him time. "Sooner or later, someone's going to find out. So unless you don't mind spending a few years behind bars for perjury, I think you better come clean now!"

He disliked the idea of threatening Bernardo with remote possibilities but was taking a gamble it would get results. Apparently, the boy would give anything not to return to the correctional facility. The very idea of additional time there might get him to reconsider, just in case he was in fact protecting someone.

Bernardo began crying. He placed a hand to his face to cover his eyes. The tears came, slow at first, then flowed heavily. John said nothing,

439

believing it a good idea to let him have his cry. Yet, something serious was at the root of Bernardo's sudden emotions. John was dumbfounded.

When his tears subsided, Bernardo spoke. John could barely hear him. His eyes still on the floorboard, Bernardo took his hand away from his face. "You're right," he said. "My sister's right." He hesitated. "I've been protecting someone all along." He raised his head and turned to face John. "But I told the truth at trial. I didn't lie. Honestly, I didn't."

He started crying again. "That's why I felt so bad when you accused me of lying in court. I was telling the truth when I said I didn't stab Ms. Gregory. I wasn't even near the place."

"But why," John said, "would you want to protect someone at the risk of hurting yourself and your family?" He shook his head in disbelief. "Risking a conviction and imprisonment doesn't make sense."

"I was hoping the jury would find me innocent." He tried wiping the tears with his bare hand.

John gave him his handkerchief.

"I was innocent and thought the jury would believe me and my family." His gaze locked on John's eyes. "I trusted you to win the case."

John forced a soft laugh. "I appreciate your faith in me," he said. "But our system doesn't work that way. No matter how good or bad our lawyering may be, the good ones that should win a case often don't. But that's beside the point. What you've said so far doesn't make sense. Not until you fill in the gaps." John shook his head. "Whom were you protecting by going through this ordeal?"

Bernardo hesitated, and for a long moment, said nothing, as if trying to find the right words. "These two guys I knew in school a few years ago," he said at last. "They threatened me. They said they'd cut Beverly and me 'to pieces' if I squealed on them. I believed them. It scared me, and I didn't know what to do." He paused to wipe more tears.

"When the police filed the charges against me, I was too scared to tell the truth. But in denying that I did it, I wasn't lying. I know I kept important information from them and shouldn't have done that. But when I was in jail, I was afraid they'd hurt Beverly. Then you came to see me and gave me hope I'd get out of this mess."

"I wish I could have done that," John said. "Tell me what happened." The youngster nodded and began his incredible story.

Bernardo walked out of his parents' house and into the shed. He relieved himself in the small bathroom there, then laid down on the bed and closed his eyes for a few seconds. But he grew restless. Yet, he didn't feel like going back into the house. He wanted to be alone.

And he felt trapped. What were he and Beverly going to do? What about his plans for a job? There were several prospects, but he had been unemployed ever since returning from California, where he had no luck getting a job. He was desperate now. Thinking it might calm him down, he decided to go for a walk.

He lost track of time as he wandered through several streets past his parents' neighborhood, going no place in particular. He walked for a long time before realizing he'd better head back, so he turned around. That's when he spotted his two former high school classmates, Enrique Ponce and Gilberto Trujillo. They were riding in a faded, old-model car.

Bernardo was somewhat familiar with the neighborhood he found himself in, enough to know Enrique and Gilberto were coming from the direction of the park a mile or so away. The two young men pulled up alongside him. Irritated for having accidently bumped into the two young men, he didn't slow his pace.

"Where you headed, Bernardo?" Gilberto, the driver, asked.

Bernardo didn't stop walking. "Home," he snapped.

"Hadn't seen you around, *bato*, since you came back from *Califas*. What you been doing?"

Bernardo continued looking straight ahead. "Looking for a job right now. That's why my wife and I came back."

"Yeah, I understand jobs aren't that easy to find out there. Enrique here just got back himself. He's looking for a place to rent. I'm driving him around." He grinned. "You know of a place he could rent?"

"No."

"Maybe where you live, there's a place."

"My wife and I are living with my parents."

"Is that where you're headed in such a hurry?" Enrique Ponce asked.

"Yeah. I was taking a walk and lost track of time."

Gilberto brought the car to a halt. "Here, hop in, man," he said. "We'll give you a lift."

Bernardo's immediate thought was to turn down the offer but then realized he had stayed gone longer than he had intended. Beverly and his parents might start worrying. He wasn't wearing a watch and had no idea how long he had been gone. If he accepted the lift, he'd be back home in less than a couple of minutes.

"All right," he said, even though reluctant. He got into the back of the car and closed the door. "Thanks."

"Don't mention it," Gilberto said. He pulled away from the curb.

Gilberto asked Bernardo where his parents lived, and Bernardo gave him their address. Enrique noted to Gilberto that the address was just down the road a couple of minutes away. As he spoke, Enrique seemed out of breath. He placed his left arm on top of the seat, turning to the left so that his back was against the front passenger door.

Bernardo noticed the fresh scratch marks on Enrique's arm. He remembered Enrique as a troublemaker in school. He bore a slight facial resemblance to Bernardo but was stockier and several inches taller.

Bernardo soon sensed he had made a big mistake in accepting the ride. He felt a knot at the pit of his stomach when it registered that Enrique and Gilberto were up to something. Had they just committed a robbery or burglary? He wouldn't put it past them; they were the sort. Why was Enrique out of breath, and where had he gotten those scratch marks?

"You can drop me off at the corner," Bernardo said, eager to get out of the car.

"Right on, bro'," Gilberto said. He brought the car to a halt.

As Bernardo leaned forward to open the door, he thought he noticed a smirk on Enrique's face.

He got out of the car and closed the door. "Thanks for the ride, guys," he said, not looking back.

"Don't mention it, bro'," Gilberto said.

Enrique leaned across the front seat toward Bernardo in an obvious attempt to make contact with Bernardo's eyes, but Bernardo didn't look at him. "I hope you don't come to regret being with us, bro'," he said, a wide smile on his face.

Bernardo turned and gave Gilberto a puzzled look. "What's he talking about?" he asked.

Gilberto smiled and shook his head. "Ignore him, *bato*." He didn't wait for an answer. Instead, he put the car into gear and took off.

The next morning, Bernardo left his parents' house to look into a job he had heard about. He was a couple of blocks away from the house when Enrique and Gilberto pulled up beside him. Enrique ordered him into the car. Feeling intimidated and not wanting to cause a scene, Bernardo complied. As soon as he entered the back of the car and closed the door, Enrique pulled out a knife. He leaned over the back of his seat, pulled

442

Bernardo by his shirt collar, and brought the knife inches away from Bernardo's face.

"The police might come around asking a few questions," Enrique said into Bernardo's face. "If they do, make sure you don't even as much as whisper our names."

"What's this all about?" Bernardo asked, frightened. "Why would they come see me? I didn't do anything."

"You'll find out soon enough, bro'."

Enrique brought the knife even closer, touching the tip of Bernardo's nose. He spit his words out. "And when you do, you better make sure you keep us out of whatever mess you've gotten yourself into."

"I haven't gotten into a mess," Bernardo said, shaken.

Enrique laughed. "That's what you think." His grip on Bernardo's shirt became tighter. "And if you even try getting us involved, my *friend*, you can bet your ass I'm going to take this knife and rip both you and your pretty white wife to pieces." He grinned. "You understand what we're saying, man?"

Afraid more than bewildered, Bernardo tried nodding, but his head barely moved. "Yeah," he managed to utter.

Enrique loosened his grip, and Bernardo was allowed to leave the car. He was too frightened to go job hunting. Instead, he went home and spent the remainder of the afternoon in the shed afraid for his life.

Later that evening, he read in the *Albuquerque Tribune* of the attack on the mayor's daughter. It made him sick to his stomach. He complained to Beverly and his mother that he wasn't hungry, and so he went without dinner.

The following morning, he wasn't surprised when the police converged on his parents' house, and Morales interrogated him about his whereabouts on Thursday evening. His worst nightmare had begun.

Bernardo was still sobbing when he finished his story. John sat there stunned. The missing pieces of the puzzle, he thought, had now fallen in place, and the case now made sense to him.

"I wish, Bernardo," he said finally, "that you would have leveled with me from the beginning."

Bernardo wiped his eyes. "I wanted to, Mr. Garcia," he said. "You don't know how many times I came close to telling you what really happened. But every time, I got scared thinking what they'd do if they found out I squealed." He cleaned his nose. "I guess I broke the law, huh?"

"You didn't commit perjury, if that's what you're getting at. No, you were right when you said you told the truth in court. But in keeping what you knew from the police, technically you violated the law. Don't worry about that, though. I don't think it'll cause a problem."

"I thought I'd be found not guilty, maybe because I knew I didn't do it. I hoped I'd be able to convince them. When Ms. Gregory picked me out at the lineup, that's when I really began to worry. She seemed so certain it was me, and so I worried the jury would believe her and not me."

"Does this fellow, Enrique Ponce, look that much like you that Patty Gregory could have made such a mistake? She was so adamant, and the jury was convinced by that fact."

"In the face. He's not only stocky, but taller than I am."

"That would explain Patty's and Carol's descriptions of a broad-shouldered and taller assailant." He paused in thought. "My questions concerning the anonymous phone call, as well as the knife, have been answered. One of these two guys made that call."

"I never doubted that."

"What about the knife Ponce pulled on you? You think it's the same one he used on Patty?"

"From the way she described it, I think so. I thought about that and about why he hadn't gotten rid of it."

"Well, obviously he hadn't the day after his attack on her. He may have gotten rid of it by now. We'll get Mr. Zanotelli to find out soon enough."

"What's going to happen now?" Bernardo asked, trembling. He had stopped crying, but John could tell he was still nervous. "I'm afraid of what they'll do if they find out I told you. But I don't want to stay in prison, either, and leave Beverly alone. She might think of divorcing me if I have to stay there for my full sentence. And she's pregnant."

"Yes, Carmen told me." He sighed. "Well, I now understand why you were so afraid to appeal. You were concerned these two fellows would feel you weren't cooperating if we tried to overturn the conviction."

Bernardo nodded. "That worried me. That they'd hurt Beverly. But I don't want to stay in prison either. I hate that place!" He rubbed his hands together. "What should we do?"

"I think there's only one thing to do, and that's to come clean with your story. I think you should give Mr. Zanotelli permission to talk to Robert Keith and Judge Walker about this. For certain, Mr. Zanotelli has enough facts on which to file that motion. He can try to persuade the judge these facts form the basis for newly-discovered evidence, which might not just get you a new trial but might be reason for Mr. Keith to dismiss the charges against you once a new trial is granted.

"Just as important, they can get Detective Morales involved so that these two hoods can be apprehended and questioned. By threatening you, they've committed several other crimes that could put them behind bars for many years to come. If that happens, I doubt they'd be in any position to carry out their threats, now that everything is out in the open."

"You think so?" He still sounded apprehensive.

"Listen. I think you're much better off right now than you were before. Meanwhile, I don't want you telling anyone else about this. Not even your wife. Let Mr. Zanotelli handle it."

"From now on, Mr. Garcia, I'll do whatever you or Mr. Zanotelli say. I'm ready to take my chances with those guys."

"Good." He started the car. "The deputies will take you back to the penitentiary. Meanwhile, I'll head on to the office and telephone Guy Zanotelli this afternoon when he returns. He's got some work cut out for him."

CHAPTER 36

LATER in the day, John telephoned Guy to tell him of Bernardo's recantation. Guy, who couldn't hide his elation, agreed to pass on this latest development to Keith and to let him know he intended to file a motion for a new trial on the basis of newly-discovered evidence. As John hung up, Chief Justice Bentson dropped by.

"Have you got a few minutes, John?" the Chief Justice asked when John's legal assistant escorted him into John's chambers.

"Of course, Chief," John said. "Please have a seat."

The Chief Justice took a chair as John sat back down. In his early sixties, the Chief Justice had the white hair most people pictured when stereotyping a learned and wise jurist. Considered a seasoned veteran in legal circles, especially in the judiciary, he had served as a trial judge in Santa Fe for almost twelve years before being appointed to the high court fifteen years ago. John found him to be easy going and not caught up with the country club groups or artsy sets in Santa Fe. In fact, what John liked most about the man was that he seemed a bit folksy, a trait some considered sorely missing in the hierarchy of the judiciary.

"You've been on the job just a few days," the Chief Justice began, "but I've got a rather delicate matter to discuss."

"Oh?" John said in a serious tone. The two visits he paid to Bernardo came to mind, but surely, he reflected, news of those visits couldn't have gotten to the Chief Justice that fast. And through what source? He decided not to ask questions but to let the Chief Justice explain.

"It's come to my attention that you paid a couple of visits to a former client at the correctional facility down the road and even participated in a prisoner transport. Is that true?"

Aghast, John stared at the Chief Justice. He was speechless for a moment. "Yes, it's true," he said. He couldn't help wincing. "But, if you don't mind my asking, how did that information get to you? And so quickly?"

The Chief Justice grinned for a split second. "Skip Davenport, the warden, is a close, personal friend of mine. He called me this morning."

"How did *he* know I was there?"

"You can bet that if a Supreme Court justice pays the penitentiary a visit, Skip's pretty well going to find out about it *pronto*. Besides, you'll soon learn that's not the sort of thing you can keep to yourself around Santa Fe."

"I suppose you're wondering what possessed me to go there?"

The Chief Justice smiled. "Yes, the thought crossed my mind. That doesn't surprise you, does it?"

"Not at all. You came for an explanation, I assume." He hoped he didn't sound defensive.

"Yes, if you don't mind. As I told you the other day during our lunch, in this job you're very much in the public eye. You'll be surprised there are those out there that'll scrutinize your every move. So you're going to have to watch your step and stay away from situations that may be perceived in the wrong way, even if you yourself are certain you'd be doing nothing wrong. You're free to visit whomever you please at the prison. But where you crossed the line, I think, is first, yours wasn't a friendly visit and second, you participated in a prisoner transport. To me, that means you were there as an attorney."

"You may not believe this, Chief, but I'm very much aware it's the appearance of impropriety that's important. I realize it may seem contradictory to say that in light of what I did. My visits there, I should add, were made against my better judgment."

He went on to give the Chief Justice a brief history of the case, including his chance meeting with Carmen and her revelation to him of the basis for her belief in her brother's innocence.

"Because I had just taken office, and I realized Guy Zanotelli, Bernardo Soliz' attorney of record, wouldn't mind, I decided it was worth the risk of someone finding out. You must understand I believed in this young boy's innocence until the very end, when he confessed to me after his conviction. Even though I suspected I was violating the Code of Judicial Conduct, I just couldn't see myself not following up on Carmen Fresquez' suspicions. Although it doesn't excuse my conduct, fortunately, those suspicions and my visits paid off."

"Oh? In what way?"

John went on to explain the fruit of his efforts—Bernardo's recantation.

The Chief Justice appeared impressed by John's willingness to risk sanctions in an obvious effort to seek the truth in a case he had just handled, and he told him so. "But surely," he went on, "that something good came of it—you're not saying that fact justified what you did?"

"No, of course not," John replied. "I've never believed the end justifies the means. If something's wrong, it's wrong, no matter the results."

"I'm glad you see it that way. So do I." The Chief Justice took a deep breath. "Well, I'm glad you were able to help the young lad, of course. But now you've created a bit of a problem for us, and we've got to face the issue of what to do about what I consider a technical Code violation but a violation nonetheless. What you have going for you, in my view, is that you took office only a few days ago and were understandably following up on a former client's case. The unusual set of circumstances you've described wouldn't happen again in a million years."

"I'd be lying if I said I hadn't hoped my visits to Bernardo would have gone unnoticed. But I decided to take that chance, and I'm willing to pay the consequences. I should add, however, that because my efforts helped Bernardo in the end, I'm glad I did it."

"Clearly, I understand." He took a deep breath. "Believe me, John, occasionally I too have had some tough decisions to make along the same lines you confronted. Good or bad, though, I didn't have the courage to follow through as you did." He paused for a long while. "I'll tell you what. I'm sure you understand that as the head of this court, I've a duty to report this to the Judicial Standards Commission. But there's nothing in the Code that says that can't be done informally. Why don't you and I pay a visit to the executive director of the Commission. You can tell him yourself the actions you took and why. Simply admit that you violated the Code. Under the circumstances, since you just got on the court, I think the worst the Commission will do is to issue you an informal letter of reprimand. What do you say to that?"

"And that'll be the end of it?"

"Of course. Let's get on it right away. Why don't you check your calendar and let me know when you have time to accompany me to their offices. We can get it taken care of in a matter of days, and then we can move on. Is that a deal?"

"It's fine with me. I want you to know, Chief, that I appreciate your understanding. I realize another person in your position might have taken a stricter view."

"Well, I'm confident you won't let this happen again."

"You have my word on that."

Friday evening, John and Demi were scheduled to attend a banquet at a local hotel. John had arranged to meet Guy after work to get a final report on the Soliz case. Guy had met with Keith and Detective Morales several times during the past two days. He had good news to report, he had said when he called John to set up their meeting at Guy's offices. Because the meeting was late in the afternoon, John and Demi made plans to meet at the bar-lounge of the hotel for a drink before the banquet. She arrived at the lounge first and had just ordered a drink for herself when John appeared.

Two agents entered soon afterward. They had followed John from Guy's office in their own vehicle. He noticed the two men join two other agents seated across the room, who he assumed had appeared soon after Demi got there. Since the expanded surveillance had been in place, they had gotten used to the surveillance teams and thought nothing of finding four or six agents close by at any given time, day or night.

As John sat down next to Demi, he kissed her on the forehead. "I missed you," he said. "Just the idea of our being in different towns during the work day is something I've got to get used to."

She laughed. "You sure can be a big baby, John Garcia," she said in jest. "Even being a Supreme Court justice won't change that."

He grinned. "No, really. When I was with the firm, just knowing we could have lunch together if we wanted to, even though we didn't do it that much, is something I took for granted. Now, you'd have to drive all the way to Santa Fe for us to do that."

"Well, don't expect me to do that often either. Speaking of the drive there, how was the commute your first week?"

The waitress delivered Demi's drink and took John's order.

"You know, it wasn't that bad," he answered. "I had lunch today with one of the fellows on the court who lives here. We agreed to car pool when it's convenient."

"Good idea."

He laughed. "He was telling me of his adjustment to commuting. What's always bothered him, he said, was that you can't run errands during the lunch hour or, for that matter, anytime during the day. Taking a pair of pants to the cleaners, for instance. That's the thing about working in Santa Fe and living in Albuquerque that seemed to bother him. The drive itself doesn't; gives him time for reflection, he claims."

"That's a great idea too. You'd be able to made good use of your driving time as well. You've always been good at that."

The waitress appeared with John's drink.

"Cheers," Demi said. They brought their glasses together.

"*Salud,*" John said.

"You're in a happy mood this evening. Things must have turned out well at your meeting with Guy."

"Very well, as a matter of fact."

"So tell me, what's happened on the case? I'm anxious to hear."

She already knew of the events that had taken place in the past few days. When John first told her of his visits with Bernardo, the news didn't surprise her because she knew his determination and loyalty to a cause often swayed him to take risks. Besides, she recalled he had felt as if he had abandoned the entire Soliz family when he withdrew from the case. So she understood why he had done what he did, even though she didn't condone it.

"The bottom line," he began, "is that Bernardo will soon be a free man. All that remains is the paperwork to get him processed out of prison. This afternoon, Keith stipulated to Guy's motion to dismiss, and Judge Walker granted it without question." He lifted his drink. "It was a happy ending to a living hell for the Soliz family. Guy said he's never seen such joy. You don't know how that made me feel!"

She lifted her glass to his. "I've got a pretty good idea," she said as they tapped their glasses. "Congratulations."

"Guy's the one who deserves the win."

"Technically, yes. But you too deserve the honors. I'm happy for Bernardo, too."

They sipped from their glasses.

She hadn't seen him so ecstatic in a long time. It soon uplifted her own mood, for she felt she was sharing and relishing in what was, after all, his own, personal victory. She could tell he wanted her to share the moment with him and knowing that made her feel almost euphoric. That was her idea of a healthy relationship.

"What I still don't understand," she said, "is why Bernardo decided to tell what actually happened when he had kept it from you and others for so long."

"I think being in prison, even for a few weeks, changed that," he explained. "He saw prison life staring him in the face, and he didn't like what he saw. Too, he grew concerned his wife would leave him. Of course, there was also her recently-revealed pregnancy. I think all that made him see things in a different light, and he was then willing to take a chance with the fellows who had threatened him."

"Before that, I suppose spending time in prison was merely a possibility. It was a gamble he was willing to take. After all, he always knew he had the option of revealing the truth if convicted."

"That was risky, though. In reality, it wasn't newly-discovered evidence because the identities of the real culprits were known to Bernardo from the start. So Guy was fortunate Judge Walker went along with Keith and granted the motion."

"He must have realized it was an unusual situation." She paused. "I still don't condone your visiting Bernardo at the pen, but I suppose in the end, you're glad you confronted him."

John nodded, recalling his philosophical discussion with Chief Justice Bentson on that point.

"Tell me about these two men. Are they in custody?"

"Morales put out a 'BOLO', a *be-on-the-lookout* bulletin, on them. They were apprehended this morning. Both men were found in Gilberto Trujillo's apartment. A search warrant was issued by a metro court judge later in the morning for Enrique Ponce's residence to look for the knife."

"Did they find it?"

John grinned. "Sure did. They even showed it to Patty Gregory."

"And?"

"No surprise there. She identified it as the knife her assailant used."

"Has she identified Ponce as her attacker?"

"Not yet, but Morales plans a lineup soon. Keith might not need it to secure a conviction, anyway, although it would help."

"Why do you say that?"

He smiled. "Because Ponce's confessed. Besides, remember that unidentified fingerprint Morales testified the FBI's analyst found on the map Patty Gregory had given to her assailant?"

"Yes. The one Morales never bothered checking up on. What about it?"

"According to Morales, a preliminary comparison revealed it belonged to Ponce. He's sent it to the FBI lab to confirm. And remember the tattoos? Patty had told police they were on her assailant's right arm, and she admitted Bernardo's were on the left arm."

"I'd guess Ponce has tattoos and that they happen to be on his right arm."

"You'd be correct. Patty thought she had been mistaken, but it turned out she wasn't."

"So the knife, that fingerprint, and the tattoos corroborate Ponce's confession. Sounds to me as if any trial against Ponce is going to be an open-and-shut case."

"Looks that way."

She reflected on the case for a moment. For the first time, she was happy he had taken on Bernardo's defense. Several weeks ago, she wouldn't have predicted she'd feel this way. She had believed all along that the case would result in a sad, even tragic, ending for the Solizes. Closer to home, she was afraid John was going to have to live with the eventual conviction, despite his initial opinion that the appeal stood a good chance of being successful. She hadn't shared his optimism, but she purposely never conveyed that to him. She was now glad she hadn't.

"I wonder," she remarked, "how Patty Gregory feels about all this?"

"Can you imagine," he said. "After being so positive Bernardo was the one who stabbed her." He paused. "Guy said he didn't bother asking Morales about her because he didn't want him or Keith to think he was rubbing their nose in what's turned out as an embarrassment for them."

"For sure. Bernardo, of course, was partly to blame for what happened to him."

"Do you mean that if he had come clean to begin with, he would never have been tried?"

"Yes." She sipped from her glass. "Don't you agree?"

"I'm not sure. So many coincidences existed in this case that permitted the system to work against Bernardo."

"Like what?"

"Well, Enrique Ponce's resemblance to him, for one thing. If Ponce had disappeared after the stabbing, I'm not sure Bernardo would have been believed after Patty ID'd him in the lineup. The D. A.'s office and Morales were so sure they had the right man. But that wasn't the only coincidence that worked against Bernardo."

"What are you referring to?"

"The fact that Ponce too had just arrived from California. He was looking for a place to rent, and the assailant told Patty that, remember? Bernardo and his wife, too, had just returned from California. When Patty identified him as her attacker, everyone assumed it was too much of a coincidence for both the real assailant and Bernardo to have moved here from California recently."

"This case is a good example of why our judicial system imposes such a heavy burden of proof on the prosecution."

"That's an important safeguard, of course. But even with such a strong burden on the state, it doesn't prevent a conviction of the wrong person. After all, Bernardo was convicted. We know now, of course, that someone else did it. Ultimately, the system didn't fail him because he was eventually exonerated."

"Yet, the fact remains that it almost failed him. That's scary." She pondered what she considered the flaws in the system. "Actually, I'm glad you followed up on what Carmen told you. Thank God for that chance meeting." She leaned over and kissed him on the lips. "I'm proud of what you did and that you stuck out your neck doing it."

He brought his glass to hers, and they toasted again. "To the Solizes," he said.

"You've made them very happy. And to Guy, for being there when you needed him."

CHAPTER 37

AS John explained to Demi the final phase of Bernardo's ordeal, in the national's capital, a nervous Vice-President waited for his visitor to arrive. He sat in the conference room adjoining his staff's offices in the Old Executive Office Building, a monolithic structure standing majestically on the White House grounds.

The dark, granite stone building with its hard edges had served the nation's executive branch for many years. The OEOB, as it was known to government bureaucrats, had fallen into disuse and for years appeared abandoned. But with the continued growth of the President's administrative offices and staff, demand for the office space in the ugly edifice increased, so that in recent years, it bustled with activity. The Vice-President's staff, as well as the Office of the Budget, occupied part of the building.

Maybe Emory Condon had been right after all, Hirsch thought as he waited. Their joint venture was getting him paranoid. He found himself distrusting his own small staff in the west wing and his larger staff at the OEOB. He also feared his offices at the Capitol and in the west wing of the White House were bugged. They probably weren't, he guessed, but his paranoia controlled his every move.

He even felt uneasy of his talk with Condon during their walk at the reflecting pool. Did government agencies possess equipment capable of picking up even those conversations? Not likely, he concluded, but that didn't quell his suspicions. But it didn't hurt to be cautious.

For that reason, he had chosen the conference room for his meeting with the person he awaited. He considered making arrangements to meet his visitor elsewhere, but that meant having his Secret Service detail to contend with. It might create unsafe speculation. He was even beginning to distrust the agents assigned to protect him.

In this building, which was within the secure confines of the White House complex, he could come and go as he pleased without worrying about that annoying and persistent presence of the Secret Service detail. He felt assured the conference room wouldn't be bugged. Here, then, he could meet in private at this late hour.

By this time, Hirsch's staff was usually gone for the day. When he had first entered the building, he noticed a scattering of his staff moving about. Some of them spotted him, and a few even greeted him. But it wasn't unusual for him to be found here at times, so they continued with their tasks, not giving his presence special notice.

As he awaited his visitor's arrival, he reflected on the necessity of spying on his confederate. Condon had been his former colleague in the senate, when he himself was a member. After experiencing considerable anxiety, he concluded he could no longer trust his former ally. He had caught him in one too many lies. His distrust may have been a part of his paranoia, he realized, but that didn't matter to him now.

What was important was that he had to be certain, one way or another. His political instincts told him Condon was keeping important information from him concerning their assassination plot. In the past, he had relied on those instincts to help him through some rough times in his political career. He wasn't about to abandon them now.

Besides, he had learned a few days ago from reliable sources that Condon indeed had a chance of winning the Republican Party's nomination for President. Condon was now considered a serious contender. In the last several years, Hirsch had heard political talk that the senator was a potential presidential candidate. He dismissed Condon's chances of getting the nomination then as pure and unadulterated poppycock, a part of the usual Washington political gossip.

A person involved in such matters soon learned that, in the place of *Potomac Fever*, as politicos often referred to the nation's capital, one couldn't rely on such gossip. But now, the political winds had changed.

And so, under these unfortunate circumstances, he had no choice. He was forced to hire a professional detective to tail Condon, hoping to learn details of the planned assassination.

As he waited for the detective to arrive, Hirsch grew visibly nervous. He knew why he was high-strung—he dreaded that his hired hand had found out the worst of his partner in crime.

Earlier, the detective telephoned him to inform him he had *the goods*— those had been his exact words—on Condon. When Hirsch probed further, he was told his suspicions were justified. The hired hand said he possessed solid evidence. Hirsch asked for specifics. The detective revealed he possessed audio tape recordings containing incriminating conversations between Condon and his hired assassins.

Before the detective hung up, the two men made arrangements to meet at the OEOB. The purpose of the meeting was two-fold—to pay the detective the remaining half of the fee agreed upon and for Hirsch to obtain the tape recording.

The visitor arrived a few minutes early. Even then, Hirsch was already agitated, for he had walked the short distance from the west wing to the conference room twenty minutes before the appointed hour and had been waiting ever since. His anxiety was caused, he was certain, by his eagerness to get his hands on the audio tape and to learn what dastardly deed of betrayal Condon was guilty of.

He had left word with the security guard at the front gate beforehand that he was awaiting a visitor. He met him at the west entrance and escorted him down the dim-lit, high ceiling corridor and into the conference room.

Upon entering, Hirsch pointed to a chair. His visitor sat in it. Hirsch sat a few feet away. He decided to stick to the business at hand and make the exchange. The man in front of him came highly recommended for this line of covert work. The Vice-President knew the man was good at what he did. But he disliked him and resented his association with the likes of him. For that reason, he thought, the sooner he dissociated himself from him, the better.

"Have you got the tape?" Hirsch asked.

"Of course," the man said. He patted his sport coat above his inside coat pocket. "Right here. Have you got the rest of the money?"

Without hesitation, Hirsch took out a thick envelope from his coat pocket, placed it on the conference table, and pushed it toward the man. "It's all there. In cash, as we agreed."

The detective began to put the envelope in his coat pocket.

Hirsch stopped him. "Count it before you leave," he said. "Just so there won't be any misunderstanding."

The man smiled. "It's fine. I trust you."

"No, I insist. Go ahead and count it."

"You don't trust me, do you?"

"Let's just say I don't want a problem to arise later that you didn't get what we agreed on."

"What do you want, a receipt? We don't use them in this business."

Hirsch glanced at his watch. "Let's cut the chitchat. Just count the money, will you?"

"Whatever you say, Mr. Vice-President," the man said, not hiding his resentment.

He opened the envelope and began thumbing through the one-hundred dollar bills. In less than a minute, he closed the envelope and placed it on the table.

"It's all there," he said, smiling. "Now we both know I got it all, don't we?"

Hirsch had no intention of acknowledging the man's sarcasm and made it rather obvious he was waiting for him to turn over the tape.

The man opened his coat and stuck his hand into the inside pocket to retrieve the tape cassette. He stood up and handed it to Hirsch, a smirk on his lean face. It was a mini cassette.

Hirsch inspected the cassette, then placed it in his pocket.

"Aren't you going to play it?" the visitor asked, sitting back down. He started to pull something out of his pocket. "I've got a tape player you can use."

Hirsch gestured. "That won't be necessary," he said. "I'll play it later." He stood up. "Now, if you'll excuse me, I've got other matters to attend to."

The detective took the cue and stood up.

Hirsch accompanied his visitor the short distance down the dungeon-like hallway toward the west exit. "I wish to remind you," he said, "that the handsome fee you've received for your efforts has also paid for the utmost secrecy. I expect you to honor the confidentiality of our arrangement." Even as he spoke, he recognized the contradiction, and it brought to mind the apt cliche about there being *no honor among thieves*.

"Of course," the man said. "That goes without saying." He grinned. "I think you'll find what's on that tape very interesting. It convinced me that I more than earned my fee."

"I'm sure you're correct on both counts."

The two men shook hands at the door.

"It's a pleasure doing business with you, Mr. Vice-President," the man said as he started to walk out the door, not expecting a reply. He walked out toward the security gate and disappeared into the darkness.

Hirsch returned to the conference room. There, he opened his briefcase and took out a portable mini tape player-recorder. Taking the cassette tape out of its plastic container, he dropped it into the small tape player and closed the lid. He put the cassette player back into the briefcase, left the conference room, and walked out of the building through the east exit into the White House grounds and toward the west wing.

The next morning in the Oval Office, President Henning sat at his desk reviewing his agenda for the weekend and a summary of the following week's schedule. He was coatless, having taken his suit coat off earlier that morning to work at his desk for a few hours before leaving to attend a ceremonial function. He was scheduled to make a speech and to participate in a presentation and tour later that morning on the grounds of the Georgetown University Medical Center.

He wore a white, heavily starched dress shirt with French cuffs and gold cuff links with the bold engraved initials "JH." This morning, he hadn't bothered rolling up his sleeves or loosening his collar or tie, which was his custom when working alone in the office for long periods. Even sitting behind his desk without a coat, leaning over stacks of paper, he appeared not only handsome but presidential as well.

The phone rang. The President glanced at his watch. It was probably his personal secretary, Evelyn, buzzing him to let him know it was time to leave for the medical center. He picked up the receiver. It *was* Evelyn. She informed him that Irving Klein, the Deputy Chief of Staff, was waiting for him in the outer office. He instructed her to ask him to come in. He then began sorting the papers scattered in front of him, placing them in a stack to one side of the desk.

Irving Klein entered. "Good morning, Mr. President," he said. "The limo is waiting for you." He looked at his watch. "If we leave now, Mr. President, it appears we'll be there on time."

The President smiled and stood up. "Let's go then," he said. "It wouldn't be such a bad idea for the President of the United States to be on time for a change." Walking over to a small table, he picked up his coat and put it on. He followed Irvin Klein out of the office.

President Henning believed it was important for him, as the country's leader, to travel throughout the country as much as possible, rather than remaining isolated in the nation's capital. Whether the events he attended were political or non-political didn't matter.

Every day, the White House staff was barraged with many requests for the President to speak at various functions throughout the country. Once in a great while, the staff would select politically low-profiled events, such as speaking engagements at a day-care center, for example, to promote health or social legislation having an impact on such facilities. But, because of distance and logistics, as well as the demands made on the President's busy schedule, such appearances had to be scheduled only on occasion.

For that reason, whenever his presence was requested at such a ceremony near the nation's capital, his policy was to attend those events as much as possible. Politically, he wanted to be known as a leader who was willing to participate in events affecting the ordinary citizen. In the past, his staff had been successful in creating that image. He enjoyed attending those events, but more importantly, mingling in the crowds, much to the chagrin of his Secret Service detail.

The presentation this morning at the Georgetown University Medical Center was such an event. The medical center, a separate arm of the university, was a reputed, world-renowned facility in the field of medical research. Long ago, the center's board of directors and the medical school's administration had initiated a joint policy. Under it, millions of dollars in funding were raised for the creation of a mecca of research facilities to augment the center's and university's educational function.

As a result, a surge of construction activity occurred in the medical center's grounds in past years. The National Research Building was built, for instance. Millions of dollars in research and grant monies were spent there every year to fund pioneering efforts in various fields of medicine. The Vince Lombardi Cancer Center became another well-known medical facility that gained a world reputation in combating cancer. This morning, ground would again be broken, this time for a multimillion dollar state-of-the-art research center for children's diseases and disorders.

The President and the First Lady were to participate in the ground-breaking ceremonies. Taking advantage of the opportunity, the President intended to announce his administration's legislative proposals for federal grant funding in child medical care and for the elderly. After the President's presentation, he and the First Lady, as well as platform guests, were scheduled to tour the National Research Building and the Vince Lombardi Cancer Center alongside it.

During the ceremonies, the President would also be presenting the medical center's administrators and Board of Directors with a proclamation recognizing the university and the medical center for their work in providing innovative children's medical care.

Although the ground-breaking ceremonies, the speech and presentation, and the tour were to take place within a period of two hours, hundreds of hours of planning and preparation were involved whenever the President attended such events. Security on these occasions was always an important consideration in making it possible for the President to attend.

Irving Klein, together with a Secret Service detail, accompanied President Henning through the west wing corridors and to the west exit.

"What of the First Lady?" the President said as they walked out to the waiting limousine.

"She's in the limo already, Mr. President," Irving Klein replied.

"And what about Vice-President Hirsch? I heard someone say earlier they couldn't find him." Hirsch too was scheduled to accompany the presidential party.

"I understand he telephoned earlier to inform his staff he wasn't feeling well. He asked that his regrets be conveyed to you, Mr. President."

"I'm sorry to hear Charles is ill," the President said. He entered the limousine. "Good morning, my dear," he greeted the First Lady. He leaned over and planted a kiss on her cheek.

"Good morning, Jim," she said, smiling. She never used terms of endearment in public or even around the President's staff.

461

The presidential caravan began its short trek to the campus.

The Georgetown district of Washington was an especially difficult area for the Secret Service to monitor and conduct surveillance whenever the President's activities required him to pass through the district. Its narrow, cobbled streets and quaint residences were the district's showpieces.

Expensive homes in the area appeared piled one on top of the other, without side setbacks and very little rear setback for anything other than a small back yard. Because the district was a tourist attraction, its narrow streets and sidewalks could hardly hold the high traffic the area experienced. The quaintness and early American atmosphere the district provided definitely benefitted the capital's touring businesses. At the same time, however, these properties created a security nightmare of monumental proportions for the Secret Service.

It was routine that, whenever the President was considering traveling to a particular location in the United States or abroad, the White House staff assigned advance teams responsible to inspect and study the proposed sites. Any site or alternative sites selected by the advance teams ahead of the scheduled event always required final approval of the Secret Service.

That agency, which ultimately had the sole responsibility of protecting the President from potential harm, had unconditional authority to reject a site, if it didn't provide the minimum security required. For that reason, the President's attendance at the activities on the Georgetown University campus this morning had come close to not taking place.

In this instance, the site itself, an open soccer field south of the medical center complex, met the Secret Service's strict criteria. But the routes available to the site were considered a security risk due to the narrow streets and compacted dwellings. Ever since that fateful day in Dallas, which had changed the course of this country's history, and some historians believed, the world, the Secret Service considered route security a high priority.

When the agency became aware President Henning himself had insisted going ahead with the presentation, it relented and didn't veto the planned route. But the agency didn't relax its security measures. Earlier that morning, the intended route to the campus was blocked off from both vehicular and pedestrian traffic. The area along the route was sealed off. It was scheduled to be reopened within minutes of the presidential caravan passing through, only to be closed again later for the return trip.

Much to the Secret Service's relief, the presidential caravan moved with ease through the Georgetown district. The caravan soon turned west onto Reservoir Road. The medical school, the medical center, and its support facilities fronted along the south edge of this road. A private, narrow road led to the south side of the medical facilities from where the soccer field was a few hundred yards away.

The caravan turned onto the private road leading to the soccer field and traveled up an embankment by way of a dirt road constructed for this occasion at the insistence of the Secret Service. To that agency, access to the soccer field from any other direction was out of the question. The road was a hundred yards or so in length and ended at the west end of the field.

For the last hour, the bleachers on the east and west ends of the soccer field were filled with throngs of people. VIP areas nearest the speaker's platform were roped off for those fortunate enough to obtain the required passes. The platform was constructed four feet above the ground. As the caravan neared the field, a "sound" person was at the rostrum, testing the PA system through the microphone.

When the President's black limousine and entourage of cars appeared at the northwest end of the field, applause and a spontaneous roar erupted from the crowd. There was no question the guest of honor had arrived. As President Henning walked across the field to the platform, he escorted the First Lady with one arm and waved to the crowd with the other. The crowd roared and applauded even louder.

Several congressional leaders seated on the platform came down the steps onto the lawn to greet the President and the First Lady. The majority leaders of the Senate and House of Representatives, along with other special VIPs, were in the presidential entourage. They disembarked their vehicles and greeted their legislative colleagues. Officials of the medical center, as well as the president of the university, also greeted the President and the First Lady. After the many greetings and handshaking, the President and First Lady were led to the platform steps.

Continuing to wave at the cheering crowd, the President walked onto the platform. A team of Secret Service agents deployed below, surrounding the platform. Meanwhile, two other teams were already in place behind and to the sides of both bleachers. These teams had arrived an hour earlier. Even earlier that morning, those same teams, together with a group of technicians carrying detectors, had combed the entire field and bleachers for explosives or other suspicious objects or material.

The underside of the platform was inspected the night before and again earlier that morning. West of the soccer field were several groupings of large trees. Those too were inspected earlier for signs of any recent or unusual activity. Even the crowd, as it had entered onto the field through the south side entrance, underwent scrutiny through portable metal detector gates installed for the event.

Every conceivable possibility of an attempt to injure or end the life of the President of the United States was scrutinized by the Secret Service. All potential risks had to be neutralized. These actions were taken for every event the President attended. The security measures taken to assure his safety at this event were no exception. The Secret Service had provided the best protection humanly possible for any eventuality the agency could conceive—except one.

CHAPTER 38

AS the President sat in the Oval Office earlier, minutes before Irving Kline escorted him to the waiting limousine, Kelly and Director Welch arrived at Vice-President Hirsch's home. Hirsch lived in the plush Foxhall residential area in northwest Washington, not far from Georgetown University.

Director Welch had been unsuccessful in reaching Hirsch at the west wing. Ordinarily, he could be found there bright and early Saturday mornings. Welch was informed the Vice-President had canceled the day's agenda due to illness. Kelly and Welch didn't want to go through Secret Service channels to get Hirsch's home phone number. Doing so would have required a certain amount of red tape and delay.

The two men didn't have the luxury of time. It was imperative they get to Hirsch as soon as possible. They knew of the detective's visit the prior evening, but the FBI hadn't installed a listening device in the conference room, thinking it was the last place Hirsch would use to discuss a sensitive matter.

Within an hour of the detective's visit to the OEOB, the FBI/CIA had a *bio sheet* on him. The night before, Kelly had reviewed it. The man had retired after many years with the detective division of the District of Columbia police department. He spent the next few years doing surveillance work for a local detective agency, then branched out on his own, specializing in techno-clandestine and covert operations. In the last several years, he gained a reputation for a high success rate. The man was a technical genius when it came to setting up electronic bugging devices.

The FBI discovered Hirsch had been careful in hiring the retired detective. Had not the agency persisted in monitoring Hirsch's every move, it would have been unable to trace the connection between the two men.

Even though Kelly didn't know what had transpired in the conference room, he made an educated guess the detective was delivering information on Hirsch's ally, Condon. Kelly long ago believed that Condon's insistent denials of any involvement in illicit Vietnam activities had aroused Hirsch's suspicions. In several of the monitored conversations, Hirsch seemed reluctant to accept Condon's denial at face value. The final straw, Kelly suspected, came during the two men's walk by the reflecting pool, when Condon kept some unknown piece of information from Hirsch.

Because of the electronic malfunction at the reflecting pool, as well as the detective's visit and other information accumulated in the last twenty-four hours, Kelly and Welch felt they had no choice but to confront Hirsch.

The two Secret Service agents outside the residence stopped the two men even before they entered the front yard. Even though one of the agents recognized Welch, they insisted to see identification. After providing it, the two men were permitted to walk to the front door. Hirsch's housekeeper answered the doorbell. Welch identified Kelly and himself and informed the robust woman it was urgent they speak with Hirsch. As the housekeeper held the door ajar, Kelly noticed a third Secret Service agent a few feet inside the entryway. These guys really did make their presence known, Kelly thought. Again, the two men were required to show their credentials to the agent, who then disappeared into an adjoining room.

"The Vice-President isn't feeling well," the housekeeper responded to Welch's announcement.

"We know that, ma'am," Welch said, "but it's imperative we see him. So I'd appreciate your telling him we're here."

The housekeeper glared at the visitors and asked them to wait in the front sitting room before she disappeared. In less than a minute, she reappeared.

"Vice-President Hirsch instructed me to ask you to please return later," she said. "He isn't feeling well enough to see you at the moment."

"I'm afraid we're going to have to insist, ma'am," Welch countered. "I'd appreciate your telling the Vice-President that we're not leaving until he sees us. Please tell him it's that urgent."

The housekeeper shook her head and bolted out of the room. She returned within seconds and asked the two visitors to follow her into the study, where she asked them to wait. She explained Hirsch would soon join them and then left the room, closing the door behind her.

Kelly thought Hirsch, apparently annoyed by the two men's uninvited appearance, would make them wait a long time. He was wrong, for Hirsch, wearing a silk bathrobe, charged into the room within seconds after the housekeeper left.

"Just what is the meaning of this, Herbert?" he shouted. "It'd better be damn well important for you to intrude into my private life when you've been told I'm not feeling well!"

Welch first apologized for any inconvenience the unexpected visit had caused, then introduced Kelly. Hirsch stuck out a limp hand toward Kelly, then sat behind his desk.

Despite the housekeeper's and Hirsch's insistence that he wasn't feeling well, Kelly pondered that, at least to him, the man looked both mentally alert and physically strong. He wondered if the illness was an excuse to stay away from the office that morning. He thought of the ceremony taking place at Georgetown University. President Henning was making a presentation there. Hirsch too was scheduled to attend. What was his and Condon's *plan?*

Kelly's instincts were alerted. He couldn't help thinking there was a connection. Could Hirsch's feigned illness, if that's what it was, be some sort of ruse to get out of attending the event? If so, why? Kelly began feeling uneasy. What was Hirsch afraid would happen on the campus?

Kelly had been troubled by that gap of a few seconds at the reflecting pool. Did their plan involve this event? Were they bold enough to take some action intended to embarrass or hurt the President? Kelly was told the Secret Service had taken additional precautions to assure the President's safety at the medical center. For that reason, he hadn't been concerned. But he had difficulty accepting what he considered incredulous—that the plan involved an attempt on the President's life. He hoped Hirsch might provide answers to alleviate what he now considered as an overblown concern. Yet, at this level, no matter how remote the possibilities, one couldn't take chances.

"Well, let's get on with it!" Hirsch said, glaring at Welch. "What's so important?"

"Charles," Welch began, "Special Agent Kelly and I realize we're intruding. But we consider this matter urgent enough to warrant that intrusion. I'm sure you too will appreciate the sensitive nature of what we wish to discuss with you."

"Please get to the point, Herbert!"

"I'm hesitating, Charles, because honestly I find it difficult to pose these questions to you. I'm sure you'll find them equally, if not more intrusive, than our visit here." He sighed. "We're here to talk to you about the individual who paid you a visit last night, to put it bluntly."

Hirsch bolted from his chair. "Goddamn you, Herbert! You've been spying on me. How dare you come into my home and insult me like this!"

"Please settle down. I knew this would anger you. But I'd appreciate it if you would listen to what we have to say."

"I don't have to do anything of the kind! And I resent your barging into my home and ordering me around like that." Still standing, he leaned forward, his two hands resting on the edge of the desk.

"I'm not ordering you around," Welch said in a normal tone. "I'm just trying to calm you down. We have important things to discuss, and I'd appreciate your cooperation."

"Did you try getting my cooperation to begin with, Herbert? No! Instead you spy on me." Fuming, he walked around the desk. "I want you out of my house this instant! Both of you."

Kelly decided the time had come to confront Hirsch with his newly-hatched theory, admittedly founded on weak inferences. Would the man fall for it? It was risky, that was for certain. After all, it wasn't until seconds ago he suspected Hirsch and Condon's plan was connected to the ceremonies scheduled this morning. Hirsch had no way of knowing the substance or amount of the CIA's intelligence. Taking the risk meant Kelly would have to assume the worst—an assassination attempt on the President. The bluff was worth a try, he concluded.

"Vice-President Hirsch, we know about the plot between you and Senator Condon," Kelly said, trying to sound convincing enough to set the groundwork.

"What in blazes are you talking about?" Hirsch barked. "What plot?"

It was now or never. "The plot to assassinate the President! We intercepted your conversation at the reflecting pool."

Looking aghast, Welch turned to Kelly. The Director appeared speechless.

Meanwhile, Hirsch's face turned ashen. "You can't possibly know anything of the kind," he stuttered, "because it's not true."

To Kelly, Hirsch didn't sound convincing. He couldn't back down now. "We've been monitoring your past meetings with the senator."

Hirsch's body appeared to weaken, and he placed his hands on the edge of the desk, as if to hold himself up.

"I-I sh-should have known," he mumbled. "How could you begin to suspect such a thing?"

Welch picked up the cue.

"Never mind how, Charles," he said. "The important thing is that we know, and it's over for you." He paused. "Now, if you don't mind, I'd like for you to sit and listen to Agent Kelly. He'll fill you in on what we've learned."

Still stunned, Hirsch said nothing. He walked back to his chair and sat, staring blankly ahead. He shook his head in dismay, as if he didn't want to hear what Kelly had to add, yet realizing he was no longer in control. He turned and stared at Kelly.

They lucked out and hit pay dirt, Kelly said to himself. That fact was written all over their host's face.

"I suspect, Mr. Vice-President," Kelly began, "that you already know we've been gathering a considerable amount of information involving Senator Condon's activities."

"The senator's denied any involvement," Hirsch muttered.

"Despite those persistent denials, I assure you we've got hard evidence. I'm certain it'll stick in any military tribunal or court of law, as well as in the United States Senate."

"I had every reason not to believe him."

Hirsch's own words would incriminate him, Kelly thought.

"This afternoon, the White House will announce a presidential news conference to be televised to the nation on Monday night. At that conference, President Henning will reveal to the nation the substance of what have now become known as the LaPierre documents. These documents persuasively implicate Senator Condon in criminal activity while serving his country in Vietnam."

Kelly paused to observe Hirsch's reaction. The man had now collapsed in his chair and appeared weakened by Kelly's deception, but what must have seemed as stark revelations. He opened the middle drawer of his desk and took out a portable mini cassette player. His hands shaking, he shoved it across the desk toward Kelly.

"It's all on that tape," he said.

"What is?" Welch said, glancing at Kelly.

"Tell us what's on the tape, Mr. Vice-President," Kelly said. "Why do I sense we don't have time to listen to it? Is it happening today—this morning?"

Hirsch nodded. "Yes, Agent Kelly," he mumbled, "it is." He raised his voice. "You don't have much time. The attempt on the President's life will take place in a few minutes on the grounds of the medical center. As you know, I was scheduled to attend the ceremonies myself." He paused. "It's all on that tape. Condon wanted me dead too. The scoundrel betrayed me!"

"For God's sake, Charles, why didn't you report it?" Welch demanded.

"Greed, ambition, I suppose, to be quite direct about it. If you've gathered the evidence you say you have, you must know I wanted the President dead. After all, it would assure me the presidency. Politically, the alternative was bleak for me. Henning planned to drop me as his running mate next year. I guess you might say I stood to benefit if I didn't attend the ceremony this morning. To be frank about it, Herbert, that's why I didn't report it."

"I find that revolting!"

"It doesn't matter what you think. What does matter is that it's now over for me."

"In more ways than one, I'm afraid."

"Just how is the assassination to take place?" Kelly demanded.

"It's all there on the tape," Hirsch said.

"Damn it! We don't have time to listen to the tape. Tell us, so we can alert the Secret Service!"

"T-t-he p-people Emory h-hired will be using an electric motor car, the kind used for grounds maintenance at the university. It's been rigged with

470

powerful explosives and outfitted with some kind of remote control that'll permit it to be controlled from elsewhere. According to the tape, just before the President begins his remarks, the vehicle will be maneuvered across the lawn to a grouping of trees a couple of hundred yards away. At some point when the President is midway through his speech, the controller, far removed from the scene, will be in radio contact with a confederate somewhere near the field. At that time, the controller will maneuver the car the final distance to the platform. It's programmed to detonate on impact. No one on the platform is expected to survive." He paused, dejected. "That, gentlemen, is what's on that tape."

The moment Hirsch finished, Kelly picked up the portable player and rushed out of the room. Welch followed. Both men ran to their automobile. Bewildered, the two Secret Service agents rushed to the car to find out what was going on.

Kelly opened the car window. "Listen, fellows," he almost yelled. "We've just learned there's going to be an assassination attempt on President Henning in a few minutes. I'm contacting our headquarters to alert your agency, but I suggest you use your radio or cellular to do likewise. It won't hurt if they hear it from both of us. But there isn't much time, so hurry! Listen to what I'm telling headquarters so you can report it to your office."

Kelly radioed headquarters and reported the information Hirsch had provided. One of the Secret Service agents pulled out his cellular phone and dialed headquarters.

Kelly started the car. The wheels screeched as he pulled away from the curb and sped toward the medical center.

Inside his home, Hirsch hadn't moved from his chair. He picked up the phone and dialed Condon's home number. Condon answered.

"Emory, Charles Hirsch here," Hirsch said into the phone.

"Yes, Charles, what can I do for you?" Condon replied. "Where are you calling from?"

"My home. I want you to pay attention, Emory, because I'm only going to say it once. Do you understand?"

"Yes, go on. I'm listening."

"Herbert Welch and one of his operatives, Special Agent Kelly, just paid me a visit."

Hirsch related what Welch and Kelly had told him during their short visit. He told Condon of the scheduled press conference to be televised to the nation Monday night. The President would expose him to the world as an embezzler, at a time when he was supposed to be serving his country as a loyal American. He then informed Condon that the CIA had learned of the assassination plot.

When Hirsch finished, there was a long pause at the other end.

Condon finally spoke. "How do they know about the assassination attempt?" he asked.

"Because, you bastard," Hirsch blurted out, "I told them!"

"You told them?"

"Yes, I only confirmed what they already knew."

"But why, Charles."

"Because you intended to kill me along with the President, Emory, that's why."

"I intended no such thing, Charles."

"Don't dare lie to me again! I've got you on tape—your own voice has incriminated you. I turned the tape over to the CIA. They know everything. They're on their way to the medical center. Thanks to your lies and betrayal, Emory, you're ruined. We're both ruined."

He didn't wait for a response and hung up.

In the soccer field south of the medical center, the crowd in the bleachers applauded as President Henning approached the rostrum. He began by thanking the administration, medical staff, and medical center's board of directors, as well as various university officials, for their pioneering research efforts. It was an impromptu speech. Those showed him at his best, and he had been successful with them in the past. He was a dynamic speaker who spoke with great eloquence, and this morning proved no exception.

As the President addressed the audience, eight black automobiles carrying Secret Service agents appeared along the edges of the lawn behind the bleachers. The vehicles traveled to various locations on the perimeter of the field, forming a barrier. For the most part, they went unnoticed by a majority of those listening to the President. But the fast-moving vehicles caught the eye of several onlookers, who turned toward the unexpected activity. As the automobiles halted several hundred yards apart from each other, the Secret Service agents, as inconspicuously as possible, exited. What they couldn't hide from the curious onlookers were the automatic rifles they carried. At the south end of the field, a van came to a stop. No one exited from it.

By now, a murmur stirred the crowd. It soon got louder as Secret Service agents rushed to the platform. President Henning, by now aware of the mysterious activity around him, began stuttering through his remarks.

He stopped when he saw several agents approaching.

"Mr. President," one of them said. "We have a Code One emergency! We must evacuate the area immediately."

The unanticipated activity on the platform caused the crowd to stir even more, for it became obvious a threat was in the making. Several persons scurried down the bleachers and onto the field. University police had been assigned to help with security and crowd control. These officers attempted to hold the swarm back. One of them shouted to the crowd at the top of his lungs to calm down to avoid a stampede. Despite the policemen's pleas, the crowd continued the frenzy.

Covering the microphone, the President yelled at the agent, "Someone will have to control this crowd before it panics!"

"That'll be taken care of, Mr. President. Meanwhile, we've got to get you and the First Lady off the platform at once, then into the limo and out of here!"

Three other agents jumped onto the platform. Two of them moved the President and First Lady off the platform. The third stepped up to the microphone to instruct the unruly crowd.

Several in the crowd began screaming in fear. Prevented from going onto the field by the policemen holding the crowd at bay in front of the bleachers, this group scattered to areas in back that weren't being policed. It was apparent that the confusion would soon make the situation difficult to control. The shouting and screams made it impossible to hear the Secret Service agent pleading over the microphone.

As the scenario worsened, the President's Secret Service detail managed to escort the President and the First Lady toward the presidential limousine.

In the confusion, few noticed the remote-controlled vehicle that appeared out of nowhere. Traveling at full speed onto the soccer field, the vehicle headed toward the platform. The remote car had the entire field in which to maneuver. It skirted around two of the Secret Service cars stationed near the south end of the field.

Two men exited the van that had stopped earlier at the edge of the soccer field. One of them carried a hand-held rocket launcher. Not hesitating, he knelt down in front of the van and aimed the launcher at the fast-moving cart. The cart now changed course, heading at an angle toward the President and the others as they entered the motorcade vehicles. Taking a few seconds to find his target on the cross hairs of the weapon's sight, the man fired the missile.

With a thunderous roar, the missile exploded upon impact with the car, creating a tremendous ball of fire in the middle of the soccer field. The loud explosion and fiery ball were followed by a billowing cloud of black and gray smoke. On detonating, the cart's explosives sent shrapnel and debris through the air. The explosion, however, occurred far enough from the panicking crowd to avoid serious injury. Some debris found its way into the crowd, causing a few minor injuries.

But that was a small price to pay, for the assassination of the President had been averted.

At his home, an expressionless Senator Emory Monroe Condon sat behind the desk in his upstairs study. A portable television console setting in front of a wide, ceiling-high bookcase was on. The senator had turned it on after receiving the phone call from the Vice-President. Minutes before, he had watched a news bulletin as it broke on the local NBC affiliate in the Washington area.

At this moment, the announcer was reporting from the affiliate's studio that its mobile unit would soon be on the grounds of the Georgetown University Medical Center. There, he said, an assassination attempt against the President of the United States had just been thwarted. The announcer, attempting to quell his excitement, promised the station's audiences that a news representative at the scene would soon be reporting live.

Condon stood up and trudged over to the television set. He turned it off and limped back to his chair, where he opened the desk drawer. He took out a blueish revolver.

There was no hesitation in his action. No deliberation. He placed the pistol against his right temple and pulled the trigger. He fell to the floor.

A neighbor across the street heard the muffled gun blast, looked up for a moment, then returned to his yard chores, dismissing the sound as coming from a backfiring automobile.

On the oriental rug lay Condon. Aware of his surroundings, he opened his eyes. He knew well what he had done and had no second thoughts. He felt no pain, only a numbness inside his head and throughout his body, as well as a tingling sensation where the bullet had entered the skull. His eyes closed. Tears formed near the corner of each eye, dropping to the rug inches away.

They were tears of mental anguish as he thought of that day long ago when he had first entered the halls of Congress on Capitol Hill as a neophyte congressman. He was so full of energy then, beginning his new career for his beloved state of South Carolina. How he was looking forward to a flourishing political undertaking when he took the oath of office after a successful military career. The new congressman was sworn in the hallowed house chamber by his senior colleague from South Carolina, who was then Speaker of the House.

His dying thoughts carried him to his boyhood days along the coastline of the Hilton Head Islands just off the Carolina coast. He remembered walking barefoot along the sandy beaches, holding his father's hand. It was during the time of the country's great depression, when Herbert Hoover lost the presidential election to Franklin Delano Roosevelt.

He recalled a few years later, as a teenager, walking the same beaches on the day President Roosevelt had died in the neighboring state of Georgia, not too many miles away from the young boy's home. Even as a youngster, the awesome power of the office had intrigued him. It was that day on the beach when he first wondered what it would be like to be President of the United States, the office few would disagree was the most important office in the world.

Lying there on the floor of his study, as the memory of that day long ago on the beach faded from his consciousness, he realized he'd never know what it would be like to be president of this great nation. The tears stopped flowing onto the oriental rug, now soaked in blood, as Emory Monroe Condon breathed his last breath of life.

CHAPTER 39

KELLY telephoned John Monday evening. By then, headline news of the assassination attempt had spread throughout the world. The electrifying news became the paramount topic of conversation in every household. John and Demi were stunned by the eventual consequences and dramatic climax precipitated by their ordeal of the last month. Their private hell had been transformed into a near national catastrophe. It was an ending impossible to predict on that day John first sought out Guy Zanotelli's help.

Kelly had first called John late Saturday evening in the aftermath of the extraordinary events of that day. Then, he informed John of his and Director Welch's confrontation of Hirsch and behind-the-scenes details of the assassination attempt and Condon's suicide.

This evening, Kelly called to bring John up to date. He spent the first several minutes answering John's nagging questions on the events leading up to the assassination attempt. He then reported the latest developments.

Hirsch had tendered his resignation. As anticipated, the news media speculated on what actions or sanctions might be taken or imposed against the Vice-President. Television networks announced that federal prosecutors were already taking steps to present evidence to a federal grand jury. The media also reported on the potential indictments that could result from a grand jury investigation. Already, various colleagues of Condon were calling for a congressional investigation of not only his part in the assassination attempt but of his criminal activities in Vietnam.

Kelly explained that the President, the Secretary of State, and a few members of the President's staff had been conferring with representatives of the People's Republic. The focal point of the discussions, of course, were the LaPierre documents implicating China as a beneficiary of the fund diversions. Other intelligence later uncovered by the CIA confirmed Henri's accusations, and the Chinese were confronted with this additional incriminating evidence.

President Henning himself was in touch with the Chinese president. The telephone discussions between the two leaders weren't without some risk of affecting the already-strained relations between the two nations, Kelly told John. President Henning had lashed out at the Chinese leader during their talk.

"How did you find that out?" John asked.

"Director Welch was made privy to the discussions," Kelly answered. "He, the Secretary of State, and our U.N. Ambassador were in the Oval Office when President Henning spoke to the Chinese president."

John had taken Kelly's telephone call in the family room, where he had joined Demi and the children after dinner. Demi now turned on the television at low volume, in anticipation of watching President Henning's address to the nation and the press conference. The address was scheduled at seven, ten minutes away. She pointed to her watch to remind John the President's address would begin soon. He nodded and took the cordless phone into the next room to continue his conversation.

"What in particular got the President so angry?" John said as he closed the door.

"For openers," Kelly explained, "even after being confronted by the President of the Tong operation directed at you, the Chinese president flat-out denied any complicity or knowledge. The President responded that we had the intelligence to prove China's involvement and insisted on an apology. But the Chinese president too became persistent in his denial."

"The fellow actually denied his government hired the Tong operatives to come after us?"

"Completely. Not only have the Chinese denied hiring Tong to stalk you, but they've denied playing a role in or even having any knowledge of the kidnapings. So the discussions became heated. There's good news, though. Despite the denials, the Chinese president turned around and promised President Henning that his government would try to persuade known loyalists and Chinese organizations in this country, like Tong, to abandon any intelligence or counterintelligence activities in the U. S. on his government's behalf."

"That's interesting. They deny involvement, then agree to use their influence to stop this sort of activity from taking place."

"That's typical international diplomacy. I come across it all the time. We've had countries tell us outright, 'We're not spying on you, but if we are, or should find that someone else is doing it for us, we promise to stop or make them stop.' By the way, I thought you'd be interested in this note. According to Director Welch, both presidents mentioned you by name in their discussions."

"Really? In what context?"

"The President, despite the Communists' denial, emphasized to the Chinese leader that future threats against American citizens wouldn't be tolerated. That's when he mentioned you and your family. He didn't bother concealing his anger, the Director told me."

"What was the Chinese president's response?"

"Something to the effect that President Henning could rest assured what happened to you wouldn't be repeated. By the way, the FBI plans to continue clandestine surveillance of your family for another week or so, just as a precaution."

"That's good news, Kelly. Sounds as if Demi's and my lives will soon be returning to normal." He paused in thought. "By the way, did you ever find out why the Chinese wanted to get their hands on Henri's papers after so many years?"

"Yes, as a matter of fact. It seems they suspected all along Condon was involved in the diversions. But they weren't positive and wanted the documents to verify his involvement. If they showed he was implicated, they planned to use them against him."

"You mean blackmail?"

"That's right."

"That's incredible. They too thought he had a shot at the presidency."

"Well, they knew that was a possibility. If he became the Republican Party's nominee and later won the election, holding the LaPierre documents over his head could prove invaluable. The Chinese could influence the shaping of this country's policy not only toward China but on foreign affairs in general. Particularly, though, they were mainly interested in our government's dealings with their government. They hoped to manipulate them through Condon."

"For sure, that threat would create an incentive for him to give in to their demands."

"For sure. Even if he failed in his bid for the presidency, the Chinese knew they could still use the documents to influence him as a U. S. Senator. As Minority Leader, he wielded a lot of power. The Chinese could have controlled his vote."

"Well, that solves *that* mystery."

"Not having the answer to that question bothered the hell out of me." Kelly cleared his throat. "Interestingly enough, despite the heated phone discussions between the two leaders, I think these events have opened some doors between the U. S. and the People's Republic."

"In what way?"

"For one thing, both presidents have agreed to continue the renewed exchange to improve relations between the two countries. What's ironic is that it took this confrontation to begin renewed communications that might end up benefitting diplomatic relations. They also spoke of each visiting the other's country in the near future. That informal agreement was reached even though President Henning informed the Chinese leader he intended disclosing his country's involvement in the diversion of funds and supplies tonight in his address."

"That was a little risky, don't you think?"

"Our President's just living up to his reputation of playing hardball. Of course, I'm not sure it's coincidental that he's doing it just a year away from the national elections. Don't get me wrong. I think he's being genuine. But I don't think there's anything wrong in milking this thing politically for what it's worth. Do you?"

"Not at all. Just politics as usual. Despite that, though, I happen to have a great respect for him and plan to vote for him again."

"By the way," Kelly said, "since the President's speech will report on the discovery of the LaPierre documents and China's activities during the

Vietnam War, my guess is that kind of public disclosure will end any future threats to your family once and for all."

"That's good to hear."

"Listen, I know the press conference's about to begin. But I've got one other piece of good news to share with you."

"What's that?"

"It seems President Henning feels indebted to you and wants to show his appreciation."

"Really?"

"You bet. Director Welch asked me to tell you that the President will be inviting you, Demi, and your children to the White House sometime in the near future. You're to be his and the First Lady's guests."

"Are you serious?"

"I wouldn't kid you about that. It'll be a small reception and dinner in your honor. Director Welch and a few other guests will be there. I understand Quigley and I may even be invited."

"Wait until Demi and the kids hear about this. I'm honored, Kelly. The end of this nightmare is turning out better than I had a right to expect."

"Someone at the White House will be contacting you soon with the details." He paused. "Listen, I'll talk to you soon. Please give my best wishes to Demi and the children. Have a good night, John."

"Thanks again to both you and Quigley. I've learned to appreciate your line of work. I've heard it said the CIA is best known for its failures and not its successes because of the covert nature of its work. I believe this case reflects one success that this country and the world will get to know about."

"Thanks. I'll pass on your kind words to Quigley. Bye."

"So long, Kelly."

John hung up and walked into the family room. He broke the news of the White House invitation to Demi and the children. They were excited.

Kelly had timed it just right. On TV, inside the press conference room in the west wing, the President's press secretary was addressing the media. He explained that the President would first be giving a prepared statement on a matter of national security. He'd then respond to specific questions. In another minute, the President appeared.

"Ladies and gentlemen," the press secretary said, "the President of the United States."

President Henning's talk, John felt, wasn't just eloquent but unique in its significance. It was significant because a talk of such substance was being given by a president who had a few days ago survived an attempt on his life. To John, that symbolized the nation's strength and continuity and the power of the presidency itself. For this country's leader, it was business as usual, no matter the threat. And the country had survived a crisis.

The man appeared at his best tonight, John thought as he heard him reveal the LaPierre documents for the first time in public. He mentioned their discovery in the abandoned railroad station, then explained a brief chronology of how the documents came to be found. He noted the courage of John, Demi, and their two children.

He went on to pay homage to Henri LaPierre. Here was a brave French journalist, he said, who gave his life in doing what he loved and dedicated his short life to—investigative reporting. What he had written in his final days had proven important to the free world over a quarter of a century later. Henri LaPierre, the President told the nation, in his death, was owed a debt of gratitude not only by this country but by the free world. Even from his grave, he said, the journalist taught us there were always lessons to be learned from all governmental action, good or bad, in times of war.

The Frenchman had labored long and hard to report on a sad chapter in our country's history—involvement in a war that had brought misery to many people, including those in this country who fought in the war and came away from it scarred for life. Some paid a heavier price and didn't return. Without brave journalists like Henri LaPierre, the world would never free itself from the greed and ambitions of those few who would think nothing of sacrificing a human life for personal gain or mere treachery. Or worst yet, for a pocketful of change.

As the President praised the French journalist, John thought of Paul LaPierre. At this moment, the man indeed had every reason to be proud of his son. He had spent many years not knowing why his son had died so young. Now, the man's sorrow would turn to joy when he heard that the leader of the free world had paid a long-deserved tribute to his dead son.

The President went on to discuss China's involvement in the illicit activities during the war in Southeast Asia. He announced the reopening of talks between the People's Republic and the United States. In an effort to improve relations between the two countries, the leaders of both nations would soon visit each other's country.

Finally, he spoke of the conspiracy between Vice-President Hirsch and Senator Condon. He followed those comments with brief references to the assassination attempt and the senator's suicide. He announced Hirsch's resignation effective that morning and closed by reminding his viewers of the hard lessons learned from these events.

"This country was founded by individuals of principle," he began. "Many years ago, these men of vision vowed to themselves and the citizens they served to create a governing instrument. One that would preserve their freedom from the tyranny and anarchy that had ruled the world through the annals of world history. The words of that sacred document, which we know as the Constitution of the United States of America, have now withstood over 200 years of change since the birth of our great nation. These are indeed powerful words that have preserved this country's freedom through many wars, struggles, and crises. Let us not ever take them for granted.

"The parchments on which these words are written have too, symbolically, withstood the ravages of time. But the words themselves, even if in time the papers were destroyed, would live on unblemished and wouldn't forsake us, for they have proven themselves worthy of preservation throughout this nation's history. This is a truth we all should vow to protect from those among us who would dishonor the sanctity of this, our most cherished document, to fulfill their own greed and ambitions. These are persons who would violate the trust of the people to pursue their own selfish goals and would stop at nothing to attain the corrupt power they seek.

"But let us not forget that, as long as the words of our Constitution are preserved and protected, they will continue to remind us of the principles under which this nation has been governed for over two centuries. As long as we live and govern under them, they will not lead us astray. They will prove victorious over the evil that often controls the minds and souls of those among us who would seek to overthrow our constitutionally-enacted government to serve their own perverted motives. Let us, then, never forget that, as long as we ourselves protect and abide by these principles, we too can claim victory, and our government as we know it will never perish."

Later that night, after Crystal and Johnny had gone to bed, John and Demi sat alone in their family room. The TV had been turned off long ago, and Demi had opened a bottle of their favorite wine. They were down to their last glass.

John lifted his. "A final toast," he said, "in celebration of our ordeal's end and to a renewed beginning for us."

Demi picked up her glass and tapped John's. "And to you, John," she added, "and to your new career."

They tipped their glasses and finished the rest of the wine.

"That reminds me. I heard from Dan. He said the funding bill for new federal judgeships has been finalized by his committee. He anticipates it'll be passed by the judiciary and budget committees within a couple of months and expects smooth sailing through the full senate and house a month or so after that. So the position will be in place much sooner than we first thought."

"That's great," she said. "When would Dan announce the position?"

"As soon as the bill passes both houses. The President's committed to signing it and the funding takes effect immediately."

"When would you break the news to your colleagues that you plan to apply for it?"

He grinned. "This might surprise you. I don't know that I'll need to do that."

"Oh? I don't understand."

"I told Dan I'd like to discuss it with you before I gave him my final answer."

"Why? I thought that was your plan all along."

"It was, but I'm considering staying on the Supreme Court."

"But why? It's a lifetime appointment. And the salary; it's much higher."

"Is the money important to you?"

"Not really, but I thought it was to you."

"It was at one point, but that's changed."

"I've always insisted this is your decision, and I want you to be doing what you enjoy; what makes you happy. I encouraged you to consider the federal appointment because the Supreme Court wasn't an option at the time."

"Granted, but it opened up. Now that I'm on the court, I see things in a different light. I now think I should give the job a chance. I realize I took it on because Guy and others, including Dan, thought it'd be a natural springboard for the federal judgeship. But I've reconsidered that;

484

I just started this job and made a commitment. I think I should fulfil it. You mentioned that once, but I didn't give it much weight at the time."

"I understand. I always sensed that might be an issue for you if you ended up getting the state position."

"What can I say? You were right. Besides, the timing isn't right. It's too soon in my tenure. Unless I reject the idea now, word's going to spread that I'm interested in it and that I'm a prime contender. I've never considered myself an opportunist and don't like the idea of being labeled one."

"I hadn't thought of it that way, but it's a valid point. In another few months, though, things might look different to you. Your present appointment's good until next year. You'll have to run for election then. No one would fault you if you applied for the federal judgeship. As you yourself said before, it's a natural progression."

"I know, but I'm concerned I wouldn't look at it that way even later. It's too opportunistic. I see that now."

"I don't disagree it might be perceived that way."

"There's another good reason for me to stay put where I'm at. I've just been on this job a few days, but already, I like what I see. I'm enjoying the pace and challenge, but more important, I think I'll be satisfied staying on for the long haul."

"That's what I meant when I said it's what satisfies you and what you enjoy doing that's important. If you feel good about your decision, you should stay where you're at."

"I'd like to know how you feel about the difference in income."

"John, I think that should be secondary in your making a decision. We both knew when you went for this position that the salary was much less than what you were earning at the firm. Besides, those long-term investments we made are paying off. We can dip into those if we have to."

He nodded. "Anyway, my gut instinct also tells me the federal job's not all it's cut out to be. The prestige, salary, and life appointment; those things don't mean that much to me."

"I'm glad to hear you say that." She shrugged. "Dan will be disappointed, of course, but he'll understand, I'm sure. Did you give him a hint of what you're thinking?"

"Not really, but I'd be surprised if he hasn't gotten some idea from our discussions. He knows I'm looking forward to this new job."

She smiled. "And that's all that matters to me, darling." She put her glass down. "If you decide against Dan's offer, I'll understand. As long as you know, there's no turning back."

"That's the way I see it. But we're in this together, right?"

"Right. I'll support you, whatever you decide."

He moved closer to her. "One other priority of mine from now on will be you and the children. I want us to plan a family vacation."

She grinned. "When?"

"What's wrong with next month?"

"What about the trip to the White House?"

"I'm sure we can schedule it around our vacation."

"Where would you like to go?"

"I tell you what. Let's all decide. We'll get Crystal and Johnny involved. It'll be fun planning it together."

"I better warn you. For them, it'll be either Disneyland or Disney World." She kissed him on the mouth. "Thank you for being a part of my life. I love you with all my heart."

"I love you, Demi. More than you could ever know."

They embraced and kissed for a long while. She pulled away.

"Hey, lover, I was just getting started," he complained, feeling the effects of the wine.

She picked up the empty bottle and glasses. Smiling, she said, "Finish what you started in the bedroom, why don't you?" She walked toward the kitchen, but turned before leaving the room. "Are you coming up soon?"

"I'll be there in a couple of minutes." He smiled at her. "Why don't you put on something comfortable—and transparent?"

Eying him with a seductive smile, she went into the kitchen, then upstairs.

Sitting there, he reflected on the events of the past weeks. Much had happened during that brief period in his life. Good and bad, but for the most part, good.

There was first the judiciary—the Supreme Court and the potential federal judgeship. Dan was committed to recommend him to the White House. Chris Dunlevy, in turn, said the President would submit his nomination to the Senate without question. Confirmation was a "cinch," Dan had said, especially with his Supreme Court position factored in.

He had wanted to run the question by Demi before making a final decision. Now that she had told him it was up to him, he decided to turn down Dan's offer. It was the right choice. He felt comfortable with his decision to stay where he was. His new job as a justice would prove demanding. Yet, it would also be challenging, which was important to him, and he looked forward to that.

Without Demi's help, he realized he would never have attempted this new chapter in his life. He had been too caught up in his work, which hadn't permitted him to see things as they really were. Fighting windmills, his mother had said when referring to his search for satisfaction in his work.

The Soliz trial had also played an important role. There were indeed ironic twists in life, he thought. Bernardo and his parents had been grateful to him for what they believed he had done for them. Earlier that evening, a happy Bernardo had visited John at home. Guy had arranged for his release after lunch on a temporary order signed by Judge Walker. The youth told John he couldn't wait to come thank him. He brought apricot and mince meat *empanadas* his mother had baked for his homecoming. He had just delivered another batch to Guy Zanotelli, he told John. They were gifts from his mother to show her appreciation, Bernardo said. The boy thanked him again, telling him the outcome of the case had changed his outlook on life. On a more practical matter, he felt certain his father had lined up a job for him with his company. And he had saved the best news for last—now that he was out of prison, he was looking forward to being a father to his first child.

John smiled as he recalled Bernardo's visit. Little did the Solizes know *he* would be forever grateful to *them*. After all, they had played a special part in allowing him an opportunity to reflect on what was important in his work. He'd be indebted to them for that one hard lesson they without knowing had helped teach him.

He thought of his mother. She had helped open his eyes to a better understanding of himself. Because she had played a significant role during his infancy and adolescence and had taught him to believe in himself, he'd always feel indebted to her.

But was she even aware, he wondered, how important she had been to him not then but now, a time when he felt as if his world was about to crumble. In his heart, he'd always cherish those two visits in particular he made to her house. It was then she had helped him the most—to see himself and his work in a way that made a difference. She too wasn't aware of the gift she had presented him with on those two occasions. He'd be always grateful to her.

Then there was his beloved Demi. She was the one to whom he owed the most. He once almost lost sight of her worth in his life. That was part of his blindness. She was the driving force that in the end caused him to reevaluate his life and to reflect on what was important.

In the past, he had been a driven man. That drive, in many ways, helped make him a successful and respected attorney. Yet, that same drive, which took over his life and work, had become a threat to him and his family. Had nothing changed, he now believed, all of them would have suffered the painful consequences. He was thankful to Demi for helping him see that a change was essential if their marriage was to survive. After all, his family was his whole world to him. Without Demi and the children, his work and life would be less meaningful.

From upstairs, he heard Demi's soft voice in the stillness of their home. She wanted to know if he was soon coming to bed. He smiled, pushed himself off the sofa, and walked up the stairs to make love to the most important person in his life.

ABOUT THE AUTHOR

Rudy Apodaca lives with his wife in his native state of New Mexico. A trial attorney for twenty-two years, he began his judicial career on the New Mexico Court of Appeals, where he served for almost fourteen years. Since his retirement from the court, he has divided his time between mediation/arbitration work and his writing. Aside from publishing various articles and essays, he published a novel, *The Waxen Image*, in 1977. He's presently working on a novel about the 200th Coast Artillery, a New Mexico National Guard unit that fought in the Pacific before its capture by the Japanese on the Bataan Peninsula.

Printed in the United States
16247LVS00001B/217-239